PROMPT
GENERATION 1

WINTER

BLUE FORGE PRESS
Port Orchard ✷ Washington

Prompt Generation 1 Winter
Copyright © 2020
by Blue Forge Press

First eBook Edition March 2021
Second eBook Edition January 2025
First Print Edition March 2021
Second Print Edition January 2025

ISBN 979-8-89439-035-2

Cover and interior design by Brianne DiMarco

For information about film, reprint or other subsidiary rights, contact: blueforgegroup@gmail.com

Blue Forge Press is the print division of the volunteer-run, federal 501 (c)3 nonprofit, Blue Legacy (EIN 83-4307421), founded in 1989 and dedicated to supporting artisans marginalized due to race, age, disability, economics or other factors. We strive to empower storytellers from all walks of life with our four divisions: Blue Forge Press, Blue Forge Films, Blue Forge Gaming, and Blue Forge Sound. Find out more at www.BlueForgeGroup.org

Blue Forge Press
7419 Ebbert Drive Southeast
Port Orchard, Washington 98367
blueforgepress@gmail.com
360-550-2071 ph.txt

for those who find solace in darkness

TABLE OF CONTENTS

PROMPT

GENERATION 1

WINTER

DECEMBER

THE PROMPT

December's prompt was a piece of piano music titled, Everything After December. To listen, visit:

http://tiny.cc/TrinityDecember

WHEN WANDA WOKE THE WORLD
BY JENNIFER DiMARCO

It's winter now. Those long, dark days after Thanksgiving but before Christmas, when no one really wants to brave the icy bite at the top of an aluminum ladder to hang seasonal lights. It's still early enough that no one is invoking Ebenezer but all the same Main Street is already lined with lopsided wreaths made by the Evergreen Scouts and cheap plastic sleigh bells that don't ring and never will.

Bundled against Jack Frost nipping at their anything, not-so-early-bird shoppers marched between mom-and-pop shops of consignment crafts like painted rocks and crocheted dog sweaters. The holiday crooning of Bing, Bruce and Willie pipes thin and unconvincing through the ten year old speakers set into the store awnings but it all sounds like lies until Ella or Louis make an auditory appearance and then shoppers turn away from one another, cheeks flush with truth as gazes divert.

Slatetown is not the town it once was. Or perhaps it's finally what it always was: Cold. Dark and cold as any grave.

They're known now. A destination. Not one to visit but one

everyone knows. They have recognition for both who they are and what they created. They're like Flint or Tijuana or Cape Town. Slatetown isn't a generic small town anymore. They're synonymous with what lies and injustice can manifest.

They're a warning sign.

Jason held an embarrassingly pink thermos in his right hand but he shoved his left deep into his jacket pocket and wondered why he hadn't worn gloves. *What have you done to deserve gloves?* he admonished himself.

The signal changed from red to white and Jason walked. But halfway across the intersection his cold fingers found the stone and he stopped. He didn't just stop walking. He stopped breathing.

The quarter-sized disc of slate, impossibly, was warm.

But *impossible* hadn't meant the same thing in Slatetown since September.

It was deep into fall when ivy becomes a gradient of green-yellow-red clinging to the aged gray grit of the contemporary Corinthian columns of the freeway overpass. Concentric ripples roil and collide across the knee-high grass, golden oak in color, each a regent jostling for position, deeded its own land root-deep and crowned, wielding a scepter of seeds at the autumn wind.

The cloverleaf of four thoroughfares that steadily funneled a stream of cars and freight in all directions (but especially *away*) was most often used to identify the meager town surrounding it: The Slate Cloverleaf. It was easier to remember that catchy moniker than the thousand-some souls who clung to Americana in the middle of the Pacific Northwest.

"Welcome to Slatetown, Washington: The Heart of the Pacific *Nowhere*." When the sheriff couldn't catch the vandal who kept changing the town's welcome sign, he finally had it taken down and from then on you either knew the Slate Cloverleaf or you had no idea where you were. You were just halfway between somewhere and somewhere else.

In the not so distant past—how distant was 1952 in the grand scheme of things?—back when TVs were black and white chubby penguins and considerably before the highway came through, the town had boasted a bustling quarry with a natural inventory of blue-black slate that rivaled the finest Brazilian imports. But after the body of little Jerome Johnston was found, devoid of life or organs, in the quicksilver moonlight pooled in the midnight tread marks of a giant machine, the quarry had been abandoned.

Right from the beginning, some thought it was all connected. Because they were both Johnstons. Because they were both black. Because the overpass was built over the old quarry. But truth be told, no one knows why or how Wanda was in the middle of the placid rainwater reservoir at the center of the Slate Cloverleaf. It simply came to be on that morning, that quintessential autumn morning, Wanda Johnston was just… there.

Someone transient—not a resident of Slatetown—made the first call and by the time Deputy Jason Landis arrived and squeezed his ten-year-old patrol car into the questionable safe zone of the berm twenty-seven more calls had been made. Commuters were either hands-free and auditioning as neighborhood watchdogs or State Patrol was lax in ticketing on a Monday.

Either way, Shirley Pickett at the front desk finally changed the receiving message to: "Thank you for calling the Slatetown Sheriff's Department. We are aware there is a woman in the cloverleaf reservoir. A deputy has been dispatched. If your call is in regard to any other matter *please* stay on the line and we'll be with you in a moment." Shirley's sweetheart grandmother tone was especially convincing when she said *please* as if actually pleading for some light arson or petty theft. If callers stayed on the line, Shirley (the only staff member) was thrilled to pick up.

Deputy Landis was the fourth generation in his family to wear a badge and with only daughters at home he might be the last. Gracie, his eldest, had inherited his carrot top and his love for police work but it would be a cold day in hell before any daughter of his put on the uniform; Jason knew things and had seen things as a deputy that would have made Gracie burn the Blue Lives Matter flag that hung in her bedroom. After all, police officers were only human and humans were just one missing link away from animals.

Jason shielded his eyes from the overcast glare and felt his forehead washboard with confusion. Sitting akimbo—his youngest, Hope, would have called it *crisscross applesauce*—in the center of the polished pewter of the reservoir reflecting the low, heavy sky was a broad-shouldered woman with dozens of delicate braids cascading down her back. She sat on the massive stone installed by the ever-helpful Evergreen Scouts to save errant deer who might find themselves out-matched by the surrounding slippery shore, otherwise stuck treading water in the surprising depths, unsettled by the speed and noise of the cloverleaf.

Even in the hot summer months the stone was surrounded by water though in the dry season it resembled an obelisk more than the flat-topped perch it was now after weeks of rain. Just a blue-black wedge of slate. A remnant, an artifact of the past. A reminder that once, almost seventy years ago, this spot had held meaning, engaged in commerce, and hosted a murder. A nameless stone in a wrap-around theatre of surround sound cacophonous traffic.

Later, whispered between the faithful sitting in church pews during the holiday months ahead, some would call the stone: Masada.

"Hello there," Jason called across the water but the woman didn't turn. Jason frowned; the noise from the continuous stream of cars had probably drowned out his voice. He immediately regretted even thinking 'drowned' and started skirting the sloped edge of the reservoir. They'd have to call State Patrol to close down at least one if not all of the 'leaves' of the exchange if they had to bring in... who? Firemen out of Port Laurel with a ladder truck? Search and rescue from two counties over with a chopper?! Just a few feet from Jason's boots the water was already deep enough that it was impossible to see the digestive benthic zone of the bed.

Jason looked back over his shoulder up at his patrol car. Closing down lanes would be a nightmare. As it was, he didn't even feel right ticketing someone if they accidentally side-swiped his car— it hardly fit in the berm even with the side-view mirrors folded in.

"Ma'am?" Jason kept walking around the curved, lapping edge of the wind-toyed water. "You can't sit there!" He jumped a little at how loud his voice suddenly was. He'd reached the western side of the reservoir and some mystery of physics and acoustics formed by the wind and the curvature of the landscape made his words bellow like a bullhorn.

Which I have in the trunk, he thought belatedly.

And then he wasn't thinking about anything procedural because the woman on the rock looked up at him and it was Wanda.

"Oh." Jason swallowed. Was 'oh' even a word? It was more a wordless sound, really. An involuntary vocalization to accompany the deep red flush of his heavily freckled cheeks.

"Hey, Jason." Wanda still had a great smile. It wasn't a toothy smile. All through school, teachers had constantly been telling her to smile as if she weren't already. But Jason had always seen what others were blind to... especially when it came to Wanda. He thought her expression was elegant or demure or whatever he thought of when he heard people more refined than him say words like that. It was a little sad, too, her smile. As if she'd always been trying to be happy, had wanted to be happy, but the weight of something—the weight of everything, the weight of everyone telling her to smile—kept pulling the corners of her mouth down.

It had been just under thirty years since they'd graduated high school—Class of 1992—and Jason had certainly seen Wanda—at the grocery store, the lumber yard, the annual tree lighting in front of the courthouse—but it wasn't since they'd last been seated directly across from one another in the round robin desks of Mrs. Weston's English class that Jason had looked at Wanda for so long. A white man—a white *police*man at that—simply didn't stare at a beautiful woman in this day and age of cancel culture and #metoo. Let alone a beautiful *black* woman.

"You haven't changed a day." The words bellowed out of his mouth before he could stop them and he instantly wanted to reel them back in and recast but, just like in fishing, he'd already given everything away. Wanda most certainly looked different at forty-five than she had at eighteen... but at the same time, she looked exactly the same. As if eighteen year old Wanda was just lightly distressed like a favorite pair of jeans.

"Neither have you," Wanda replied and Jason could hear the humor in her voice as her sad/elegant smile widened. "You're still awkward as fuck."

Jason laughed. He laughed so hard and so completely unheard by the anonymous masses passing them in droves, witnessing this strange and unusual discourse as they banked around the cloverleaves and were carried north, south, east, west and away each with a soundtrack all their own, each writing their own script to the unique tableau.

"How'd you get out there, Wanda?" Jason was less surprised by his break with protocol this time though, again, his words lacked premeditation as he shifted from foot to foot and noticed Wanda's blue jeans and black boots were dry and her russet, jersey-style shirt seemed too lightweight for an autumn day.

Wanda didn't answer. She looked down at herself, pressed her hands to the rock on either side of her, then looked back up at Jason with that same smile... except it wasn't the same. The clouds shifted and the day brightened, sparks catching in the dark water and for a fleeting moment, a moment far too brief to be real, Wanda looked... confused. As if she were asking herself—and maybe even Jason—how *had* she come to be here? But then the clouds closed again, sealing away the sky, and the moment, with all its portent, was gone.

Wanda's silence brought Jason back to the matter at hand and he drew himself up. She'd always been taller and even with the three inches he'd gained after graduation, she still had him beat. Lucky for Jason, she was seated. And thirty feet away in the middle of the flooded graveyard that was the center of the Slate Cloverleaf.

"You really have to leave, Wanda." But the wind shifted and physics and acoustics were no longer on his side. Wanda just watched his mouth move without any sign she'd heard him.

Twenty minutes later, they were both still staring at each other when the news van arrived.

Rebecca Bland rolled her eyes and Jason remembered the time the other cheerleaders had dropped her on her head. He had double-timed it up the slippery slope back to the highway as soon as he'd spotted the green and white KJAX van.

"Probably wasn't the first time," he'd overheard Nadine Mueller snarl to Charlotte Edmond who, normally mild-mannered, had added, "Probably won't be the last." Rebecca truly had a talent for bringing out the worst in people. Her default attitude was privilege, being owned something, everything, by literally everyone around her.

Then she'd gone and married into the type of out-of-town money that comes with a job in the family business. She'd once called the cloverleaf a "clusterleaf" live on the air yet here she was, still employed by King Broadcasting and still sporting a microphone that, in her hands, resembled nothing more than a dick on a string.

At least she doesn't live in Slatetown anymore. Jason made himself find a positive.

"So what's the scoop, Jace?" No one ever called him that except Rebecca. She didn't even look at him as she snapped her gum, the perpetual teenager bit wearing a little thin coming from a woman who hadn't been an ingénue in twenty years, let alone a teen. Jason wondered if blunt trauma to the head could cause that.

Rebecca squinted down at the reservoir, the rock, and Wanda. "I heard she was speeding and went over the rail going westbound."

The KJAX van was squat and bulbous, dangerously overflowing into the curved lane of the eastbound leaf.

"You can't park there," Jason called to the cameraman and with a lull in traffic he was pleased how far his voice carried across the concrete.

Rebecca just pulled a face and rolled her eyes again, motioning her one-man crew impatiently to her side like she might use hand commands with a dog. She turned her back on Jason with a swirl of her TRESemmé blonde locks as the camera came up and she was on. Or recording. Or whatever the heck small-time reporters did when they showed up uninvited. (Did reporters ever get invited?)

"Slate Cloverleaf deputy, Jason Landis, witnessed the harrowing event as a daily commuter failed to obey—"

"What? No!" Jason clambered up the final few feet of the embankment and came around the end of the guardrail. "That's not—"

"She's baiting you."

Jason stopped. Rebecca's back was still turned. Chad (Jason named him just then) was grinning at him very unpleasantly. The camera wasn't on.

Jason turned his head. Wanda was facing him. Looking up at him. How had she warned him from so far away? Her voice had been soft, smooth, as if she'd been standing right behind him.

"Then how—exactly—did *Wanda Johnston* wind up in the middle of a lake?"

Jason's attention snapped back to Rebecca. She was staring openly at Wanda now, recognizing her. The camera was finally on. Jason cleared his throat. "I'm *Deputy* Landis with the *Slatetown* Sheriff's Department. This morning at approximately 7am, we received a call informing us that a woman was sitting—"

Rebecca cut him off with a snort and closed her eyes as if his ineptitude was unbearable. "How! *How* did she get there, *Deputy?*"

Jason blinked. "Well... at this time...." Jason cleared his throat again. He looked back at Wanda.

"Everyone will watch."

Jason had felt a cold chill before but this was the opposite. He heard Wanda's voice, calm and clear, even as he was looking at her face and her mouth didn't move and when she 'spoke,' a warm wave went up and down his spine.

The wind bowed the tall grasses and created ripples that wrinkled the surface of the water in an arrow that pointed to Wanda on her rock. When had it become hers? Jason remembered how hard she'd laughed when he'd read an essay aloud in class. She'd been the only one who got his humor.

"I suppose," Jason turned and gave Rebecca a smile that he hoped was charming. "Good things come to those who wade."

Any shred of friendliness fell from Rebecca's face but Jason wasn't done. He looked into the camera lens then pointed too, for good measure. "And you can't park there. It's a public safety hazard. Now move along."

As Jason turned away from both of them he was almost certain Rebecca had frozen and shattered in shock and Chad was biting off his own tongue to stop himself from cracking up. Rebecca may have grumbled about going to find the sheriff but Jason was already halfway down to the shore and fantasizing about impounding the fat-bottomed van on her father-in-law's dime. When Chad honked obnoxiously as they pulled away, Jason shot them his best country hick smile accompanied by a double thumbs up. She wanted to pretend she was some city-slicker better than everyone else? Fine. He could play the part. But he was not smearing Wanda's name all over network news. Especially when he still had no idea what was going on!

What had gone on?

What was going to go on?

"I guess not giving her a sound bite really got her goat."

"She can keep her damn goat. You did great."

"Thanks." Jason smiled a real smile at Wanda. This time they were really talking, back in that golden zone where voices carried over water and distance and snuck beneath the choppy waves of combustion engines.

Wanda shifted, letting her long legs dangle over the side of the rock while she leaned back on her hands. "Do you remember the time Nadine and Charlotte dropped her on her head?"

"Probably wasn't the only time," Jason quipped, coining the old joke.

"Probably won't be the last."

They shared a smile then and Wanda cocked her head to the side.

When a few minutes passed and she didn't speak again, Jason

tried, "Should I get a raft?"

Wanda leaned forward again and laid her hands on her thighs. Was she getting cold? She was contemplating him... or looking right through him at her own thoughts.

"I heard you," Jason's voice came out a whisper. He couldn't seem to will it any louder. "I heard you up on the road. Even though your mouth never moved."

"You married Debbie." It wasn't a question.

Jason nodded slowly. Keep the—victim? suspect?—talking. "Deb, yeah. Twenty-seven years last June. We've got two kids. Two little girls."

Wanda was definitely looking at him now, not past him. Her eyes were the same rich brown as the mahogany desk he'd inherited from his grandfather two years back but had never used. *I'm not worthy,* the thought came from nowhere and disappeared almost as fast.

Wanda tipped her head to the side and Jason remembered her doing that—and biting the eraser on the end of her pencil—when she was writing across from him in Mrs. Weston's.

Jason exhaled. He knew what she was asking without asking. "We..." He looked down at his boots. He'd have to polish them tonight. They were scuffed from the gravel and silt of the embankment. "Deb and I lost the baby. It was pretty bad. Deb was... we were...." He looked up at the sky, trying not to feel what came along with these memories. "I didn't take the scholarship."

The clouds were racing and Jason had the strangest thought that time was passing differently. That hours, days or even weeks had passed since he last saw someone other than Wanda, that they were back in class, sharing glances and wordless, private conversations when they understood a story at a different level than the rest of the students.

"I'm sorry, Jason."

Jason felt almost hesitant, almost shy, to look away from the clouds and meet eyes with Wanda again but she had no judgment for him.

"There is no greater pain," she continued. "Than losing a child."

She got it. She knew. And Jason knew as if she'd said his name that she was thinking about Jerome. He hadn't been her son, of course. He would have been her uncle had he lived. But he hadn't. But in some families, every lost child was your own.

"You always understood me," Jason purposefully projected his voice, he made himself not whisper, he made himself be brave. She had the right to know.

Wanda smiled her perfect smile. No teeth showing. The corners of her mouth turning down just a little but it was a smile nonetheless and it showed in her eyes and the little crinkles between her brows. Had those been there back in high school?

Jason's cell phone rang and he nearly jumped out of his skin. *I'm not cut out for this anymore.* Where had that come from?

Mumbling a pardon, he fished out his phone and slid his thumb across the screen to answer. "This is Deputy Landis."

"Deputy, hello. My name is Walter Bingham. My father, Anthony, opened the Slatetown Quarry in 1941."

Jason's eyes darted to Wanda. Facts and images came back to Jason in jumbled flashes. Ancient town history that was far from ancient and seemed far too gruesome to even say the word 'quarry.'

Jason lowered his cell and motioned to Wanda that he'd be right back, better reception up the slope. Walking away from her felt incredibly wrong but he forced himself to do it.

"Yes, Mr. Bingham. How can I help you today?"

"Are you still at the quarry, Deputy?"

Jason stopped. He'd only gone a few feet. From this angle, Wanda was in profile but no further away. Jason lowered his voice a little. "How did you know that, Mr. Bingham?"

"I saw it on the internet. That local girl that grew up to be a reporter?"

Jason closed his eyes and pinched the bridge of his nose. So Chad was streaming live to some local news website? "Rebecca Bland."

"Deputy, I was quite dismayed by how... jovial... you were."

"I see. The situation—"

Walter cut Jason off as if not hearing him at all. "Quarries— even former ones—are extremely dangerous places, Deputy. The drop offs and deep water, the sharp and jagged fragments of rock, abandoned wire and bits of equipment. Industrial waste even. All industries have it, you know. You can't entertain the idea that a quarry is a place of recreation!"

Jason slowly exhaled. This was all part of the job. Older citizens especially liked to call Shirley and ask to be directed to a deputy to offer pertinent insight into anything Jason was working on. Mid-way through his forties he'd assumed this would stop, but now it was just prefaced with, "With my thirty years of experience, I thought you'd want to know..." preambles that only made Jason sad. Did these seniors all feel so marginalized and under-utilized that offering unsolicited advice to on-duty officers was the only way they felt heard?

"I promise you, Mr. Bingham," Jason used his most deferential voice, heavy with respect and appreciation. "The sheriff's department doesn't want people picnicking in the middle of the cloverleaf either."

Walter made a wordless sound that was either the wet crackle of clearing his throat or an abject snort of distain. "My father had the whole quarry surrounded by barbed, electric wire, you know? Slate in

Washington is rare and the deposits weren't as plentiful as promised when he moved the family here from Utah."

"Mm-hm." Jason kept listening but he was looking at Wanda now. She'd turned her head to watch him.

Mr. Bingham continued: "Less than one percent slate was what he found. Mostly he had argillite and siltstone. Ordovician rocks. Middle Ordovician. In 1943 he finally discovered ledbetter slate—used to be called mission argilite but no one says that anymore. A thousand meters of it with a band of quartzite. But that was it. That was all he wrote, as the saying goes."

"Ask him." Wanda's mouth didn't move but it was her voice, the voice Jason had loved to listen to every day in class when they read their essays and stories aloud. Jason was certain it was her.

"Mr. Bingham. Did you know Jerome Johnston?"

Wow. Out of nowhere. Out of thin air. An out of the ordinary question for an out of the ordinary day. Extraordinary? Had we crossed over into extraordinary yet?

The line snapped, crackled and popped between them. But other than that there was a long silence.

"Mr. Bingham? Did you—"

"No."

It was a single word. A complete sentence. A full stop. Jason was listening to the open line again, the faint sound of the older man's breathing but Jason's eyes stayed on Wanda's. Her face wasn't as full as when they were younger, her cheekbones were more pronounced, but the way her raven-wing braids spilled over her shoulders and one another whenever she moved her head softened her somehow. She was arguably more beautiful at forty-five.

Jason pushed because he didn't even know why he'd opened this door. "But you went to school together, yes? Crest Ridge Elementary was the only Slatetown primary school until Boulder was built in '81."

"We didn't socialize."

The response was quick and clipped. Jason could tell the conversation wouldn't continue much longer. He wondered at Mr. Bingham's meaning. 'We' as in Walter and Jerome? As in the Binghams and the Johnstons? The Binghams and any family of color?

"Good day, Deputy." The other man ended the call without a word more and Jason wasn't surprised, didn't really blame him.

Jason's phone chimed. A text message from Shirley. It was a link followed by a smiley face emoji. Jason tapped and grimaced. The title—assigned by some creative internet troll no doubt—was: Small Town Cop Tells Off Bubblegum Reporter. The short, looping clip showed Rebecca snapping her gum and rolling her eyes then Jason shrugging, "Good things come to those who wade."

Jason scrolled down. The meme had already been seen by a few thousand people... and rising.

Shirley texted again: *I sent it to my granddaughter. She says you're a hero. No one likes the media anymore.*

Jason's eyebrows went up. They like the media less than cops? Will wonders never cease!

"So the quarry wasn't doing so well."

Jason turned his attention back to Wanda when she spoke, tucking his phone away. He had no idea that Shirley, her granddaughter, and hundreds of other creative trolls were busy making his face and good-ole-boy demeanor a trusted global brand.

"I guess not." Jason almost stumbled walking back to where the acoustics were best. Wait. How had Wanda heard Walter's side of the conversation? "He said the quarry didn't have the slate deposits his father had expected."

"Anthony Bingham."

Jason was back on the western shore. "Yeah. Died back when

we were freshmen, remember? Richest family Slatetown ever saw."

"Stock market."

Jason tried to remember. Yeah. Some adult in his life back then had mentioned that once. To most Slatetown residents playing the market was somewhere between alchemy and sorcery. "Must have invested after he sold the quarry."

Unspoken truths passed between them. Slatetown might have been the last place in America where an act of violence shut down commerce. So many locations and businesses just cleaned up, painted over, and powered on. The capitalist way of the Western world. Jason had always felt closing the quarry was justified and *right*.

"Washington annexed the quarry in 1973. Imminent Domain. None of the Bingham money came from the sale of the quarry because the quarry was never sold."

Jason blinked. He shifted. His mind started to file, sort, shift and rearrange facts. "I... didn't know that."

Wanda held her hands palm up as if offering just the truth. "No one cared to know."

"I care." The words were instant, out of his mouth before he could think them.

"I know." And she smiled.

Jason was back in class. It was 1992, senior year. The bell rang, everyone rushed from their desks and jostled through the narrow door into the hall, all while Mrs. Weston called frantically after them to remember their reading assignment over the weekend.

Jason lingered behind to return a borrowed book from the teacher's small library of translated classics. *The Unbearable Lightness of Being* hadn't impressed him as much as he'd wanted it to but it was a unique glimpse into Czechoslovak culture and society in the 1968 Prague Spring. He might be a small town boy but he didn't want to grow up to be a small town writer.

"You dropped your pencil."

Jason looked up from his stack of notebooks. Wanda Johnston stood a head taller than him, holding out his favorite Palomino ForestChoice Number 2. "Thanks."

Their hands brushed. Wanda didn't leave.

"Congratulations on your scholarship to U-Dub."

"How did you—"

"Hey, Jace! You coming to the banger at Bobbie's?"

Jason did a double-take, almost giving himself whiplash as he looked between Wanda and Rebecca Bland, a varsity cheerleader, leaning around the doorframe and pointing at him with a pink-painted fingernail.

"Huh? What? What banger?"

Rebecca laughed and looked over her shoulder at someone. "Told you! He probably holes up in the library all weekend."

"Hey. I don't—"

Debbie Stone, a transfer from out of state, her father in the Navy, stepped around Rebecca. "I'll be there, Jason."

Jason just looked at her. They'd never spoken before. Why would her presence make any difference? Wanda shifted her textbooks and Jason stopped being oblivious. "Are you going, Wanda?"

"She's not invited," Rebecca injected then popped her gum at Wanda. "Sorry. Bobbie's party. Bobbie's rules."

"Bobbie Bingham and I don't really..." Wanda was looking at Rebecca, holding her gaze and making her uncomfortable but talking to Jason. "...get along."

"Oh." Jason fell silent. He just felt... lost. Out of his depth somehow. Maybe he was working too hard? Focused too much on college in the fall. But he didn't want to go to a party if Wanda wouldn't be there. Sure, they'd never hung out before. As a matter of fact, this was the longest interaction they'd ever had! But he was still pretty certain she was the only person in school who knew the different between narrative and essay, high lit and creative memoir, or an em dash and an en dash.

"Book worms," Rebecca snarked but Jason caught her mouthing 'losers' before she sashayed away blowing a bubble.

"You really should come, Jason," Debbie implored one more time and this time Jason's eyebrows shot up as he understood. "Bobbie's dad let's him drink."

Jason frowned as Debbie left. He hadn't meant to cause the look of dejection on her face but girls weren't a topic he was well-versed in. Debbie was literally the first one to ever proposition him... if that was what this was.

Unless... Jason looked back at Wanda. She was still standing with him.

"Jason? I want you to have something."

Wait. She'd never said that.

"My pencil?" Jason tried to sound smooth and charming. "I already have it."

"No. A hundred thousand dollars."

What?

Jason returned to the present as the wind whipped the water up enough that a fine sheet of cold misted his face. His cheeks felt especially hot and he knew he was blushing. He'd gone to the party at Bobbie Bingham's but only because Debbie had called him, crying, begging him to come get her.

"Did you hear me?"

Jason looked at Wanda on the rock in the middle of the reservoir. Had she spoken aloud or in his head or not at all?

"Take the box, Jason." She was so adamant and she was

definitely speaking aloud. Her tone left no room for argument, her sincerity and urgency were both unmistakable. "When she offers it to you. Take the box."

"Wanda... what—"

"You'll need it."

Jason was about to press her for more when she looked up toward his patrol car, toward the eastern leaf of the exchange. A green sedan was pulling over into the berm. Another lookee-loo, most likely, posing another very real safety hazard.

"I'll be right back." Jason excused himself and headed up the embankment, getting his exercise in for the day. Did the incline count as extra steps?

On a whim, an old habit of collecting mementos, Jason snatched up a small stone maybe an inch across and a half inch thick. It was very black, blue-black even, and from the smooth layers he guessed it was slate.

Feeling particularly spry, he vaulted over the railing this time and jogged over to the driver's side of the sedan as the driver was just getting out of the car. Jason stopped. It was a regular high school reunion.

"Nadine. Hi."

Nadine Mueller looked at him without a shred of recognition. Which was fine. He was a water boy for one year but that was as close as he'd ever been to her glamorous world of varsity sports. Jason was pretty sure the only thing they had in common was a shared dislike of Rebecca.

"Is it true?" Nadine strode toward him with such purpose and intent that Jason almost took a step back. Almost.

"You saw the video."

"The whole world has." Nadine stopped in front of him and sized him up without hiding it. Jason tried not to look confused or startled—both of which he definitely felt. Nadine wore men's cargo pants and a tight purple shirt with a woman singer Jason had never heard of holding a guitar and raising a fist. Nadine had cut her fine black hair very short and the collar of her open bomber jacket was curled up against her long neck.

Jason grasped for anything. "Do you and Wanda know each other?"

Nadine's scrutiny turned decidedly hostile. She couldn't stop the anger and accusation—and sorrow?—from transforming her face the way wind makes tall grass bend to its will. "Yeah. We were married. For twenty years."

Jason was silent, flooded by a chaos of hot and cold shock shot with a thread of shame. He should have known that, right? Two classmates. And one of them Wanda whom he'd always… what? Whom he'd been in love with from fifth grade until he'd stepped in and offered to be the man that Bobbie Bingham wouldn't be? Until Jason had fallen in love with the naive and sweet-natured Debbie Stone, pregnant with another man's baby, desperate for a hero, who always looked at him like he was the only good thing that had ever happened in her transient, military kid life.

But when he opened his mouth, the only word that came out was, "Were?"

This didn't endear him to Nadine. She reached into her bomber jacket and he didn't even respond. His training, his instincts, everything was numb. "She died in June. Breast cancer."

Jason's world slanted. His body tilted, almost fell, his thigh just above the knee catching the railing and holding him upright. *No, no, no….*

Everything in him, every cell in his body, positively screamed for him to look down into the center of the cloverleaf. But it wasn't will power that kept him from confirming what he knew he would find below. It was Nadine.

"Take it already," Nadine groused. "She wanted you to have it."

Jason looked down at the slender metal box—a vintage pencil box with a Coke-a-Cola swish and the motto in cursive: Delicious. Refreshing.

When he didn't take the box immediately, Nadine shoved it toward him more aggressively and Jason looked up at her face. Wanda had never spoken of him until the end. Nadine had never known they'd even known each other. Jason had never dined with them or celebrated a holiday. He'd never wished them a happy anniversary or offered to take Wanda to an appointment when Nadine had to work. Because after Bobbie Bingham goddamn banger, Jason's entire life had changed tracks. His entire reality had derailed.

Was it derailing again? Or was he being placed back on his original tracks?

"It's a hundred and fourteen thousand dollars," Nadine told him, her voice so flat, so devoid of anything pleasant, and Jason understood. He couldn't possibly understand her pain but he understood it was there. He was shaking his head, still not taking the pencil case, even as Nadine continued. "I tried. I tried to get her to spend it. To pay for treatment. But she wouldn't. Never. Not a penny. I don't even think she ever counted it."

Tears left wide trails down Nadine's cheeks. She cried silently and without sobs but she cried hard. The tears were in her voice and on her face. "She told me: Give the box to Jason Landis. He'll need it to find the truth."

The box. Take the box.

Jason looked past Nadine. Her car was full of cardboard boxes and bags and linens. Packed so full that opening any door other than the driver's door would have resulted in twenty years of life spilling out onto the freeway. Nadine was leaving Slatetown.

Jason took the box. He stared at it while Nadine stared at him. In the edges of his vision he saw her move to the railing and look over. He thought she made a small sound then, a small sob, but he could've imagined it. She seemed made of ice or stone or steel.

"I thought," he heard her whisper. "For just a moment, when I saw that video… that she was the woman on the rock."

Then Nadine turned on her heel and strode back to her car. Standing between her open door and her vehicle, she paused only once and called back to him, "Jason."

He looked up at her.

"It's blood money. Hush money. Someone left it for her family. Ten years after Jerome was killed."

And with that, Nadine got in her car, started the engine, and took the cloverleaf away from Slatetown, away from her past, away from the love of her life and the dark secrets of a long dead quarry.

Jason was left alone with the box. Cars of strangers passed him. Too many cars. He was standing here, frozen, for too long. His phone rang. Then a text chimed. Then another. A semi driver honked at him and laughed, giving him a quick double thumbs up.

Jason looked at the sky. The clouds were gone. The night would be cold but the stars would be brilliant. What time was it? He walked to the edge of the railing.

There was no one on the rock.

Shirley texted him: *One million views! What will you do next?!*

"Yay! Daddy's back!" Hope broke away from Deb and pushed through the little crowd of thirty or so people gathered outside the Slatetown courthouse.

Jason smiled at his youngest and willingly relinquished the bright pink thermos. "Can't have the tree lighting without cocoa, right?"

Hope beamed. "Right!"

Jason took her little hand wrapped in its teal mitten and together they joined Gracie and Deb.

"Thought you'd gotten lost," Deb teased and kissed his cheek. She wasn't the naive schoolgirl she'd once been. She was an outspoken advocate for women's rights, a counselor at the same high school they'd graduated from, and a fantastic mother. "Or caught up in work."

She meant his writing. And researching. The long, countless hours of searching archives and interviewing neighbors who turned out to be strangers. The weeks become months of uncovering the truth... or rather fragments, remnants, artifacts left behind by the truth. Jason was afraid, some nights when the work had yielded precious little, that he would search all his life and not find justice.

But then there were days when a trail of virtual crumbs or some misfiled, newly reclaimed document would spill its secrets across his grandfather's desk and entire regions of the puzzle would come together, clarified into perfect, brutal sense.

Jason had called Rebecca to break the story. He didn't know any other reporters. Chad had come along and both of them had been very willing to ride the wave of exposure and titillating drama. But Jason wasn't titillated. Nor was he kind. He spared no one during his first live announcement and the immediate condemnation out of the sheriff's office and his forced 'leave of absence' wasn't a surprise.

Perhaps the surprise was that he'd continued. That Deb had stood at his side. That even as their bank account had dwindled, as Jason refused to spend the hush money, as he worked ten, twelve, eighteen hours a day on the case that was no case, he wouldn't stop. He dissected every Slatetown family that could even tangentially have been involved in the exploitation and dehumanization of the Johnston family, the unforgivable murder and profiteering off a child.

"I walked," Jason offered as explanation and Deb nodded. She knew he walked to clear his head. She knew a lot more about him since that day back in September when he'd come home with an antique pencil box filled with a hundred and fourteen thousand dollars and tears dried all over his face.

"Do you want cocoa, Daddy?" Gracie held up the thermos cap. Hope was eyeing it jealously but Gracie had grown particularly attentive to Jason after he'd turned in his badge.

Jason had been down the hall in the study they'd converted from their guest room when Gracie had taken down her Blue Lives Matter flag. Hope had asked her sister why and Jason had listened, his Palomino ForestChoice Number 2 held between his teeth.

"Because," Gracie explained with her new-found logic. "Blue lives have always mattered. Blue lives are there to protect all the other lives. Blue lives choose to be blue."

She was only twelve and her logic was oversimplified but Jason knew she'd seen the tip of the iceberg and was considering what lay beneath the surface. Killing a police officer was a capital felony, punishable by death or life in prison without the possibility of parole. But killing an unarmed black man? The average sentence for an officer was probation.

So which lives were we worried about mattering? Police *chose* to be police. No one chooses their skin color.

Jason looked down at his eldest daughter and saw himself. Not just in her ginger curls and freckles and but in her loyalty, in her fealty. She was not one to be led blindly. She would do what was right not because others said it was but because she knew the difference inside herself.

And even here, standing among the stares and frowns of other Slatetown residents that resented Jason's videos and hated his continued scrutiny and dogged persistence as he dug deeper and deeper, even literally surrounded by all this anger and resentment, these grumbled commands to leave well-enough alone, Gracie's face said it all: *Well-enough is not enough. Show them all how it's supposed to be.*

"How is it supposed to be, Mr. Landis?" Rebecca had asked so respectfully last Sunday during their weekly video update. Checks had started to come in. From all over the world. Large and small and very large. Famous private investigators were offering their services. Jason set up a trust and reached out to Nadine. She was coming back in January.

But the video had focused on comments, answering viewers who had asked Jason how he would change the police force if he could. How it could ever be possible for justice to be found. Jason was all too aware that he would always be what he was—a white man in a position of privilege, entrusted by a black woman to make a difference. He would not let her down.

Chad had moved a little closer to the wooden table at the park. It was cold and their breath all came in frosty clouds but Jason had insisted they film there.

"Protect and serve. That's how it's supposed to be." Jason looked right into the lens. "I wanted to be a writer. I became a deputy instead. But I'm also a father, a husband, a Washingtonian, and an American."

He'd looked down at the W+N carved into the table top and placed his fingertips in the grooves. This had been just one of the many discoveries he'd made. Maybe it meant nothing. Maybe it meant everything. Maybe it just reminded him that love was love and everyone deserved it.

"In the end, I don't think I had the ego to be an officer. I don't think my life matters more than someone else's. I don't weigh my life or the lives of officers heavier than the lives of firemen, librarians, store clerks or dog groomers. Protect and serve is what appealed to me. In a way... I've been doing it all my life."

Jason looked back at the camera but he imagined he was looking at Nadine, imagined he was looking at Wanda. "I can't bring back Jermone. I wish I could but I can't. But I can do everything in my power, everything for the rest of my days, to search for justice. To ensure that Wanda Johnston won't be silenced. Not by brutality. Not by hush money. Not even by death."

One September morning, two months after she drew her last breath, a woman appeared on a rock in the middle of the Slate Cloverleaf and set in motion a chain of events unlike any other. On that morning, Wanda woke the world.

WHAT REMAINS
BY LAUREN PATZER

King Dolnar walked into the charred and destroyed remains of the throne room for what seemed the hundredth time. He carefully navigated the broken stones and broken beams to the front of the cavernous room. Big enough to fit a dragon, his father had said when he built it decades earlier. Unfortunately, he'd been only too accurate.

His feet came to rest at the foot of the shattered throne. The scent of the room still made him gag, but the smell had faded. Even so, his memory of that day came flooding back to his mind.

Queen Alorra had been sitting here in his stead while he chased the winged beast of the neighboring mountains. He'd failed to anticipate the giant lizard's intelligence, thinking it no more than an oversized winged rat. But it knew all along where he resided and, somehow, what he cared for most. Oddly enough, the Queen's death was the price he paid for success.

"And yet, I feel I've lost everything," he whispered to the empty room, appealing to the ghosts of the great hall.

Ten months had passed since the attack from the great wyrm, Charos; an attack in direct response to Dolnar's assault on the beast's lair in the mountains, the crushing of the dragon's eggs and slaughter of her fledgling young. They'd struck while she was out hunting and feeding, assaulting the King's lands yet again. Dozens of assaults from above had seen the disappearance of hundreds of livestock, the burning of farms and loss of many villagers. They were the simple yet brutal actions of a mother caring for her growing brood.

He'd done what he needed to do for his kingdom. Destroy the nest and, ultimately, the dragon. He'd expected to do the last act there on the mountains, not chasing the rising smoke from his own castle through the night. While the beast eventually died from the wounds she took attacking the keep, she had already exacted her revenge by then.

Why hadn't his love sought refuge in the dungeons below or in the escape tunnels? Why she had remained here in the great hall he'd never know. Everyone here had perished long before his rescue party arrived.

As always, he hadn't been gone more than fifteen minutes when Sir Bendell found him. His second hand emerged from the broken hallways beyond, crawling amidst the fallen stones with some difficulty. The leg injury he received during the destruction of the dragon hive had left him with a noticeable limp.

"Sire," Sir Bendell began.

"Save it, Ben," Dolnar replied. "I don't need the lecture."

Sir Bendell pursed his lips and nodded. He looked around at the charred room and then back at Dolnar, his eyebrows raised. Dolnar sighed.

"It's time, Ben."

"Time sire? To rebuild?"

"No, I weary of this burden," Dolnar said. He walked to the

edge of the ruins and looked down into the town square where Charos' curiously preserved body lay. "It's time Evan took the reins."

"But sire, he's only sixteen," Sir Bendell scoffed.

"Was I so much older when I ascended the throne?" Dolnar replied, still looking down at the fallen foe.

"But… you were battle tested! A leader!"

"Evan has been in the field for two years. Do you forget it was Evan who saved your life in the hive?" Dolnar turned and glared at Sir Bendell.

"I apologize, sire," Sir Bendell replied looking down. "I'm not ready to see you go, I'm afraid."

"Ben, don't you see? My soul left months ago. My body just hasn't realized it yet," Dolnar turned back to the window. "Perhaps a fresher perspective, a younger mind can solve the riddle of the dead dragon."

"As you wish, sire," Sir Bendell said. "But where will you go? Will you remain to advise the Prince?"

"We, Ben, will be traveling to the North. It is time to enjoy wandering the wastes and finding adventure again. Somewhere far from this kingdom is our destination. We're leaving the past behind."

Sir Bendell walked slowly to the edge of the room, staring out at the town below. The morning sun struggled to pierce the clouds above, leaving the buildings below bathed in a dreary light, the morning mist failing to burn away. He rested his hand on the column still standing there, holding up a non-existent roof.

"The beast has not decayed, sire. What if it isn't truly dead?"

"Then the new king will have a different puzzle to solve. How to kill the unkillable," Dolnar muttered. He turned to his advisor. "Make the announcement. Arrange the coronation. We leave in a fortnight."

"Sire!" Sir Bendell protested. "That's barely enough time to alert the other kingdoms!"

"Then, my good man, you'd better hop to it."

Dolnar turned to Sir Bendell, who had not moved from the spot. He frowned as he noticed Sir Bendell's gaze remained on the scene below. He looked to where his good friend stared and saw the cause for his attention. The upturned crow headdress was unmistakable—Ariastheni had returned with her brood of witches to visit his court again. He watched them examine the dragon's inert body. Ariastheni placed her hand on the flesh of the beast and a bright green glow emanated from the spot. Ariastheni removed her hand and then looked up at Dolnar, unerringly finding him amidst the ruined part of the castle. When she looked at him, he shuddered. It was as if she peered into his very soul. He refused to shy away from her gaze. After what seemed like hours, but could have been no more than a few minutes, Ariastheni dropped her eyes and walked away from the dragon, heading to the right. Dolnar sighed. She meant to have an audience with the king.

"Ariastheni beckons, Ben," he said as he turned away. "Let's go see what the old witch has to say."

"Sire," Sir Bendell responded as he turned and watched King Dolnar retreat from the room with haste. "If you but wish it, I shall send the old hag away."

As they deftly navigated the fallen debris, King Dolnar laughed.

"Send her away?" the King responded as he reached the intact part of the hallway. "Why should I do that when it was I who sent for her?"

"Her sorcery has no place in civilized society," Sir Bendell responded and spat on the ground. "Superstitious nonsense."

"In months of consultation with all the clergy from our kingdom and those surrounding us, not a single person came forth with any credible theories about why the dragon remains," Dolnar said as he strode toward the banquet hall. "I sent for her shortly after normal means failed. Why it took her six months to respond is beyond me, but now that's she's here, I will certainly lend her an ear."

"Sire, you're leaving in a fortnight. Surely you can leave the matter to your son," Sir Bendell murmured.

Dolnar stopped in his tracks and turned on his advisor who shuffled to a stop.

"I'm the King," Dolnar said in a tone dark and dangerous. "Until that changes, keep your head about you lest you lose it permanently."

Sir Bendell paled. "Of course, sire," he said and bowed his head.

King Dolnar nodded at his friend and smiled warmly. "Good." He patted him on the shoulder and turned away, heading for the banquet hall again.

Sir Bendell stood motionless for a few seconds and stared after his king. He blinked a few times, shook his head and then followed after him.

When they reached the banquet hall, the King sat in the slightly raised great chair he currently called his throne and awaited the arrival of his invited guests. Sir Bendell walked in stiffly and sat to the king's right hand at the long banquet table.

A runner came in from the gate and bowed as he entered the room.

"Sire," the young man said. "There are some strange people—"

"Yes, Tommy, a strange woman with a crow on her head and four equally strangely dressed women wish to see me. Send them in."

"But how," Tommy began and then immediately bowed again. "Of course, sire. As you command."

The boy turned straight away and ran full speed toward the front of the castle.

The king turned to Sir Bendell.

"That boy's got a lot of promise," Dolnar said. "Quick thinking, fast on his feet. Does Evan have a squire yet?"

"No, your grace," Sir Bendell responded. "That is, the last one took a bad spill and has become lame. We had to move him to the kitchens."

"Well, he certainly can't take Tommy's place with a bum leg. But see to it that Tommy gets a move to Evan's side. Do Evan some good to see how quick a commoner can be. Keep him on his toes."

Before long, the feathered headdress of Ariastheni bowed low upon entering the room. She was followed by four more women dressed in various skins, furs and feathered attire. People of the wild, they were called in more polite circles. Others called them witches, sorcerers and consorts of the devil. The four women kneeled down and Ariastheni stood in front of them, still bowing her head.

"Arise, Ariastheni," King Dolnar said and she raised her head, her sparkling blue eyes taking his breath away. Faint tendrils of her golden hair peeked out around the headdress. He closed his eyes and took a breath. She was always a temptation but never a prize that could be won without being taken against her will. She'd always been off limits even before the King had met Alorra. Still, she made something stir deep in his soul and in his loins.

"My king, I have come at your request," Ariastheni said. The statement was plain, quiet and sullen. It wasn't the usual bubbly, upbeat song of words she normally set forth when she came to court.

"You're troubled," Dolnar said. "That much is plain. What troubles you?"

"You sent for me and I at first did not come because I thought there was nothing I could do for you. Dragons, after all, are magical and my expertise is in the natural. Still, I know something of curses," Ariastheni stepped forward and leaned on one of the low-backed chairs on her side of the table.

"A curse?" Sir Bendell stood up. "Of all the preposterous-"

"Sit down, Ben. I don't need your counsel just yet," Dolnar said with a chuckle.

Flustered, Sir Bendell bowed to his king and sat down. He frowned at Ariastheni.

"What is the curse?" King Dolnar asked.

"I don't know," Ariastheni said. Sir Bendell strangled a reply but still made a small squeak of contempt at the woman.

"I don't understand." Dolnar frowned.

"I can tell you who is behind the curse, but I know not the nature of it. Only that it involves the beast in the courtyard," Ariastheni replied, bowing her head once more.

"Who, then, is behind the curse?" Dolnar said leaning forward.

"The spirits whispered to me the name Zettelek," Ariastheni said almost unsure of the pronunciation.

"The sorcerer?" Dolnar sat back with a groan.

"We put him to death a decade ago." Sir Bendell spat on the floor in disgust. "He put his dark magic to the ill of this kingdom one too many times and got his just reward. Anyone wielding magic is just as tainted by evil."

"Surely, no one of non-magical persuasion could do any evil then, lest all be accused of being the same sort," Ariastheni retorted.

"Enough, you two," Dolnar growled. "We're not here to debate the nature of all magic, just the nature of the magic surrounding Charos."

Dolnar turned and shouted at an open doorway to the left of him. "Fetch the Royal Scribe!"

"Yes, your majesty!" came the shouted reply from an unseen

servant. Running footsteps could be heard disappearing into the distance.

"Why did you come?" Dolnar asked.

"Well," Ariastheni looked around at her companions, confused. "You sent for me."

"Six months ago," Dolnar said. "As you're not a subject of my immediate kingdom, I could not compel you to come forth by penalty of death, so…"

Ariastheni looked down. She stared at the ground for a good minute, gathering her thoughts.

"I had a dream, an ill omen," she said and looked up at the king. "There was a dark shadow looming over you. Death is near. I feared the worst."

"I'm still quite alive," Dolnar said.

"Yes," Ariastheni nodded slowly, "and so is the dragon you told me was dead."

Sir Bendell jumped from his seat. "You'll not call the king a liar, regardless of whose kingdom you set forth from!" Sir Bendell shouted. "You'll be put in chains and tortured for such insults!"

"Ben, sit," Dolnar said calmly, setting a hand on his friend's shoulder.

"But sire!" Sir Bendell said and turned to his king. "This witch has insulted you!"

"Have we not been able to pierce the dragon's hide, even though it has fallen?" Dolnar said. "Has its flesh not rotted as a dead beast should? We may profess to know the ways of the normal world, but a dragon has special properties you and I may not understand. A few wise men have proffered the same advice."

Sir Bendell grimaced, recalling his words just moments ago in the broken throne room. He turned and gave Ariastheni a menacing glare.

"You'll keep a civil tongue around his majesty," Sir Bendell growled and sat with a huff.

"I meant no disrespect, your majesty," Ariastheni said and bowed her head in apology. "But..." She raised her head. "Though it appears to have been dealt a mortal blow, it simply hibernates and heals as would a bear through the winter. I know not why, nor why it hasn't moved, but it is still alive."

The royal scribe arrived, sporting a long flowing white beard and wearing a dark red robe. "You called, your majesty?"

"Tellosh, tell me what we know of the trial and execution of the sorcerer Zettelek?" Dolnar asked. "I recall there being something we worried over after his death, but I can't recall the details."

"Oh, the curse?" Tellosh asked.

"That would fit the details we're after, yes," Dolnar said.

"Let me retrieve the records," Tellosh said. "Even though I think I recall it, my memory is a bit fuzzy and it seems the details would be important, yes?"

"Indeed," Dolnar said waving him away. "Best speed, scribe."

Tellosh bowed and turned, running away as fast as his old legs and sandaled feet could carry him.

"Humph," Sir Bendell said. "I'd forgotten about the curse. I was so filled with hatred at Zettelek's actions that I felt contempt at his final words, not believing them at all. I don't remember the details, but when his curse didn't come true… we all forgot about it."

"Seems that he'd send a dragon immediately if that was the curse, possibly to free him before he was executed," Dolnar mused. He turned back to Ariastheni.

"Tell me, why did you never entertain the idea of being my queen?" Dolnar sat back and enjoyed the blush that came to Ariastheni's cheeks as she quickly averted his eyes and looked at the floor.

"Your majesty is too kind," Ariastheni said. "I'm but a simple druid. I could never hold court with you. This is not my world."

"Tell me about your world," Dolnar said.

Ariastheni looked up at Dolnar. She glanced at Sir Bendell who just shrugged his shoulders.

"Well, we commune with nature," Ariastheni began. As she continued to describe her world of trees, healing, praying and caring for animals and the common people who sought her out, her voice lilted back to the sing song voice Dolnar so admired and fell in love with nearly twenty years ago.

"Sounds wonderful," Dolnar said.

"It is, your majesty," Ariastheni blushed again and bowed her head. "But it's not the life for a king, forgive me for saying so."

"I agree," Dolnar said. "Your reasoning is sound."

"Thank you," she replied.

"Sounds dreadfully boring," Sir Bendell murmured.

"Ben," Dolnar said disapprovingly.

The scribe reappeared at the doorway, out of breath, holding a bundle of manuscripts in his grasp.

"Your majesty," Tellosh gasped, out of breath. "With your permission?" He held up the bundle.

"Of course, Tellosh," Dolnar said, waving his hand at the table.

Tellosh stepped forward and dumped the manuscripts on the table. He spread the five sets of papers out and began leafing through them, every once in a while muttering something and then moving on to the next pile. In the middle of the third pile, he slapped his hand down on the page and turned to the king, beaming.

"I've got it!"

King Dolnar smiled and inclined his head forward.

"Oh, of course, your majesty!" Tellosh said and turned back to the page. "It says Zettelek said 'With my death, you will seal the curse and the beast shall hunt and destroy everything you care for until the end of your kingdom.' And then you nodded and Marvin cut off his head."

"Marvin?" Sir Bendell asked.

"Ah, yes, my brother Marvin was the executioner. Unfortunately, he's since passed. Died of consumption while I was away at the monastery studying several years ago."

"The end of my kingdom not my death?" Dolnar asked and stroked his chin.

Tellosh looked back at the manuscript. He traced the words carefully with his fingers. He turned back to Dolnar.

"That's what was recorded and it's accurate if my memory serves," Tellosh said. "All kings reign until their death or so it's been recorded."

"Thank you, Tellosh," Dolnar said. "You may return to your studies."

Tellosh bowed his head, gathered his manuscripts and hobbled out of the room. Ariastheni looked at Dolnar with a sadness that shook the monarch to his core. He chuckled nervously.

"Not to worry, my dear, I'll be abdicating the throne in a fortnight and then we can permanently dispatch the beast where it lay."

The look of sadness did not dissipate, but was accompanied by a shaking of the head. Again, Ariastheni looked at the floor.

"I can only advise, milord, but the beast will be up within a few days' time if not sooner. That wound is nearly fully healed. Even now, I can barely sense the damage and the injury is no longer visible on the dragon's hide."

"We noticed the wound healing," Dolnar sighed. "I remember the day the shaft from the ballista bolt slid from the wound nearly three months ago. The wound has been closing ever since, but we thought it some minor magical trickery. Turns out it wasn't minor at all."

Dolnar looked at Sir Bendell, who had been strangely silent the last few minutes.

"What say you, Ben?"

Sir Bendell looked up with sadness in his eyes as well.

"I can find no fault in your logic, sire, nor that of the maiden druid." Sir Bendell stood up. "I would be the first to advise you to never give up your throne, but under the circumstances, I…" His voice faltered and he found he couldn't finish his sentence.

"It is well, Ben," Dolnar said softly. "Tommy!"

The young runner appeared almost immediately.

"Yes, sire?"

"Tell Sir Frederick, Prince Evan and Lady Drea to attend me at once."

"As you wish, sire!" Tommy bowed and turned on his heels faster than anyone Dolnar had ever seen. He turned to Sir Bendell. "Ben, make the arrangements. The coronation will take place in an hour's time. Have all the people we need, but forgo the decorations. Speed is of the essence."

"Of course, sire." Sir Bendell bowed and headed out immediately.

"You see, Ariastheni, nothing to worry about. In an hour's time, the beast will no longer be protected by this curse and we can dispatch it safely," Dolnar said smiling.

"But, what will you do then?" Ariastheni asked, a look of shock on her face.

"I thought perhaps I might visit the wilds of Oakendell to see what might interest me there," Dolnar said. His low rumble caused Ariastheni to lower her eyes to the ground once more. However, he heard her breath catch at his comment and he smiled.

Sir Frederick was the first to arrive, half in his armor and half out.

"Sire, my apologies, I was just readying myself for some exercises with the men," Sir Frederick said. His woolen trousers hung loose beneath his breastplate of iron.

"I'm abdicating the throne in an hour's time, Frederick," Dolnar said. He held his hand up at the anticipated objection from Sir Frederick which immediately quelled his protest. "The reason the dragon still lies in wait upon our grounds is a curse that can only be broken by me giving up the throne. It's time, Frederick. The ghosts of the past must be laid to rest. As God is my witness, my reign is one of those ghosts."

Sir Frederick nodded. "Your grace, shall I assemble the men for an honor guard for Prince Evan then?"

"Prince Evan shall be attended by no more than ten men. The rest will ready themselves to slay the beast. There's a chance even now that it will awaken before we've completed the coronation. Ready the ballistae. We may have a bit of fighting before the day is done. My last command as king will be to slay that foul serpent with all your might and prowess."

"So it shall be, my liege," Sir Frederick replied and exited hastily.

Prince Evan arrived with Lady Drea in tow. Behind them, Sir Bendell escorted Cardinal Archibald into the room, followed closely behind by Tellosh, carrying another manuscript as well as a pen and quill. All was ready for the signing and ceremony.

Cardinal Archibald approached King Dolnar immediately.

"This is most unusual, your highness. Never before has a king of the realm abdicated," Cardinal Archibald protested.

"Abdicated?" Prince Evan cried out. He immediately strode

forth, running his hand through his blonde locks. "Father, this can't be true! I'm not ready!"

"Can either of you fine, upstanding members of society give me a way to end the life of Charos who still haunts our grounds?" King Dolnar said, standing up and thundering in a commanding voice.

A cry rang out down the hall. "The beast moves!"

Ten of Sir Frederick's men arrived to surround and protect Prince Evan.

"Quickly now, while we still have the upper hand!" King Dolnar shouted. "Lady Drea, my apologies. It appears we won't have time for a celebration feast until the beast is slain."

Lady Drea bowed her head and the Cardinal stood before King Dolnar and Prince Evan and repeated the words Tellosh read from a manuscript. Within moments, Dolnar signed the decree, the task had been completed and the former Prince now wore a crown signifying his coronation.

"Be strong, noble and wise, my son. Lead from the heart as well as the head," Dolnar said as he grabbed his son's shoulders and pulled him in for a hug. "Now use that wisdom and get to the safety of the dungeons, my king. Lord knows what this beast has in store for us in its final moments."

The men and the new king rushed away and Dolnar picked up his scabbard from next to the chair. He looked at Sir Bendell and smiled.

"You ready for one last fight at my side, Ben?"

"Always, sir!" Sir Bendell shouted and rushed out after his lord into the night.

WANT SOME T?
BY HIROMI COTA

Eh? I'm just winding things up. Shutting it down. At least until the passes clear. Might be awhile. You, uh—if you don't mind me sayin' so—don't look like you're from here. Not that that matters a bit. Lots of folks from here leave and don't find their ways back here. Don't know how they're doin', but I'd imagine—I'd hope—that they found someplace else that suits them better. And other folks wind up here without knowin' exactly where here is and makin' it their home. What I'm tryin' to say here is that if you're meaning to stay here a spell, that's just fine. And if you're waitin' 'til the passes clear up so's you can make your way out somewhere else, that's okay in my book, too.

Not that you need my approval. You're a grown person. You can do as you please. That's somethin' most folks don't take to heart these days. Or any day, truth be told. Humans are social critters. We always want to make sure that what we do's okay in the eyes of other people. And, that's a good thing. It helps to make sure that we don't hurt no body.

We're still gonna do some harm. Ain't no gettin' 'round that.

Harm happens. Hurt happens. All we can do is try to keep it to a minimum. So, like I was sayin', you're your own person and you can do what feels right for you. If that means stayin' here when the weather gets better, well, plenty of space here for more folks.

And, hell, it don't even matter if you don't know whether you're stayin' or goin' right now, either. Or if you change your mind. Heh. I've been sayin' that this place isn't quite my home for years, but it's the closest thing I've found. It feels good. Solid. You say somethin' like that long enough and it stops being something you think about. It's just somethin' I say now. I know I'm not gonna up and leave here. I'm not too old to learn new things, but I know I don't want to find myself someplace that's not right again.

You know the feeling.

You sit down and everyone looks at you. Maybe they say that they're okay with you. Maybe they have daggers hidden behind them. Maybe the daggers are out in front, in plain view of anyone who thinks to look. Maybe everyone's fine, but only that: fine. Okay. Not bad. Not good. Things sit just well enough with you that you don't want to tear your heart out and cry your soul away. You can live like that. But you know in your heart of hearts that you don't want to. Something's gotta go. You or your surroundings.

I know you've felt that. I have. Hell. I—

No. We don't need to talk about that. If you want to later on, we can. But I don't need to know, and you don't need me to put any weight on your back by spillin' my guts before we even rightly know each other. Point is, there's a choice: move or don't. And "don't" means you don't make it, for the biggest definition of "make it." Self-harm, takin' one's own life, endin' it all, takin' the easy way out, suicide, whatever you want to call it.

Nothing easy about any of it. But, when you're a square block and all the holes around you are circles, the balls don't know you have it rough; they can go back and forth, no problems a'tall. Try as you might, you're not gettin' through those holes and it's no one's fault.

Whoever made those holes didn't know folks like you and me were around. Hmm? No. I don't blame them. They're just ignorant. They didn't know. They should'a. But, they didn't. If you tell 'em now? I don't know. Maybe they'll learn. Maybe they'll cut out a square hole and a triangle hole. Maybe they'll do the right thing and level out that playing field. Maybe they won't.

That's what being an activist is. Talkin' out loud and hopin'. Hopin' that someone'll listen and get those square and triangle holes cut. If you could do it yourself, that'd be even better, but not everyone can. It's hard. Too damn hard for me. You know what happens to most o' those folks who just do the work first without askin'? Well, they wind up in jail. Or worse. But, that's how fast change happens.

You know the first Pride was a riot? True story. Buncha trans ladies o' color got mad. Got real tired of bein' punished for not looking like balls. They were done being pushed around and started doing some pushin' of their own. Lotta people got hurt. Lotta people got arrested. Was it worth it? I think so. But I wasn't there. I wasn't one o' the ones getting hit by the cops. For me, it was just a story in the newspaper. It was just an action that started leading to folks like you and me not having to worry about as many of those daggers I was talkin' about.

Would I do it? Heh. I think we know now that I wouldn't. Or I'd be in jail right now. Does that make me a coward? I don't know. I hope not. I've spent my bravery doing other things. Some days, just gettin' up and lettin' other folks see my face is pretty brave. Maybe no one else thinks so. That's fine. They're not me. I know what it feels like to be me. It's hard bein' me all the time. But, that's why I'm here. Halfway between somewhere and somewhere else. Neither of those places'd suit me. But, here? In the neither here nor there? It's good. I like it.

Could it be better? Yeah. Probably. But I'd have to find that place first. And that's a whole mess of work that I know I'm not ready to handle. So, yeah. I'm home.

I hope this is your home, but if not, I hope you get there soon.

Want some tea?

A GIFT
BY AMBER RAINEY

I hate this song."

I winced almost immediately, hoping Allison hadn't heard my outburst. I pretended I hadn't said anything, continuing to stare at the crossword puzzle I had been solving on my phone. I suppressed a sigh when I heard her daintily walking across the floor towards me. She'd heard. She came around the couch and plopped down on it, propping her feet in my laugh and staring at me. I was still patently ignoring her, even though I had moved my hands out of her way, but I knew she had raised her eyebrow at me in that way of hers. It meant she was waiting for me to elaborate. When I didn't take the bait after a few minutes, she nudged my phone with her foot. I put my phone down and looked over at her, still not answering her unspoken question. She shook her head in an amused way and ended our staring contest.

"What, my darling Scrooge, do you dislike about the song?"

She laughed at my scrunched up face and the middle finger I shot in her direction. I listened again for a moment, my discomfort clear, and then shook my head. It was almost Christmas and I did not want to start another argument.

"Forget it."

"Nope. Not this time. This time you have to tell me."

"Allison…"

She jerked her legs back from my lap and tucked them under her body. It was a clear sign that my desire for peace would not win out. Allison hated it when I kept things from her and she hated it even more if I ignored her desires for closure before bed. She went by the *don't go to sleep angry* motto, whereas I was more a *let me cool off and forget it* kind of person.

"Fine!" I snapped, just a little too harshly—judging by the way she jumped back in surprise.

I swallowed heavily, wishing my hatred of the "Christmas" song had not burst out of me. I silently berated myself for my inability to just stay quiet for the few minutes it would take for the song to play out and switch to something more pleasant. Already, a new song was playing through our smart speaker and I would have given anything to have been still solving my crossword while listening to Allison hum to the music while wrapping Christmas gifts. I would have helped her but our first Christmas together she saw the haphazard way I wrapped presents and then banned me for life.

I adored the hours it took her to wrap the presents. They were works of art and it was a shame they were destroyed so quickly by those who did not appreciate art. Allison used double-sided tape and wrapped each seam so carefully, she even made sure the paper continued so it was nearly impossible to tell there was a seam in the first place. She also wrapped each present in a different paper, meaning we had a veritable treasure trove of wrapping paper. One entire closet was dedicated to paper, ribbons, bows, and other decorative items not normally found on a package but artfully placed on Allison's gifts. The memory had me smiling, which did not sit well with the seething I could feel coming from Allison and I resigned myself to the argument we were about to have.

"Honey, I don't like it when you call me a scrooge. I'm not a scrooge, I just feel like we should acknowledge one holiday before we go worrying about the next. Christmas has encroached upon Thanksgiving for years and then it started in on Halloween. *This year* there were decorations in the store before Labor day! It's getting out of hand."

Allison shook her head at me and I knew right then she had seen through my attempted diversion. She was not easy to throw off the scent and I was not giving her the explanation she wanted. She crossed her arms and glared at me. Daring me to either go on with my bogus detour of the topic or actually address the elephant in the room that had brought her to the couch in the first place.

"It's just a song."

"Nice try…"

"Why is it a Christmas song? Just because it has Christmas in the title? Just so they could capitalize on the holidays? They couldn't make something catchy and cute?"

"It is catchy," she shrugged.

"But… for all the wrong reasons. The tune is catchy but the sentiment is horrendous. I mean—just bear with me here—he says he will give his heart to someone special this year. It begs two questions: one, why didn't he give it to someone special last year and two, he is clearly still hung up on last year's person so this year's person is just a rebound so does that mean the very next day he will break their heart? It's preposterous… oh and *three*, Christmas isn't a time for romance!"

She huffed and stood up. She opened and shut her mouth a couple of times, trying to find a way to poke a hole in my argument but I could clearly see she agreed with me on some level. Then I saw it in her eyes. My third reason had hit and she was even more livid than before when I'd tried to change the direction of our fight.

"Christmas is a *perfectly* wonderful time for romance! Otherwise, we wouldn't have Christmas romance movies."

I opened my mouth to give my opinion on that particular topic but caught myself just in time. Or so I thought. She'd watched me too closely. *Great,* I thought, *now we are going to argue about that, too.* I wasn't wrong, though it did not please me to be right in this instance.

"No. You will absolutely not get out of this by just pretending you weren't going to say something. Spit. It. Out."

"Very well, those romance movies are too sickly sweet and way too formulaic. No one falls in love in just one month. Everything is just too easy in those movies. Those relationships could never work. It's all chalked up to the magic of Christmas but Christmas isn't usually magical. It is stressful and time-consuming. It's not a time for romance. It can be enjoyable but things that are too easy don't last."

"You only say that because you make everything so difficult!"

Allison's voice had started quivering and I could see tears welling in her eyes. I wanted nothing more than to wipe away those tears and hold her close to me but I knew she was too wound up for that to happen. Once again, I yelled at myself internally for pointing out the ridiculous song. It was not worth fighting over and yet, we were.

"Sweetheart, it's just a song and I am sorry if I offended you. December is not my favorite month but that doesn't mean you can't enjoy it and I can't enjoy watching you have fun. Can we just forget about this?"

"I just... I need to go out for a while."

I looked out the window. It was a little fogged up from the heat inside and I could tell it had probably gotten colder since the sun had gone down. I hated the cold, too. I just hated winter in general but we'd had that argument enough and I knew how to tamp down my feelings on that topic. I looked back at her, tried to give a reassuring smile, and nodded. I watched her retreat into our bedroom, heard her rustle around for a few minutes, and then return wearing her winter gear.

"I could come with you."

She sighed and shook her head.

"I need to cool off and it is pretty chilly. Just give me a bit, okay?"

I nodded and watched as she grabbed her keys and left the apartment. I let out a long, shaky breath and squeezed my eyes shut, trying to picture a reset on the pleasant evening we had been having. My mind wandered to Allison, mentally following her as she walked. I knew exactly where she was headed.

Whenever she needed space, Allison always walked to the Bridge of Glass. It was an odd obsession she had but she was an artist and I knew she appreciated the beauty of all the pieces on the bridge. I'd once caught her lying under the "Seaform Pavilion" staring up at the various pieces and smiled. When I had hovered over her, blocking her view, she'd pulled me down to lie next to her, talking about the various pieces. I stared at her, falling more in love with her, a feat I'd never thought possible. She finally noticed me staring instead of listening.

"What?"

"Why do you like to stare at these pieces? You come here so often."

"I'm looking for possibilities."

"It's just sand…"

"That sand never aspired to anything. It didn't know what it would become. Now, look at it, so beautiful and yet so fragile. The sand never asked to be turned into glass but it was and now it is possible for it to shine."

I laughed and she blushed. I held her hand and stared up at the glass pieces, trying to see what she saw. I never could see anything more than colored glass pieces. My mind was too analytical and too caught up in order to see the beauty in the chaos. I knew she could tell I did not enjoy it as much as she did but she didn't say anything and I was content to lay on the ground and hold her hand because my joy was fulfilled by lying next to her. She was my possibilities.

I came back to myself in the apartment and chastised myself for letting her go out walking, alone and in the cold. Time was a vague construct to her and if I didn't remind her it was freezing outside, she would lay on the bridge for hours at a time, the cold from the concrete seeping into her bones and giving her a chill. The last time we had been on the bridge at night, we were out so long, I didn't think I could feel my butt for three days, even after sitting on a heating pad. I got up and went to find some warm clothing.

I stepped outside, already regretting the decision not to take some hand warmers. Luckily, the promised rain had not yet started and I was hoping to retrieve Allison and make it inside before that luck ran out. I walked swiftly down our block and across the street, hopping back and forth to stay warm while I waited for the pedestrian light to allow me to cross. Once across the street, I walked quickly to the bridge but frowned at the start of it. I didn't see anyone there. Allison was not lying under the "Seaform Pavilion", nor was she standing by the "Venetian Wall." I turned around under the pavilion and looked back the way I had come, wondering if I had missed her somehow, but I did not see anyone else on the street. Everyone was in for the night, anticipating the forecasted wintry weather.

I turned back around and scanned the bridge once more. A sudden wave of unease fell over me and I balled my hands in my coat pocket, dreading the walk across the bridge for an unknown reason.

As I passed under the pavilion, a dark figure emerged from the side of the bridge near the crystal towers and ran off in the opposite direction of me. Fear gripped my heart and I forced myself to continue to the spot where the man had just run. Adrenaline took over the moment I saw a foot sticking out from the side of the only obscured spot on the bridge.

"Allison!"

I rushed over and knelt on the ground, ignoring the slick, almost black liquid on the cement. My brain refused to acknowledge what it knew to be blood. Her blood. I checked for life and was relieved to find that she was still breathing. I swore under my breath, a quick check of my pockets revealing I'd left my cell phone back in our apartment.

"Allison, it's going to be okay. I need your phone. Just stay with me."

She reached out and grabbed my arm, the one I was using to pull her phone out of her pocket. She looked at me and at that moment, I realized she was going to give up. She tried to talk but I wanted her to save her strength and use it to fight for her life. I wanted her to fight for us. I didn't want fighting to be the last thing we had done.

"I need to call an ambulance. You need to rest. It's going to be okay."

"Virginia... I just wanted to help... him."

"It's okay, sweetheart. I'm here. It will be okay."

"He didn't believe I didn't have... cash... I tried to tell... him... "

She broke off coughing and I refused to acknowledge the blood on her lips. I didn't want to admit she'd been hurt. Intrinsically, I knew it was bad but I wanted to deal with the situation in a calm manner. The trouble was, my usual calm in the face of danger was crumbling in the face of the impending death of the one person I loved most in the world. I sat down fully and cradled her in my arms, trying to yank off my glove at the same time in order to use the phone. She put her blood-stained hand on mine and shook her head.

"It's too late."

"It can't be."

She nodded, her strength for arguing waning with each labored breath. She closed her eyes and I started sobbing, stroking her hair and hoping the approaching sirens were coming to save her. She squeezed my hand and I hugged her to me, as tightly as possible, trying to make my sheer force of will keep her alive. She chuckled for a moment and I looked down at her. She raised her eyebrow a little.

"Darling… Scrooge… it's everything after December…"

"I don't understand."

"One day… you will…"

Paramedics arrived and the adrenaline overtook me. I crumbled into a sobbing mess while they worked on her and rushed her off to the hospital. The policemen tried to console me but they did not understand anything I said. They wrapped me in a blanket and took me to the hospital.

In February, I sat on the sofa and stared at the window, cursing the falling snow. I'd sloshed through the rain to get home before the snow had started but I'd wanted to be out longer. I'd gone to the bridge, just as I had done every day since the one that took Allison from me. I'd try to figure out what she meant, looking into the glass but only feeling her ghost everywhere. It was the only place I still felt whole and leaving made the emptiness grow larger and larger each time. I looked around at our apartment. The Christmas tree was still in its spot, the timer turning the lights on each evening. The presents Allison had been wrapping before our argument were still in their original state of either being wrapped or partially wrapped and decorated. I hadn't been able to touch anything as if Christmas were a perpetual holiday in our house.

I ignored our friends. I knew they wanted to help but I couldn't stand their looks of pity or even the genuine offers of help. Our neighbors would bring little doggie bags of food, ring the doorbell, and then set the bag outside the door. They'd learned it was the only way I would take the offering as I refused to talk to anyone. I was a shadow of myself, convinced there was no way to live in a world without Allison.

By March, my friend George had decided enough was enough. He barged into our apartment, technically he used the key we had given him, and announced we were going to start the healing process. He practically forced me to take a shower, threatening to put me in it with my clothes on if I didn't do it myself. When I was done, I came out of my bedroom and gasped in horror, the Christmas tree in a half state of being undecorated.

"What are you doing!?!"

He shrugged, "It needs to come down. You can't heal if it doesn't."

I glared at him and stomped my foot.

"I don't want to heal!"

"But you must. Allison would want you to heal."

Angry tears began flowing down my face.

"Don't," I growled.

George came over to me and gave me a hug, letting me cry on his shoulder. When I could stop, I tried to pull away but he just enveloped me tighter. He waited until I hugged him back and then released me.

"Go out for a walk, honey. Clear your head and then, when you get back, we can work on everything else in the apartment. We'll make a plan. Baby steps…"

I nodded and went to put on some warm clothes. I knew he

was just trying to get me out of the apartment so that he could de-Allison it. I knew that it was for my own good, even if I didn't like it. I yelled at him in my head, not wanting to yell at him in person. I was done trying to argue and George was a good friend. I hadn't already run him off with my behavior for the past three months so chances were pretty good he wasn't going anywhere. I looked up and sighed, realizing my feet had taken me back to the bridge, again.

I laid down under the Seaform, remembering my darling Allison and happier times. I couldn't stop the tears from coming. A man and a woman stopped for a moment and then quickly walked past me, whispering to each other, probably about me. I gathered myself up and rose, walking down the bridge, ignoring the spot where Allison had been shot. I had never been able to look at that spot, clearly seeing the pool of blood on the concrete in my mind, even though, rationally, I knew it was cleaned long ago. I stopped in front of a green vase on the wall. I could feel her presence and almost see her in the glass but she wasn't there. I collapsed into a heap and began sobbing again. I don't know how long I was there. It had gotten darker and colder and yet, I did not feel it. I only felt my overwhelming grief.

I felt a hand on my shoulder and looked up to see George, holding a candle, and smiling at me. He pulled me to my feet and I took me over to a group of others, all holding candles. It was all the friends I had neglected. Those who were hurting by the loss of Allison, just as I was. George and the others all hugged me and I listened as each one told me what Allison had meant to them. I allowed myself to be consoled for the first time since she had died and it did not feel as unsavory as I thought it would.

After a while, George walked back home with me and let me into the now clean house. George had put away all of the decorations and stowed the presents, all save one. There was a beautiful green package, adorned with a red, glittered butterfly sitting on our table. I sighed and started shaking my head, backing away from the present as if it were a snake ready to bite me. George stopped me with his hands on my shoulders. He leaned into me.

"She took the time to chose it for you. I think it will help you move on to see her final gift to you. She was very excited about it."

"You know what it is?"

"I do. I'll leave it up to you. I'll be back tomorrow."

I nodded and listened to him leaving. I stood by the now-closed door and stared at the package. I don't know how long I stood there but I eventually went over to the package and sat down at the table. I put out a shaky hand and lovingly caressed the paper. The design was subtle but I knew that no matter how hard it was, Allison had matched that design so perfectly I would not be able to easily find the seam. I picked up the package and put it in my lap. She'd probably wrapped it right under my nose while I did crossword puzzles. I laughed a little, hearing her chiding me in my head for hoping to keep it as pretty as possible.

"They are made to be ripped open."

"They are too beautiful. Works of art."

"Here, I'll help you tear it."

"Don't you dare! It's my gift."

I smiled and laughed because she would smile and laugh. I took a deep breath and tore into the paper, just to make her proud— if she were watching from above. The thought brought tears to my eyes and I closed them, trying to chase away the sorrow and enjoy what she got me. When the feeling to cry subsided, I opened the box and stared down at the gift. Love filled my heart and I finally understood. Everything after December was the key. I put my hand on the gift and sent a silent thank you to Allison, knowing she could feel my gratitude and my love.

SOOTHES THE SAVAGE BEAST
BY MARSHALL MILLER

Joe Handel covered his eyes as the darkroom was flooded by light. "Assholes," he mumbled while he blinked his eyes in automatic attempts to focus. He had been in the lightless room for an indeterminate time, ever since unknown people had grabbed him after the concert.

One minute Joe was walking his lanky frame out of another successful Rock concert venue as an opening act in Las Vegas, and the next moment someone with bulging muscles grabbed him. Another person placed a black hood over his head. He had tried to fight back (being a former Roadie he had learned the rough and tumble), but some chemicals inside the hood made him zone out within seconds. The musician woke up in a totally dark room. The only thing that kept him from thinking he was blind was the florescent bracelet some female fan had given him that night. If he ever saw the young hot body again, he would give her such a hug and a kiss.

He had called out in the darkness, demanding answers. Joe received a high pitched electronic howl like in feedback from a lousy speaker/microphone mix for his efforts. THAT had hurt his ears, so no more complaints. So he sat and tried to count seconds and minutes. After a tedious passage of time, he started composing new songs in his mind.

Joseph Handel was a musical savant. His family believed a direct familial connection with *the* George Frederic Handel of 'The Messiah' fame, but nobody had ever done an ancestry workup. However, for as long as he could remember, he had an ear for music. Joe could play most instruments by ear, learned to read music so he could write songs. He preferred to play his own songs, not someone else's.

He had completed a five-minute guitar and drum riff in his head and was trying to figure out how to add some orchestra violins (he loved to jam together classical sounds and nasty rock and roll) when a door opened. The pitch blackness had hidden the access point. At least those in control had a subdued red illumination from the other side of the door, so Joe's eyes had a chance to adjust without pain. The musician blinked a few times then stood up.

"If I'm being held for ransom," said Joe, "forget it. I'm not worth that much."

Two red light outlined figures came through the door. As Joe's eyes focused, he saw one character walked; the other was in some kind of motorized chair. Joe stood silent as dim lighting began to fill his confinement.

"Hey, this has been giggles, but..."

"Mister Handel, this is no joke," the walker spoke. Then the person in the motorized wheelchair came closer. Joe could barely hear the motors of the conveyance hum as the operator moved to within a yard.

"You're brave to approach a mad kidnapped musician," said Joe as he saw that both the seated and the upright persons were female. Now the chair-bound woman spoke.

"You won't hurt me, Joseph Handel. I have been a fan of your music for quite some time. I know you inside and out. Literally."

"What?" Joe asked, now even more confused. "You grabbed me because you like my music?"

"Not me, my talented friend. Them."

The room was now well lit, so the large photograph the standing woman was holding was easily seen. The—thing- in the picture had way too many limbs, appendages, and what passed as a head had two large batwing ears. Joe was known throughout the music scene as a bit of a UFO aficionado, so the photo itself did not shock him. The fact that clearly, some government officials were showing him the being as an official document, that shocked him.

"Alright. Enough with the bullshit. I don't know who you are, not even first names…"

"My name is Eve Aden," said the clearly disabled dark-haired woman.

"And I am her sister, Karen," added the standing lady. "We are both exobiologists, doctors, assigned to a select SETI working group. I believe you know what SETI does based on some media interviews and a song or two you wrote—and broadcast at Burning Man five years ago."

"Burning Man?" Then Joe remembered. A week of partying and counter-culture debauchery in the desert in Northwest Nevada out past Reno. He and the band, the *ALTERNATES*, had gone there as a media gig to launch another attempt at quasi stardom. Some guy had hooked up an odd-looking machine with antenna, with a sign stating he could broadcast anything to the Heaven. So Joe and his buddies broadcast two songs referring to Outer Space, and Aliens. A local news station had interviewed them and the 'scientist' resulting in some entertainment agents contacting the band soon thereafter. The rest was history.

"Yeah, the band and I did that. That scientist guy said he beamed the songs using a laser and also broadcast them on the good old FM band. I never gave it much thought, other than it helped us get the opening act gig in Lost Wages."

"Well," said Eve Aden. "Someone else was paying attention when your 'scientist' friend beamed the signal out towards the Proxima Centauri B area. It is a discovered planet about 4.2 Lightyears away from us near the well-know Alpha Centauri."

"So," interjected Joe, " our new friends with the enormous ears heard my songs and came a-running. Just like that."

"Yes," my fast learner fan," said sister Karen with a smile. "The Dumbos, as some wise alec named them, came zipping our way."

"Faster than light, hyperspace travel, what are they using to get here this fast?" asked Joe.

"We will know that when they get here," said Eve as she adjusted her motorized chair. "Why we grabbed you and brought you to Area 51, Dreamland, is that your music—well, it seems to speak to them. You are going to help us find out how and start a conversation."

Joe did not protest about being grabbed once he learned he would be talking to real Outer Space Aliens. However, he did drive a hard bargain for compensation for himself and the band. After all, he told the Sister Scientists he needed them to help communicate.

"Why?" Eve, his biggest music fan, asked. "You wrote these songs."

"And the band, Mike, Janice. Peter and Archie, they MAKE it. They help give birth to the sounds. Without them, it's all in my head, trying to beat its way out."

The two sisters looked at each other. Then Karen walked to the single access door.

"Please wait with my sister. This will take some—work."

Eve ordered some coffee and light snacks while they waited. A large man pushed a serving cart into the room, gave Joe the message with a single glance not to try anything stupid. Joe poured himself and Eve some coffee. The wheelchair scientist took it black, which surprised Joe. As the two humans sipped at their beverages, Eve looked at Joe.

"Please, go ahead and ask. I know you are thinking about it."

"Thinking what, Eve? I can call you by your first name, right? "

"Of course. Your biggest fan is flattered. Now, ask it."

Joe paused for a moment. How to ask this without being too rude and crude.

"Well, you and your sister's faces," said Joe. "You could be Twins."

"We are. And yes, you are thinking, how could that be? Well, let the scientist explain."

Eve Aden explained they are started like as Conjoined Twins. In old rude and crude days, they would have been called Siamese Twins. Because of the way they were joined, at the pelvic region, with their organs twisted around. Originally, it was thought Eve would have to be sacrificed so that Karen could live.

"Our parents, our father, an Air Force Colonel, our mother, a school teacher, said Hell No. They said all or nothing. This was at a military hospital, so you can imagine how that conversation went."

Joe snorted, then commented.

"Yeah. I did a short stint in The SandBox. Three years as a Marine Rifleman. I know all about military medicine. Good with shrapnel wounds, limited with everything else."

"Yes. Your records said you have a Purple Heart."

"I should have known, Eve, when you said you knew everything about me, you weren't kidding."

Eve smiled.

"All except why you joined, being a musical savant and all."

"Hell, Eve. I had something to prove. You know how many times punks tried to beat me up for carrying a violin, or a clarinet?"

Eve laughed as Joe chuckled. He liked the sound of her laugh. The exobiologist continued with her story.

"Karen got the working legs out of the deal. I got a chance at life."

"You don't seem—bitter, Eve. Some people would be."

Eve shrugged, then sipped he coffee.

"It could have been worse. There are cases where one twin has the remains of the other inside their body. This way, we each have a twin who lived."

The two very different humans made what was often referred to as small talk while they waited for Karen to reappear. It soon revolved around the band's music.

"I like it because you are not afraid to mix classical type orchestration with good old hard rock and roll," Eve said with a twinkle in her eye. "I may not be able to dance, 'cut a rug,' as my Grandparents might have said, due to my limitations, but I can still enjoy it."

"You know, not to get personal," said Joe, "but I saw a beauty contest for wheelchair-bound women where they danced. So, don't sell yourself short."

Eve's mouth formed into a sly grin as she looked at Joe.

"I never do. And I also know that you have sides to your person you very rarely show to others. Like now."

Joseph realized he had not been this relaxed talking to a professional woman since he could not remember when. He was used to groupies, fans, music executives who looked at him and the band as pieces of meat. Eve looked and talked to him as if he mattered beyond his loud music. Before Joe could continue, the room door slid open again ala *Star Trek*, and Karen Aden entered.

"Your bandmates are en route. They should be here in a couple of hours."

Joe frowned, then asked, "Did you use the hood routine again? They will NOT like that."

Karen gave him a sly smile, which was a duplicate of her sister's.

"Ask me no questions, and I will tell you no lies, Joseph Handel."

Joe's bandmates did arrive in record time, but without the drug-induced unconsciousness. Some Men and Women In Black had contacted them as they were looking for Joe when he failed to attend a meeting with a music agent. The music agent was quickly hustled off with the fear of God in him about a story of terrorism, 9/11 stuff, and how would he like to disappear. There was almost a fight as even Janice was ready to punch someone when the black-suited personnel told them Joe was at Area 51, and they had to come with government types if they wanted Joe to be returned safe and sound.

"I told Joe all that UFO crap would get him in trouble!" Archie McNab, the beefy redheaded drummer, opined.

"Well, if he is in trouble," said the mixed-race bass player Peter Johnson interjected, "the band is all for one and one for all. So, we fight our way out."

Mike Yamato, the Okinawan-American jack of all trades with instruments, like Joe, chuckled.

"Well, I have some tonfas in my gear. So I can bust some heads without breaking our instruments."

Janice Page flipped her dark striped blonde hair back and stared at the Men and Women in Black who were escorting them to some black SUVs.

"Joe is okay, right?" Janice said with her best growling vibrato voice. As the main vocalist, Janice had a range in her singing that was seen as near supernatural. Joe oft said when she was not in earshot that if not for her, they would be just an average club band.

"Don't tell her, she may get a swelled head and leave," was a frequent statement from the titular leader. Joe had brought the band members together, and they all knew it.

Some two hours later, the final quarter-hour under black hoods, the Alternatives were hugging and scolding Joe in a large briefing room. There were a couple of military types with lots of ribbons and shiny rank along with the Agents in Black. And of course, Eve and Karen Aden were there with a set of briefing charts. The two exobiologists explained in more detail what they knew about the aliens called Dumbos.

"They look like odd Centaurs," said Janice. "Four legs to walk on, two muscular looking arms with what, six-digit hands at the end? If they had human-looking heads and not the big ears, they could come from Greek Mythology."

"I see we have someone educated in something other than rock and roll music in our midst," said Eve with a smile.

"Hey, Doc Wheels," began Archie. "Just because we are headbangers doesn't mean.."

"Watch how you talk to her," snapped Joe. "Keep it up, and your drum sticks will be where the sun don't shine."

"What? You her boyfriend now?" Archies snapped back. Joe growled and saw red. Then two large Agents in Black were between them.

"Alright, gentlemen," said the General in a Marine Corps

uniform and a high and tight haircut. "We do not have time for bull—crap. Our alien friends will be in Earth's orbit within twenty-four hours. We need to figure out if they are as peaceful as they are acting—so far."

"And that is where you all come in," said Karen. "The video and audio they sent us show our Centaur neighbors communicating with what to us sounds like songs and with body motions like dance moves."

"They did this to our songs, also?" asked Mike.

"Yes," replied Eve. "They pay recordings of your song and move with the rhythm. Then they sing or talk to us. We just cannot quite get what they are trying to say. So, since they, like myself, enjoy your music, we thought why not contact them with something they like."

"You're a fan, also, Professor?" asked Peter.

"I have all your recordings. Including I believe some bootleg ones."

"Hell, we're famous in interstellar space," quipped Janice. " Time for a new music agent."

"What General Jamison said about being Earth's orbit, that is going to happen in twenty-four hours?" asked Joe.

"Yes, Joe," answered Eve. "General Jamison and USAF General Hargrove are here on direct orders from the President. If you can establish a dialogue with the Dumbos, great. If not, then they have to plan for the worse."

"Which is?" asked Joe.

"Terminate contact. With prejudice, if necessary."

The band was soon in a large auditorium containing every kind of musical instrument imaginable. The musicians were like five-year-olds in a toy store at Christmas. There was even a Theremin electronic music maker. Joe whistled as he examined it.

"Man, shades of *The Earth Stood Still, Forbidden Planet*. We can make some weird music with this".

"So, where's the Alien music?" Janice asked.

"Watch the large video screen," Eve answered as an oversized section of the wall slid back. The five musicians were soon transfixed as a group of six centaur Dumbos appeared on the screen. A melodic sound that seemed to be coming from the large teeth filled mouths of the aliens filled the room. There was an undercurrent of bass which vibrated the humans and an overcurrent of what seemed to be Soprano singing. Janiec began to sway with the rhythm.

"This is nice. Could be good dance music," she said.

"Sounds like a bit of Mongolian Throat Singing going on in a supporting track," stated Mike."

Joe looked at Eve.

"Those teeth say they re predators, flesh-eaters."

"Which is why, Joe, the Military is involved. We do not want to be on the menu of a more advanced species."

"You know what they say," interjected Peter. "Music soothes the savage beast."

"I think the original quote was 'Music has charms to soothe the savage breast' from the old play *The Mourning Bride* by Cosgreve." Said General Jamison. "It is often falsely attributed to Shakespeare.

"Ah, a Renaissance Warrior," said Archie. "I thought Marines were all about bayonets and blood."

"Ignorant soldiers get you killed and defeated, son."

"Peace is our Profession. War is just a hobby," General Hargrove said with a smile.

"So let me get this straight," said Joe. "In less than a day, these people from way out into Space will be in orbit around Earth. Then we are expected to use music as a universal language to communicate with them. What if it all goes wrong? What if we royally piss them off?"

"Then we nuke em to they glow, then shoot them in the dark," replied General Hargrove.

Karen ensured an excellent food and drink spread was provided for the band. As the musicians took a break from examining and tuning all the instruments, they talked in low tones, although all five of the group realized the room was probably wired, and they were being recorded no matter what they did.

"So mankind's fate is in our hands?" asked Pete.

"Womankind's also," said Janice. "We can do this. They said computers would be helping to find patterns and put them into a language. We just need to keep them singing and playing."

"The Dumbo's rhythm and tunes are catchy," said Mike. "Plus, they all rock together as they sing, communicate."

"They move with the music. Like dancers at a Rave," said Joe. "They like our stuff, so there is that."

"You forgot one item," interjected Archie.

"What's that, Arch?" said Joe.

"What if they are actually interstellar music critics who came to shut us up?"

The musicians watched and listened to the alien recordings over and over again. Joe, in particular, listened to those instances when they sent back the band's original music. Eventually, his trained ears discovered some nuances in the rebroadcasts of the Burning Man songs.

"Here, listen to this," he told the others. "Is there an everso slight background track they added here?

"Yep," replied Janice. "I can hear it. Maybe a vocalization?"

"Let me get a hold of the head shed, tell them."

Joe was quickly in a conference with Eve and Karen.

"I'll run this thru a program I developed based on your music,

Joe," said Eve. "I may obtain an impression as to what they are trying to communicate. I'll be right back." Eve maneuvered her motorized chair down a hallway to a computer room. Karen spoke as Joe watched Eve disappear down the hall.

"My sister has a bit of a crush on you, Joe."

"Hey, she's nice."

"Do her sister, me, a favor."

"Shoot."

"Don't lead her on. She has a disability that makes normal life difficult. Especially relationships with the opposite sex."

"You're the protective sister, I get that," said Joe. "But just because I'm a headbanger with groupies who throw panties at me does not mean I'm an asshole. Eve is a good person who I like. I won't do anything to hurt her, or you."

Karen examined him for a few moments, then spoke.

"You surprise me. I see a person who is not the stereotypical drug-using rock and roller."

"Never touch the stuff. Dulls my music playing. A glass of Merlot once in a while, that's it."

They heard Eve's approach. The exobiologist entered the room with a grin on her face.

"Bingo! The program seems to have identified a buried background track when the Dumbos broadcast your song back. And it may correspond to verbiage meaning 'friend,' or 'friendship.' It is not easy understanding a language when you do not even have an alphabet."

"How about the band, and I try to come up with a bit of a musical reply?" Joe asked. "We can try to elicit a response."

"Let me tell the Military what we are doing," said Karen. "I don't want them to be caught off guard with any response." The twin walked out towards an electronic surveillance room set up down another hallway in the underground complex. Joe had figured this hidden installation in Dreamland covered miles.

As Karen left, Eve spoke.

"My sister was protective again, wasn't she?"

"Hey, she loves you. You're family."

"And I have some severe limitations. I know that, Joe. But I can still handle myself."

"I figured that, Eve. Hell, anyone who likes our music must be a cut above the norm."

That elicited a laugh from Eve.

"Not egotistical, I see," the young lady said with a smile.

"All Rockers have egos. We all think our music is better than other bands and groups."

"Well, Joe, you have a unique chance here. You can prove that to an interstellar audience."

The *ALTERNATES* listened to the music and the hidden track over and over again. No one felt like sleeping, they were all so pumped. After all, they had a chance of playing for an actual out of this world audience. Janice was working on some vocals when General Jamison burst into the auditorium with a couple of military technicians in tow.

"Showtime, people. The bastards suddenly hauled ass, and are nearing Earth orbit. And they are broadcasting up a storm."

"But we haven't talked, sang back at them yet," protested Mike.

"But everyone else imaginable is trying. That ship of theirs is the size of a Kennedy Class aircraft carrier. Can't hide that in the sky when they are also broadcasting out music."

"Music?" Joe said.

Just then, the technicians had the video on the oversized wall screen. And there they were. Six almost lifesized centaur aliens. The

General motioned the technicians out of the way of the video camera hookups. The six Dumbos were swaying in perfect unison, using their arms and hands to seemingly spell out intricate symbols of some such. From beneath each of their oversized ears was a thin tentacle with also seemed to vibrate. Joe looked at the General as Eve and Karen stopped by the double entrance door. Jamison pointed at the band and gave the thumbs up to Joe. The band leader took a deep breath, then said, "It's showtime."

He pointed at Janice, and she began a rhythmic chant similar to the beat the Dumbos were using, Then all the band members were grabbing instruments. The next couple of minutes was pure experimentation. Joe signaled the band to form a line and to begin swaying in unison to Janice's vibrato. Joe had an electronic keyboard in front of him, and he started an attempt to reproduce the 'friend' music. The Dumbos froze.

"Oh shit," mumbled Joe. Had he insulted them, scared them?

Then a wave of sound vibrated across the room from the screen speakers.

"It's the 'friend sound,'" yelled out Janice, as she began to twirl around with a tambourine in her hand. Suddenly, one of the Dumbos made an attempt to copy her twirl, which with a six-limbed creature, was a sight to see. The next quarter-hour became a blur as the members of the two different species tried to match each other's musical communication. The Dumbos kept with the rhythmic line dance but began attempts at individual moves as they seemed to copy Janice. Of course, this fed into the female singer's excitement, and she began to laugh and twirl even more.

Joe led individual riffs but tried to end with a variation of the "friend" chord. The Dumbos caught on and were soon doing the same. Joe sensed someone behind him and glanced to see Eve had slid up behind him. She had earphones on and displayed a broad grin.

Eve mouthed. "They are talking through the music. The computer program understands." Musicians learn how to read lips to overcome loud music and noisy fans, so Joe understood immediately. He grinned back and began another variation on the "friend" sound, now a song. The centaur aliens matched him, and their teeth filled mouths seemed to be formed into grins matching the humans.

Then, just as the humans were on the verge of exhaustion, the Dumbos stopped. Joe chopped with his hands to signify the band must stop also. The two species stared at each other through the electronic screen connections as they both regained their breaths,

"They are oxygen breathers," Joe said under his breath. Then he flashed the famous "Live Long and Prosper" hand signal, why, he could never explain. All six of the Dumbos copied him, their large ears flapped out as if to catch any possible sound. The video signal faded.

The band all flopped into seats, bathed in sweat. Then, they all began to giggle like school kids.

"Man, what a JAM!" Archie bellowed.

"You just established communication with a completely alien species," interjected Eve. "You have done what no person has ever done. You will be famous."

"Yeah, but will we get record contracts?" Peter said with a grin. They all laughed, and Janice began to hug them all, ending with Eve.

"This could not happen without our Number One Fan here," said Janice.

"The computer did all the work," Eve replied.

"But it was your program," said Joe. "If you hang around with headbangers, you have to lose your humility, Eve."

"Alright," interrupted General Jamison. "Rest time. You have to be ready for another attempt. Head back to the dining area, We have some comfortable recliners set up for your use."

Someone jokingly mentioned 'overtime pay,' and the General smiled. As they began to settle in the dining and now rest area, General Jamison and Hargrove approached Joe.

"You and your comrades in music just did something unique in human history," said Jamison. "Will you shake an old Jarhead's hand?"

Joe shook the proffered hand, and then General Hargrove's.

"Hell, General. We just play music. You guys put your ass on the line all the time."

"We do that so you can play music," said Hargrove. "Thus, things like this can happen."

"Now what?" asked Joe.

"We wait," said the Marine. "Eve and Karen are working on a lingua franca for the Dumbos. They definitely use sound more than we do. Their eyesight seems weak, and the small nose structure in the center of their faces seems small and crude. Thus, audio, and maybe touch, has special uses in their culture. Those small tentacles by their huge ear structures seem to sense vibrations as well as produce them."

"Well, if you need our music again, just holler. Our music is our life, so this may seem like work, but to us, it's a blast."

Joe went for a short walk with an energy drink in his hand. His mind was working overtime replaying every bit of music in his head as he tried to figure what the aliens were saying without using a computer program. As he strolled along, Eve came up the hall, saw him, and grinned.

"Out for a walk, I see," said Eve. "I call it a wheelie when I do that."

Joe laughed. "Being called Doctor Wheels by Archie…"

"Hey, I've heard that nickname before. I kind of like being special."

Joe stepped closer and looked into her eyes.

"Excuse me," said in a low voice, bent over and kissed Eve. She returned the affection with a bit of fervor. Then their lips parted.

"When this is all over, will you go on a date with me, Eve?"

"Of course. You can even take me to dinner and dancing."

"I'd like that. I'd like that a…"

A klaxon went off, shattering the moment. Personnel the band had not seen before were suddenly dashing about, some with weapons. Joe automatically stood in front of Eve's wheelchair so no one would knock her over. Then Karen came running up to them.

"The damned Dumbos," she said between pants. "They are five minutes out in a high-speed shuttle of some sort. We barely stopped the missile defenses from shooting then down."

"Now what?" asked Joe.

"Why you meet them. The computer developed language seems to be a demand that the Dumbos meet you five."

"Ah, shit. And me with no special party clothes."

Karen managed to grin.

"The Generals have that covered."

In ten minutes, the five band members were in some sort of combination hazmat and space suit to meet the aliens.

"We need to pass on smallpox as we did with the Indian Tribes like we need an interstellar plague from them," Karen said. Luckily the gloves were flexible enough to allow some instrument manipulation.

With nervous grumbling, the five musicians were transported slowly on the equivalent of an oversized golf cart. The alien shuttlecraft looked like many an aerodynamic Sci-Fi CGI-generated craft. However, this was real, not some movie fiction. Joe carried a small speaker connected to Eve and her computer-driven translator. The other band members brought some string guitars and a clarinet if some new music was needed. However, it was hoped Eve's program would be able to provide the necessary communication.

It was hard to tell, but Joe thought the six Dumbos who exited the craft, now being referred to as Centaurs in official communications, seemed to be the same six with whom they had sung and dance. The aliens were clad in their own versions of protective suits, with air tanks attached as they came down the ramp from a large access hatch. Joe knew a Main Battle Tank unit had them targeted in case things went wrong. That gave him little comfort as he knew they would be blown apart also if necessary.

The six Centaurs formed a line some two yards from the humans. They then began what was later identified as the Greeting/ Welcoming Song and Dance. As they swayed in unison, the humans tried to match the motions. Then Joe held up the speaker as he knew Eve would broadcast the "friend" song to the visitors. One of the Centaurs held up their version of a speaker. From it came singing, in a very human-sounding voice.

"We came to make music, Can you make music with us??"

"Hell, yeah!" Joe said aloud before he realized it. "Let's rock!"

Five years later, and Joe was waiting in the back of the Univesity Auditorium with Eve's and his twin boys. Their initial date had led to one thing after another, then marriage, then children. Centaur science added some expertise that helped Eve carry the children to near term and then placed in a special growth tank to continue the birth process. Two bouncing baby boys were the result, with none of the problems Eve and Karen had at birth.

Eve was finishing up with her current rendition of "MUSIC. THE INTERSTELLAR LANGUAGE," a series of lectures based on her best selling book. As Karen and Eve had predicted, the band was famous. With in a month of the First Contact, the *ALTERNATES* had a best selling album of "Out of This World Songs." Then they collaborated with the Six Centaurs to create Interstellar Rock Sounds, which now included some five albums. An investigation soon revealed the Centaurs lived for their music, their songs, as that was how they transmitted their culture. Developing on a world shrouded in darkness, the sense of sound became all-important.

The music industry had a colossal rebirth as the aliens loved to hear new music, songs. Thus, they bought up everything and sent it back to their home solar system. They had a form of hyperspace propulsion which shrunk travel between systems down to a manageable time duration.

The band still played together when possible, as well as attended all the Science Fiction Conventions. After all, they had met and played with actual, real, intelligent outer space aliens. The members now all had families of their own. Funny how meeting an alien culture made one think about the human family.

The applause came as Eve finished her presentation. As she walked from the stage, pieces from "Out Of This World Songs" played. Joe took the twins and met her in a Green Room set up especially for her. The two boys were soon clamoring to ride on Mommy, as the Centaurs had adapted a four-limbed exoskeleton for Eve's use. Her work in translation had made her a First Human in their eyes, and in their Songs.

"Want to get a sitter and have a date, Eve?"

"Yes. I could do with some fun. This lecture series is becoming a drag."

"No rest for the famous, my dear. Welcome to the world of music entertainment."

As the twins sat on the artificial flesh-covered exoskeleton, Eve looked at her husband.

"Honey, ever wondered what might have been? What if your songs had not been broadcast from Burning Man? What if no one heard them?"

Joe shrugged.

"I'd be playing Lost Wages, beating off groupies and their panties. But that wasn't going to happen."

"Why not? "

"Because, my dearest Eve, God is a Headbanger Rock and Roller. The Almighty would not let good music go unappreciated."

Eve laughed.

"Still with the oversized ego."

"Of course, Goes with the territory. Now, time to get the show on the road…"

In the deepest darkest interstellar space, sounds of rock and roll travel between the galaxies. And then, they find a new ear…

KILL TICKET
BY ELIZA LOEB

Cecilia Meyers drove along the coast line with the windows down. The ocean breeze swayed through her ebony hair as the smell of brine filled her senses. For at least a moment, she could consider her options. She could consider more honorable paths that didn't involve her needing to spill blood or possibly having her blood spilled if she stepped out of line. And in all honesty, she had been in a desperate situation when she had first joined the mafia. Sure she knew what that sort of thing meant. She had even considered the risks and the consequences when she had so much as decided that she no longer wanted to starve. And not even fast food places had been hiring at the time, especially for people on the streets. And surely no one would want someone jobless moving in without *proper* means of payment. She was too prideful for that sort of thing.

Most nights she would go about her business without a hitch. She loved that. She loved not having to attend to the beck and call of her boss, loved not staining her hands with any more blood than she was ordered. The ability to roam free had enticed her beyond belief.

And dancing as though no one had been watching or preparing to kill her on sight had called to her more than once. However, it was often nights like these ones, where the illusion of choice and freedom, had been little more than sickeningly sweet dreams. Gone was the humanity of a hit man, who as a grunt bore little to no importance or footing. When told to jump, Cecilia was to respond with "How high?" And when men like her boss, when men like Marco pointed at a target, the option to say no was dangerous. Family stopped being family. Friends were no longer friends. If a person went so far as to anger Marco to land on his black list, however deep the rabbit hole had gone dependent on how terrible the offense... whether or not the act of offended were petty or not.

When this happened, no one was safe.

She merged into the next lane and turned in to the nearest exit, crossing the Golden Gate Bridge just moments later. Thanking the travel time to allow her to turn her emotions off, to the rest of the world and prepare herself for the scene she would soon walk in to.

His new catch of the day mewled and writhed beneath him as he had bent her over the table, thrusting in a flurry of anger and frustration at how submissive the bitch had been. He despised how she begged for his attention and practically chased him to and fro about the office. Next he would hear about how he got her pregnant and demand repentance.

He hated women like this one. He hated how much they would beg for him to get to his money and hated that they pined after him. He hated easy targets and often wished that killing them on sight wouldn't expose his underworld activities. Expensive prostitutes were untrustworthy. His assistants were far too uppity to bother with him unless it involved scheduling a meeting and ensuring that his meetings went along smoothly. Honestly, he despised them almost as much as the easy little harlots who flitted after him.

"Come in," he growled as a knock came to the door.

His thrusts grew more and more violent as the woman beneath him cried out. Her nails dug in to the paper schedule atop his desk, protecting the cherry oak beneath as yet another woman entered his office. Her expression was cold and off putting as she slowly closed the door and waited for his completion in silence. He gave her a cocky grin as he felt a mild wash of lust fall over him. Her silver eyes were unmoved by his antics, and if anything the air of disgust that she tried to hide from him only managed to turn him on even more.

"I didn't think you would be here so soon," he huffed. "I've always liked that about you, Morpho."

The way her lips formed into a pout as she tried her best to remain unshaken from his statement had been rather adorable. He lived for subjecting her to any form of mental and emotional torment as he saw fit when she met alone with him, and never bothered with hesitation. He could see her muscles tense and contort as discomfort overcame her and the idea of the woman beneath him... he stopped his thoughts as only the thought of finishing crossed his mind. He proceeded to grab his latest catch by the hair and continued to batter her from just over his desk.

"Tell Morpho she's beautiful," he commanded.

The woman let out a low murmur, whimpering a protest as she grit her teeth.

Marco slowed to a halt and the woman nearly cried out, begging him to continue. There was a displeased expression on his face as he glared down at her.

"I see."

The woman turned around to face him, opening her mouth to argue right as he pinned her back down by the throat.

"You know, I really fucking hate women like you," he chided. His fingers squeezed harder as he felt her attempting to fight him. "You come to work for my company, suspecting nothing, following orders until the situation suits you best, and then you fucking turn around and disobey."

Cecilia shuddered at the venomous edge in his voice. He had intended to kill the woman beneath him and it scared her for the reason he would do it.

"And not only do you disobey, you insult my woman."

She had to remain calm at this moment. Any reaction could mean her life. She cared little for how he was treating another life and wanted little to do with the fact. She had to turn a blind eye. She had to ensure that she stayed safe above all else and could not risk her life for someone else's over being treated as though she were the product of some sick mans fantasy. She couldn't object. But she could, in the very least collect a payout to deliver. Some sort of settlement to which could set her free, she hoped.

A loud snapping sound echoed through the room and caught Cecilia's attention. The woman that had been enjoying herself on her bosses desk now lay dead with her head faced down. The psychopath who had killed her merely adjusted and straightened himself out as though what he had done were meaningless. But... she drew herself in. Wasn't this always how he had been with her? Always doing something to get a rise? Always trying to get a reaction out of her to prove how soft she was and to remind her that at the end of the day, she was always nothing more than a woman to him? She held her tongue as he continued to straighten himself out and brush the dead woman off the desk. His eyes were, if anything, cold and unfeeling.

"Now..." he began. "I'm sure you know why I've summoned you here?"

The sudden change in his moods had scared her. And the very

idea that he was of the more mercurial sort would send a chill down anyone's spine.

"Actually sir, I was hoping you would tell me?"

Marco paused, sneering over at her as if questioning him were going to be the last thing she had ever done. His gold eyes fixed on her, eyeing her up and down as he tried to make a move before her. Yet found nothing of interest.

"I called you here to talk to you about your younger sister."

Finally, she had lost control and gave him a reaction. What had her sister done to warrant Marco's attention? What could Cecilia do to get her out of the situation? Did she have to kill her?

The mafia boss smiled at her, as if she had given him something he wanted.

"Amelie has wracked up quite a debt with the company, and it's become a bit of a bother."

She didn't like where this is going.

"I need you to take her out for me."

This was one thing she had hoped she would never have to do.

Finding a replacement had been a difficult endeavor to say the least. The decoy had proven to be quite resistant in their procurement. But Cecilia wondered when her targets had ever been easy. So as she paced back and forth while the young woman of perhaps nineteen or twenty swayed her head to and fro. With how long the girl had been out, it had been no surprise that she would soon begin to panic. Finding herself in a dimly lit room with nothing more than a swinging light and the sound of footsteps tapping in tune with distant dripping and splashing noises. She wouldn't be able to move much beyond twisting and writing within her binds. And if she tried to scream, she would only run out of energy and ware down to a panting and writing mess.

In fact, that is exactly what the young girl had done as Cecilia remained in the shadows. Not responding to her targets protests and bargains.

Sounds like internal or external pandemonium had always managed to trigger some sort of animalistic instinct within Cecilia. As if prolonging the targets inevitable demise would somehow make the kill sweeter, more purposeful on both parts. And she often wondered if that instinct had been something she had been born with or if it had been learned.

"Please," the young girl begged.

"Please, don't kill me, I will do anything."

Anything? No. No, no no. That won't do. Anything is for those who have freedom to move around without fear or repercussions. Anything is for those who have done nothing to warrant being killed or getting anyone else killed. And the poor girl just happened to be one of the unlucky ones to obtain someone else's kill ticket.

Cecilia would work toward amends to her family once she managed to leave her predicament, but for now... for now, she had at least one final job to do.

Once Cecilia had found she had had enough she began to get to work. She started with removing one of her victims fingers. Slowly tearing the skin from the knuckle as she imbibed in the act of torture. Her heart leaped with sadistic frenzy as the younger being screamed in both terror and agony. No one could hear her. No one would come for her. Just as no one had heard or come for Cecilia. Why should this unlucky target of a black lottery be any different? And she rather enjoyed the trepidation of those who fell beneath her knife. And the more that the girl screamed, the more joy she felt. Yet her face would remain blank, still and unfeeling. She wouldn't want the poor dear to know how much she liked the girls slow and methodical torment, it would make her lose hope.

No.

She couldn't allow that.

Instead, she proceeded to break her targets fingers and look in her eyes as she decided she had grown weary of her screams. The girls lips were then sewn shut with little regard and she couldn't vocally express her agony as it came. Hours would soon pass as the flow of time took its course. The girl had eventually succumbed to a brain aneurysm. Cecilia guessed that such extended torture had proven too much. Still, it was pretty impressive that she had managed to survive as long as she had. Her murderer acknowledged that much.

Still, she wondered what the girl could have achieved with that kind of will power. She wondered what sort of life could have been achieved in what life she had had left.

Either way, it was her younger sister who dug this girls grave. Cecilia remained responsible for the clean up and went into another room three walls over, where a mattress with moss and overgrowth lay bent over a pitch black trash bag. Peaks of green could be seen through the stretched out plastic, yet not for reasons one would think. The old building that the hit man had tended to her work had officially been set ablaze with no signs of a corpse. Cecilia's clothes had been changed and then burned within the dumpster nearby. The finger had been placed in a Zale's box along with a ring and fancy wrapping. Her heart feeling the tinge of what was to come.

She had been gone for hours, he thought to himself. He had so hoped that she had quickly done the deed so to get it over with, and just bring him proof of her sisters death. Yet she had proven just how stone hearted she could be. Which is why he liked her so much. He wanted her attention on him. He wanted her to obey him and show him some iota of warmth on a cold day. He would lovingly bend her over any desk or surface she would allow him. He danced for the idea of her falling to her knees after wearing her down. And god, he lived for the idea of her. She was a good girl.

She was his good girl.

She just didn't know it yet.

His office doors swung open and she entered the room with stride. There was a look of defiance on her face as she approached his desk with a briefcase in one hand, and a zales jewelry box in another. He leaned back and watched her with subtle praise as she sat in front of him. She walked with some form of newfound confidence for some reason or another, which as odd as it was, had been nothing short of attractive. She set the brief case on his desk and then placed the zales box right next to it. He reached for the box and opened it slowly, finding a freshly cut finger with a gold band on it. It seemed she had done the job with gusto.

"Morpho, baby..." he crooned. "You're too much."

"Don't call me baby."

Marco looked up in shock at his interest as she stared down her nose at him. The sheer expression of disgust toward him had been enough to make him want to strike her. What right did she have to talk to him like that? His boss? She was lucky that he liked her enough to remain silent for a brief moment as he thought about her words.

"Should I call you a dog then?" he half joked.

"Because only bitches give orders."

Now his Morpho's expression grew cocky. Perhaps because of what the suitcase contained?

"You're not to call me anything, Marco," she said to him. "I'm leaving and I'm turning my life around."

She could feel the air thicken around the room as his eyes filled with fire. His hands slammed down on the desk as he quickly rose and reached out to her.

"I could give you anything," he growled at her.

"You could have the fucking world if you wanted."

She looked to the briefcase and sighed. Marco seemed to think that she belonged to him beyond just working for him.

"There is enough in that briefcase to pay off my cut."

Her eyes narrowed at the overgrown man child as her stomach filled with disgust. She wanted nothing to do with him, let alone be in the same room with him. Yet here he was, enjoying himself with his late fathers mediocre empire. She wondered what he did to earn it, what work he put in after lazing around all day and night and sipping cocktails like some millionaire playboy from the projects. Were he to grow up with nothing, were he to have been cut off and penniless, women like her would eat him alive and dump him in the streets with the skin off his bones.

Cecilia could feel the sadistic frenzy tickle at the back of her shoulder as she smiled at him. The mans shitty way of begging was enough to make her laugh, and she almost couldn't believe how long she had allowed him control over her. Instead she turned her back on him and proceeded to walk out.

"*I fucking own you!*" she could hear him shout beyond the door.

Night had fallen and Cecilia had settled in a nearby smoke bar. The smell of cigarettes and clove wafted through the air as she crossed one leg over the other. Soft blues played through the vicinity with a slow and mellow beat cooled her nerves while she took swig after swig of a twelve year scotch. She spied her reflection nearby and smiled. She had never seen herself so relaxed in ten years. She had often found herself tense and looking over her shoulder every five minutes. She just needed that moment. That was all she needed and had been one of the little things she had taken for granted in her youth.

BANG!

Her eyes shot open as she set her glass of scotch down, looking over the back of her seat as a man exited a vibrant red car outside of the bar window. Another man stormed out and touched his head in frustration. The other man standing beside him touched his shoulder and passed his card over with ease. Likely exchanging insurance information so that he could take care of a situation that he had unwittingly caused.

It wasn't a gunshot.

Cecilia gave a soft sigh of relief.

It wasn't a gun shot.

She went back to lounging in her seat with ease, taking her scotch back up and slowly sipping away at it. She closed her eyes and took in a breath. All was calm. There was no violence for now and her past experiences would one day prove to be a world away.

APOCALYPSE YESTERDAY: A COLLAGE
BY SHEILA MENGERT

The quest for reality and for truth statements about reality is an elusive one, so elusive in fact that the great philosopher Immanuel Kant finally surrendered and admitted that what things are in themselves is unknowable. What emerge instead are various assessments of the phenomena of existence and these in turn are further modified by the limitations of the language by which we communicate those assessments. Beyond even these we have the various arts that attempt to illumine reality by a mimetic translation of reality into various mediums that highlight and emphasize various latent aspects of the whole.

This would be difficult enough but in addition the would-be knower must deal with the phenomenon of change; things do not remain static but transmute into other things; as every physicist knows the arrow of time points only in one direction. The general law of entropy yields increasing overall disorder in a system. Yet despite all of this metaphysical humility history speaks confidently of progress attained through a fundamental and gradually acquired knowledge of the past. The historian is not a mere archivist; he assumes that patterns can be discerned in history and that eventually history can become a proscriptive science.

This was what George Santayana meant about learning from history. Of course what he forgot to explain is why we *never* have collectively learned from history. Perhaps this is because historical problems always emerge in new guises just as viruses mutate season by season. The temptation to exceptional exclusion from general laws is insistent and overwhelming. Historians like to think of themselves as scientists, although historical writing is more akin to the arts. If history is storytelling, then does the plot come after the events in question or is the form imposed upon the raw data of events even as they occur? The question is a significant one because it bears upon any judgment that the discipline of literary criticism imposes after the fact upon the amorphous mass of writings that claim to be literature.

The literary arts have never existed in such low general esteem. They appear to be so steeped in subjectivism that they appear to be inapplicable when plotted along a pragmatic continuum. If this applies to the novel it is even more likely to be the assessment of the short story. The short story is remarkable among literary forms for its brevity, its impact, and its ability to allow character to manifest itself under the stress of a dramatic situation. Judging by these criteria the present story, one that will dispense from the ordinary convention of characters, must be content to proclaim its universal applicability for what "apocalypse" can live up to its name if it is not universal. We expect a certain extravagance and grandeur from our apocalyptic candidates.

However, there has grown to be a marked tendency to see such candidates as shrouded in the misty confines of the future and for this reason the title of this submission to the reader's discerning judgment must consider that an apocalypse coyly situated in the past as in yesterday may be viewed with suspicion or at least with curiosity. Have events so far eroded the normal cause and effect relationships upon which tranquility rests that, unbeknownst and as it were stealthily, apocalypse crept in among us unremarked and did its mischief while our eyes and senses were distracted and engaged elsewhere? If things are out of order at precisely the moment when progress appears poised to shift into overdrive how did this situation come about and why was it not more attentively examined when its nefarious influence began? Perhaps our collective immune system has been sleeping. If so, and having concluded this much, our weary narrative voice, one still echoing with the sonorous periods of the prose of one of the founding fathers of American literature, Nathaniel Hawthorne, we will proceed not deterred by disillusion to do what art always does: to express the reflected shadows of reality as persuasively as possible.

The three unities being long since discarded, the storyteller, balanced along the edge of irony and deconstructed discourse, must assemble a narrative out of fragments. The borders between the arts are dissolving so that rather than assembling a chain of incidents into a moral narrative of cause and effect leading to a moment of revelation and insight beset with questions of setting, dramatic motivation, and point of view the author may look instead to music and the plasticity of art here for inspiration. At once many problems of narration vanish to be replaced by effects of assembly, rhythm, juxtaposition, and contrast. The narrator need no longer be identified or to explain how she knows what she inexplicably knows about the personages or inner mindsets of her characters. Artistry in any case consists in tonality and the ability to suggest, to tickle the outstretched antennae of perception not all of which are within the parameters of the conscious mind. With this inspiration and stimulated by a Freudian spirit of free association and accompanied by a silent drum roll the camera slides backwards to reveal what follows...

Out of a soft haze emerges the head of the last male of the northern sub-species of white rhinoceros hunted into extinction by poachers to feed an Asian market that covets its horns to stimulate fertility and sexual potency in the human male. Is it imagination or does the dead eye of this ancient creature manifest a sorrow and pain beyond its mere animal mentality? "How," it silently asks, "Did we come to this? What fate has condemned me to perish with my seed still intact so that the entire species and the long history of my kind must die with me? Where is the Sophocles to tell my story?"

Across an ocean and by the sluggish flow of the great Amazon River comes an answer from trees rooted in soil long adapted to nurture the canopy where bright birds flash in the sun from limb to limb. The Amazon Rainforest is a sculpture, a system of perfect efficiency and exchange between sun and soil, wind and cloud, plant and animal. Presiding over it is a force that exceeding all lesser forces embodies origin and process that contains it all and yet stands separate from it. Such is the imagination of symbol-making humans that the indigenous tribes called it woman and made it visible. They called it Pachamama. It was as real to them as to industrial man are the names of the great oil companies, the corporate entities that in American law are defined as 'persons' with full rights under the law. There are no statuettes to symbolize these entities but they are held to be real none the less and they are worshiped and served by countless acolytes.

Across the ocean we pass again to where a Pope, a man drawn from the Pampas, has tried to awaken his ancient church to the challenge of the times. In the course of the recent Amazonian Synod and as a gesture of cultural respect he allowed into the sacred precincts of the church the bowed maternal head and figure of a Pachamama statuette that was later stolen and thrown into the Tiber River. This is the preferred tactic of those who are unable to distinguish degrees of symbolism and the artificiality of ritual when it attempts to grasp transcendent reality. Under the belief that the Pope was sponsoring and promoting idolatry conservative Catholics have demanded his public penance. It is characteristic of the formalist and essentialist mind that it cannot see behind prohibitions to distinguish the policy or purposes behind those prohibitions, therefore anything that comes within the gravitational pull of a concept is included within its presumed domain. The worst part of this type of reasoning is that it is non-relational and fragmented so that the deity is encapsulated and eclipsed by utterances that are viewed in themselves as absolutes. This leads inevitably to fundamentalism and eventually to attempts to justify religious terrorism.

Meanwhile back across the ocean the Brazilian President, anxious to clear away the rubble of the rainforest to stimulate cattle ranching and oil drilling sees these same indigenous people as obstacles to the growth of national prosperity. Forest fires are the chosen means to manage cheap brush clearing. The great businesses are served by this but of course this service is not ritualistic idolatry and no voices of opposition or demands for penance are raised to oppose it. To the conservative religious mentality ritual always trumps reality. A list of prelates and concerned conservative lay Catholics have demanded that the Pope must do public penance for the sin of idolatry over the Pachamama incident or suffer the pain of eternal damnation. Many members of the same group, of course, see no problem in promoting the Trump brand on every occasion, discerning no idolatry in the various Trump-rallies with their chanting and vulgarity.

But stop; these linear contrasts already have drawn us into the balanced dialectic of opposing forces that like a ticking clock advance us towards some great conflagration while as the title indicates the planet is already living out a disease process long since begun somewhere along the corridors of yesterday. Besides, what we pursue is not linear but rather emergent as when a system undergoes a phase change to a new order or as is the case where an energized atom steps down from one valance orbital to another emitting a photon of light.

We move the camera once again along a circular track and focus on the fact that the past, already frozen into unalterable lineaments, hangs about us like a shroud. The generations spring up constantly so that any dividing line that we choose to impose to define epochs must be deemed somewhat arbitrary. The sheer density of events appears to give a degree of absoluteness to the happenings that occur in real time. We at least expect the cast members to stick around for the conclusion of the play. We do not expect the stage hands to whirl away the setting while the dialog is still being exchanged and while the audience, remaining in their tiered seats, is still engaged with the action on the stage.

All very well but what if one play merges into another imperceptibly so that a question remains whether one is watching scene five of act four or on the other hand scene one of act one of an entirely new play. The surge of events allows no time for an intermission. Would pausing and taking advantage of such untimely timeliness not be ... well, somewhat apocalyptic? So that even before receiving an answer to the above question we rush onwards in our devising of new forms to contain old events and to constrain the ever evolving permissibility of innovation (and we are not even dealing yet with artificial intelligence but only with the creative mind run amuck). These new forms that beckon to the backs of the patrons of the literary circus as they make for the exit (disappointed that there are no trained elephants or bears to perform but only dusty grim old T.S.

Eliot or an artist drawing his designs on the sidewalks soon to be effaced by the December rains). No concert hall is to be found here filled with well-dressed men and silken ladies gracefully taking their seats as the lights dim about them. No, there is only the dark undercurrent of the withdrawing tide past the old sea-weary barnacles and mussels that cling to a long abandoned boat-hull or pier.

We gaze about us. It is closing time at the pub and the patrons walk out one by one into the solitude of a night in Belltown or in Pioneer Square. The old signs of a bathhouse beckon to no takers, the denizens being long dead victims of one of the scourges of history. So we wander about Seattle with an old Modern Library copy of Joyce's *Ulysses* or maybe one of Kerouac's *Visions of Cody*. We pass an old plate glass window in a vacant building and see our reflection distorted back to us, perhaps on the edge of tears … Okay Boomer, no time for self-indulgence, it is time to move along now; pack up your troubles. We were unable to update your app because of insufficient memory. For technical assistance please call the 800-number provided to India or the Philippines where our call center will be happy to serve you.

We walk up to Boren Street. There is the old brick building where a student rented a room once on the first floor (wonder what rents are like now)? Remember the old movies at the Harvard Exit and years later climbing the stairs on Pike to sit on the old couch or a straight-backed chair in a circle with boys who wished they were girls. Afterwards we could dance until after midnight at one of the gay bars on the hill or eat fancy food in one of the new gentrified eateries if some rich John picked us up and paid. Gone now or did it ever happen? No one recalls a past not worth recording. From here we can look back down Denny or Pike to where the downtown skyscrapers pierce the mists coming up off of Puget Sound. The fog has made

Bainbridge Island invisible tonight. The ferries work the docks like an old streetwalker crying unremarked by the passers-by.

But we are falling into the old trap of locality that leads eventually into naturalism; better to stick this side of surrealism. Genre traps exist everywhere for the unwary. Suddenly words emerge out of the darkness and arrange themselves on paper to be fed on later by the ghouls of interpretation. Who can separate the sign from the signifier? Who can distill significance from an inconclusory epic? William Blake and all the mythmakers before and after him groping for universal applicability must finally yield to the ever onrushing flood of the circumstantial. We turn in vain to the old sources of interpretation; data multiplies beyond our ability to find categories for it. First there comes redundancy and then inapplicability. Finally a red-line is reached and the system collapses.

(Pause here to change the reel)

And again we begin: perhaps the poets have the answer after all, poets the ultimate custodians of language. Perhaps life's experience should be divided into cantos; Ezra Pound thought so. Or perhaps it is sufficient to leave a case-hardened image as Amy Lowell sought to do. The poet is unperplexed by questions of before and after; there is only the now of suspended apprehension. Is all of poetry one long lamentation? One need only read the poets of the Tang Dynasty to know the answer. The poet pleads for understanding and sympathy.

Life is like this (he cries): times were once better and now I am old and I don't seem to understand things as once I did. It is estrangement the finally engulfs us. I thought to return home only to find that it had dissolved away in my absence.

(Ah at last we have a narrator, you heard him. He said "I.")

Too late he has disappeared once again and we are plunged

into the rush of images and oratory. A student once set herself the task of reading and understanding *Finnegans Wake.* No apostrophe in the title to indicate possessiveness because Finnegan is universal. Even the genders merge and waver and the family is merged into one amorous and amorphous whole. After nightfall all boundaries waver and dissolve. The elm and stone discourse together by the river filled with all the soil and refuse of Dublin. Images emerge out of memory and then vanish before the recording angel can note them down, all to be recapitulated on the Day of Judgment.

(We dare not make literary use here of the Koran and suffer the fate of condemnation exercised towards Salman Rushdie. Let us rather remain within our familiar zones of late stage religious freedom in America).

"We do not serve sinners here, so tell me have you done anything wrong lately? If your sins are different than my sins I reserve the right to refuse you service as a testimony to my own righteousness."

Korea… "Our patience is not unlimited. Our dear leader will not delay to bring retribution upon America beyond its worst fears if this warning is not heeded."

"The Democrats are planning a coup attempt in collaboration with the deep state to deprive the people of their right to choose a President. We need a true authoritarian to get thing done. There is too much talk in a democracy. We are better armed than they are and the liberal Dems better remember that we'll fight to keep Trump in office. God has chosen our President, just listen to Rick Perry, if you don't believe me."

Whose were those voices interrupting our narrative?

(Flap flap flap … time to change the reel again? No just a break in the continuity as we sit in the private theater showing this day's rushes.

No editing yet; that comes later when we choose between multiple takes. 'You were looking down again dear. Try and remember your character. Alright company let's try it again. Lights, camera, action!')

"No everything is fine so where were we? Oh yes we were discussing the treatment that was submitted to our Culver City Offices, or well somewhere in L.A., about an apocalypse that just went unnoticed until its effects began to show up ... hmm interesting concept but film is about showing and all you've brought me is an idea. Besides, religion is a touchy subject right now; we don't want to alienate key sectors of our potential audience. Don't forget the Red States; they buy popcorn too. Maybe we could just suggest the idea by a creative musical score for the picture, borrow a little from Strauss or Stravinsky. Look what they did with the music in *2001: A Space Odyssey*. Nobody even knew what was happening in that film but it sure made money. Man that's entertainment. A rose is a rose is a, hell whatever that old lesbian in Paris said: you get my drift anyway. People don't need an explanation; they need experiences. Okay that's it. Look I'll talk to our people in production and see if it flies, alright? Hey, stay in touch."

Thoreau went to the woods to live deliberately within the ambit of a particular time and place and in the custody of his own conscience. Emerson, another great individualist, tried to imagine an oversoul that is distributed among all persons. Whitman believed in a natural adhesiveness that draws all people together in sympathy and finally evolves a unified democracy as the best form of government. Compare these great prophets of the American ethos to the pseudo-populism of dictators whether actual or aspirational who seek to draw an equation between their own particular personhood and the unified will of the people. This is a false symbolism and in the end this alone may bring forth the apocalypse.

"Fractional distillation allows us to separate a fluid into its separate viscosities. When applied to the newsfeed our task is to confirm our readers in the opinions they already hold. Please try and remember staff that America no longer has a univocal point of view grouped about a mean. We are a country without a centrist group to moderate between the extremes so we simply have to choose: who are we trying to reach?"

The death rate of young adults is rising in the United States due primarily to obesity, addiction, and suicide. This trend has an inverse ratio to years of education. This is what allows the schools to use tuition to leverage a generation into debt and so to control them throughout their years of rebellion and vigor making them a subservient mass. By the time you hit forty and are debt free it's a little late to take to the barricades.

It is projected that most people who reach their full retirement age will live for another twenty years and most of these will not continue to work. Thank God for the kids! When they finish paying off their own debts they can support us.

"Hey that was one great putt! You have the honors on this hole. It's a four-par dogleg left."

Russia claims to have a new guided nuclear deterrent that can elude our defensive missiles. Maybe he whispered something to Trump at the last summit. "Got you sucker!"

A collage is made of many different materials or pictures affixed to a backing instead of encased in a frame. The different textures add contrast and color to exemplify a theme or idea without explicitly stating it. What looks like chaos may have an underlying strange attractor present and paradoxically be more orderly than a deliberately ordered but mendacious creation. The art of framing involves selection; the subject is confined by the scope of the lens. It should always be kept in mind however that behind the camera another world exists that is not observed. This means that there is no real escape from the laws of perspective. The mere fact of selection introduces an artificial barrier.

"You know I could just listen to you all night honey. Where do you come up with all this crazy stuff?"

(Now who was that speaking?)

"Hey did you read about the Catholics and those Pachamama things? Well its getting a lot of air-play. They're these naked mother things out of the Amazon." "

"Is that so?"

"Sure is. So the real die- hard conservatives are really upset about these things; claim they are idols and the Pope is a big sinner because he allowed them in Rome. Yeah, they think the Pope isn't even Catholic. Besides they can't stand his lifestyle; he's too much like Jesus: cares about the poor, doesn't start every sentence with an accusation, you could see how that would piss them off."

"I've known lots of people like that for instance…"

"Hey don't break my train of thought. Anyway, here's my idea: we trademark these Pachamamas and sell them. Yeah, it could go viral! Auto supply houses could sell them; hang them from your rear-view mirror. Toy stores, novelty shops, you name it. Yeah, and hey if it gets more controversial great; we hit the religious freedom angle. Hey who's going to knock motherhood right; besides these things are topless, you know always a winning point. Yeah well I'm looking into it, first kid on the block, get the early sales in the big box stores. Okay so we'll spell it funny like Pa Cha Mama; don't settle for any imitators; we're the original. Right, okay, I'll make the pitch and see if it flies with the finance people but hey keep this under your hat okay? Great, see ya."

A latent infection is one where the alien organism has been

introduced but has not yet manifested itself as overt illness; the body's defenses have managed to hold its onslaught to an equilibrium, a *modus Vivendi,* a presence without any harm instilled beyond that sense of apprehension elicited by any foreign agent when inserted into the calm and oceanic integrity of the organism. Similarly, what we have called a premature apocalypse or apocalypse yesterday describes a catastrophe that has become so normalized and habituated that its signs, even when they become overt, will be overlooked by the usual guardians of sanity and health in a society. In fact the first signs that something is very much amiss will appear disconnected to their ultimate cause. The swirling currents of cause and effect may hide a larger even if latent force that is everywhere operative among us.

Thus the magician, loath to be coy, might explain in no uncertain terms the inspiration that lies behind all sleight of hand for the success of illusion always depends on distraction. In multitudinous juxtaposition there is a great weariness. We depend upon the magic of art to synthesize our intuitions for us into one great insight. The tension that exists between the real and the imaginary is resolved by a sort of crystalline process into clarity and resolution.

We will even forgive the artist his little unresolved discrepancies for the artist is only human after all. We will allow him or her a few editorial comments drawn from the insistent wellspring of an everyday life. One need only think of the constant wear and concatenation of molecules bombarding the delicate circuits of the brain year after weary year. Who can blame the artist, musician, or writer for including something of these in the very public arena of his discourse? What power has the artist to command attention or regard let alone respect?

Out of the solitary workshop of the creative mind things multiply and distill themselves into one medium or another and then the creator stands back to judge or to forgive and this before even its exhibition or publication: already it is distant from the hand that crafted it. Even the artist knows not whence has come what stands before him just as God for all of his advance warnings of the deleterious fruit of knowing the difference between good and evil could preserve the innocence of the first couple in Eden. If the artist feels that somewhere a great and fundamental disharmony has set in he would be well-advised to keep his suspicions to himself.

The only people who enjoy apocalypses are those who are let into the secret in advance so that they know when to build an arc and hoist sail for Mount Ararat. But if the apocalypse is so latent that it has already occurred, why then everyone is in the same relative position to each other and no one will be spared. Crisis will follow crisis and each will appear to have been resolved in a timely fashion, while hidden in the darkness below the infestation will multiply and spread its toxic effluvia. Tiny fissures will appear in even the most sacred and unquestioned of our certainties until at last, its force, long gathered, breaks suddenly forth in storm and destruction. Dismay will yield to a forlorn isolation and a blackened sea vessel beset by hideous and multi-legged worms that will seek shelter again in the mass of mussels and anemones that clinging together retard all progress.

Even thus do metaphors multiply so that even a possible good ending is wasted and to no avail. An apocalypse does not always imply closure; it may just as well merely mean that things become so fragmented that integrity, whether structural or merely in the form of a literary discourse becomes impossible. This process was attempted to be contained through deontology and the method of the deliberative deconstruction of all texts. It was always assumed however that the text could be re-integrated and re-inspired so that the corpse would breathe again and rise up from our dissection table and go about its business as if nothing untoward had ever occurred. This is what lies behind our ultimate fear of insight: that we might inadvertently discover that our nature is inadequate to support the full extent of our knowledge let alone our suppositions and our dreams.

Story depends upon the preexistence of a set of uniform expectations in a discerning audience for the interchange of meaning to occur. If this uniformity is lacking the exchange of contrasting and of sympathetic viewpoints does not occur. The problem that the author faces at the present hour is finding a target audience in the face of societal drift and fragmentation. The only authorial hope remaining therefore is either to adopt an overly simplistic narrative or to appeal to the subconscious mind by reducing logical narrative to a mere collection of symbols or stimuli and to push the interpretive task onto the reader, to allow his unique subjectivity to make of the literary object whatever he or she pleases.

The trend is towards the ultimate in objectivity and abstraction wherein the narrator as narrator disappears and all that remains is a suggestive artifact that escapes clear definition. It is in this spirit that reflexively speaking "Apocalypse Yesterday" is written. If this seems an abdication of the authorial role it is an abdication that is forced upon the author by the sheer number of empty seats in the theater of the mind. The basic contractual agreement between writer and reader has been severed by technology and by social drift into various polities that approach the world and the act of interpretation with widely divergent tastes and presumptions. This phenomenon forces the author inwards to confront his or her own inner experience and perceptions in all of their primal and decompensated nature.

Out of the ur-text and raw data of the ever suggestive mind arise thoughts and images out of the vast whirlpool of language that form wholes through sheer proximity and the bonding tendency of association. Literature like science advances by degrees as new forms are created to convey content. To speak of the form in the very act of evolving that form is less an act of transgression than a frank confession of what the author is about even as he does whatever authors do. The problem of the unreliable narrator disappears as soon as the author peaks from behind the curtain and unveils the machinery behind his own creation. Like the Eiffel Tower the difference between structural elements and ornament disappear when they become one and the same.

The ultimate question for the conscious mind is whether it exists in isolation. We depend upon communication to form linkages—we seek communities of interpretation. Even then the question remains: how do we ground our ethical and epistemological insights in some sort of ultimate guarantor of verification. An unprofitable enterprise entirely is literature unless it is termed to be revelation at one end at least, at that spectral zone where color fades into blackness. History has yet to escape the impact of its sacred texts because to do so would cause us to collapse into ourselves like a collapsing star forming a black hole leading to some inexpressible singularity. Humans cannot exist alone floating in endless space/time without direction or orientation without experiencing overwhelming anxiety. Deprived of beginning and end, lost in a sea of indeterminacy, brought into conscious agency and then as abruptly plunged into insensibility without hope of one last review and summation we are forced to adopt a position towards ourselves and to all questions whether asked or still forming themselves somewhere in the floating ether of the mind. We balance our absolutes each day with our morning coffee.

What if Moses or centuries later St. John of Patmos had suffered writers block? But then if words are being forced into your mouth like a set of oversized dentures I guess you just write what you're told to write by God. Anyway there's still time for correction (isn't there) just in case you misunderstood something or placed the wrong emphasis on something that was merely a parenthetical illustration of a more important but unstated point. In any case one apocalypse is enough. I mean a general ending for humanity includes everybody so that we don't need to worry about getting the daily rushes edited for our hypothetical film or who got the best distribution deal because it just won't matter anymore will it after the final waves of the metaphysical tsunami advance and then retreat?

Anyway I'm pretty tired as you can perhaps tell and I'm running short on paste and materials for the collage and hell you can overdo anything if you stick with it too long. I'd like to enshrine all the things that upset me, what the French call my *bête noire* but who'd listen even having come so far intrigued and yet bewildered. They'd figure they had the drift of the whole apocalypse thing anyway before we even started. Apocalypses are about endings...

DREAM
BY CARRIE AVERY MORIARTY

That was amazing," the man with the conductor said.

"Thank you," Christie replied. "I'm glad you liked it."

"We'll let you know as soon as we've made a decision," the conductor said.

"Thank you," Christie said. "I hope to hear from you soon."

With that, she placed her violin into its case and snapped it closed, dropped her music into her satchel, picked them up and walked off the stage. Ever since she was a child, she'd always dreamed of performing on stage, playing her own music for everyone to hear. While this wasn't going to be for that, it was a step in the right direction.

She'd been gaining respect within the music community, and this audition was for a steady paying gig. Those were so few and far between that she had almost given up hope in getting in with this particular orchestral group. Oh, sure, she'd had the paid gigs, quartets for weddings and other events of that sort, but this was for a spot with the big guys. Richard Bowman was one of the most prominent conductors in the area, and the fact that they even had an opening for her to audition for was a miracle in and of itself. Now, she just had to hope her piece was sufficient to get her in the door.

As she walked the few blocks to the subway entrance, she thought back over the audition. She'd been in key, on tempo, and had performed flawlessly, even if she was sweating like a whore in church. No, she couldn't look at the negatives, she had to stay focused on the positive part of her performance. The other man in the audience had seemed impressed with her piece, even if Mr. Bowman wasn't forthcoming with his opinion.

"Breathe," she told herself as she bounced down the stairs to the station.

"Spare change," an old man that sat at the bottom of the steps said, holding out a paper cup that looked as if it were ready to fall apart at any given moment.

Christie reached in her coat pocket and pulled out the two quarters she'd stuffed in there earlier, knowing he'd be there. "Here you go," she said, dropping them into his cup. She knew it wasn't much, knew it was likely going to go to booze of some sort or another, but she just felt like giving today.

She slid her Metro Card and went through the turnstile to get to her train. It would be there shortly, so she pulled out her phone and opened it up. Pulling up her social media, she posted a status about the audition, saying she felt it went well, and asking for positive vibes to be sent her way. Hearing the train coming, she locked her phone and stuck it in her pocket, and waited to get on.

The trip home was just as boring as it always was, and she stepped off the train to go up the stairs to the street, walking just a few blocks to her brownstone. Keying into the building, she stopped at the mailboxes and checked for anything. Unfortunately, the only things in there were bills. The city was getting expensive, and her job at the bistro was not going to get her where she needed to be. If she got this position, though, things would turn around quickly.

Walking up the stairs, she keyed into her apartment, closing and locking the door behind her. Taking a deep breath, she dropped the mail into the basket on her kitchen counter that doubled as a breakfast bar and walked to the closet in the corner. The one room space was sparsely filled, just a full-sized bed against the wall with the window, a small chest of drawers at the end, a night stand with her lamp and alarm clock on it, and the stools at the bar. She barely had enough space to turn around in it, but it was hers. She put her violin into the closet and stepped into the bathroom to splash her face.

She stripped from her performance black dress and hung it up in the closet, pulling out jeans and a shirt to replace it with. Once she was dressed, she went to the kitchenette to put the kettle on the little two burner stove. Tea was always a way to get through the waiting process, and this was one of those times. It wasn't as if she expected to hear anything today, but she needed the relaxation the chamomile tea offered. She got everything ready to wait for the water to boil, and went to her bed.

Her laptop was still sitting on the top, so she opened it to see what other opportunities she might find in the city. Spring was usually the time when she could bet on gigs becoming available, and her small group of four that played together often was always on the lookout for something. When she pulled up the internet browser, she saw she had an email waiting. Clicking to that tab, she opened it.

Ms. Butler:

Thank you for your time today. We appreciate your interest in our ensemble. There are still several additional applicants, so will not be able to make a decision until we have heard them all. You will be informed if you are chosen to fill the position we have open.

Sincerely;

Richard Bowman, Esq.

Her kettle began to whistle, so she closed the email with a sigh. She knew it was too much to hope for an answer that quick, but seeing the email lifted her heart just enough for it to plummet when she read the contents. Flipping the stove off, she picked up the kettle and poured the water into the pot for her tea to steep like her grandmother had shown her, then went back to the bed to look for other openings. Hopefully, there would be some folks looking for music for their events in the upcoming months.

"You still haven't heard?"

It had been a week, and she'd planned this lunch with Darci to hopefully celebrate her getting the position she'd auditioned for.

"Just the formal response thanking me for the audition," Christie said. "I guess I didn't get it."

"They don't know what they're missing," Darci said as she took a sip of her ice tea.

Christie laughed at the grimace she made. Being from the south, nothing Darci drank up here was sweet enough.

"There's always next time," Christie said, though she knew the next time could be a long time coming.

"Who is that?" Darci asked, looking over Christie's shoulder, nearly swooning in her seat.

Christie turned around to see the man who had been at the audition last week. Not the conductor, but the one who had said her music was beautiful.

"That's one of the guys from the audition," Christie said, then turned back around. "Wonder what he's doing here."

"Looks like he likes what he sees," Darci whispered behind her glass. "He's coming this way."

"Ms. Butler, right?" he asked as he stepped up to their table.

"Right," Christie replied. "I'm sorry," she apologized. "I don't remember your name."

"Not surprised," he said. "Charles Ward, assistant to Richard Bowman, at your service."

"So," Darci began. "When are you going to tell Christie that she got the job?"

"Darci," Christie seethed.

"That's quite all right," Charles laughed. "We haven't made a firm decision, yet. But you are at the top of the list."

"I am?"

Christie was shocked. She knew she was good, but to be at the top of the list for a position within Richard Bowman's orchestra was more than she ever dreamed.

"Yes," he said. "Trust me when I tell you that if it was me, the decision would have been made the moment you finished your piece."

"Told you," Darci said, smacking Christie's hand.

"You're serious?" Christie asked, still not believing what he had said.

"Look," he said as he sat. "I've been in the business for quite some time. Been working with Dick for nearly ten years. When I tell you you're good, believe me."

Christie just stared at the man, dumbfounded.

"I shouldn't have barged in on your lunch," he began.

"Please stay," Darci said. "I'm sure Christie won't mind."

Christie looked at her friend, then at the man who was watching her. "Stay," she finally said.

"If you're sure," he replied.

"She's sure," Darci said.

"What can I get you?" the waitress asked when she came back to the table.

"Just coffee," he replied.

"Cream?"

"No thanks," he said. After the waitress walked away, he asked, "Have you been in New York long?"

"I went to Columbia," Christie began. "It was a lot of work, but I fell in love with the city and decided to never go home."

"Your hometown's loss is our gain," he replied. "When were you at Columbia?"

"I graduated a couple of years ago," she explained. "It's been a struggle making ends meet, but I'm hopeful that I get this position and will be able to move from the starving artist role to something a little more permanent."

"Do you have an agent?" he asked. "I mean, someone helping you find places to play?"

"I don't have the money for that," she replied.

"She's just using her good looks, charm, and amazing talent," Darci threw in.

"Darci," Christie seethed.

"What?" her friend replied. "It's true. You're gorgeous, funny as hell, and ridiculously talented. You could compete with anyone out there. I'm surprised it's taken this long for you to get noticed."

"So am I," Charles said.

Christie looked at him, dumbfounded.

"She's right," he added. "You have the kind of talent that comes along once in a great while. I honestly don't know what's taking Richard so long to snatch you up. If he doesn't, he's nuts."

"You really think so?"

"Absolutely," he replied. "If he doesn't bring you in, I will find you a place. There's no reason you shouldn't be with the biggest orchestras in the city. You really do have that much talent."

"Told you," Darci said.

Christie sat there, stunned. She knew she was pretty good,

but to hear this man who just met her and only heard her play one piece say she was great was more than she could handle.

"Here you go," the waitress said as she set a cup of coffee in front of Charles.

"Thanks," he replied, then added a packet of sugar in the raw to his cup.

Stirring it, he watched Christie struggle with the truth, that she was a remarkable musician who just hadn't caught her break. Yet. His phone began to buzz in his shirt pocket, so he pulled it out.

"Speak of the devil," he said before answering. "Mr. Bowman. How can I help you?"

Christie sat in silence as she watched the man sitting next to her. His eyes widened, then he smiled like the cat that ate the canary.

"I am actually sitting next to her right now," he said. "I'd be happy to tell her in person."

A couple more moments, with him giving the affirmative "uh-hu" before he hung up.

"Well?" Darci prodded.

"Welcome to the Bowman orchestra, Ms. Butler," he said with a smile.

"I got it?"

"Like you should have a long time ago," he replied.

"Oh my god," Darci said. "You got it!"

"I got it," Christie mumbled. "I really and truly got it."

Tears started rolling down her cheeks as she looked at her friend, then at the man who had given her the best news she'd received since the acceptance letter from the college came.

"Hey," Charles said. "Are you all right?"

"I can't believe I got it," she stuttered.

"Cupcakes all around," Darci shouted, then got to her feet to go get the confections she mentioned.

Christie had her hand to her mouth, holding back the sobs that were threatening to break free. She had truly made her dream come true. She was going to be playing with one of the best orchestras in the country. Her daddy would be so proud. The thought of him missing this milestone in her life by just a few months pushed her over the edge and a sob finally found its way out.

"Hey," Charles said, unsure what was wrong with her. "Here," he said, offering her his handkerchief. She took it and proceeded to wipe her eyes, but it did little good. Her tears were falling too fast for her to gather then in the small cloth in her hand. Charles opened his arms and she leaned in from the side, putting her head onto his shoulder and let the tears fall.

"What happened?" Darci asked when she came back to the table.

"Don't know," Charles replied. "It just started."

It took a couple of minutes, but Christie was finally able to pull herself together and pulled away from Charles.

"I'm so sorry," she sniffled.

"It's quite all right," he replied. "Are you…"

He left the question hanging, unsure exactly what he wanted to know.

"Yeah," she sniffed again, then wiped her eyes with the only dry spot on the handkerchief. She then looked at it and realized that it was a very nice cloth, monogramed with his initials. "Oh god," she said. "I've ruined your handkerchief." When she looked at him, she saw she'd smeared her makeup onto his shirt as well. "And your shirt," she said with a hitch.

"It'll wash," he assured.

"No," she said, pulling another napkin. "I got mascara on it. It's waterproof. It'll never come out."

"I can buy another one," he said. She looked up at him

confused. "Seriously," he offered. "I just want to make sure you're okay."

All Christie could do was nod, her throat growing tight again with emotions.

"An official email will be sent out," Charles said. "I'm really glad I got to tell you in person, though."

"I've got her," Darci said, seeing the worry in his face. "Don't worry. She's thrilled, I promise."

Charles looked to Christie again, and she nodded. "If you're sure," he said, clearly waiting for a response from Christie, not her friend.

"I am," she squeaked out, trying to smile.

"Then I'll see you at rehearsal," he said, standing with his coffee and making his way back to the front of the café.

Once he was far enough away, Darci scooted closer to Christie and whispered, "He is super cute. You should totally go for him."

Christie slapped her friend's hand and laughed, finally able to get past the knot in her throat.

"You are something else," she said.

"I am," her friend replied. "It's an acquired taste, but once you get it, you can't give it up."

The both of them laughed again, easing the tension that had come upon Christie. She'd done it. Honestly and truly, she had made it to the big time.

"You need to cut back that much?"

"I know it's short notice," Christie said to her boss. "I just got this position in the Bowman Orchestra. The only days I don't have rehearsal or performances are Mondays and Thursdays."

"Does this mean you'll be leaving us?" her boss asked.

"Not yet," she replied. "I want to keep this until I know for sure that the orchestra will work out. That, and I have to make sure I can make ends meet.”

“Well,” her boss began. “I’d hate to lose you. But I am so thrilled for you, at the same time.”

“I can’t tell you how thrilled I am,” she said as she put her apron on.

“When do I need to change the schedule?”

“They said rehearsals start in two weeks, so that gives you a little time,” she replied.

“I should probably get your autograph now,” her boss said. “So I can say I knew you when…”

“Very funny,” Christie replied. “I’ll still be by to get coffee every chance I get.”

“I’ll hold you to that,” he replied. “Now, get to work.”

The order was issued with a smile, and Christie knew it was all in fun. As she worked, she wondered if this was the beginning of the end of normalcy for her. What would it be like when she was recognizable? Would people hound her every time she went to the grocery store? Maybe she wouldn’t even be able to come here and see her friends. But she was getting ahead of herself. She was still the same girl who came to New York to follow her dreams.

“Americano,” the man at the register said.

“Room for cream?” Christie asked before she looked up. “Oh, hey,” she said, recognizing Mr. Ward, the assistant to Mr. Bowman.

“I didn’t recognize you,” he said. “No cream, but thanks.”

“Absolutely,” she replied, ringing up his order and placing the sticker on the cup, handing it off to her barista. She told him the price and he offered her his card. Sliding it through the reader, she asked, “Receipt?”

“Not today,” he said. “You’re all ready to start next week?”

“I thought it was two weeks,” Christie said, confused.

"We begin rehearsals on Tuesday," he said. "Did you not get the email?"

"I did," she said. "I'll have to read it again to make sure I have the dates correct."

"I would hate for you to miss the first rehearsal and be cut," he offered. "You're far too good to be left on the sidelines."

"Thank you for letting me know," she said.

With that, he walked away from the register to wait for his order to be ready. By the time she got her first break, her boss had already left. She pulled out her phone and pulled up her email. Sure enough, she was supposed to start next week, not the week after. She sent a quick text to her boss, apologizing for the mistake, then went back to work.

When her shift was over, she hung her apron on the hook in the back room, picked up her purse to slide over her shoulder, then made her way back up front.

"See ya," she called to one of her coworkers.

"Have fun," Penny replied.

Walking the couple of blocks to the train, she was lost in herself, humming a tune she made up as she went along. Down the stairs, swipe the Metro Card, through the turnstile, and wait for the train. It was a daily thing, something she didn't even have to think about, she'd been doing it so long. She hopped on the train and stood next to the door, knowing her stop was just a few down the way.

"Ms. Butler?"

She looked up from her phone to see Mr. Ward stepping into the car.

"Hello," she said, scooting over to give him room.

"I wonder whether we've ridden the same train for days and never seen each other," he pondered.

"Definitely could have," she replied.

"Even in this big city," he began, "it's still a small world."

"That it is," she said. "So," she began after a pause. "Going home?"

"I am," he replied. "You?"

"Same," she said.

They rode in comfortable silence for a while before Christie's stop was coming up

"This is me," she said as the train slowed.

"Me, too," he replied.

"Shall we walk together?"

"Sure," he said. "At least until we have to separate."

Up the stairs to street level, the turned the same direction. They made small talk about their mutual love of music, and discussed their history in getting to where they were. His predecessor had died suddenly just two years earlier, and Richard had given him the position because of how well liked he was by the members of the orchestra. It hadn't been his intention to be second to the top, but the position was growing on him.

"This is me," she said as they came upon her building.

"No way," he replied.

"Wait," she halted. "You live here, too?"

"Next door," he said, pointing to the brownstone building next to Christie's.

"Well isn't that fun," she said.

"I knew someone musical lived in this building," he said. "I've heard you playing. Always wondered whether it was a recording or live, but when I heard the same piece being worked on, I knew it was a musician."

"Why didn't you come over?"

"And say what?" he asked.

"Oh," she colored. "Guess that would probably have been a

bit awkward, huh.”

“Probably,” he laughed.

“Did you want to come up?” she offered.

“Nah. Gotta finish up some work. See you next week.”

“Unless we end up on the train together,” she laughed.

“True,” he replied. “Have a good evening.”

“You, too,” she said, then keyed her way into the building.

Once she was inside, she grabbed her mail, what little there was, then bounced up the stairs to her studio. Pulling her phone out, she dialed her friend.

“What’s up, buttercup?” Darci answered.

“You’ll never guess who lives next door,” Christie blurted out.

“The Pope?” Darci laughed.

“No,” Christie said. “I’m serious.”

“I have no idea,” Darci said.

“Charles Ward,” Christie said as if that made all the sense in the world.

“Who’s that?”

“The dude who we ran into at the café,” she replied.

“The hot dude?” Darci asked. “The one you’re going to hook up with?”

“I’m not going to hook up with him,” Christie said.

“You should,” Darci offered.

“He’s kinda my boss, now,” Christie said. “That’s usually frowned upon in polite society.”

“Doesn’t mean it doesn’t happen,” Darci countered. “Actually…”

“Not gonna happen,” Christie interrupted.

“Seriously,” Darci said. “I have to live my life vicariously through you. I can’t do that if you’re not gonna bang some sexy guys.”

"You could go out," she countered. "You know, find a guy. Go on a date and get yourself laid."

"You gonna watch Robbie?"

"Not on your life," Christie said. "Your kid is too wild for me."

"He's a little angel," Darci cooed.

"When he's sleeping," Christie laughed.

"Speaking of," Darci said and Christie could hear the little boy in the background calling for his mama.

"I'll let you go," she said.

"Think about what I said," Darci said. "I expect details."

With a laugh, the call ended.

"That girl is gonna get me in trouble one of these days," Christie said to her empty studio.

She dropped her backpack onto her bed, then pulled out her violin and began to learn the music she'd received for the upcoming week.

"What do you think?" Charles asked Richard after the first week of rehearsals.

"She's good," Richard replied.

"I told you," he said. "Are you going to move her up?"

"I can't do that to the guys who've been here longer," Richard explained. "It wouldn't be fair to them."

"So she loses out when she's better than them," Charles began. "Just because they got here first? It isn't her fault."

"Let's do this run and see how things turn out," Richard offered. "I know she's good and will do well. I just can't upset the whole apple cart at this point."

"If you don't," Charles said. "She's likely to be poached."

"That's what I'm worried about," Richard confessed. "If anyone else sees how good she is, they're likely to offer her more than I can. If I were her, I'd jump at the opportunity."

"So do something about it," Charles said.

"Give it another week," Richard said. "Then we'll reevaluate."

"How's it going?" Darci asked.

It had been two weeks since she'd started rehearsals, and Christie was loving every minute.

"I'm better than some of the chairs ahead of me," she confessed.

"Are they moving you up?"

"I doubt it," Christie sighed. "It's seriously an old boys club thing in this industry. Because I'm the new kid on the block, I get the back of the bus."

"That's stupid," Darci complained.

"It is what it is," she said.

"It shouldn't be," Darci said.

They sat and drank their coffee in the little shop they'd been meeting in for years. It was their home away from home, close enough to the theatres, yet still close enough to where Darci worked for them to grab a quick visit between their shifts.

"Ms. Butler," Charles said as he came up to the two of them.

"Mr. Ward," she replied. "What brings you in?"

"I wanted to tell you," he began, then looked at Darci.

"Oh," Christie said. "This is my best friend. You might as well tell me in front of her, cause I'm gonna tell her anyway. That way it'll cut out the middle man."

Charles laughed, then sat in one of the vacant chairs. "I don't know if you're aware, but I've noticed some other composers have been in attendance at our rehearsals."

"Really?" Christie asked. "I didn't know they were open to the public."

"They're not," Charles explained. "But composers are connected. They know when there's fresh blood, and they like to come in and check out the competition."

"And Mr. Bowman is okay with this?"

"Not really," Charles said. "But he doesn't really have a choice. If the theatre owner is willing to allow another composer to come in, the one who is in residence doesn't get to say no."

"What does that mean for Christie?" Darci asked.

"That there have been people talking," Charles said. "And they are saying that they like what they see."

Christie looked at her friend, then back at Charles. "What does that actually mean?" she asked.

"That what I feared would happen is likely to," he said.

"You mean she's being fired?" Darci asked.

"On the contrary," he said. "You're going to be poached."

"Poached?" she asked. "What does that mean?"

"Someone is going to put you in the first chair," he said.

Christie looked at him, baffled.

"That's good, right?" Darci asked.

"That's very good," Charles replied, still watching Christie.

"First chair?" Christie whispered, blinking.

The smile that spread across Charles' face was enough to make it clear that he was not kidding, but was honestly thrilled to be the one to tell her the good news.

"That means you're not gonna be her boss anymore?" Darci asked, and Christie looked at her with daggers, knowing just what her friend was thinking.

"Unfortunately," Charles said. "I feel like I've been witnessing the birth of a new star. You're going to be talked about for years to come. You know that, right?"

Christie blinked at him, still stunned with what she was

hearing. She'd always been told she was good, but to be taken from the back of one orchestra and placed in the first chair was something completely different.

"Here," Charles said, handing here a business card. "I really want to keep in touch with you. Let me know how things go."

"I haven't changed orchestras, yet," she said, eyes wide.

"Expect to get an email or call soon," he replied.

Just then, her phone pinged with an incoming email.

"Told you," he smiled. "Call me. We can go to dinner some time and talk about what it's like at the top."

As he walked away, Christie opened the email on her phone. She read, then reread it several times, her mouth falling open with each line. She looked at her friend and said, "He's right."

"About?"

"Look," she said, turning her phone around so her friend could read the email.

"Oh my god," Darci said, looking between her friend and the phone. "They're gonna pay you that much?"

"I get to do solos," Christie said. "And they want me to start right away."

"Email them back," Darci said. "Don't let this opportunity pass you by."

Before she had a chance to respond, her phone pinged another incoming email, and then another, and another. She looked up at Darci and smiled.

"I think I'll have several to choose from," she said.

"Let's look," Darci replied.

They spent the next hour pouring over seven different offers for positions in orchestras from all around New York. She even had a couple from Europe come in.

"How am I supposed to choose?" she asked when she felt like

they'd all come in.

"I know someone who could help you," Darci said, holding the business card Charles had left on the table out.

"I couldn't ask him," Christie said.

"Why not?"

"It would be unethical."

"Since when?" Darci chided. "He offered to help, wanted you to stay in touch. Here's your chance to kill two birds with one stone."

"You really think he'll help?"

Darci looked at her friend. "Do you really need to ask me that?"

Christie sighed, then picked up the card and dialed his number.

"Hello?"

"It's Christie," she said. "Christie Butler?"

"Hello," Charles replied and she could hear the smile in his voice.

"I have a problem," she said.

"How can I help?"

"There are too many offers," she said.

"That's a good problem to have," he laughed. "What do you say to dinner tonight?"

"Um," she hedged.

Darci looked at her and she mouthed that he wanted her to go to dinner. Nodding, Darci pushed her friend to say yes.

"Strictly professional," he said hearing the hesitancy in her voice.

"I'll buy," she insisted.

"Or you could come over and I could cook" he suggested.

"I can't ask you to do that and help me," she argued.

"What if I insist?"

"I guess I can't refuse," she replied.

"Good," he said. "So, why don't you plan to come over in say, half an hour?"

"You'll be ready by then?"

"I'm ready now," he replied.

"But," Christie began.

"Look," he said. "When I talked with you in the café, I knew you were going to be getting offers for most of the afternoon. Richard told me he'd been approached by several conductors and head hunters. It was only a matter of time before you were overwhelmed. I stopped on the way home and picked up some stuff to cook. Bring your friend," he offered. "There's plenty to go around."

"Oh," she said, stunned.

"Say you'll come?"

"I guess it would be rude to refuse," she replied.

"And your friend?"

"Let me ask," she said, turning to Darci. "Dinner with Mr. Ward?"

"Not on your life," Darci replied. "This is all you and him."

"I guess she has something she is doing," Christie said into the receiver.

"Maybe next time," he said. "I'll text you my address so you have it. You already know how to get here, so it should be fine. See you soon."

"See you soon," she echoed, then disconnected the call.

"I want details tomorrow," Darci said.

"Shut up," Christie laughed. "It's professional. Nothing more."

"But it doesn't have to be," she replied. "Take the plunge, jump in with both feet."

"He's helping me with my career," Christie said. "I don't want to lose him because I push something that isn't there."

"Babe," Darci began. "I saw how he looked at you the first time I met him. He wants you. Trust me. I know that look."

"We'll see," was all Christie could say.

They left the café and headed to the subway. Bidding her friend farewell, she got on her train and rode it to her stop. She pulled up the text when she was close to her building and saw that he did, indeed, live right next door. She climbed the steps and pressed the button for his apartment.

"Hello," she heard his disembodied voice.

"It's Christie," she said.

She heard the buzz and the click of the door. Pulling it open, she stepped inside. Taking the stairs to the left, she climbed the first flight, then walked around to take another. On the third floor, she looked at the numbers on the apartments, determining which way they were going, then turned left and walked a couple of doors down until she saw 3B. Raising her hand to knock, she gasped as the door opened.

"Hey," he said. "Sorry, didn't mean to scare you."

"How did you know I was here?"

"I didn't," he replied. "Just wanted to have the door open when you got here. You're faster than I thought."

"Years of doing stairs," she laughed.

He held the door open, allowing her entrance to his apartment.

"You have so much space," she said as she looked around.

"It's one of the nicer ones in this building," he replied. "Can I take your coat?"

"Sure," she said, slipping it off and handing it over. "Smells good."

"Hope you like pasta," he said.

"More than you know," she laughed.

"It's just about done," he said, stepping into the kitchen. "Make yourself at home."

"What can I do to help?"

"Oh, no," he said. "You're a guest. My mother would skin me alive if I allowed you to help."

"Alrighty then," she said, walking toward the windows on the back of the living space. "Great view," she said as she looked out over the city.

"It's even better at night," he said. "The lights of the city are spectacular."

"I bet," she said.

"Wine?" he asked.

"Oh, no," she said. "I'm good with water, thanks."

"Sure thing," he said. "Whenever you're ready."

Christie turned around and walked back to the table set near the kitchen. He had a much larger apartment than she did, with actual divided spaces for each room, even with how cozy it was.

"What offer has you most intrigued?" he asked after they'd begun their meal.

"They're all so different," she replied. "This is really good, by the way."

"Thanks," he said. "My grandmother taught me to cook, insisting that it would be a good thing to use to catch a girl."

"She was right," Christie said. "You'll have to tell her."

"Back to you," he said. "How many offers did you get?"

"I think there are ten total," she said. "I'll pull up my emails after dinner."

"Are they all from here?"

"Four or five from New York," she began. "There are a couple from out in California, then a few from Europe. It's a little overwhelming, honestly."

"Well," he said after a few more bites. "I can tell you who to stay away from here. The California ones will be harder to know, and those in Europe, unless they're really big ones, I will be of no help."

"You never did tell me how you ended up here," she said. "What's your story?"

"I grew up in the middle of nowhere," he began. "My mom loved music, and always wanted to be in a big band. Growing up, she watched those shows on the TV, dreaming of sitting behind one of the podiums, playing beautiful music. Unfortunately," he laughed. "She couldn't carry a tune in a bucket."

Christie laughed. "That was my dad," she said. "Tone deaf doesn't even begin to describe it."

"I know what you mean," he agreed. "Dad was a professor at the local university. One day when we were visiting with him, I found my way to a piano and started plunking away. Apparently I was pretty good, because a crowd started to form, and everyone watched in amazement as I fiddled around with a song I'd only heard on the radio."

"Sounds like me," she said.

"I bet," he agreed. "Needless to say, there was no doubt I had a natural talent. My parents cultivated it and pushed me to pursue music. It paid my way through college and found me moving to New York before I realized what was happening. I was grabbed by Richard as an assistant with finding new talent, because he said, 'it takes someone with great talent to recognize it in someone else.' That's one of the reasons I was so shocked it took him so long to offer the spot to you."

"Why did it take that long?"

"He said he wanted me to be sure," Charles said. "He knew, though. He also knew that you wouldn't be with us long once word got out."

"About that," she said, wiping her mouth. "How did word get

out? I mean, I know that conductors talk, but it seemed like this went really fast."

"With New York, everything is fast," he said.

"It does seem that way," she agreed.

"Let's look at your offers," he said.

For the next two hours, Christie showed him the emails that she'd received, and Charles told her which ones to stay away from and which ones were good options.

"I just wish I didn't have to choose," she said, frustrated.

"But you do," he said. "What do you say I make a few calls and see if I can find out anything?"

"You've been more than kind," she said. "I couldn't ask you to do that."

"Why not?" he asked. She didn't have an answer for him. "Look," he continued. "I like you. You're a good person with a smart head on your shoulders. You're beautiful and talented beyond anything that should be legal. I can't just watch you go out there and end up in a horrible situation. I'd feel responsible."

"How would you be responsible?" she asked.

"Because I'm the reason people know about you," he confessed. "I asked Richard if it would be all right if we invited a couple of other conductors in to listen to you after your audition. He was hesitant, but saw exactly what I saw. Raw, pure, tremendous talent. He knew it would just be a matter of time before you were poached outright. This way, he could have a hand in trying to find the best fit for you."

"I'm afraid I don't understand," she said.

"Like I said," he said. "New York moves fast."

She sat there, looking at the man next to her, completely confused.

"Tell me what to do," she whispered.

Charles reached out and held her hand. "Sleep on it," he said. "Give yourself at least one day to bask in all that is the wonder of being so wanted that people are fighting over you. Then," he continued, "sit down with someone you trust and go over what they've offered, and what I've told you. Do some research, see what there is out there about the ones you want most, and make a decision."

"You make it sound so simple," she said.

"It is," he replied. "If all else fails, tack them up on the wall and throw a dart."

She laughed, then said, "Thank you. Not just for this, but for dinner and for being so nice."

"I like you," he said. "Now, go home and sleep on it. The decision doesn't have to be made today, or even this week. Give yourself time."

Standing, she thanked him once again, then made her way out the door. She walked down the steps, out of the building, and down the block to her own place. Keying her way in, she bypassed the mailboxes and made the climb to her studio. Once there, she checked the time, and decided she'd call Darci in the morning. Yawning, she undressed and climbed into bed, plugging her phone in so it would be ready to go when she got up. Tonight, she would dream of all the possibilities, and tomorrow she would make a decision.

Christie's phone began blaring before it was even light out, and she rolled over to peer at it. Darci. Of course it was her.

"Hello," she mumbled as she answered.

"About time," Darci said. "You didn't call last night and I was worried."

"It was late when I got home," she said. "I didn't want to wake you up. Unlike you, who has no problem calling when normal people are sleeping.”

“So,” Darci prompted, waiting to hear the details of the night before.

“We talked,” Christie said, yawning. “And he gave me some great insight into some of the offers. He also told me to talk to someone I trust. I guess that’s you.”

“Those aren’t the details I was hoping for,” Darci sighed. “Did you kiss? More?”

“Good lord,” Christie mumbled. “No. It was a dinner with a colleague. Nothing more.”

“You’re boring,” she replied. “Seriously, he isn’t your boss anymore, so you should go for it.”

“He did tell me he liked me,” Christie said.

“Woah,” Darci said. “Liked you as in *liked* you?”

“I guess,” she replied.

“And that didn’t give you incentive to kiss him?”

“It was dinner,” Christie argued. “We talked about work.”

“Which doesn’t involve you two together anymore,” Darci interjected.

“It’s too early for this conversation,” Christie yawned again. “Can I call you when I’ve had more sleep?”

“Fine,” Darci said. “But if you’re not gonna kiss him, then you are doing it wrong.”

“Good night, Darci,” Christie said.

“Night,” Darci replied.

Christie disconnected the call, then saw that she had more emails. Deciding that she really couldn’t sleep anyway, she pulled the app up on her phone. Blinking, she counted the unread emails. More offers had come in, ranging all across the US, Europe, and even Asia. She just stared at them, unsure what to even do. Deciding she needed more help, she sent a text to Charles, hoping she didn’t wake him, but also wanting his help with this. She didn't wait long before she got a reply saying he was awake and she could call if she wanted. Booting up her laptop, she stepped into the bathroom to take care of business before getting on a call. When she came out, her phone was ringing. She looked at the screen and saw it was him, so she answered.

"Sorry," she said by way of an answer. "Had to powder my nose."

"It's all good," he replied. "How many more did you get?"

"I lost count after about a dozen," she said.

His low whistle was the reply.

"This isn't fair," she said. "There are a lot of other talented people out there. Why am I getting all these offers?"

"Word is out," he said. "I say pick from one of the first ones you got. Unless there's something that really catches your eye in one of the new ones."

"Maybe I should just stay where I am," she sighed.

"And give up on this amazing opportunity?"

She sighed, then said, "I guess you're right."

"I know I am," he replied. "Do you want me to do anything?"

"Make the decision for me?" she asked.

"I can't do that," he replied.

"Sure you could," she insisted. "Then I wouldn't have to make the decision myself. You have no idea how bad I am at decision making."

"Tell you what," he began. "You let the offers sit, no answering any of them. And we will meet with Richard on Thursday. It's not a rehearsal day, so he'll be available to talk. You can show him every offer you have and ask him his opinion. That way you'll get the best guidance anyone could. He knows almost every conductor in the states, and some of those who are in Europe. Can you do that?"

"Thank you," she said. "You have no idea how helpful that is.

It makes it seem possible, now.”

“Happy to help,” he replied. “Rest. We’ll talk again in a couple of days.”

Christie hung up the phone and looked at it again. Three more emails had come in while she was talking to Charles. How was she ever going to decide?

The days flew past, offers piling up one on top of the other, until Christie couldn’t keep track of who was who, which offer had multiple requests, and where all the offers were from.

“Hey,” Darci said as she sat down next to her friend.

“Hey, you,” Christie replied.

“Today’s the day?”

“Yep,” she said. “I’m meeting Charles here and then we’re going to see Richard.”

“You think you’ll stay in New York?”

“I’d like to,” she said. “It’ll depend on what is the best option for me, though.”

“Christie,” Charles said as he came in. “Darci.”

“Hey,” Darci said. “Don’t steer my girl wrong.”

“I wouldn’t think of it,” he replied. “You ready?” he asked Christie.

“I guess,” she replied.

“Break a leg,” Darci said.

“That’s only when you’re actually performing,” Christie laughed.

“Whatever,” she replied. “Don’t forget us little people when you’re world famous.”

They left the café and walked down the street.

“Did you figure out which ones you like best?” he asked as they got closer to the theatre.

"I couldn't figure it out," she said. "I really would like to stay in New York, though, and there are several offers from orchestras here in the city."

"We'll be sure to let Richard know," he said.

They stepped into the theatre and made their way to the office area. Knocking on the door to the conductor's office, they heard him call for them to come in. When they walked in, he wasn't alone.

"I'm sorry," Charles said. "I thought we were scheduled to meet."

"Come in," Richard replied, standing. "I'd like to introduce you to Margaret Schofield."

"Hello," the woman said. "It is truly a pleasure to meet you. I hope you don't mind me barging in on your meeting, but I wanted to offer you a position face to face."

"Okay," Christie said, shaking the woman's hand.

"It's a little unorthodox," Richard said, sitting down and indicating the others should follow suit. "I was to give you some guidance on what offer might be best for you, and here I have another to show you."

"It really is my fault," the other woman said. "I insisted he invite me when I found out you were meeting with him."

Christie sat with her hands in her lap, twisting her fingers around each other, more nervous than she'd ever been in her life.

"Margaret has an offer that you haven't yet seen," Richard said.

"And one I hope you will consider seriously," she added.

With that, she began to lay out an offer that was not only a good fit for Christie musically, but it was more money than any of the other offers she'd seen. Add to that, the opportunity for her to travel not just around the states, but abroad as well.

"It will, of course, also include your own apartment here in New York, as well as all travel and lodging for shows outside of New York," the woman concluded. "You would be allowed to have a significant other join you on the trips abroad, if that becomes a factor as well."

She was stunned. This was almost everything she'd ever wanted.

"What would be the chances of her bringing her own music to the group?" Charles asked, knowing that it was one of the things that Christie had wanted when they'd talked the other night.

"We would be delighted to look at pieces you've composed," Margaret said. "Each one would be considered on their own, and added to the score on a case by case basis. Richard indicated that you played your own piece when you auditioned for him. He was kind enough to allow me to view that when I asked."

"You listened to my piece?" Christie asked.

"And it was remarkable," the other woman replied. "You truly are a gifted musician, and I am very hopeful that I will get the opportunity to work with you."

"Thank you," was all Christie could say.

"I'll leave you to it," Margaret said as she stood. "So good to see you again, Richard."

"And you," he said, ushering her out the door. He closed it behind her and went back to sit behind his desk. "Well?" he asked.

"That was rather bold," Charles said.

"It's an offer that she didn't want to make unless she was sure she would be heard out," Richard said. "When I told her that I was meeting with you, she said she had to meet you as well."

Christie looked between the men. "She's serious?" she asked.

"Absolutely," Richard replied.

"This is a wonderful opportunity," Charles said.

"But it's more than I'm worth," Christie argued.

"Nonsense," Richard barked. "You're worth that much and more. The problem is, you can't see your own worth. That's not a bad thing, either. It will keep you humble, which will make you all the more valuable."

"You think I should take it," she said. It wasn't really a question, though she wasn't confident in her convictions, either.

"Unless you have an offer that can match it," Richard said. "I say take it as soon as possible and run away with it. I would if it were offered to me."

She sat there, looking between the two men, pondering the offer. It really was a good offer, and it would be awesome to have a bigger place. The opportunity to compose her own music was the tipping point, though, and she smiled.

"There it is," Richard said. "The moment she picked her destiny."

"And we can say we knew her when," Charles chimed in.

"So," she began. "Should I call her? Or are you going to? I don't have a number for her."

Richard picked up his phone and dialed. "She's in," he said after a moment.

"Oh my god," Darci said. "Look at this place."

"I know," Christie replied. She'd only been in her new place for a week, and already it felt like home. She had a three bedroom with a bath and a half, and an open floor plan. The extra bedrooms had been a must, as she said she needed a place for a friend to stay.

"And you're sure they're okay with us staying here?"

"I told them I had someone who I needed to stay with me," she said. "Why would they worry? They said a 'significant other' was allowed."

"But I'm not your significant other," Darci insisted.

"They don't need to know that," Christie insisted. "Besides, you're as close as I'm gonna get for a while."

"What's wrong with Charles?"

"We've had this conversation," she insisted. "I can't go there."

"But he likes you," Darci offered. "You told me yourself. I think you should go for it."

"You are incorrigible," she said.

"I'm amazing," Darci retorted.

Her phone began to ring, so she looked at it, then slid to answer.

"Ms. Schofield," she said.

"I take it you are all moved in," the other woman said.

"I am," Christie replied. "Thank you for checking."

"You should be receiving a package with your music for this next month," she said. "Along with the schedule for when and where you'll be needed. We have three orchestras working in unison, and you are leading one of them. We'll need you at rehearsals starting on Tuesday."

"Thank you," Christie said. "I'll watch for the package, and begin rehearsing at once."

"I'd also like to see the score for the piece you played for Richard," she said. "We might just want to add that to the next set of music we use."

"I will see if I can find a copy of what I wrote," she said. "Again, thank you for this opportunity."

"You deserve my thanks," the older woman said. "I never thought I'd find another one who was as good as our last lead. It was a breath of fresh air to listen to your piece."

"I appreciate your vote of confidence in me," Christie said.

"I'll see you soon," the other woman replied, then disconnected the call.

"Slave driver?" Darci asked.

"The opposite," Christie replied. "She's so nice, it's impossible to not do what she asks."

Darci smiled at her friend. "I'm glad you like her. It would suck for you to work with an ogre."

"Something she definitely isn't," Christie said.

Days turned into weeks, which moved to months. Christie was busy playing and traveling. Just as Charles had told her, she was wanted all around the world, and was beginning to lead a very different type of show, one where her music was front and center, and the orchestra was accompanying her rather than her simply being one of the pieces.

After three years she was back in New York on a month-long break to compose and rest. Darci and her son continued to live with her, sharing the space while she was in town, and enjoying it while she was away.

"Christie," Darci called. "Someone's here to see you."

She came out of her room and turned the corner to see Charles standing in her living room.

"Hey," she said, walking over to him.

"You look amazing," he said, giving her a hug.

They'd kept up conversations over the phone, but hadn't seen each other since her first big tour took off about six months into her contract.

"Back at you," she said.

"Dinner?"

"You cooking?" she asked.

"Or we could go out," he suggested. "You can afford it, right?"

Christie laughed and said, "Absolutely. What do you want?"

"You're paying," he said. "You choose."

Christie grabbed her purse and phone and said, "See you later," to Darci.

"Have fun," Darci replied, giving a little eyebrow wiggle when Charles had turned away.

Christie rolled her eyes, then followed him out. They walked down the street to a deli that was on the corner and stepped in.

"Miss Christie," the manager said as they came in.

"Raul," she replied, giving him a hug.

"Who is our friend?" he asked.

"This is Charles Ward," Christie said. "He's the reason I come here."

"He is bad for you at home?" the manager asked, confused.

"No," she laughed. "He's the one who discovered me."

"Oh," he said, drawing the word out. "I have you to thank for my best customer, when she is in town."

"You have her to thank," Charles said. "She's the talent. I just helped her find a place to shine."

"Thank you, thank you," the other man said. "Your usual?" he asked Christie.

"Please," she said, then made her way to a corner table. "So," she began once they were seated. "How has New York been treating you?"

"I wanted you to be the first one to know," he said. "Richard is retiring, and has asked that I take over his orchestra."

"Seriously?" she squealed.

"Right after the first of the year," he said, smiling.

"I'm so happy for you," she said.

"And I was wondering," he began, then stopped.

"What?" she asked, curious.

"If you would mind doing a special engagement with my orchestra," he said.

"Have you talked with Margaret?" she asked.

"She said she would love it," he said. "But that it was completely up to you."

"When?" she asked. "And what would we play?"

"I know you have a huge tour for Christmas," he began. "But after the first of the year, Margaret said she could spare you for a month. I'd like to do February with you in the lead. And if you wouldn't mind, we could do the piece you played when you auditioned."

She looked at him and smiled. "You're nervous I'll say no," she said. "Why would you think I would say no?"

"You're kind of big time," he said.

"But you are the reason I am," she replied.

"Nah," he began, but she interrupted.

"Seriously," she said. "If it weren't for you, I wouldn't have had the confidence to accept any offer, let alone the one I did. I feel like I owe it to you to help out. I'm in."

He smiled just as the manager came over with a couple of plates.

"For the beautiful lady," he said, placing one in front of her. "And for her charming partner," he said, placing the other plate in front of Charles.

"Oh," Charles said. "We're not..."

"What?" Christie asked when he stopped mid-sentence.

"Well," he said, looking at her.

"What?" she asked again, clearly confused.

"I don't want this to come off as pushy, but," he stopped again, not really finishing his sentences.

"Just come out with it," she said.

"What would you say if I asked you out?" he asked.

"We are out," she countered.

"I mean on a date," he said. "Like a romantic date."

She looked at him and smiled. "I thought you'd never ask," she smiled.

SUNRISE
BY DAVID MECKLENBURG

for H.M.

The direct flight on Alaska Airlines dropped me off in Palm Springs, which, even in the beginning of December was light and pleasant. But I wasn't staying in Palm Springs. Instead, I sat sideways in the back seat of a Mercedes convertible climbing out of the smoggy Coachella Valley, up through the Morongo Pass and into the high desert of the Little San Bernardino Mountains. It's a beautiful place because you can see how the land is tortured from below. Being a desert, the thin layer of Joshua trees, acacia and chaparral cannot hide the youthful, rough angles of naked rock. Back home, in the Pacific Northwest, I live on an equally broken land, but that land, like the true thoughts and desires of its inhabitants, lies hidden beneath layers of clothing, glacial till, Douglas fir, pretense, Himalayan blackberry, caution, and Western Red Cedar.

Both places embrace their ghosts but in different ways. In the forest, each nook and hollowed out place hides something, whether human in origin or not. The rain and moss make the dead unclear, and there are no shadows beneath the ever-present gray, making the differentiation of living and dead, and the immensely populated frontier between them, a useless endeavor. In the desert, though, the dead fly at night like bats from their homes among the deep rocks and add their voices to the wind as it searches across the stones and distance. In the middle of the day, the shimmer of heat and mirage is a perfect home for regret and memory to stand and dance or sweep across the arid floor in the swirl of dust devils.

My human perception of change—let us call it what it is, *mutability*—is both like and unlike. In the gray and green expanse of forest, redundant bourgeois suburbs and now uniform density of the Northwest, the growth of things, whether it is a plant, mud or redevelopment, obscures and unifies the forgotten and disposed. You have to look hard for ghosts.

In the desert, it is different. Once shorn of water, the livid, flirtatious footprint of life, the desert's things, whether rusting trailer, redundant bourgeois suburbs, or garbage *remain*. Hulks of old aircraft, metal signs, plastic milk bottles slowly disintegrate beneath the distant thermonuclear lamp of the sun, in a timeframe more geologic than human. Only the Joshua trees seem to grow quickly as they throw up their arms in praise and prayer of the sun and its intense dominion. Ghosts are everywhere, but so denuded that you cannot see them, save those who manifest themselves in desire and rage.

Uncle Louis and Bruce's place was in Cholla Canyon, a little desert town on the north side of the plateau that makes up Joshua Tree National Park. In fact, the park itself was the next-door neighbor. Uncle Louis concentrated on the road, the radar detector. He scanned the gauges and knew the temperature of the coolant water and the rate of fuel consumption as we crested the pass near Yucca Valley. My Uncle Louis is a retired engineer.

His hair was a rough mop of iron filaments fluttering in the wind: striking against the yellows, ochres and winter greens of the desert. Both he and his husband Bruce wore leather jackets when they picked me up. My uncle's is brown, like an aviator's. Bruce's is black and cut like a sport coat. Neither are campy enough to wear a leather daddy jacket, but as it is, they have a certain antique class about them. That day, I closed my eyes and imagined we flew over the desert in some fantastic airplane, like a flying boat only it was made for landing in the sand. Bruce is bald, but because it was cold, he wore a Ralph Lauren baseball cap and sunglasses.

Bruce was not paying attention to the road. He was paying attention to me.

"This is so awesome, Ada. We can't thank you enough, you know." Bruce didn't really have to flatter me, but he also knew that a bit of flattery was exactly what I needed at that point. "This will be a great break for you, I think. Kind of a reboot. You don't mind being alone?"

"Ada loves being alone," my uncle said over the wind.

"He's right, Bruce. And I'm sort of in between *that* and *whatever's next*," I said.

"Which means *nowhere*, if you keep up with that," Bruce said. "But look where you came from, I'm sure it's depressing and miserable up there. Cold…"

"…it gets pretty damned cold down here at night."

"Oh yes, I forgot you must be loving that rain and the dark at 4:30?"

"Touché."

"Besides, Mimi needs a friend." Mimi was my uncle and Bruce's 100 lb Akita and was ostensibly the main reason I was coming down to house-sit for them. "Now don't worry, Mimi distrusts everyone she doesn't know. But you're family. Once she figures that out…"

"There are a few t-bones in the fridge. Just give those to her and she'll love you. Dogs are mercenaries," Uncle Lou said.

"Anyway, there's plenty to do around here if you want and plenty not to."

"And you promise to be back by Christmas?" I asked.

"Yes, Bruce and I should be at the airport on the 22nd. You're picking us up." We roared off the main road at that point and left the pavement. The rest of the trip up the Cholla Canyon was on a dirt road. I'm not sure how much my uncle's tires were on the road. Bruce looked back at me, my hair must have been waving crazily in the wind.

"He always drives this fast up this road. Louie..."

My uncle thereon entered into a sort of monologue, fascinating perhaps for its steadfast focus on itself; as it was the subject matter which had a lot to do with velocities and lateral vectors reaching a point wherein the speed ensured less repetitive variance fatigue through irregular impacts.

"Is this like a horse not having all its feet on the ground in a gallop?"

"Well, Muybridge proved in the 1870's..."

"Why did you ask that?" Bruce asked me, his eyes rolling. "Supposedly it's easier on the car if we speed through here. I still suspect Louie is full of shit."

My uncle Louis was my mother's younger brother. In terms of thermodynamics, my uncle acted as a sort of heat-exchange between my mother and me. He'd always played that role in my life and was probably the closest thing I had to a father... but not quite and that was fine by us. My mother and I don't get along and do not speak to one another although I always sense there will be a rupture in this perfectly suitable arrangement. I still check in on her thanks to the Internet. She's a big-shot professor at UC Santa Barbara in their Chicano Studies department. Uncle Louis keeps me abreast of other items, and while he may harbor a spark of desire for my mother and I to make things better, he knows his older sister too well to allow her to sneak by his stoic regard.

"If you expect her to get any better you are at the mercy of the expectation, Ada. I've learned that a lot of life is like that."

From Japanese food to old movies, my uncle was an important influence on me, and while it took him a long time to come out, he didn't seem all that different and remained Uncle Lou, who was there to take care of me when my mother would go on her weeklong dates. House-sitting for them through most of December was really an adult modification of that relationship.

And I loved his boyfriend, now husband. Gregarious, cheerful, and possessive of a vast generosity and energy, Bruce truly loved my uncle.

"No one's really admired him, I think. Except you of course and that's why you're my favorite niece. So I want to make it up to him, for the world's sake, not mine and the best part is, I get to enjoy it all and the world just la la las along not knowing what it's missing, but I do and I'm a silly little bitch but who cares? There, that should work fine. Go to the circuit breaker and turn it back on."

Bruce said that to me once when an outlet in my crappy old apartment had blown out. My landlord wasn't doing anything about fixing it and such was the case in Seattle that you never really wanted to remind your landlord that you even existed. At best, you might be able to just deposit the rent straight into a bank account because if you reminded your landlord of your existence, your rent was bound to increase at some point in the following six months.

And so it had and I had lost my job because I was old and even worse, of the Old Regime at the Foundation. The new Executive Director, like many, had favors to bestow on other, younger peers and did not like anything that reminded anyone, especially major donors, that there had been a Foundation before him.

The house was enormous, but much of it was tucked back into a fold of the hills and waited behind mesquite oak and acacias. There were some towering palm trees further back beyond the dappled white walls and I remembered from pictures that they surrounded a courtyard and pool. We drove up a steep concrete driveway and into a garage that could have held several of my apartments. There was a blue 1966 Jaguar E-Type my uncle had been slogging around since he turned 55 and a Mini Cooper: Bruce's "runabout." Sturdy metal shelves lined the garage, holding motor oil, anti-freeze, and spare parts I couldn't even begin to identify.

"You still have the Jag," I said.

"Except it works now."

"Really?"

"Well, as much as any English car can be said to 'work,'" Uncle Lou said. "Actually, it's a great ride. Solid. Gas guzzler, and an oil burner, but it corners better than this Mercedes."

"Can I?"

"No," My uncle said, and the garage door started to close.

Bruce just looked at me and winked.

The door closed in near silence. I didn't even notice it until the absence of the sound arrested my attention.

"So how much of this did you two add and how much was here?"

"We've done remarkably little."

"I thought you said on the phone this place was a steal."

"It was."

We walked into a dark hallway of beautifully laid sandstone and stuccoed concrete, a tunnel really, and yet in the ceiling very high above us was a railing and beyond that skylights. The feeling was one of being both underground and coursing through the dark and holy air of some forgotten temple.

"The developer finished most of it," Bruce said.

"Developer? I thought you said you got this in a distressed estate liquidation." I said this to Uncle Lou who opened another door. On the other side was Mimi.

"Is that the story you told her?" Bruce asked, and Her Majesty then entered.

Her Majesty completed the Trinity. While my uncle possessed a Roman sort of *gravitas,* and Bruce possessed boundless charm, Mimi was simply *Imperial* in her dignity. There was no sense of entitlement in Mimi, because that word always conjures up the subtexts of underlying fragility; as though when challenged, the entitled person will throw a tantrum. Rather, Mimi sat on the throne because the destiny of the universe was reflected in her brown eyes and she did not even *know it* but resided in the rarefied realm of pure *a priori* Being—beyond the morality and ontology of the quotidian masses whom she benevolently tolerated. Especially when they had steak.

Mimi sniffed my hand with suspicion and looked up at Uncle Lou first. "See, she knows you're family," Bruce said. "I'm sure you two smell the same."

"Is that a compliment?" I asked Uncle Lou.

"It's as good as you'll get right now. C'mon, we might as well get this over with now. Let's go get something to eat, Mimi."

And she led us on a direct, albeit informative tour of wide hallways, and a gently spiraling grand staircase fashioned from custom tile to the sprawling kitchen. The island was about the size of a stage and lit like one. One could conduct all the acts of a grand dinner there, for there were at least three stoves (one gas, one electric and another was a built in AGA cooker.) The whole thing was made of hard-rock maple and granite, finely polished and lit by a number of recessed lights and track lighting that blended in with the prodigious pot rack.

"Do you even use a third of these?" I asked Bruce. All the copper had come from France and I could have cooked the Foreign Legion a six-course prix fix meal with them.

"No. Some of it *is* mine, the Mauviels down there, but a lot of this was here with the house."

"Really?"

"Yeah. Obscene, isn't it?"

"Here, Ada, give this to Mimi." My uncle brought out a plate with an enormous t-bone steak on it. "Tell her to sit."

I picked up the tail end with my fingertips and turned to look at Mimi. She must have been hungry because she didn't even have to be told to sit. She licked her lips.

"She won't bite your arm off," my uncle said, "unless I tell her to." He smiled and winked.

I swung the steak off the plate and Mimi watched the drops of blood fall on the floor, but her main focus seemed to be on the steak. She opened her mouth: huge white canines and a healthy pink tongue.

"Don't worry about the blood, she'll clean that up later," Uncle Lou said. Bruce shrugged and sighed. I knew the droplets bothered him. "Go on."

I held the bloody piece of cow out for her "good girl." She leaned forward, looked at me and then the steak and paused. And then, she slowly leaned forward and licked the meat. This went on for a minute until I felt my hand cramping. Sensing this, she then gingerly took the meat out of my hand and wandered off to her mat by the kitchen door and started to eat it.

"She's very ladylike," I said.

"Oh yes. No houndish gulping cha-lupping for my girl." Bruce said. "Well, that went well. There are three or four more in there. I suggest you give her one when you get back from dropping us off."

Bruce then took me on a tour of the house, showed me how the heat and light controls worked, where the circuit breaker panel was, the water shut off, the bathrooms, the stereo system that could play all through the house, a workshop, the cable and network closet. "Your uncle doesn't believe in Wifi, although I told him you would need it. So, he's installed a hotspot here in the center of the house. I don't know if it reaches everywhere, but you're more than welcome to plug in your laptop in my office."

Bruce's office looked out over the valley and was appointed with beautiful, understated prairie style furniture. I looked down the canyon, past the acacia trees and at the garden of stones sprouting up near the bottom.

"Is that a graveyard?" I asked.

"Sure is. Santa Margareta. I think it was Catholic a long time ago, but a lot of people were buried there. The former owner of this place is down there somewhere."

"The developer?"

"No, the guy who built this house in the first place." Bruce didn't say anything else because his mobile phone was buzzing in his pocket. I looked down into the beautiful valley. It seemed strange. Watchful.

"Yes, she just got here. No, not at all. You two should meet up as soon as you can. When do you? Oh, yeah, that's fine."

"Who was that? You're not setting me up with someone, are you?" I asked.

"Jack? Ha! Well, I don't know, maybe you would be a cute couple but he's about twenty years older than you. Jack is a friend of ours and lives down in Yucca Valley. We would have stopped at his café but he's at a gallery opening in Irvine I guess and won't be back until the day after tomorrow. That's one of his right there." Bruce pointed to what I had thought was an abstract oil painting.

"He paints," I said. The painting was actually more of an expressionistic portrait of the desert. I noticed a small figure in the painting, just off to the right looking at the enormous disc of the sun as it set. It was a woman half-nude half wrapped in a flowing serape.

"Jack actually uses the studio out near the guest house sometimes. The light is fantastic. He's a good guy and can help out with anything you'll need. You should just go down there and meet him. His café's a great place to write if you want to get out of here. Oh, you two will just love each other, I know. You're both in the *effete corps of impudent snobs who characterize themselves as intellectuals.*"

"He sounds wonderful, then" I said, and we laughed.

They even had a gym with a Pilates machine. Bruce knew I was into it, but I couldn't afford one of my own. "Oh, it's all for you, honey. Lou and I just use the elliptical, but I thought you might like this."

I unpacked my suitcase in the guest bedroom, although like everything it seemed over-sized with a California King sized bed. I walked over to the window and noticed it too looked down on the graveyard, but by now the sun was beginning to set over the San Jacinto mountains which lay southwest of the San Bernardinos and separated by a deep tectonic gash.

"It's a beautiful bedroom, isn't it?" Bruce said. We were sitting together at Charango—what passed for a fancy restaurant in Cholla Canyon. But the food was excellent: a mix of Mexican and California haute cuisine. I had pork medallions with achiote-sherry butter sauce, grilled delicata squash and mizuna tossed with a maple raspberry vinaigrette. Neither Bruce nor Uncle Lou wanted to cook that night because they were leaving the next day.

"You're spoiling me. If I hadn't seen the master bedroom, I'd have thought that was it."

"It used to be a long time ago." Uncle Lou said.

"Before the developer?"

"Kind of," Bruce said.

"Kind of? You said there was a story, something Uncle Lou didn't tell me." I said. Uncle Lou frowned.

"Louie…" Bruce said.

"The property has an interesting history, that's all. Well, probably for you. I think it's a beautiful place and wait until you see the sunrise tomorrow."

"What sort of history?"

"It wasn't much of anything I guess, back in the 70's. Just a big lot with a cinder-block house. The first owner, well, of the house, was a retired marshal with the Newport Beach fire department. He started to build a very nice home. Really, it was the bones of what you see here. I guess he had a lot of trouble with the permitting department, because they weren't used to anything like that up here. Issues with the cistern, the septic system. It all works. Very well after the second owner."

"Was that the person you got if from for a steal?

"Yes. That one. Anyway, the fire marshal and his second wife never really finished it. He kept changing plans, adding a room there, tearing out another one. When he died, the widow and his children from another marriage got into a real tussle over it all because he'd bought it before marrying the townie or whatever she was. There was a rumor she destroyed the will, too."

"Family squabbles. It's like *Wuthering Heights*," Bruce said.

"And the second owner got it in the estate sale. Undervalued because the widow was so difficult, I guess. The kids wanted to live here but she wouldn't hear of it."

"So how is it that you got it so cheap? I would think the developer wouldn't let that happen."

"No one knows that. It was rather unexpected. Too bad, it

was nearly finished. I guess he wanted to turn it into a corporate retreat center."

"What happened?"

Uncle Lou was silent. Bruce drank down the last of his wine and looked at me:

"The developer never finished it because he put a shotgun in his mouth and blew his brains out."

"Jesus, here?"

"No, down in Yorba Linda, I guess. Anyway, nasty business," Uncle Lou said.

"Do you think this place had anything to do with it?"

"Of course not. He was probably clinically depressed," Uncle Lou said, but Bruce went on.

"The guy was your classic developer, one peg down the coatrack from a plutocrat's step-n-fetch-shyster, in my opinion. His family decided to fight over other things. They really didn't want the place. Someone said it was haunted."

I was tired by the time we got back and after saying goodnight, I went back to my room. Nothing seemed odd, and I took off my clothes, put on my pajamas and crawled under the big down comforter. The night was cold, but I loved the contrast of the dry cool air and warm bed. I looked at the window, wondering if Cathy Earnshaw was going to tap on it.

The next morning there was chorizo, eggs, coffee, toast, and the spectacular sunrise waiting for me when I got up. Bruce called the house *Amanecer*, or 'sunrise' in Spanish. The dishwasher was already humming, and my uncle was fiddling with suitcases by the passage to the garage. Bruce leaned against the island while I ate.

"You know, you don't have to go back to Seattle if you don't want to. I think it would make Louie feel better if you regrouped here for a while. We have plenty of space you know, enough for two introverts like you and Louie. You can stay after Xmas. We can pack up your stuff in Seattle in storage."

"What does Mimi think?"

"Well, she will be the deciding factor, but I think she wouldn't mind."

"Is she an extra or introvert?"

"Oh, Mimi is beyond all of that human duality," Bruce said.

"How does she like this place?"

"It's hard to tell, actually. She's fairly indifferent to a lot of things."

"Any rooms she won't go into?"

"Ha, I don't know, now that you mention it. Honey, we've only been here for a little over 9 months and look at this place. I suspect there are some rooms *I* haven't been in. But maybe you'll have to check it out. Anyway, seriously think about my offer. Don't worry about Louie, he'd love to have you here."

"Thanks, Bruce. I appreciate that. I'll... have to think about it."

"You should. I think the change would do you good."

After a final litany of chore-schedules, key locations, security codes, passwords, systems review (the water system that heated the place was geothermal and complicated) and a grocery index (the fridges and freezers were full), we finally all packed in the car. Just as Uncle Lou roared off, Bruce reached over the seat and slipped keys into my hand.

"The Jag?" I mouthed the words to Bruce who just winked.

I drove back, speeded really, because like my uncle, my foot is heavy and the Mercedes was fast, responsive and sure-wheeled even as I rattle-battle flew over the dirt road back up to the house. I had to give Mimi her morning steak, according to Bruce, and I didn't want her to wait. Besides, I had to figure out what to do with myself.

The desert is so different from the desert of the Central Valley where I grew up: hot, flat and low. Los Angeles is the same, but then there are the high deserts like this one. I was wearing long underwear and my jeans, a turtleneck and Norwegian sweater, down vest and an old surplus Navy Pea coat. I kept the cold at bay with these items and walked around the property.

The property was a large swath of ground, mostly slope that hugged the west side of the upper valley with a switchback dirt trail that led into the National Park. And it was green. Not a powerful evergreen or tropical green, but it wasn't the endless wheat -gold sand colors I had expected of a desert. I should have known it would be green in the winter and I suppose I expected the desert of Estremadura.

No, I haven't been there, but I've watched a lot of spaghetti westerns, many of which were filmed in Spain. I looked over the desert, with the sun arching just out of 10:00. I felt alone and I *was* alone. The wind blew over the stones and through the Joshua trees, and I should have felt its companionship, but such was the clear winter light and cold, such was *the only* other sound of my boots on the coarse, loamy sand, that I could not tell which of us was alive and which was a ghost: the wind or me?

I turned and looked down on the house. I was finally high enough to see all of it. It had been made of several terraced levels. The top level had a guest house and large patio with an attached dry garden, perfect for stargazing I thought. There was a large swimming pool that curled into the hill. It was beautiful and looked almost like a natural pool because the bottom was finished off in the same colors as the surrounding sandstone. Rocks from the area dotted it like a Japanese garden. There was an outdoor shower area near a large spa, finished like the pool.

And then, the first movement of something alive I had seen all day. A shape, so quick its shadow moved with it as a corroborating blur, bolted from under an arched loggia. It skirted the pool, quickly climbed a palm tree and disappeared over the wall. It had a big tail. It was on four legs. And Mimi was chasing it. A feral cat.

I walked down and realized there was no gate in the wall on that side, but it would have been locked anyway. The third terrace level was the wide garages where the Mercedes, Mini and the Jag lived. I walked into the supernaturally clean garage and shut the door and then followed the catacomb tunnel up to the kitchen which obliquely faced a small, sunny part of the pool terrace.

Mimi turned around when I walked out and wagged her tail. A good sign. There must have been some private entrance for her (I wouldn't dream of saying something as vulgar as a "dog door.") She then trotted back to a bed that had obviously been laid out for her with southern exposure and took up a horizontal repose. The sun was warm there and I wanted to sit with her.

But I was drawn out to the pool. It was beautifully done, like it should have been in a first-rate zoo or a Dubai emir's palace. Bruce told me to keep the fountain and filter running and the spa was mine if I wanted to use it. "the controls are easy and over in the cabana." I imagined how beautiful it must be at night—there were lights submerged in it everywhere and built into cunning, theatrical locations on the sheer rock wall above it. My eye followed the stones out across it; they nearly bisected the pool, providing a bridge across to cut out enclosures under the rock wall.

And then I was reminded of Japan. There was no Torii gate. There were no winds screaming down from Alaska, but there was the mood of solitude and transition, as though the World Just Over There was as near to me in this place as it had been on a beach in Hokkaido a long time ago. I was alone then too, save for the ghosts who decided to meet me there.

I sat down and watched the water reflect the sky. I reflected. The thought of staying in Cholla Canyon appealed to me and for a moment, I even envisioned myself growing old and into some wise woman of the desert with long iron grey hair and a leathery stomach.

"Could I live here?" I directed my question to Mimi but she was already blissed out in sleep.

What is the difference between a house and a home? Our basic categorizations are simple enough. A home can be many things: an apartment, a suburban rambler, a castle, a ship. A house is something more specific, and more generalized at the same time, elucidating the fact our language derives its meaning from use. A house can be a home, but it can also be a family. There is the architectural description of a house whereas zoning laws may describe it as a single-family residence. Most people are content to leave it at that. But again, if a family makes a house, what is a family? What does it mean to reside?

I had many reasons to mull all this over. As the sun warmed up the patio, the memories of cold Hokkaido remained. I was 27 then. I was rebuilding my life and trying to find my way off the island I had landed on. Not Hokkaido itself, but it stood in admirably at that time. I remembered the ghosts of what-could-have-been came to me in the darkness and I wrapped myself up in the cozy frigidity of self-deprecation.

Just as the desert was different, so was my life. I was pretty lucky, and I knew it, but that meant I was utterly terrified. I was 49, single, childless and going through menopause. A complicated formula for the concept of Freedom.

When Bruce called to invite me down our conversation had turned to my welfare: "Louie's going to take care of you, Ada. He won't say it, but you know that. And you don't have to worry about me. I've seen enough of how families destroy each other after someone dies, no thank you. And I'll take care of you if Louie goes first."

"I'm not worried about you, it's your son and his wife I can't stand."

"Me neither," he joked, but there was enough of an undercurrent of sadness in Bruce's voice—usually so ebullient—that lent the joke a greater portion of truth than even jokes usually permit. "But Jilly will be on your side." Bruce meant his daughter, an unmarried radiologist living in Santa Monica.

"You mean when they sue us?"

"Hopefully it won't come to that."

I spent the rest of the first day getting used to the house: retracing the tour Bruce and Uncle Lou had given me. This afforded me the occasion of avoiding doing anything "productive." I learned that Mimi did have her own way out to the patio area through door cut into the wall near an entertainment room that fronted the pool area. She still liked, expected, rather, to be let out from the Kitchen, but when the need arose, she would go out that way. I suspected it was a private exit because Mimi hated taking shits—not because of any filth aspect (she was a dog after all, whose notions of filth are quite different than ours) but that it somehow lowered her to the realm of Mortal Beings and the preposterous pose one assumed was even more insulting. She often went out to the cactuses on the far end to take care of this evidently leveling requirement.

I worked out for an hour or so on the Pilates machine and finished on the elliptical trainer, then made some spaghetti and a salad for lunch. The rest of my first day was uneventful. I made a sandwich for dinner out of some brie and prosciutto along with some pomegranate and honeydew melon. The house was quiet. Almost too quiet and I wondered… sure enough when I went out on the patio the wind was blowing down the canyon from the park. It sounded lonely and had been shut out of the house by the thick insulation and masonry walls. Just then Mimi began a slow, careful stalk out toward the cactuses near the pool and suddenly I saw a flicker in the lights to my right by the pool and watched the feral cat dart off toward the wall.

The next day, I got a text from Uncle Lou.
```
Got here fine. Long flight.
I bet
When you drive the Jag, be sure and put a
quart of oil in it after 300 miles.
```
Bruce then chimed in:
```
be sure and check the closet in the garage,
honey we luv u
```
I went down to the garage and found the "closet" Bruce was talking about. Inside was a brown military-style leather jacket from Chanel. "Merry Xmas" was on the tag.

Enzo Ferrari once said the E-Type was the most beautiful car ever built. The transmission was clunky and chunky, but solid, so different from the Mercedes. My uncle didn't believe in automatic transmissions unless 'one is a soccer mom in some Toyota', and the clutch was a bit tricky. It was so low I had to crawl into it, but I wore my new jacket, the sweater, fleece-lined leggings and sunglasses and let my hair loose in the wind.

I figured I would take Highway 62 out to Vidal and then down 95 along the Colorado river and then come back on Interstate 10 from Blythe. I'd then make a circle and go back on 62 from North Palm Springs near the huge wind farm.

Once I got to pavement the big cat really stretched out and roared along. The air was bright, clear and terribly cold but the open land was too beautiful, so I kept the top down and got used to the wind. I stopped, got some coffee in Twentynine Palms, and made sure I had enough gas and then let the rest of the day unfold before the car. I drove through the day, was honked and winked at by at least six men and two women, and finally stopped for dinner in Palm Springs: braised rabbit braised with a mustard sauce, black sticky rice, and organic pea greens. I only had one glass of Pinot Noir but made sure to drink an espresso to carry me back up to the lonely house.

I didn't feel particularly drowsy. Perhaps I was lulled under by the beautiful sunset over Mt. San Jacinto, the purple sky, and the strange giants spinning their blades in the wind. I stopped just before the climb up the Morongo Pass to put the top up because by now it was freezing cold. The cockpit was so low I had to scrunch down to see out of it, and the headlights weren't very illuminating either. I hadn't even bothered with the radio through the day. The hum of the engine was enough, and I left it at that as the shadows deepened among the Joshua trees and rocks. When I finally turned on the old Cholla Canyon road it was really dark, and I did not follow my uncle's theory, but took it easy over the old wash outs and ruts. *Amanecer*—I was getting used to the name—had timers on many of the lights so it glowed upon the canyon's westward slope but turns and twists in the road hid it from view. Maybe that's why I didn't see her at first on the last straightaway before the side road up to the house. But no. I know better.

I was lost in thought when I passed the Santa Margareta graveyard entrance—a decaying Spanish arch in need of new stucco and broken iron gate when I saw someone ahead of me on the road. I slowed down and could see spiky brown hair, tight white jeans and pink Crocs. It was a woman, and as I got even closer, even the Jag's bad headlights could illuminate her. She didn't seem to be in trouble. Didn't even turn around. I decided she must be out for some weird walk in the darkness, although her neon green tank top didn't seem like something one would wear for December up here.

I didn't want to choke her with dust, and she wasn't moving

too far off the shoulder to let me pass easily, so I let the Jag glide up to her. And then she turned around and walked straight out in front of the car.

I am not really certain as to where the dividing line between waking life and dream is because I question the existence of any 'line' beyond the metaphor itself.

In retrospect, which is suspect and circumspect, again, relying upon vision and not the feel of blank air—that there is simply *a there* which can also mean a *not here.* I would have to go back with some kind of Universal felt-tip marker and actually draw the semblance of a line between my present self which is constantly falling backwards into the company of my other selves. Occasionally a potential self still mulls around, bumping into others and shoegazing while she is considering her options.

I felt that way, as though I'd passed between this world and "that one just over there," as the Japanese say. I had felt it before in my life: very strongly in Japan which was a place in my life that both resembled and did not resemble where I was. Maybe that's why I hesitated to slam on the brakes, but I did and the Jag simply ground to a stop and stalled.

My heart whacked against my ribs and my breath was sharp and shallow. *My God, I hit her.* I thought of the glass of wine. I thought of her round, pinched angry face. She had fake eyelashes so big I couldn't miss them. But I did. Her mouth was open, not in fear but in rage and beyond her missing teeth was a blackness deeper than the entire night of the desert around me.

I got out of the car as best I could and turned to look. There was no black lump in the road. The lights from the car reflected enough for me to see the windshield wasn't broken, the hood wasn't dented. I stood there perhaps for a moment or two and went around to reach into the glove compartment and look for a light. Sure enough, Uncle Lou had a powerful LED light, but I hesitated again. *Should I just leave? Why in the hell am I thinking that?* I could then hear Mimi barking and it broke my freeze. In a cowardly, frightened pass, I waved the light beam over where I thought the woman would be. There was nothing but settling dust from the Jag.

There was no one, not anything there. *What the fuck!?* I walked toward the place she should have been and shone the light along both sides of the dirt road. Nothing in the acacias or junior Joshua trees among the rocks. I didn't think of Jacob Marley then, not consciously, but it was December and so the rational Ada kicked into gear and began offering explanations. *You're tired. You drove all day and you're seeing things. Maybe that rabbit was bad. More of gravy than the grave.* That last line of Dickens finally knocked me back into a semblance of this world and I still found myself panting and full of adrenaline. I looked around a little more, looked back toward the graveyard, but there was nothing. No person. And yet I felt something wasn't right. I shouldn't speak and did not. I quickly got back in the car and sped back up the hill to *Amanecer.*

When I got there, Mimi was unusually welcoming and licked me as though she were a puppy. I decided I'd tell Bruce and Uncle Lou all about it when I could and that would explain the big glass of Bourbon I nipped from their bar. And maybe the second one. I sat on a high barstool in that room. A row of them stood against a thin railing and floor-to-ceiling windows that looked down into the dark canyon. Mimi lay down near my feet and I'm not sure at all how long we remained like that.

I woke up the next day with a start. I was sure I had hit someone, and it took a while for the sunrise to reassure me that whatever happened last night, it was in a dream. Maybe. I went and took a long shower and then made coffee, fed Mimi and thought about the night. Maybe it was Uncle Lou and Bruce's perfect house.

Maybe it was the darkness. I thought about the artist Bruce had talked about when I strolled out by the pool. I didn't see the cat.

Later, after much cajoling and negotiation, I got Mimi into her walking harness and took her with me down the hill. If it hadn't been for the fright last night, it would have been a nice walk in the cool sunshine. We got down to the stretch of road where the 'incident' should have occurred. Even though it was broad daylight and the desert canyon floor looked utterly lush and different, the spot wasn't hard to find. The marks from the Jaguar's tires were still in the road. Mimi promptly walked over to a spot on the right and peed. It was where I had seen the specter, if I could call her that, but there were no footprints. Mimi took an especial interest in the place which unnerved me. She peed on several bushes like a male dog, although her approach was more of straddling than lifting her leg. There was no sign of blood, and again, not even a footprint save for my boots. I still dreaded finding some aging, ugly woman, a pulp after the Jag had hit her, now lying stone dead among the grasses and sand, but no. Nothing.

The rest of the week proceeded with nothing unusual except the furtive visits of the feral cat who made sure to never show itself when Mimi was alert and watching the pool. I realize this only in retrospect because I didn't notice it at first. Everything was calm, clean and contemplative. I had plenty of time to work on the writing project I had in front of me and answer a few emails and of course waste time on social media. I worked out every day and followed the impeachment hearings until it all got too sickening and then went back to reading, making my meals and relaxing. Bruce sent me texts, mostly pictures of himself and Uncle Lou smiling: selfies at the Acropolis, at Mycenae, Delphi and other locales of classical interest.

Until the night of December 11th.

The day had been fine. I reread most of Emily Wilson's new

translation of *The Odyssey* and worked on my own piece. I worked out and then made a lunch and stared out the window at the shifting light on the green Cholla Canyon. I remembered earlier in the year going to the restroom at work to pee. I wound up spacing out by staring at the door in the stall. The writing should have been on the wall, but I was looking at a door made out of recycled pop bottles: it was a beautiful sworl of greens and purples. My future at the foundation swirled down into oblivion: a sort of marble Charybdis. They laid me off three months later.

The Odyssey remains one of my favorite stories. I still fondly remember watching an Italian *pepla* film of Kirk Douglas as Ulysses at Uncle Lou's place when I was a kid. It must have been Channel 40, the local UHF station, showing it on a Saturday afternoon, because I spent a lot of Saturday afternoons with Uncle Lou; my mother had other things to do: study, research and men. I was in the way. I was not in the way with my uncle which explains much. My mother was obviously Penelope except she liked sleeping with all the suitors and somewhere in the wide world, my father the sailor was trying to come home.

The rest of the day was productive insofar as writing. The feral cat did not make an appearance. When the light failed, I made a light dinner, and I followed Uncle Lou's ridiculously perfect directions and fired up the spa. After my meal and giving Mimi another steak to work on, I slipped outside with a glass of Gigondas and my bathrobe. It was freezing cold outside, but I didn't mind. I turned off the lights outside, slipped out of the robe and then naked into the spa and spent an hour watching the stars and trying to figure out my course through them.

Maybe it was those stars, or the solitude or the hot water, but a languid sensuality seemed to steal up from the water. Maybe it was the old lovers who seemed to cross my way in the course of thoughts: the way Astrid looked when she went down on me. The irregular rhythm of Wolfram's hips when he was about to come, and the strange high pitch cry Matthew would make sometimes. *Who cares, there's no one here anyway.* I hadn't felt sexy in a while; the desires just never came on strong like they had before and I knew my age and mutability were to blame but I simply imagined myself in a river, somewhere in ancient Greece. I liked this pastoral and used it often. The tan younger man was hirsute enough to be a satyr but without the goat feet. I was simply a priestess coming to bathe in a sacred pool and he was going to take me. But I made him worship first. He would have to come into the water with me and I would tantalize him to the point where he came a strong jet in my hand at the slightest touch. All well, he would last longer the second time I thought.

I was almost *there* when Mimi started barking. She had a deep, booming bark and seldom used it. The last time I had heard it was the night I driving-dreamt hitting that woman. My Attic lover did not run away into the forest, he just disappeared as I opened my eyes. The stars still wheeled around but I got the sense of *not* being alone. Not watching, but a presence. I crouched low in the spa so only my nose was above water and I looked around. The feral cat was there in the shadows by the pool gazing deeply into it, but I couldn't make out any details since the faint moonlight was shining behind it.

The cat's head shifted then and I saw the lights in its eyes. They were wrong somehow. I couldn't tell. Its head looked misshapen. Mimi continued to bark and then fell silent and I knew she was probably making for the exit in the other room. The cat continued to look straight at me with just the glowing eyes until Mimi boomed out. Then it turned in profile and I saw... a nose. A flat face and a nose. A human nose and lips. It hissed and bounded away into the darkness with Mimi hot on its tail until I heard her crash into the bushes and the creature—I didn't want to call it a cat anymore—clambered up a palm tree and to the safety of the other side of the wall. Or the other side of here.

I got out of the pool immediately and grabbed my robe and the air was wrong. It wasn't the bracing cold I had been expecting but something cold, clammy and dead, like the embrace of a corpse that washed up in the Puget Sound. I ran into the house and the air felt better. In a minute or two, Mimi walked up, unscathed and naturally victorious. Through the window, she gave me her characteristic look that meant "open this door, houseape, my task is done." I went and drank more bourbon and watched the patio for a long while. When I finally grew drowsy and concluded my eyes were playing tricks again and it was some horribly mutilated cat that had survived getting hit by a car or a coyote attack, I went to bed and Mimi followed me. This was also not her custom. She usually slept in Bruce and Uncle Lou's bed, but this time she crawled in and slept at the foot of mine. With the bourbon lulling me further and comforted by Mimi's even breathing, I fell asleep.

The next day a number with a 760 area code showed up on my phone. I didn't know who it was, so I let it roll over to voice mail. When I listened, a smoky, mischievous old voice explained.

"Don't blame you. Probably think I'm some goddamned robot. Anyway, Ada, my name is Jack Harper. I think Bruce and your uncle Lou mentioned me. I was thinking about coming up to say hello. Maybe do a bit of painting and see how you're doing. Call me back…"

I hung up and called him.

"So you're Lou's niece! Glad to meet you, over the phone at least."

"Jack, it's nice to talk to you too. Bruce said you might want to come up here."

By the end, I had decided to go meet him. I remembered being in the spa and seeing the weird cat. I wanted to get out of the house anyway and this was a perfect reason. I made sure the place was locked and Mimi was comfortable and went to the garage. The Jaguar was dusty from the long drive. I knew it had gas because I had to stop and fill it up in Desert Center. But I was momentarily afraid to drive it. *But there was nothing wrong,* I told myself. *That was nothing, just a weird daydream. I was probably already falling asleep.* I got my purse, threw on the jacket and drove off in the Jaguar.

"Oh no, Jack's not here yet," the barista said. "Were you going to meet him? I'm sure he'll be here soon. You're not from around here."

"No, I'm house-sitting for my uncle. I flew down from Seattle."

"And here I am making you coffee, jeeze, I hope it's okay," she said. Her cappuccino was really a latte, but I didn't care.

"I'm sure it's fine. This is a neat place. All of the cute little places like this in Seattle are pretty much gone now," I said.

Not one piece of furniture matched. This was not some pretensions hipster café striving for authenticity. Jack's place was simply unchanged. One wall was done over in imitation wood paneling and the other was still the original bare cinder block of the old garage. Frank Sinatra was singing Christmas carols on a CD player. There were tuck and rolled couches, metal chairs and even a Wassily-style chair in the corner. I went there first.

Jack's paintings were on the walls, but so were some from other artists. Jack's were fairly easy to espy, not that they "looked alike," rather, they shared the same brush strokes, the same generosity with paint, and the same compositional features: lots of women and men looking off at the horizon in the desert, but a few were turned around and looking past you. As though you weren't really there or part of their concern.

Around 11:00, an old white man with a neatly trimmed gray beard and short hair walked up and stopped to look at the Jaguar. He then turned and saw me. This was Jack. The mischievous voice harmonized with an even more mischievous grin. He reminded me of what Dean Martin would have looked like with a beard and he had the same deep tan. He was dressed in a black turtleneck, ratty navy sweater and khakis. He was too skinny to be Santa Claus but in robes of green, purple and red he would have been a passable Father Christmas, but one with a bit of edge because you suspected the Krampus was waiting just behind him with a black tongue, horns and a whip.

"I'd know Louie's girl anywhere. You must be Ada," he said. His hands were long and weathered, with prominent knuckles but they didn't seem like they were wracked with arthritis: simply long life. Jack's eyes were a piercing blue that must have once shaded over to violet. He smelled like turpentine and Old Spice. Tall and lanky, and slightly bent, Jack still had a grace about him that most young men could never have. I could see why Bruce joked about us being a couple. If Jack had been my age... and where did that come from again?

We talked about Bruce and Uncle Lou and I brought him up to speed on where I thought they were and showed him the pictures on the phone.

"Looks like they're having a grand time. Now, the important stuff. How's Mimi."

"Haughty. Indifferent mostly. Except for this weird cat that keeps coming over the wall."

"That cat. Get a good look at it?"

"Um. No. It was dark the last time I saw it. Kind of up close. Usually I've just seen it running away."

"Yeah. Feral thing. I'd stay away from it. It's been there a while, but always acts that way."

"But Mimi doesn't seem to be afraid of it."

"What is she afraid of?"

"Good point."

Jack then looked at me. Like most people we had been bouncing our gazes around the room and back at each other. I've dated an artist, and so I knew *that* gaze: a strange mixture of ascertainment, proportional judgment mingled with a fickle weathervane of desire that moved with the wind. But not at that moment. This gaze locked with mine and remained steady.

"Seen Maxine yet?"

He didn't explain further.

"No, there's no one there. I haven't seen anyone up there at all. I had this weird dream though that I did. That I hit someone with the Jaguar."

"This dream. When did you have it?"

"A few days ago. Sort of stuck with me."

"Is that because it wasn't really a dream?"

"What do you mean?"

He stared at me a bit longer with only one glance at my fingers fidgeting with the handle of the coffee cup.

"I hope you don't play poker. You'd lose a lot." And then he smiled. "Don't worry, Ada. I've seen her too. And that cat. If you want to call it that."

The café got suddenly busier and I realized it was noon. Lots of locals—everyone knew Jack—came in and I felt introduced to a greater part of Cholla Canyon. Eventually the barista got swamped so Jack got up to help her out. But Jack hadn't forgotten our conversation.

"Nice to meet you Ada. I'm bit busy here, but mind if I come by tomorrow? I've got two folks on here, so it won't be a problem. It's usually my day off anyway and I've got some work to do."

I drove the Jaguar back to *Amanecer* without seeing the

woman on the road. Once in the garage, I fed the Jaguar its oil. My uncle had so many quarts of synthetic oil, I guessed this was as much of a ritual as feeding Mimi the steak. The darkness had fallen by this point and I made myself something to eat and gave Mimi one of her steaks. I figured out how to run the complicated stereo system, although just barely. The first thing I listened to was Brigette Engerer's recording of Chopin's Nocturnes and it set me at ease almost immediately, so much that I gave the finger to whatever it was outside, dismissing it as only in my mind and I turned on the spa.

This time, I walked out into the freezing night with only my bathrobe and a glass of Pinot Noir, but I let Mimi come out as well. And I left all the exterior lights on. The water was sumptuous and relaxing, but I could never really let my guard down. I simply sipped from the glass of wine and silently watched the patio garden. The cat never made its appearance, but Mimi was sitting in the spot I had seen it when it was gazing into the swimming pool and me. Perhaps she was keeping it away or perhaps my magical-thinking brain made that up. Regardless, the charm, or spell, kept either my demons away or whatever it was in The World Just Over There. I pruned up on my hands, and got out, shivering a bit and my cold bathrobe didn't help. By that point, I was tired, and felt sufficiently safe when Mimi and I went back in. I got into my pajamas and laid down to sleep.

I don't usually remember my dreams unless they are of a particularly terrifying nature or I have to pee, and I wake up. In the latter case, I most often wander through vast architectures trying to find a bathroom. In this case it was *Amanecer*, although it had grown beyond its already imposing size. I was naked and cold and wandering down a long trapezoidal hallway. I came to a solid bronze door and gently pushed it open. Outside was not outside, but rather a discovery that *Amanecer* was simply a vast house built inside another, larger building composed of steel reinforcing beams and a soaring metal roof. It reminded me of the baseball stadium in Seattle, only it was bigger.

I walked out into that greater darkness, which was tempered by moonlight streaming in through openings in the two-hundred-foot walls. At last, I came to a row of seats and there was my mother.

She and someone else were sitting in two seats, again, much like the seats in the Mariners' ballpark. The figure next to her was shadowy and indistinct, but human. The person had short-cropped black hair so that the faint light reflected off her hair, casting the ends in luminous silver. They were both angry. I could tell that.

"Is that the *puta-cunt?*" The figure asked my mother. The voice was feminine, but with a masculine overlay of dismissive antipathy.

"Yes, that's her. Naked as always. Probably looking for some cock or maybe another Nazi woman to fuck. She's always been a self-centered little bitch."

"Not so little anymore."

"Yes."

"She's quite beautiful."

"She could be. I tried to talk her into modeling, but she was always so stubborn. She just slunk back into her slouch and her gothic clothes to fit in with all the other bourgeoise white girls that hated their daddies. I quit trying, especially after she got those stupid tattoos."

"And then what?"

"And then she went to college. To study philosophy of all things. How useless and not even worthwhile philosophy but the patriarchal dronings and mazes of those fucking Germans."

"She speaks German."

"Yes, she learned it from my father and brother to shut me out of her life."

"It's a hideous language," the figure said.

"I know."

Throughout this whole conversation I was silent. I stood there before them, having to pee, and holding my hands in front of my vagina and breasts as though I was some obscenely demure statue. I remember the paradox of that pose distinctly.

"And even when she got into graduate school, to study English and Critical Theory, I thought she might make something of herself. She started reading Beauvoir at least. And Foucault. But then her proclivities got the better of her and ruined it."

"She fucked her professor, didn't she? Got caught doing it in his office and was disgraced."

"Yes. I almost quit talking to her then, but she was still my daughter."

"But you never really loved her."

"No. I never have. She almost derailed my career by coming into this stupid world. Then she was so demanding. You have no idea how awful children can be."

"But that wasn't the final straw."

"No, it wasn't. It wasn't even when she ran off to Germany when she was twenty-seven. I think she was trying to find that asshole father of hers. But she found someone else who filled that willing pussy full of venereal disease. She lied to me about it."

"How did you find out?"

"I suspected as much in hints from her uncle. Then later I found out she was dating some Nazi woman."

"She's a traitor to *la Raza*."

"Yes, and then we argued. I at least wanted some grandchildren, maybe I could make their life better and have comfort in my age. I knew she would never do that. How would I ever be an *abuela* if she had some Nazi woman's hands up her cunt? And then she said it was too late for that anyway. She's sterile. Has been since that trip to Germany. I think she's proud of it. Probably lets her fuck any man she wants."

"She did it to hurt you."

"That's how she's lived her whole life."

"And now?"

"She's standing there like an idiot. The *baño* is over there you stupid bitch. Why don't you go now before you piss yourself like you did in junior high?"

And then their hold on me relaxed. I can't say it was broken because I tried to run, still shielding myself but I couldn't find the bathroom. That was when I opened my eyes. The waxing moon had filled the room with light, and I was alone. I thought.

But when I stuck out my arm to prop up and get out of bed, I felt the depression on the mattress next to me, as though someone had rolled away from me. Just past the bed, for a brief moment, a shadow stood in the moonlight. It was only five-feet four or so. It had spiky hair and I knew instantly it was that woman. I shook my head and she was gone. There one minute and gone, like the shadowy ghosts we see in the corner of our eyes, but this one had disappeared right before my full gaze.

I quickly got out of the bed, but the moonlight had filled the room with a present clamminess, like the moist hand of some presumptuous fat man who was pressing his palm against my naked back. I left the room and started turning on lights and went as far from that bed as I could until I was in Bruce and Uncle Lou's room. Mimi was on the bed looking at me. I ran past her and into their huge bathroom and finally relieved myself on the toilet. But I was shaking the whole time.

I washed my hands and face with cold water, which gave me enough courage to peer out into the bedroom. Mimi still lay on the bed like a sphinx, looking at me. I crawled up onto the bed and she came over and started licking my face and climbing into my lap. I probably sat that way for an hour. I could see the shift of the moonlight across the floor.

The rest of the night passed without incident, but I couldn't get my mother's face out of my thoughts. It was her face now. I must have been reconstructing it from her faculty photography. She was a pretty woman, but I hated every inch of her face. I just remember that sneer. I seldom saw her smile in the old days. I remembered how much she hated the fact I had dated a German woman for three years. Which was too bad, I think they would probably have liked one another.

Eventually, Mimi curled up in the crook of my drawn-up legs and I fell asleep as well.

"Hello, Baby Girl. How is Daddy's little girl?" Mimi fawned over Jack's attention, licking his hands and face. As with everyone else, he had an offering for She Who Must Be Obeyed, in this case a slice of pepperoni pizza.

"Drives your uncle nuts. Says the cheese is bad for her but look. She loves it, and Georgie makes a damn fine pie. You should order one some time."

Jack had arrived at 8:00 AM. We walked out to the pool area and over toward the guesthouse. I hadn't used it much, but had peeped in. There was an unfinished canvass with only the first coat of gesso on it but there were many others drying in racks.

"I like your art, Jack. The figures, how small they are and often out of center. Ever been to Berlin?"

"Once, a long time ago. Wish I could have gone to Dresden as well. Take it you have? You speak German like Lou?"

"*Nicht so gut, aber ich kann das gut verstehen.*" I remembered the accusations from the dream as I said it.

"*Genau.* That's about all I learned." Jack said. "Couldn't speak a lick of it myself. But I met this young woman there. It was during the seventies when the West German government was paying people to live there. It's where I saw my first Caspar David Friedrich. But you knew I was going to say that" and he winked. "But don't take me for psychic. Lou's told me a lot about you. And you're just as pretty as he said. I like how Friedrich's figures are always looking off at something else. Like the one with the woman in the green dress and that hiker in the mountains everyone knows."

"*The Wanderer Above a Sea of Clouds.*"

"Yes, that one. The first thought a lot of people have is that you're sharing the view with them. But that's bullshit because you can't. You're not in their heads. You don't *really* know what they're looking at. You can only guess. I think that's what I've tried to do all these years. The desert's good for it because the space and light are right for expansive guesswork."

We continued to talk as he set up his work area, and eventually he got around to what I wanted to know.

"The woman? Maxine. Yeah. Well, you see this place here has been here for a lot longer than we have. We don't know what this desert slope really looked like and never will. I can guess in my artwork. Maybe you can with your words. Lou gave me your book about the notary in the mountains. I don't usually like fantasy work all that much save Lord Dunsany, but I liked your book. Lot of Heidegger, but you could make heads and tails of it for once."

"Thank you."

"Anyway, I may look old, and I am, but I had just gotten here when Dan Kershaw did. You knew he retired from the Newport Beach Fire Department, right? Yeah, well, he had this almost Hearstian dream of making this place into a palace. I don't think it started that way, but the house kept growing with additions and stuff. I know because I worked on it. I was younger then and just starting out as an artist, so I was broke, and he paid me under the table to help out with labor and painting.

"Dan was a restless man. I really liked him and there wasn't anything better in those days than sitting up here after a long day, drinking beer with him, and watching the sun set on the canyon. But damned if he could finish anything. I suppose for his work that made sense because a lot of what he did was check other people's work and he was good at it. The trouble all started when he started dating Maxine."

While Jack unfolded the story of Maxine, he laid another coat of gesso on the canvas and put it on a drying rack. "Sometimes I like to work *alla prima*, but sometimes it takes time.

"Dan Kershaw's first wife stayed mostly down in Orange County and during the trips up here, Dan began to have an affair with a townie named Maxine. I don't know what he saw in her. 'Cept sometimes I think people like to have their monsters on the outside so they don't have to look at the one's inside of them."

"A very artistic statement. Is *she* a monster?" I asked, pointing at the picture he was now working on. From what I could see it was a young woman wearing nothing but a smile and cowboy hat in the middle of a desert.

"Her, no. She's Venus."

"Some people might say she's a monster. She's staring straight at us. She's got a nice rack, too."

"Hell, Ada, she's Venus. She's going to have great tits. These are like my first wife's, which were always my favorite. You can write that down for posterity. Might make this daub more valuable when I'm dead. She's asking you 'what's over here in this grave? What have you buried?'"

"That's a grave?"

"It will be. See, here's the pencil study."

Sure enough, stark-naked Venus was holding a shovel and standing in front of what looked like a newly dug grave. There was no name on the marker.

"So, it's open ended. I like the modeling and the Joshua trees. They look better than her. So what's been buried up here?"

"Ask what hasn't. That developer, named Steve Fairbanks, I think. He isn't over in Santa Margareta."

"Is Dan Kershaw?"

"Yeah, he's there if you want to say hello. He won't answer."

"Is Maxine?"

"Ah, no. See, the problem is, she's still alive."

We drove down the canyon in Jack's Jeep which made the ruts and the gouges in the road seem even deeper.

"Don't worry about Mimi. She'll be fine," Jack said.

"I thought you needed to work more."

"Nah, the light's shifted. Besides, I think you should know. Bruce never told you about this? I mean, I can't imagine Lou bringing it up. He's never seen them."

As soon as Jack said that I felt drawn to look into the rear-view mirror and something moved across the road behind us. It looked like an animal, but it didn't move on all fours the right way. It looked like a person using their legs and arms to run like a spider across the road. The Jeep heaved up again and whatever it was had disappeared.

"There. Stop!" I said and Jack hit the brakes.

"Something behind us?" We both turned around and looked at the Jeep's dust cloud. Once it had blown off the road, we could see nothing. "What did you see?"

"It looked like a person, running across the ground like a spider."

"Probably nothing, Ada. Hope not. You need to eat something. We'll stop at Francesca's. Best tacos along Highway 62."

We stopped at Francesca's, a small storefront in a stripmall on the main highway and ate the best tacos I had tasted in years. I found myself hungry and piled on the radishes and onions.

"What do I need to see?"

Jack sipped at a Pacifico beer and looked at me.

"Maxine, who else?"

We drove along the highway for a while longer until we came into Yucca Valley. Jack turned off the main road and wound through a series of unremarkable desert streets, with houses set well back and crowded with acacias and the ever-present Joshua trees. Finally, we came to a wide drive up to a large two-story building. 'Canby Retirement and Nursing Home.'

The only thing that set it apart from the rest of the landscape was its relative newness. It was white and made out of cinder blocks with a wide, overhanging flat roof covered in fake Spanish tiles. We got out in the parking lot and I could see the wind driving dust devils up the valley toward us, but the strange thing was, when we entered the lee of the building all the noise seemed to switch off. The only thing I could hear was the angry whining of the HVAC compressors.

We went through the automatic doors of the entrance and up to a wide desk, the kind of greeting place you see at any rest home, hospice or urgent care clinic. A woman with a huge hairdo of piled black curls sat at a computer.

"Esme, hello." Jack said.

"Hello, Jack. What gives me the pleasure?"

"Maxine still here?"

Esme, short for 'Esmerelda' which was on her name tag, frowned and looked at the screen, then back to Jack.

"Yeah. Why do you want to see her and who's this?"

"This is Ada, the guys who own the big house in Cholla Canyon's niece."

"Oh, um. Jack, you're not exactly family."

"Maxine's got none except that daughter in Missouri. We're standing in. C'mon. We just want to say hello."

It took a while for Jack to convince Esme that we were up to nothing but curiosity, but eventually she gave us clip-on badges and let us through the doors."

"If you see Dr. Martin…"

"Don't worry, Timmy won't care," Jack said and turned to me: "Timmy Martin grew up here. Went to med school at UCLA. His mom's a neighbor of mine."

We walked down a long hall of open doors and in each dimly lit room was some human figure in a bed. Most were draped over save for their gray heads, most of them watching Fox News' propaganda-coverage of the impeachment hearings. The place smelled of Pine-Sol, the saccharine-acid odor of medications, and urine.

"Ugh. Depressing." Jack stopped by one door. "This ain't her, but I want to say hello. Hi, Mabel, how are you?"

"Montrose? A voice said coming from the bed. "They're still trying to impeach Nixon you know."

"I do."

"Will you come back tonight? We can have the room to ourselves."

"Sure thing Mabel, I gotta go. 'Cmon let's get out of here. Ever since the Alzheimer's set in bad with her she tries to sleep with every man here. We're all Montrose. Concrete contractor who died about twenty years ago. They were having an affair behind her husband's back."

"Better than in front," I said. "Jack you seem to know everyone."

"That's the worst part of being me in this place. I *do* know everyone and there's no privacy in a small town."

At last, we came to Maxine's room. I couldn't see her right away because a large medical machine blocked the view of the bed. It quietly hummed and pumped oxygen into the shape beyond it. When I got up the guts to look past the machine, I could see her.

The woman's eyes were closed, and she was lying face up with the oxygen mask over her face. There were other machines, an IV regulator, and two others I had no clue as to their function.

"C'mon over. She won't bite. She can't anymore." And there was the woman from the road. The same spiky hair, only gray now. The same angry pinched expression, as though the doctor had rammed a dead rat or lemon onto her face in the shape of the oxygen mask. Her face, sunken in around the mouth from a lack of teeth, was covered in wrinkles, and her skin had that light, translucent quality of the end, as though it would just dissolve away to reveal gray desiccated muscles and tendons. Even like this, and even though I had only a brief glimpse of that face on the dark road in the Jaguar's headlights, I knew it was the same person.

"What is it?" I whispered.

"What do you mean, this is Maxine."

"No, what's she… dying from?"

"Three strikes: emphysema for one, Alzheimer's and a stroke that should have finished her off in the single-wide. But she's a tough old stubborn girl."

I breathed deeply and looked at her.

"Hello Maxine. Why don't you leave the house alone?"

There was no answer, and I wasn't expecting her to sit up and explain her deep abiding love for Andy Williams or anything, but I wanted to see some flicker of REM behind her eyelids, some form of presence.

"You said three strikes."

"Yep, but she won't go back to the dugout. Timmy Martin says he's stumped. Thought she'd be dead four months ago."

"I need a drink," I said. "You must know a good bar nearby."

"Of course."

The bartender, a ludicrously good-looking man named Enrique poured a strong margarita for me and a Black Russian for Jack. The bar was nice and dark with old captain's chairs from the 70's. There were velvet paintings of Popocatepetl and Iztaccihuatl on their frozen way to becoming Volcanoes, a Spaniel, a Matador and The Spirit of Mexico holding up the Red, White and Green. Her breasts were nearly pouring out over her bandoliers, but I loved the defiant look in her eyes.

"If she had bangs, she'd look a lot like you," Jack said.

"Thanks. So what's the deal? I thought Maxine would be dead."

"She sort of is, really." Jack went on to explain though that he'd seen her shadow up there for quite a while. "Sometimes I think it was actually her. Steve, the developer who bought the place from the estate sale said she would come up there and bang on the door and threaten to call the Sherriff to throw him out as a trespasser.

"The Sheriff's men eventually learned to quit paying attention to her calls. My guess she'd been slipping for a while after Dan died and the court case went on for a year. She really went down hill then. I never got along with her much. I knew what she was. I think she burned Dan's will. Don't know why he never had the damn thing recorded. Anyway, when the court ordered the sale of the house, she slipped fast.

"I remember seeing her up there when I went with the appraiser and Sheriff. They thought I could talk some sense into her. But she just stood out by where the pool is now glaring at us. Finally,

Steve had her arrested once for vandalism and that sort of did it. He went on to build up the place, more or less the way you see it now. That went on for two or three years. One day she wandered into my café wanting to buy a gun so she could 'shoot that sonofbitch who stole her property and that little bitch.' I think she meant Dan's daughter by his first marriage. I took her home and had to listen to her rave. I remember calling her daughter in Missouri because I could see something had to be done soon. The next day she had a stroke and wound up in Canby.

"Two days later I saw her walking up there, right as rain. At least I thought I did."

I gulped the margarita. "When did the fucking cat show up?"

"That thing's been there all along. I never saw it much. Then only glimpses. You've seen it up close."

I explained the night in the spa and Jack shook his head and ordered another Black Russian.

"I'll be damned if I know what that is, Ada. But… it's not natural."

"Supernatural?"

"Well, you said back at the house you were a philosophy major. Can we even hope to understand the supernatural?"

"By definition, I'm not really sure. But there are more things in heaven and earth…"

"Ha, that line of Old Bill's sure is useful. I don't know what that thing is. It doesn't sound like it belongs here. Or maybe it did once? I don't know."

"It leaves a trace."

"Really? How do you know?"

"I saw scratch marks up the side of the palm tree from when Mimi chased it."

"Probably a good thing she didn't catch it. Hmmm. But if it

leaves a mark maybe it can be killed. Thing is, it might use ways around us we don't even know about. Hey, what's say I go back up there with you. No funny business, you know what I mean. We're wanting to avoid that."

"I would really appreciate it, Jack. I don't want to be alone up there."

"You've got Mimi."

"I'm afraid of what might happen to me and her."

"I wouldn't be too sure about that," and Jack winked at me.

We stopped at Jack's house where he threw some clothes into a bag, grabbed a bottle of Chivas Regal and we headed back. Mimi was there, happy to see us in her reserved way, but nothing seemed amiss. We went through the whole house and there was no door open. Even the feeling of clamminess was gone in the bedroom I'd been in. I told Jack about the dream in certain details.

"Well, you're leaving some embarrassing stuff out. You didn't pee the bed, did you?"

"No!"

"That's good. This place is rather strange. I always got that sense when I was up here. Part of the reason I like to paint."

"In a haunted house."

"Ahh, I wouldn't say that. I wouldn't say this place is haunted or evil. It's just on the edge of things and that's beyond what we know. Ever been in a place like that before?"

I remembered the Torii Gate in the water near the beach where I had stayed in Japan. Jack and I sat down in the massive living room and talked about it for the rest of the night. I told him about Hokkaido, the English class I tried to teach and how lonely it all was at the New Year holiday. After two glasses of Chivas, I even told him about seeing all the ghosts of what could have been in my life rise out of the ocean, perform their brief play on the beach and disappear back into the dark water.

"Sounds like you stood on the brink of *anoyo*," he said.

"You know the word."

"A lot easier than the World Just Over There."

I fell asleep on the couch and Jack must have wandered off to one of the other bedrooms. In the morning I smelled melting cheese, tortillas, beans and freshly brewed coffee.

"You slept well," he said.

"I did."

"I thought it best to just leave you there. Mimi was curled up near you on the couch and I figured everything would be fine."

"Did you see anything?" I asked.

"Not last night. But I saw something crawl over the fence out there this morning when Mimi went out to take care of business."

"Was it?"

"I can't say. You know, there are some feral cats around here and it could have been one of those. Now here, eat."

Jack was kind enough to stay for several days with me and we never saw anything. He would go out to the studio and paint and I would stay on the patio and write. But we didn't see anything. Occasionally he had to go back into town and I went with him.

"Did you ever model, Ada?" He asked me one day.

"Yes."

"I don't mean for clothes and fashion, I mean for an artist. You're very beautiful in a different way."

"That's what she said."

"The artist?"

"My mom. And the artist."

"Ah, then that's something interesting. Who was she?"

"You might know her work, her name is Astrid Pauli. A photographer. She painted too, but that was just a hobby she said."

193

"Were you her muse?" He asked. He was applying the last touches of the lean layer to *Venus in the Garden*.

"I don't know. I would have said yes once, but I sometimes think it was the other way around. Except Astrid wasn't a muse."

"What was she then?"

"A terrible Goddess with bright shining eyes. The old Greek kind that would flay you as soon as fuck you."

"You mean Athena then. I can't say I know Astrid Pauli, although that name sounds kind of familiar. Black and white?"

"Yeah, mostly."

"Hmmm. Maybe I've seen her... oh yes. Oh lord! You're the girl in the agave plant! I knew I'd seen you somewhere before, but that sort of thing is hard to assemble right."

"Yes, the agave plant." It was one of her most famous recent pieces and helped her break out to a bigger audience. We'd been in Quintana Roo together and she got me to pose nude in an agave plant. The blood from the scratches was real and I remembered everything about that trip.

After a while, Jack asked: "You were lovers, weren't you?"

"Yes. For a time."

"What happened?"

"I bored her."

"Fair enough. You don't bore me, but there's no accounting for people in the world."

"Why do you ask?"

"Ask what?"

"If I had modeled."

"I was hoping you might model for me."

I sighed, but Jack didn't look at me. He kept looking at Venus, or rather one of Her Joshua Trees.

"Nude?"

"How else?"

"On one condition."

"Of course. Well, you can throw in more than one."

"I want to be a *Rückfigur*."

"Oh, that's what I was thinking of."

And so for the remainder of the days he was up there, I modeled nude for Jack. He had me stand with arms akimbo facing away from him.

"I get to ask what it will look like," I said during a break. I was standing behind him back in my bathrobe.

"This one's different. You don't really belong in the desert, least ways not this one. I see you somewhere else. Looking out over an ocean, but maybe in a desert, like Namibia."

"Namibia?"

"Place I've always wanted to see," Jack said. "The Desert comes right up against the Ocean. Talk about natural chiaroscuro."

"I hope you get to go there."

"I can with this painting."

"So, what am I looking at?" My portrait, if you can call it that, was straightforward. I was naked, but at peace. There was a tension, but not one derived of fear. My hair was down and he captured the tattoos on my arm well.

"That's up to you. I just told you to stand there however you wanted. I might as well have taken a photograph, but I'm not Athena. It does look like something out of *The Odyssey*, though. You could be Penelope, of course, but I don't think so. You could be Telemachus looking for his father, somewhere out there on the waves. Or maybe you're Odysseus, looking for a way home."

Jack had some business with a gallery dealer, the same one in Irvine, I gathered, and he had to leave. There were only five days left before Bruce and Uncle Lou returned and I realized that aside from a few selfies in Crete, I hadn't heard from them. When Jack had gone, and I was alone I felt the creep of the house. This time I was sure it was nerves. Jack and I had both been vigilant for the first few days of his stay, but neither the cat, nor whatever the projection of Maxine was appeared. Still, I wanted to hear someone's voice: Uncle Lou's rationality washing over me like titanium armor. Or Bruce's ebullience and understanding like an enormously soft bed.

`Are you awake?`

It took an hour for him to return the text.

`yes, how are you doing honey bruce`

`Can I call`

`Yes`

"What's wrong?" Bruce immediately asked when he picked up the receiver.

"Mimi's fine."

"I'm not worried about her. Should I be?"

"No, it's... how come you didn't tell me about this place?"

The line had a faint hiss of static in the silence that followed.

"You've seen Maxine, then?"

I didn't answer. I was too afraid from hearing the name all the way from Crete.

"And pussums too, I suppose. They won't hurt you. They don't come in the house."

"Is Uncle Lou there?"

"He's in the gym running on the treadmill. Ada, we only have a few minutes. We're leaving port and the reception might die out."

"I suppose he'd say it's nonsense."

"Of course. He never sees them."

"And you do?"

"Once or twice. They seem to vanish. I thought Maxine was a real person the first time."

"So did I."

"But then she just disappeared."

"Yes."

"Are you alone?"

"Now I am. Jack had to go to Irvine."

"Oh good, he's been there. Well. Gosh, I just don't know what to say except again, they never come inside."

"I think Maxine was in the guest bedroom with me. I went to sleep one night and I woke up with this presence in the bed…"

The signal clicked. The call dropped. I could not get him back.

I looked at Mimi. "It's just you and me tonight."

But it wasn't just me and Mimi. They were subtle and they took their time. I wondered if time worked the same for them. I warmed up some chili that Jack had made and poured it over spaghetti for dinner. In addition to getting me out of my clothes again for modeling, he even had convinced me of the virtues of Cincinnati chili and so it was comforting to eat his food.

I turned on the big TV and tried to find something to watch. The news of the day was too dreary and familiar, so I watched old movies from Uncle Lou's BluRay collection. Being out in the main gathering room had the advantage of not being in line-of-sight of the patio. Halfway through *Sunset Boulevard* I remember spacing out and thinking about Jack. Had he been twenty years younger we'd probably be having sex.

Or would we? I didn't really feel like it. I simply liked his company. Maybe I would have had to be twenty years younger and that took me back to those days: the miserable porch before thirty when I was freshly sterile from chlamydia and had no idea what I was going to do with myself. I would be fifty the next year, and perhaps this was part of menopause. If it was, I didn't mind it. Having a man near that I found sexy, even in his geriatric years, was enough. I didn't have to go to bed with him and the practicalities of such arrangements—surely rife with embarrassment and pharmaceuticals—made it silly to think about. That wasn't the important part. Jack seemed to know me, or at least *knew how to know me* and that is what mattered more. I needed to get to know him better, I thought. What was he like as a boy? What was his first broken bone? When did his mother die?

I asked myself that last question when Mimi began barking. You might be able to guess why. She had been curled up around my feet but was now standing half on the coffee table and half on the couch. Her hackles were up, and she had transmuted again into something not quite domestic, but not wild. And she saw something Just Over There.

In the window was Maxine. She glared at us and I shrank back. It was a window set high above the alcove for the TV and to stand there I knew *she was floating outside.*

'*You little bitch*' I could read her lips. 'I know who you are. You'll never get this place, you *puta-cunt*' and her expression cranked into a sneer. I knew the sneer. But she did not come through the window. Mimi continued barking. On the TV, Gloria Swanson kept sliding down her own dark hole.

I don't know how long it took, but slowly Maxine faded in the window until only the reflection from the interior lights illuminated the glass.

"I saw her last night, Jack, so help me God." I called him the next morning.

"You got a rosary?" He sounded tired.

"Fuck you, I'm not Catholic anymore."

"You Catholics are always Catholic. I doubt it would do much good with Maxine, but it'd probably make you feel better. See the cat?"

"I didn't check the patio."

"Hmmm. I think…"

"…think what?"

"I have a theory. It doesn't really make much sense and I can't tie it together. I don't think we're supposed to in this world."

"Are you still in Irvine?"

"'Fraid so. I can't get back there today. I have two big sales. Did you talk to Bruce? I got a weird text from him. Asked me if 'they ever came inside.'"

"What did you say?"

"Not that I knew," Jack answered.

"Not yet."

"We don't know that. You said she didn't come in." Jack said.

"I have a feeling it's a matter of time," I said. That was it. "Do you have a spare key at your place, Jack? I don't want to stay here anymore. I'll take Mimi down there."

"Sure, there's a pot of marigolds near the back door. It's in there. And this night's a full moon. I wouldn't stay there."

"Jack, what's your theory."

"Get rid of that cat."

"That's it?!"

"I'll see you tomorrow. I gotta get going or I'll be late here and then late there."

"Fine." And I hung up.

At first I began to hurriedly pack up, but then realized I had to take Mimi along and so I'd have to find her accoutrements if necessary, so I packed some steaks and her bed into the back of the Mercedes—I could just see the Jaguar dying on me on the deserted road and then they would find me.

I needed to be calm, though. I needed some music. I figured something on the stereo would be good. Something that reminded me of Uncle Lou. He had to have some Bach on that system somewhere. I went into the entertainment room and clicked on the system and turned on all of the speakers which went through the whole house. The display panel lit up and I began to look at playlists. There was Bach, but just a ways below was something else.

"Playlist for Ada" The description next to it simply said: "For when you need it: Uncle Lou"

I pressed play and then it began. The solitary trumpet slowly marched up and down exclaiming the fanfare until the rest of the Berlin Philharmonic joined in the defiant crash that cranked up past glory into a realm of pure power.

I smiled and looked up and around me.

"Fuck you!" I yelled as loud as I could. I could not let them win. I would not let them drive me out again. All of them.

"Mimi, we have to be careful about this." She stood next to me in the garage. I was taking out her bedding and food when I saw the lines of motor oil cans Uncle Lou kept for his thirsty Jag. I didn't know if it was going to work, but I could still hear the music seething courage and decided it was at least a plan.

"To catch a cat, you need to use another cat."

I calmed down and made my plans while the 5th Symphony finished, then I made a ham sandwich. And I waited.

I finished up the necessary preparations on the stones near the pool while it was still light outside. Mimi watched me with curiosity, but without judgment. I couldn't tell if she understood what I was doing but it didn't matter. I decided to skip my work out and drank black coffee while I waited for the darkness to fall further and the hot tub to warm up.

Just before the last light failed over the mountains, I walked out to the guest house across the patio carrying my bathrobe. I changed out of my clothes and stood naked before Jack's painting of me. Although it was still in its bare infancy—he'd prepared the canvass and made a sketch outline—I could look at the detailed graphite sketch. I looked pretty good, not a day over 40, at least from behind and I wondered if I really looked as good as Jack had rendered me, or it was a courteous flattery on his part. I then picked up the robe and went outside into the chilly air.

The water in the spa was warm and inviting, but I was finally feeling my initial rush of adrenaline and concomitant guts melt slightly. My stomach turned in knots. I decided not to drink, so there was no glass of wine or whisky nearby. I figured I'd need my wits, so I simply lay back and waited. The full moon rose over the San Jacinto mountains and I didn't need the lights to see around the patio and pool area.

Maybe it was fine I didn't have kids, I thought. "I still have this body" and reveled in the insult I presented to my mother. I wondered over who the other person in the dream was. At first, I dug through my memories of the Internet articles about my mother I'd read and thought I had concocted some phantasm of her PhD candidate/ assistant researcher: I think she was a girl but she may have been trans. That didn't matter. He, she, they were the child my mother always wanted. Or thought she'd wanted. I remembered how my mother suddenly began taking Spanish lessons again, around the age I was now. In our last big argument, I asked her why English was the only language she spoke to me when she "raised" me. She followed with a string of invectives in Spanish, which she seemed to forget I understood.

But I was off on a tangent. The other person wasn't her researcher. I knew who it was because she was in this spa waiting for destiny or insanity or whatever it was that lay before her. I had to turn my back on my mother and that other presence. To see where I was going next.

And then I felt it. In spite of the warm water, my neck felt cold and the chill descended down through the rest of my body. They were here. I opened my eyes and there was Maxine. I could hear Mimi barking at her furiously through the sliding glass door. There was nothing but her solid silhouette, with her ugly hair, ugly body, ugly face. I then looked across the pool and there it was. It came down from the high point of the rock wall and circled the pool until it reached its accustomed place. There, the moonlight bathed its face and it *was* a human face. Neither male nor female. There was no race. No age. It was a plain face. Hideously plain and it looked at me with heavy eyelids. Its tongue came out and wetted its lips.

I did not know how long this would take. Perhaps this would go on all night: Mimi barking, her rage fixed on Maxine so the cat could do as it pleased. How would they kill me? Would I stay here? With them?

The moon continued on its course and the shadow of the cat moved across the stones. I looked back and Maxine was now coming closer. Her mouth was moving but I couldn't understand or even hear anything she said.

"You're not even here," I said. I stood up in the tub and this seemed to enrage her even more. She began to walk, as solidly as she had before when I ran her through in the Jag. I took one step out of the tub and she moved closer. The cat seemed to enjoy this. Its grotesquely human face smiled in a leer and I had no idea what I was going to do.

"You little puta-cunt. You want to stay here so bad, then fine. You'll stay here alright." It was the harshest whisper and sounded as though it came through a plastic mask. A small thought then rose, and I remembered the trumpet fanfare from the 5th Symphony growing in memory. I had to go to the swimming pool and get her further from the door. She kept putting one foot in front of the other as I side-

stepped towards the pool. Finally, she crossed into the full light of the moon and I could see it now shone through her and that was enough. Mimi had stopped barking.

Maxine, or whatever she was, came closer. Her face was a mixture of gray death, like a bloated body pulled from Puget Sound and she lifted up one arm to point at me. One step. Two more steps. *"You little bitch, I've never loved you."* And her finger extended, her arm stretched unnaturally, and I could count the few teeth left in her open smile. Spittle clung between them and her lips and glimmered in the moonlight. She reached further to touch my heart and I then let myself fall backward.

I could hear Mimi bounding across the yard and I heard the claws of the cat-thing turn, but then I hit the water and closed my eyes in reflex. I felt Maxine on me then, or perhaps in me, a strange wriggly anger that scratched and constricted all over me. I touched bottom and pushed up, glad I hadn't fallen in the deeper end because whatever Maxine was, I could feel her on my breasts, my stomach and my legs. I breathed hoarsely for the water was terribly cold and I felt my heart knocking. I was dying.

But then a strange mewling screech cried out over all of us. I could only look to see the cat-thing. It had slipped in the motor oil I had poured on the stones between its escape route and the wall. It had made the wall but not in time. I watched Mimi bite its leg and then she began to whip it around in the bushes. The hands of Maxine lessened in their grip until there was just the cold water. I clambered out of the pool and still heard the sounds of the thing dying in the bushes and Mimi's terrible silence: she killed without sound, without remorse and in the purest form of rage that went beyond into the World Just Over There.

The wind returned at that point. Perhaps it had always been there, but I did not only hear it, I felt it on my naked skin.

I lay like that, freezing cold for a while. I have no idea how long it was. It wasn't until Mimi came up and began licking my face that I recovered enough to stumble over, wrap myself in my robe and go back to the house to pass out on one of the couches. In the morning I heard Jack knocking and ringing the bell. I ran to the door, pulling the robe around me as much as possible.

He took a step back when he saw me.

"Ada, your face. Come on back in…" I was covered in blood from where Mimi had been licking me, and had it been anyone *but* Jack I would have been carted off for psychiatric evaluation to whatever godawful mental hospital San Bernardino County had waiting.

"Well, I don't know that I would have gone about it that way, but I don't think I'm the one to do it and that's why." After Jack had cleaned me up and made sure I was alright he went out to mop up the motor oil from off the stones as best he could. I just sat there, better dressed now in the cold December desert air drinking a liberally spiked tumbler of coffee.

"What?"

"Motor oil. Ha. Gave Mimi just that extra time." Mimi was buoyant. Her tail was coiled up tightly and she sat with an alert expression watching every stroke Jack made with the mop. "Told you she was the one. But maybe not the secret weapon. I think that was you. I have to say I'm proud of you. I'd have lit out. What made you stay?"

"I found some courage."

Bruce and Uncle Lou returned two days after that. By that point I had recovered enough from everything to do the only reasonable thing: pretend it never happened. Jack and I agreed that was probably the best strategy, but Bruce figured out something had happened. He fawned over me worse than usual and finally on

Christmas eve he leaned over and asked: "they're gone, aren't they?"

"Yes."

"What did you do?"

"*We*, took care of it. Jack, me, and especially Mimi."

"Maybe I don't want to know." *You don't* I thought in answer to him. I thought of the mangled body, the mutilated human face on the thing Jack and I found out in the garden and how we burned it in an incinerator down in the town.

"You'll drag it out of me," I said, "but as a Christmas gift, I'll let you squirm a bit for not having told me in the first place."

"I am so sorry honey."

"I know."

Uncle Lou pretended to nag me about the Jag, but I knew he really didn't care. Jack and Bruce had wanted to come along to see me off to Seattle, but I wanted some time alone with Uncle Lou. We drove back down Highway 62 in the Mercedes, mostly in silence.

"The desert's beautiful in the winter," I said.

"Yes. I'm glad you came. And I'm glad you're okay." Uncle Lou then turned on the stereo and turned it up. It was Mahler's 5th Symphony: Berlin Philharmonic.

"You knew."

"Ada, we don't *know* anything. I seem to remember a strapping young philosopher telling me that after she had discovered Wittgenstein's *On Certainty*. But I did know Bruce had been acting weird about that place since we bought it and Jack wouldn't say anything. You all must think I'm incredibly dense."

"We do."

"Yes, I've heard the stories, but I've never seen anything up there. Nothing's ever bothered me. Nothing I had to waste two quarts of Jag Juice on," and he looked at me and winked. "But if it had to be figured out, my little Ada would, because she can do anything."

JANUARY

THE PROMPT

The night was bleak and biting like only the middle of winter can be and the sky, cluttered with stars, was wide and cloudless. It was as if the moment was frozen, preserved for posterity by some unseen and all-powerful force that knew what was to come.

HANNAH AT NIGHT
BY JENNIFER DiMARCO

All you have to do is write one true sentence. Just one. Not a million words. Not new words. Just your words.

You'll know it's real because it won't be easy. It won't be painless. It may not even be pretty or lyrical but rather devoid of all alliteration and destitute of charm. But it will be the truth and, in the end—your end, my end, the end of us all—that will be the thing that people remember. That will be the moment, indelible on the black papyrus of the sky, that burns like a new constellation—intimate and universal and, beyond everything else, true.

I loved Hannah but only at night.

I think that might be my sentence.

She said things like that—quoting Hemingway or Whitman or Angelou or Sarton, usually without knowing it, usually just proving the adage that the same stories are told, the same advice is given, over and over again—that made me fall, head long, into her midnight of discontent. Those times when she'd lean back, exhaling an ethereal cloud of blue haze and dispense the wisdom of the ages. The cumulative knowing and doing of seemingly every sage before her. As if she'd been their lover, their father, their best friend. As if she'd inhabited their bodies and rode as a guest (or more likely to her personality as a host) for long enough to discern their drive, their fear, their passion—the building blocks of their lives. It wasn't really a surprise the way she effortlessly, almost lazily, conjured the greatest minds into our bed; if anyone could do it, it would be her. I think she could raise the dead with her scarlet lip and lace and leather corset. Arguably, raising the dead was her profession, after all.

But I'm starting at the end and the beginning is much better.

"Another."

The bartender—I think her name was Karen—acknowledged my order with a bob of her chin in that way that tells you someone's mind is elsewhere. I'm not offended; I'm a regular. She knows my drink. Plus I do that at work all the time. I can't imagine mixing drinks is more mind-numbing than designing logos but I couldn't imagine a lot of things back then.

The music was too loud, as always, making conversation next to impossible. But I assume body language is heard with the eyes and no one comes here to talk. It's not a classic dive bar but it tries really hard with the antiquated jukebox in the corner, the half-broken pinball machines and scratched pool table. Come to think of it: It's the definition of a dive bar. The only difference is the clientele.

"...is both mask and unveiling."

My whole body jumps and I almost take a header off my bar stool. She's standing so inside my personal space I can smell her perfume. It's lilac.

"Excuse me?"

She's staring at my mouth to read my lips and her hand is still spread open on my notebook in front of me. Her hands are small and square. Her olive skin streaked with neon from corporate breweries and local IPAs and her hair is a mane of chestnut ringlets that spill over her bare shoulders and brush the top of her strapless satin halter. She wears gold hoops and thin gold bangles. She pats my page.

"Writing..." She leans into me, fully committing so her scarlet lips brush my ear when she speaks. "...is both mask and unveiling." A beat, a pause in the narrative she's weaving. "Is it a novel?"

She hardly leans away then as if she can absorb my response directly into her body. She seems to be made entirely of curves, lacking hard lines or sharp angles. God, was that the wrong first impression; *Everything* was a hard line with Hannah.

But that night, she fit perfectly against my side as if we were two pieces of the same thing.

"It's a grocery list," I tell her, matter of fact and mundane. "I'm out of coffee." And I meet her eyes for the first time. I'm trying to be witty, maybe even debonair. I don't stand a chance and I fall instantly, irreconcilably, into her copper penny gaze.

Some emotion moves across her face. Is it surprise? Irritation? I'm watching her and not breathing. Does no one counter her? Does no one else play her game? She glances down at my notebook— clearly showing prose—then back up at me. And then she smiles. She smiles all the way up to her remarkable russet eyes and I'm almost certain my fate is sealed. Her smile is predatory and precious in equal measure. Like a little girl about to rip the wings off a butterfly. Except this little girl is all grown up and looking at me like a challenge she didn't know she wanted.

"I have coffee," she offers, making the game her own. "Come home with me."

I'm still not breathing. She's backlit, haloed in fiery tones like a fallen angel. I manage a shrug, my exterior nonchalant as my heart pounds in my chest. "Why not?" I murmur, her reading my lips. "I've always hated shopping."

And so, I go home with Hannah that first night.

It's like I'm hovering above the city, suspended in the inky night above the skyscrapers and the streams of midnight traffic in the distance. There's the disconcerting juxtaposition of the entire tableau reflected, upside down, in the still, dark waters of the Puget Sound.

"And the sea and sky are as one." She does it again. Catching me off guard as she appears beside me, sliding into my reality soundlessly. "Brandy."

It's not a question and I take the offered snifter. We stand together for a moment, unmoving, the floor to ceiling windows radiating cold beside us, framing the black heavens and blacker water with their shared swath of city and cars. Her condo is Frank Lloyd Wright meets Denise Scott Brown, a master class in clean lines, pale walls, and glass and metal accents.

I drink. "Oh."

She smiles, like a secret between us. She drinks.

This isn't off-the-shelf brandy from the corner store. I taste earthy apricot and savory fig, smooth honey and the tang of green fennel. I'm not uneducated in the ways of a good cognac but this one is beyond my ken.

"Delamain."

She dispels my curiosity with the brand and my eyebrows lift. So much for playing it cool. I try to recover: "Are you trying to impress me...?" And I lose my composure again as her smile broadens. Damn it; she keeps the upper hand so easily.

She closes the space between us, leaving no room for anything but breathing in tandem.

"Hannah," she grants me and the boon of knowing her name emboldens me. I kiss her.

There is something arresting, alluring and undeniably unknown about Hannah. She never answers an asked question and always answers the unspoken ones. She loves being a mind-reader but despises banal inquisition. If I say to her, "What do you like?" she ignores me. But if I hesitate above her, wondering, she pushes me down her body and nestles my head between her thighs. This wordless interplay fascinates and frustrates me moment to moment and it's one of the many reasons I'm never bored of her.

She reveals nothing and everything. She keeps me in the dark and shines light on her deepest vulnerabilities even in those first few days. And I am liberated by the truth that after that first question—"Is it a novel?"—she never asks me another. Ever.

Sunlight slides across the wine red sheets turning merlot into chardonnay. I reach out one hand and feel her warmth already gone from the satin. It seems a shame and a loss; her mere presence is a treasure to me.

I roll over onto my back and stare past the ornate cherry posts of the bed to the eggshell white ceiling. When did she wake? I vaguely remember six in the morning. Or was it seven? Does she work? A condo like this, with a view like that, doesn't pay for itself. But what does she do?

I find myself sorting through fantasies of her day job. I weigh each option against her predilections last night. The way she pulled me down on top of her. The sound of her voice rich and honest filling the room. Her desires uninhibited, unbridled. Playing with stereotypes, I imagine at work she's in power but silenced by corporate politics. The burden of responsibility rests on her shoulders; Atlas carrying the world.

It's amazing how wrong I was. And how right.

I should have gone home. At noon or one or certainly by five, I should have gathered my clothes off the floor and the chaise lounge, stripped the bed, washed the sheets and the snifters. But the etiquette of the situation—what was the situation?—was lost on me. I felt like I'd fallen down a rabbit's hole into another world where everything was surreal and enticing, where messages of "Drink Me" were met without hesitation and whispers of "Eat Me" were permission to feast.

In short: I didn't want to leave.

I rose from Hannah's bed only after the sun had poured across my entire body and then spilled away, luxuriating in memories of her that seemed glided in dreams, as if I'd slipped in and out of the nether while I touched her though I knew very well I'd been entirely present. Perhaps more present than ever before.

She had a plain cotton robe—black with a tie—hanging behind her bathroom door and I wrapped it around myself like a cloak of invisibility. I noticed it was a men's medium but instead of letting this bother me I decided instead to be grateful it was my size.

The stairs from her open loft bedroom were Gabon ebony spiraling between chrome bars and glass panels. My eyes half closed as I descended remembering kneeling at the base of the flight, her knees wrapped around my shoulders. My face had showed concern; that can't be comfortable. But she only made a low sound in the back of her throat; a plea for more action and less thought.

I was famished but also uninterested in food or drink. I smiled to myself; after Hannah, even ambrosia paled in comparison. I felt blessed. I felt chosen. I felt full. But I wanted more of her.

Apparently, she knew a painter. Someone who worked in acrylic, as throughout the condo were black and white abstracts. They evoked emotion and movement and reminded me of film noir until I caught one at the end of the hall reflected in the mirror across the living room. I turned in slow motion, afraid I'd somehow scare the image away.

Seen in reverse, the painting was far from abstract. It was a nude. Of Hannah. Her body arching back and revealed, a study in exposure and offering. She was beautiful. Utterly vulnerable but entirely in control.

Finally I made a cup of black coffee in the Italian percolator on the counter then stood on the balcony for an hour taking in the view in daylight. Work called—it was Monday—but I was off for four days so they could learn to live without me.

I explored with my eyes but never my hands. I imagined what everything felt like but chose not to touch anything. I didn't want to overstep my bounds; maybe just staying was too much already. I held onto the fact that she'd left no note. No missive of: "Coffee's in the kitchen. Help yourself then help yourself out." Certainly she didn't want me to leave the front door unlocked.

There were no photos anywhere. But on the tempered glass shelves in-set to either side of the gas fireplace, there were small statues and curios from around the world. A Grecian Olympian, wearing only a laurel crown as he readied a discus. A reclining Venus, resplendent with curves, stroking the head of a fawn. A Nigerian shikra in bronze. Cristo Redentor carved from Brazilian tigerwood.

Was Hannah the traveler? Or perhaps her painter bestowed these gifts as symbols of longing when far away or as souvenirs of times together? I searched for a unifying theme among the figurines but came away only with global appreciation. A woman versed with the world.

At sunset, umbers and golds seeped throughout the condo and strategically placed mirrors and other reflective surfaces filled the space with molten light. I walked up the stairs to the loft to get above the almost liquid blaze. I wanted to take it all in without drowning or incinerating or both. When my hands wrapped around the brushed chrome railing was when the front door opened and Hannah came home.

Except it wasn't Hannah.

I really should have left. No one wants to come home after a long day at work and find their lover's one-night stand wearing your robe and drinking your coffee. But certainly, that was the predicament. I stared, frozen, not in fear but in dread. What a truly unfortunate turn of events after such a remarkable evening. I admit I was without remorse but that's the power she held over me. My willing subjectivity.

His wore straight-legged Levi jeans cuffed once over heavy motorcycle boots, worn and creased from actual use. Likewise his riding gloves that he pulled off and tossed casually, with belonging, onto the pristine chrome and glass sideboard. The sound of his keys landing in the cut crystal bowl that a moment ago had been a basin of prisms filled with arcane light almost deafened me. His jacket, at least, was hung up in the hall closet, and when he emerged from the long hall he shrugged out of his hoodie... and shook out his chestnut curls.

For just one moment I thought: "She has a brother." And that would have made everything so much easier but that brief illusion evaporated as I watched Hannah pull off her white t-shirt and unbind her chest. She sat on the couch by the fireplace, nude from the waist up, her breasts small and full and chilled in the air. She leaned back, resting her arms along the back of the couch in both directions. At the curve of her hip, far above her low-slung jeans, rests the slender strap and D-ring of a harness. My eyes move to her crotch.

Hannah looks up at me, pinning me in place. "Guess what I do for a living."

Our first moments together, I was breathless. Now I'm breathing so fast I feel faint; a dangerous proposition when standing at a loft railing but seemingly not as dangerous as joining this stranger in the living room. I catch my own thought the moment after thinking it. I didn't think of Hannah as a stranger until she walked in with a cock.

"Something corporate." My voice sounds thin. There's a feeling in the pit of my stomach. A coiling, writhing thing made of all those ugly human emotions that we all pretend we don't harbor. I'm starting to hate myself a little bit.

"Wrong."

She crosses one booted ankle over her knee, her eyes unrelenting. Her mannerisms, her gaze, even the confidence, dominance in her tone belie her bare breasts and cascading ringlets. She is a dichotomy and I'm struggling with it.

"Come here."

I absolutely don't move. I'm more likely to pitch forward over the rail then voluntarily walk down the stairs to her.

Hannah shifts, uncrossing her legs. One hand falls to rest against her thigh, almost cupping the impressive though not unrealistic package her button fly conceals. I start to see spots.

"I said…"

Time has no meaning. It folds in on itself. Space and distance change their rules. I am kissing her, buried inside her, listening to her whisper in my ear even while her shouts fill the room. I might be losing my mind.

"…come here."

And, of course, I do. But not by choice. It becomes an autonomic response. My body overriding the cultural basis of my brain. Last night I'd followed a dozen commands from her without hesitance but now….

Hannah doesn't get up. I loom over her, a substantial figure despite my borrowed robe, and she doesn't change her smile. If anything, nearer to her like this, I can see her amusement more clearly. She revels in my uncertainty and disconcert. She feeds off it. And I realize I want her to. I want her to swallow these feelings I'm having whole, consume them entirely and leave me without shame or betrayal. I don't want to be 'that guy.'

"Come closer."

I stand between her open knees. I'm struggling with what to say. The past and present collide in the now and the cacophony is painful. "I'm…" Oh, God. Am I speaking? Why am I speaking? "I'm not into boys."

I want to crawl into a hole and die. I literally wish, in that moment, that I didn't exist.

And Hannah just wets her lips. "You don't say." She's snide but somehow not unkind, I think because of the passion and patience on her face as she leans forward, running her hands up my bare thighs, finding me beneath the robe—her robe?—and holding me in both her hands. She seems curious and amused to find me unaroused.

Hannah exhales and stands, moving me aside with her own body but only enough to make room for her. "Lucky for you," she tells me, her hands already at her jeans. "I'm not a boy… at night."

And deftly, with the slick sounds of denim and cotton, her belt, then her jeans, then her boxer briefs hit the hardwood floor.

Finally she's standing almost nude before me and I feel like I should do something, anything to prove I'm not some unenlightened Neanderthal who blunders through life in binary absolutes. I want to drop my gaze and look at her equipment, maybe even reach out and touch her but instead I just drop my robe.

Hannah gives me her patient smile again. She steps against me so our bodies touch almost everywhere at once and then reaches down between us and unbuckles her harness. Leather and silicone join our clothes on the floor and she kisses me soft and sweet as if I'm delicate but now I'm growing hard against her and she's still smiling.

"Let's get high."

She walks away from me and I look down. It's like he melted on the floor and she rose from his demise. I look back up at her. She has a great ass.

She turns at the top of the stairs, looking down on me. "It's been a long day." Her voice is steady and sure but I imagine a weariness behind it. "Come upstairs and fuck me."

And I do as the lady commands.

She's leaning back against pillows, the bed sheets tangled, as thoroughly under the influence as she had been under me an hour before. It's somewhere past midnight but nowhere near dawn. I am captivated by her entirely.

"I think I'm most afraid of onism. The looming boredom of being forced to be just one person, just one body."

I want to understand. She's so beautiful. Like looking at a painting or a tapestry. I have known her for twenty-four hours and she is art to me.

"I realized when I was sixteen…" She pauses to take a deep, slow draw from her thick blunt. I have no idea what strain it is but it tastes and smells like mown grass with lilac beneath. After two hits, I can fold time like origami. Hannah continues, "…that women would pay me to fuck them."

"As a boy?" I'm trying to comprehend and having no sense of self or gravity or direction isn't helping me. Or maybe it's exactly what I need.

"Not at first." Hannah passes me the joint and I take it because I feel on thin ice, barely allowed in or worthy of her presence.

"But that became my angle." She laughs a little. "My special niche."

"Why don't they just…" I lose my ability for words because my third hit has left me floating somewhere near the vaulted ceiling looking down at both of us. If this is what death feels like, it's not half bad.

"…hire a real boy." She finishes my sentence as a statement and laughs but I'm not sure if her mirth is spurred by my inability to handle my THC or her own Pinocchio reference. She pins me with a gaze so direct and sensual that I'm back in my body with a snap that's positively audible. "Endurance. Consideration. Focus. Knowledge. Novelty. Poetry. There are things women can say to each other that a man never will."

I'm almost completely mute. Unable to make any sound, only able to want her so utterly one hand falls to cover myself, as if—lying naked in her bed—I can hide anything from her.

Then it happens. Time folds in on itself like a paper crane and the present moment becomes the past and a hundred futures repeating just the same: That young man coming into the condo. Dropping his keys in the crystal bowl. Throwing his jacket on the couch.

I lean over the bed and throw up.

Occhiolism is realizing the smallness of your own single perspective. It wasn't a state of being I discovered until many, many years later when politics and world events turned the world upside down and pink. It knocked the wind out of me. My ignorance. My bigotry. My loss.

Fate or chance or some nameless gods amused by my infinite stupidity had handed me my soulmate and I had thrown up on her hardwood floor.

And mine wasn't a graceful exit. There were no insults slung (though I deserved them), no questions of my own inadequacies as a man if I was so easily threatened by a girl wearing a dick. I didn't even have the self-respect to wipe off my face and slink away.

I stayed. I stayed the four days I had off that week. Hannah left in the morning while I was still naked in her bed, exhausted from pot and cognac and the best sex I'd ever had in my life. And when I woke, I'd wander her home, drink more, admire the view... And conveniently be in the shower when she came home as a boy.

Liberosis is the sincere desire to care less. I wish I could say I prayed or wished or bargained with those merciless gods to care less about something that—twenty years later—seems trivial and even petty. Such a small thing. Maybe... eight or ten inches.

When I vomited that second night, Hannah actually laughed at me and her laughter was nothing but kind.

"It's okay, Michael," she assured me as she helped me into the bathroom, cleaned my face like a mother and child, gave me a toothbrush and mouthwash. "You don't have to keep pace with me."

She had no idea how much of a problem that was.

I suppose that's why I decided to write about this. To write my one, true sentence. Because I created a problem where there was only perfection. And Hannah, if you read this somewhere, somehow, someday, please know: I was an idiot. I should have been stronger. I should have returned your calls. I should have gone back to that dive bar and found you again. I should have gotten over my damn self and seen you for everything you were: A goddess. A god. A creature made of mercury as fluid as only quicksilver can be.

I loved Hannah but only at night. And that was my mistake.

FATHERHOOD
BY LAUREN PATZER

I looked into the dark night sky, slightly emboldened that we could see the stars again after so many years. It was strange to me how a constant overcast sky could affect your mood. Behind me, Anna worked with the rags we'd scavenged, taking care of her new development—menstruation.

I'm torn between relief that she's grown up, survived in this hellscape and appears healthy and normal. The past 11 years had been a learning experience I never thought I'd live through. I looked out from the hilltop we retreated to, watching for any signs of trackers, the humans who'd risen to the top of the wild packs due to their sense of smell, hearing or eyesight. If they found us, I'd be the next meal while Anna would become a breeder. Not that she would escape that fate anyway, but I could do my damnest to make sure it didn't happen in a tracker pack.

"I think that's it," Anna whispered, coming up behind me quietly. I honestly didn't hear her. Whether that's a testament to her stealth skills or my wandering thoughts, I didn't know. I'd like to think I taught her well enough to sneak up or away from anything this new, desiccated world could throw at her.

I took a whiff of the air and nodded my head.

"It's barely noticeable now," I said as I turned my eyes to the north. "We need to keep moving."

"We're not making camp here?" Anna asked. There was a hint of worry in her voice. I shook my head.

"That last tracker pack was only half a day behind us," I said. "It's best we not take any chances and keep moving. We can move faster and they can't move at night as easily with a large group."

"But our chance of injury," Anna began.

"I know, but especially now, we can't risk any encounters with trackers. It will end badly for both of us."

Anna nodded and we made our way north, using the stars as our guide. After a few hours, we happened upon a complex of caves in a cliff face and I selected the one with the best chance of escape and least chance of ambush. I explained my reasoning to Anna; this passing of knowledge could be what allows her to survive where billions had perished before her.

As we settled down in the cave, she snuggled up next to me and I rested my head against the cave wall. My mind wandered back to when I first found her, sitting in the back of an SUV amidst the ruins of Vegas. How she survived with what I assumed were her dead parents in the front of the vehicle for a week after the disaster, I didn't know. She was a hardier breed than most, I supposed. My first instinct was to run. I knew there would be scavengers, wild people for whom all hope was lost and desperation the only emotion they knew. They'd come, perhaps they'd save her and take her in, but just as likely she'd meet a savage end. One look into her blue eyes and I knew I couldn't leave her there to die.

It took some wrangling with ropes and defunct power lines to create a rickety rope bridge across the chasm that had been created a week earlier when the earth's crust had been torn asunder. I worried she would cry out and fuss, drawing unwelcome eyes to our situation, but she remained silent, watching me work my way to her. That patience and ability to keep quiet contributed to our survival all these years.

I fell into a fitful sleep until shortly before dawn when rodent activity alerted me to the ending night. Anna was already awake and had caught two wood rats. I heard the fire crackling from deep inside the cave, but didn't smell anything or see smoke. My lessons on how to stay hidden were well absorbed by my young protégé.

I moved deeper into the cave and found a larger cavern that could capture and hold the smoke, at least until it could filter out through the fissures in the granite and limestone above our heads. Anna was on the far side of the cavern, deeper into the cliffside. I noticed she used some of the herbs and plants we gathered along our travels. The thin metal pot we scavenged years ago still functioned well for most of our cooking and water sterilization needs. I noticed the rats had been skinned and dangled over the fire at just the right distance, impaled on thick wooden sticks. All of this reminded me in a flash that, if I were to succumb to some illness or mishap with wild life or the even worse and more ruthless human adversary, Anna would survive if she could escape.

We ate in silence. Anna read from one of the many books we scavenged from a school years ago. It was simple and elementary, but I'm relieved to see she enjoyed consuming the written word. I can only hope she'd taken in enough with my impromptu instruction to someday produce content or at least pass on the skills to her offspring.

"What are these?" Anna handed me the kindergarten book we found just weeks ago. It was the first time she'd opened it. I looked at the flying machine and understood why she didn't recognize it. She'd never seen one flying through the air unless she'd possibly noticed one before the cataclysm. Even then, she probably wouldn't remember them.

"Airplane," I said.

"I know how to read the word airplane, but I don't understand what the object is," Anna said. She chewed thoughtfully on a bit of wood rat meat seasoned with dandelions and chicory. "What does it do?"

"They flew through the air, transporting people long distances," I said. She didn't look convinced.

"Like magic? I thought you said there was no such thing as magic." Anna drank some dandelion tea and looked at me expectantly.

"It was a machine that used scientific principles like lift, air flow, wing design and jet propulsion to rise into the air." I shrugged my shoulders. "I don't have a scientific background, so I can't explain exactly how that worked. It was like the cars except it traveled through the air."

"The cars." Anna raised her eyebrows. "They still sound like magic to me."

"I know," I said. I looked at the fire and realized it may make the lesson a little easier to understand. "You know how there is something rising from the water when you make it hot?"

"Steed?" Anna said and frowned.

"Close, it's steam." I pointed at the pot of tea she had made. "That steam rises. Some people know how to harness that action, capture that energy and use it to run an engine or mechanism."

"Why?" Anna asked. She was intent on my every word, so hungry for knowledge I could barely provide to her.

"It's a tool for accomplishing something with better efficiency than can be accomplished with one person's or even many people's power and energy."

Anna nodded her head.

"Like the bow and arrow is more efficient for hunting and the snare is more effective at catching small game than running around trying to smash them with a rock." She looked at me and smiled.

"Well," I said. "I didn't expect you'd remember that particular hunting lesson word for word."

"I went hungry that night and that's a great memory maker," she said.

"We went hungry and it's a great way to remember," I corrected. "OK, so we may find someone where we're going that has tools running on steam or something else. It's good you're aware of what machines are."

"Where are we going?" Anna said as she began to pack up our foodstuff and cooking utensils.

"You remember the old man we came upon last winter?"

"He died," Anna said. There was no emotional component to the statement, but it still jarred me. My old sensibilities still grieved for the loss of human life, even more so given the devastation that appeared to happen to the human race. It seemed like every loss of life now was another nail in the coffin for humanity.

"He did, but before he died, he mentioned a friend of mine. At least, I'm hoping it's my friend and not someone else. Daniel Casson. You remember?"

Anna nodded and stood up. She finished packing.

"Time to check for safety," she said. I nodded. We ended the conversation and we both crept to the front of the cave and looked out. I saw a thin column of smoke rising far in the distance. I waited for Anna's assessment.

"Nothing close," she whispered. She nodded in the direction of the smoke. "The tracker camp is behind us and a bit off to the right."

"Which means?" I asked.

"They've likely lost our trail," Anna said. "We should continue to head away from their camp and put more distance between us to ensure we don't run into them."

"Perfect," I said. Anna smiled at me for the compliment of her abilities. I saw at that moment that she was indeed growing up before my eyes into an attractive woman. My heart swelled a little and then darkened. If we met strangers in the wild, her maturity was a liability to her and to me as well. She wasn't just another mouth to feed as she had been before. Now she was an asset as well as an object of desire for breeding and other things.

"Best we get moving as quickly as possible," I said. Anna and I both crawled carefully from the mouth of the cave, still watching the surrounding landscape for any signs of movement. There were none and we completed our exit and descended back into the high brush surrounding the rise.

Travel over land was as fast as we could possibly make it. Our northward trek didn't seem to concern my companion as much as it did me. She'd never seen summer on the plains. It was still spring, so the heat wouldn't be sweltering yet. As we walked I thought about the wisdom of my musings and realized I was projecting pre-cataclysm memories on the environment. In truth, I didn't know what the northern climes would bring in terms of weather anymore.

We passed by what I remembered as Yellowstone. For two weeks, a collection of charred daggers pushed up through the earth into the sky. The disappearance of cloud cover might regenerate the barren landscape, but I wasn't hopeful. Most vegetation higher than three feet barely clung to life through the last ten years. A suddenly rejuvenated forest would take decades but might never happen in this area. I didn't think I'd see a lush forest again, at least not in my lifetime.

Halfway through the wilderness, we came upon the tell tale signs of an old road. I stopped and pulled out an ages old map. Unfolding it carefully, I did some triangulation with the forest and the road. I figured it was state route 20. The old man said Daniel was somewhere south of what used to be Billings. I did my best estimation and changed our trajectory. I showed Anna what I'd done even though the landmarks of old would be lost on her. Maybe someday she'd teach the next generation how to make maps.

As the weeks of travel dragged on, Anna got a better handle on handling her monthly visitor. We approached a large rock outcropping that somewhat resembled a mountain that had broken through the earth's crust. I recognized the two-story high walls built from gravel surrounding and blocking off most of the path to the mountain, just like the old man described it. This would lead into a labyrinth of sorts—a defensive configuration meant to slow down attackers and put them at the mercy of defenders. I wondered how Daniel had managed it; it was an enormous amount of earth to move without the benefit of bulldozers and dump trucks.

"Keep your weapons stowed," I reminded Anna. "We wouldn't survive an attack even if we had them out."

"Don't provoke them," Anna said, nodding.

We walked to the edge of the first wall. I heard sounds above us, but the echoing confused my senses and I was never sure where our observers were exactly, which was just the way they wanted it. As we moved into the interior, we had to pass through gaps barely large enough for a single person, again defensive design meant to slow down anyone entering the labyrinth. All the while, the sounds of moving rocks above us meant our progress was being monitored closely.

When we finally emerged from the six interlocked walls of rock that made up the labyrinth, we came to an array of construction machines. After eleven years, they no longer had usable tires and rested on tire debris mashed under the rims. Looking at the array of machinery, I understood how they moved so much earth and rock to make the walls behind us. Arrayed in a semi-circle around the exit from the labyrinth, I could also tell this was yet another defensive position for Dennis' home base. Depending on the number of people he had inside, I could see the defensive corridor he'd setup could repel an incredibly large number of invaders. I don't think I'd seen a tracker pack large enough to make it past the labyrinth much less this next line of defense. I hadn't seen any weapons yet, but even the heavy rocks thrown down from above would damage or kill most would be invaders. Perhaps this last line was where the projectile weapons would come into play or some other weapon I hadn't considered yet.

High above our heads, in the cab of a large earth mover I'd only seen in mining quarries before, sat a man with long dark hair observing us. He waved.

"Hank?" the man shouted down to us.

"Howard Ferber, but my friends called me Hank years ago," I replied.

"Friends?!" the man said as he laughed, "I don't recall you having any of those!"

"Dennis, I presume," I replied.

"Probably," the man responded, not moving from his perch. As I watched him, I noticed several heads appearing between the crevices of the machinery in front of us, wielding what looked like bows and arrows. "You'll have to forgive my caution. We don't get many visitors that don't wish us harm or want to take what we've built here."

"Understood. I come wishing only peace." I bowed. "And perhaps a bit of Jamaican jerky?"

The man nodded. "That's something Hank would say, but also something that could be tortured out of him." He stepped out of the cab onto the surrounding decking. I noticed the age lines now and the graying hair. He was in his forties like me. "What was the first course we took together at Antioch?"

"English Lit, but it wasn't at Antioch, it was at Villanova. Third class of the day."

"Correct. And the teacher's assistant's name?"

"Frederica. Her sister wound up being your wife."

Daniel began to climb down the steps of the mammoth vehicle.

"She was indeed."

"I'm sorry," I said.

"It was another time, another place," Daniel said as he hit the ground. "Another world, really."

Daniel walked up to me. Involuntarily, I stepped back with a barely perceptible flinch. He didn't seem to notice and just engulfed me in a hug. I awkwardly hugged him back. I'd more expected him to deck me at the least after all these years. Daniel stepped back and held me by my shoulders.

"You look like hell," Daniel said. "Come on in—we've got a spring. A cool drink will do you good."

He turned and shouted "Guardia!" Four kids moved from their perches on the equipment and ran to ramps along the sides of the immense cavern that took them up to the tops of the rock barrier walls behind us. Daniel walked forward. Anna looked at me and I nodded. I followed Daniel as another five people, three of them adults, ran ahead and into the opening in the wall that led to the interior of the immense complex.

As we passed the orange and red walls, the interior revealed itself to be more of a dark brown color. The walls appeared smooth as if polished by water, but there was none present. Daniel gestured overhead. "The remains of an aquifer the earth belched up during the event," he said.

"It's cooler than outside," I noted. Anna looked in wonder at the walls. This was completely alien to her. "An aquifer was an underground reservoir of fresh water."

"Oh," she said and continued to glance around. "Where did the water go?"

"Some of it," Daniel answered, "is still here. But the greater majority of it burned away up into the atmosphere. The rains have picked up though, so it will be coming back, but clearly it will never fill this space again as its above ground now."

We entered some winding paths in the cavern walls and came to a room where water bubbled from a hole in the wall down along a trench and into another hole where it splashed somewhere below into a larger pool of water. Daniel grabbed a cup from next to the hole and filled it up with water. The cup looked like it had been carved from stone. He handed it to me and I drank readily, closing my eyes and savoring the cleanest water that had passed my lips in a decade. As I was gorging myself, Daniel filled another cup and handed it to Anna. She looked at me briefly and then followed suit, drinking in the precious fluid.

"So, what brings you to our humble abode?" Daniel asked. He took our cups and refilled them, handing them back to us as we drank our fill again.

"An old man let me know about this place," I said. Daniel looked down.

"Albert Foster, the only person who left us for different pastures," Daniel said. "He's dead then?"

"Yes," I said. "But how did you know?"

"It's the only way he'd let slip his knowledge of this place."

"Oh, I didn't kill him," I said quickly. Daniel laughed.

"No, he would've directed you somewhere entirely different if you'd tortured him. I suspect you saved him from some calamity, but his injuries were too severe to recover."

"Tracker pack," I said. "I flew into a rage when I saw them torturing him. Killed a few and the rest ran off. I guess I lost control that day."

Daniel nodded and then turned to Anna.

"And what's your story, miss?"

Anna looked at me and I nodded.

"My name's Anna. I travel with Howard," she said. She looked back at me and shrugged. I chuckled.

"I saved Anna when she was quite young, after the cataclysm," I said.

"Cataclysm?" Daniel raised his eyebrows. "That's a catchy term for it."

"I pulled her out of a wrecked SUV in what was left of Vegas," I said. Daniel motioned to some rock outcroppings that were the right height for sitting or even laying on. He sat and we followed his example. "Do you know what happened? I never found out."

"The reports I heard were only a few hours old before everything went to hell," Daniel said. "Drilling for oil, gas, whatever else they could find beneath the earth's crust. I guess there was some kind of offshore drilling race to claim the most of the new oil fields they'd discovered. The ocean started boiling around one of the oil rigs and then several of them. Some of the countries were using explosives and it escalated to cracking the crust just right to release a volume of magma the likes of which probably hasn't been seen since the time before the dinosaurs."

"Did they try to fix it?" I asked.

"Once that genie had been let out of the bottle, well..." Daniel shrugged. "I tried the math once and figured a quarter to a third of the Pacific ocean probably boiled away into the atmosphere. With the weight of the ocean's diminished on the floor of the ocean, that lead to the big eruption or cracking of the crust or whatever it was. Maybe four hours passed from the first signs to all hell breaking loose. I had a refuge, you know. Designed it for just this occasion."

"I remember," I said. "Didn't you call it Hell Hole?"

"Right," Daniel sighed. "I just thought I'd be using it for a political nightmare. I didn't realize the earth would fight back so hard. I survived, but just barely. Hell Hole is no more, but it served it's temporary function of keeping me alive. I emerged, surveyed what there was left of the landscape and the resources and managed to devise our little getaway here. 40 people live here now. 25 originally and as time, illness, additions and subtractions affected us, we grew to 40."

"That's less than most tracker packs," I said.

"We haven't been adding women fast enough to keep up with the attrition," Daniel said.

"I thought that might be the case," I said. "It's one of the reasons we came."

Daniel looked at Anna and then back to me. "Does she know that?" Daniel asked.

"Some, not all," I said. "It's a little complicated."

Daniel nodded.

"I'll be a breeder?" Anna asked. "That's what you're talking about, isn't it?"

"Yes, but Daniel and I aren't sure you have all the details you need to know about it. It can be a bit of a shock."

"You didn't want me to be a breeder with the tracker packs," Anna said. "Is being a breeder bad?"

"Uh..." I scratched my head.

"If I may," Daniel said. "All the young women learn what it means to be a breeder in consultation with Rebecca."

I breathed a sigh of relief. Being a father figure was hard enough. Explaining propagation of the human race? That was well beyond me. "If that's all right with Anna, I don't have any objections," I said.

"Okay," Anna said. "If Howard comes with me."

I nodded. "I had a feeling that would be the case."

Daniel led us through a labyrinth of tunnels until we came to a medium sized cavern. Rebecca was an older woman, in her 50s. She turned to watch us as we entered. Another young woman moved about in the cavern behind her. I noted she was with child.

"Rebecca," Daniel shouted out. "Come meet my old friend Hank and his companion Anna." Rebecca came toward us. Daniel turned back to us and smiled. "Rebecca is what we would call a midwife in the old days. She's also our primary medical expert."

Rebecca reached her hand out to shake and I reciprocated. Anna watched us both curiously. I thought I might have seen a momentary flash of jealousy cross the young girl's face. It was then that I realized we hadn't spoken with other people often, perhaps a handful of times, in the last ten years. All of Anna's social interaction had been primarily with me and I hadn't made much of an effort to teach her manners; most of the time, I just advised her to remain silent. But her face betrayed her thoughts.

"Welcome, Hank and Anna. It is nice to meet you both," Rebecca reached out to shake Anna's hand and Anna looked at me, waiting for a nod before she complied. "How long have you been travelling?"

"Ten years," I replied.

"I see," Rebecca said and looked at Anna. "How old are you, my dear?"

Anna looked at me again for permission to speak.

"Anna, you can speak freely with these people. They are friends and this will be your new home," I said. Anna's eyes didn't leave mine.

"I may be twelve years old, maybe less, maybe more. You didn't say our new home." Anna didn't even look at Rebecca. I sighed.

"I may not be staying long," I said.

"You're welcome to stay as long as you like," Daniel said.

"Crowds," I said. "They're still a thing."

"Some things don't change," Daniel replied. He moved behind Rebecca and took a seat on a large rock. "Anna, your companion, Hank here, has had a history of being a loner. I was quite surprised to see him travelling with anyone else."

"You've always been with me," Anna said. "What did I do wrong?"

"Nothing, Anna," I said. "Now that you're a woman, it's not safe to travel with me anymore. It will be so much safer for you here."

"I wish we'd never come here," Anna said. She turned to Rebecca. "Can you teach me how to not be a woman?"

Rebecca looked at me. "I'm afraid that's not how it works, Anna," Rebecca said as she returned her attention to Anna. "Time marches on, we grow older, our bodies mature and things change. Come meet Tanya." Rebecca held out her hand. Anna took it without looking at me. They walked over to the pregnant young woman and chatted with her for a while.

"You could stay," Daniel said. "Ten years travelling with another person is amazing. I never thought I'd see you share your life with anyone."

"I didn't feel like I had a choice," I said.

"Perhaps it's better if you don't have a choice then," Daniel chuckled. "You care for her, otherwise you would've left her to the tracker packs. You cared for someone, Hank. That's huge."

"I've been trying to find a way to let her loose the entire time, Daniel," I said. "I haven't changed except to save her life."

"That's better than you did fifteen years ago," Daniel said. I didn't say anything, but I knew he was right at least in that sense. Fifteen years ago, I would've left Anna to die in that car just as I'd left Frederica.

Later that night, as I lay looking at the stars through a hole in the rocks, Anna came and lay with me. A week later, I left the complex, never to see them again. I know she watched me as I entered the interleaving walls of rock, but I never looked back.

INSIDE THE BLUE CIRCLE
BY HIROMI COTA

The bathroom faucet dripped languidly.

Tip-tap

Tip-tap

A cat loafed on the edge of the sink, her paws tucked underneath her body as she observed each pair of drops. Her eyes gazed into the string of twin worlds created by each faucet drip. Birthing as individuals. Chasing one another as they fell through the air. Fracturing into dozens of new worlds on the basin. Looking up to their descendants as the cycle begins anew. Astra's furry tuxedo bristled and relaxed with each cycle, her tail marking time as morning crept into the tiny apartment.

Tip-tap

Tip-tap

Astra stretched a curious paw towards the faucet's drips, experimenting for the millionth time with what the water would feel like against her fur. A shift of the air injected warnings into her mind and she froze before making contact with the water. Her head flicked to the side and stared at the bed. One of the human lumps she shared the apartment with had begun stirring. The lump stretched and resumed lumping with exasperation.

"Meow?" Astra questioned of the human.

& groaned, rolling out of bed, barely escaping the mattress that felt more like pudding than foam this morning. Their feet entered an uneasy alliance with the floor, chilly faux tile on concrete that extracted heat as its part of the bargain. Each passing moment made the alliance more bearable, but not less regrettable. & pulled their body to the elderly folding table that had long dreamt of being a kitchen.

"Oh, good," & sighed as their bleary eyes found focus on the viewport on the side of the electric kettle. There was still water. & flicked the kettle's switch, the first step of the tea-manifesting ritual. Forcing their eyes to take in the rest of the items on Kitchen, they found the bag of buns. But, before their hand could close on it, the world of sleep took one last shot at &.

A sudden yawn forced their eyes closed and their mouth open to noiselessly roar at the morning for interrupting dreams. They retrieved two buns from the bag and looked back at the bed. A smile birthed on their face as @ scooted closer to the warm spot that had, until recently, held &. They could see @'s face swirl through disappointment to the inevitable and annoying conclusion that it was time to be awake.

Neon Gods, they're cute.

"Tea?" the annoyed @ in the bed inquired.

"Just started the water. Give it a few."

"Bleh. Who the hell invented mornings, anyway?"

"I mean, you know my feelings on time."

"Pfft." @ forced their feet to join the alliance with the floor. Their feet stretched and flexed before striding to the plastic shelving beside Kitchen. Dancing their fingers along the drawers, @ found and retrieved the perfect bergamot tea for banishing the morning brain fog. "Are those European buns still good?"

"I hope so. I don't think European-style buns needed to be refrigerated." & gave them a quick sniff and squeezed them. Generally, wheaty, yeasty, and sweet with a soft, dry texture. "Yeah, they seem fine. These might actually be American."

"What's the difference?" @ scooped up a pair of mugs and trudged to the bathroom to rinse them under the faucet. The sudden change in water pressure earned a dirty look from Astra, who hopped off the sink and sauntered past @, slowing to flick the human's ankle with her tail on her way out. The cat flounced to the bowls, arriving just in time to sit and look annoyed, despite & already having Astra's food bag in hand before the cat even left the bathroom.

"I don't know," conceded &. "Maybe it's like the difference between Japanese gyoza and Korean mandu?"

"Tofu?"

"No, I mean- never mind." & arrived at Astra's bowls, topping both the food and water off, though they knew the water would go untouched so long as the faucet's show continued. "You're such a weird cat," chuckled &. They scratched Astra behind her ears, and then began excavating the pile of clean laundry. & struggled into their binder, squeezing their body into something like the right shape. After a few moments, a gray hoodie, and a pair of ill-fitting blue jeans, Alex&er stood frowning near the pile, his fingers twisting through the air, seeking seams in the fabric of Reality. Golden sparks rained down from where & bruised Reality.

"Alex&er? What are you doing?" asked @, buying time to back up to their dresser, perfectly knowing they weren't going to like what their partner had to say.

"Oh, I'm gonna break it, babe."

"Break what?" they asked, already dreading the answer. They jerked open the dresser and dragged clothes onto theirself.

"I'm gonna break time."

"Again?"

Alex&er nodded and grinned.

"All right, but I'm not putting on a gender this time," @ sighed as they shoved their body into a soft black long-sleeved top.

"You don't have to. You never have to do that for me," winked Alex&er.

"Ugh. Fine." M@ threw a scarf around his neck and crammed his feet into boots.

"I meant it when I said you didn't have to," Alex&er said during a brief window of seriousness.

"Yeah. I know. That just makes it-," @ cut theirself off. "Never mind." N@alie tugged a beanie onto her head. "Today's not a scarf day."

"Not a boy day, you mean?"

"Shut up. Let's go break time or whatever."

Alex&er and N@alie started cleared off the ritual space. Astra supervised. They shoved their various belongings out of the way and fought back the accretion of random junk. Books to the left. Cords to the right. Things that looked edible under Kitchen. Whatever the hell that thing with the knobs was into the trash. After a few minutes of something resembling cleaning, they had freed the vaguely defined circular region of the apartment dedicated to magic. The untiled concrete area bore signs of years of weirdness. Smeared remnants of chalk circles splaying out in overlapping arrays. Salt stains. And an outer circle of blue paint surrounding it all.

The lovers stepped over the blue line.

N@alie knelt. Her part in the spell was security. It was her job to keep Alex&er safe while he screwed with the rules of this dimension. Her hands folded against each other, as she centered herself. Alex&er began crawling around N@alie, orbiting between her and the edge of the blue circle. His fingers traced the inner edge as he moved. Visual echoes of his fingertips started drifting behind them. Soon, an uncountable number of translucent Alex&er fingers followed the presumably real ones attached to his hands.

He swung his hands apart, outlining a circle's arc, and the world outside the blue circle drained of color. Kitchen looked muted. Grayish. Reality itself began to surrender its hold on the apartment, while Alex&er and N@alie became crisper, better defined and more vibrant. The concrete beneath them dropped away, revealing the Milky Way. Yet, they did not fall. Their place in the universe had already been found. Instead, the circle expanded and swallowed the entire Earth.

Alex&er stood in the vacuum of space, his hands glowing with nameless colors, tones that reality had forgotten millions of years ago. N@alie twirled as she rose to her feet, swirling in a full circle, watching the ancient colors surge upwards with her. The pair turned around each other, twin planets orbiting the center, while the universe outside the circle faded to pencil sketches.

&@ opened their eyes. Or at least something that worked like eyes. Their vision flooded with the blackness of space, the nuclear energy of stars, and the dreams of trees. A celestial tapestry wove itself in every direction. Towards @&. Upwards. To the left. Flirwards. To the zir. Even as they gazed upon Reality shaping itself, writing and rewriting itself, they saw theirself embedded within it, the universe stretching towards an understanding of itself. A sphere of life and energy with neither an inside nor an outside. A Klein bottle of energy, matter, and things unknown. The fabric of the universe fluttered as if in response to something beyond &@'s perception.

Motes reclined and tumbled past @&. Lavender ones glittered with secrets untold. White ones danced to an unknown beat. Green motes sailed in random arcs, like lightning swinging from pendulums.

Are those stars? Dust? Souls?

Who knows?

Neither of us apparently. Neither of me?

&@ would have shrugged it they'd had a body.

How long will it take this time?

For Time to repair itself? No idea. I don't even know how much time is passing now.

If those things are stars, we've been here longer than the Earth has existed.

Is that scary?

No. Because I'm not alone. We're not alone? How many of us are there?

Does it matter?

It does. To me, at least.

I was two when we dropped through the seams. I think it's just me in there. Us, I mean.

The Universe roared, stabbing Reality through with tremors. The motes exploded in fragments. And the fragments unified.

Everything fell.

Tip-tap

Tip-tap

"Mew?"

Alex&er and N@alie woke gasping on the floor, their bodies limed in sweat, smoke, and magic. Not for the first time, N@alie wondered if what she'd experienced were real. She rolled her eyes at herself. *Does it really matter? I experienced it. Hell, we both did. If that's not real, what is?*

N@alie pushed the floor away, arriving at a sitting position, looking at her still supine partner.

"Why do you keep wanting the break time?"

Alex&er flopped onto his side, looking up at N@alie. His eyes held swirling galaxies as he fumbled for an answer. He ejected his hoodie and dug his fingers into his binder to peel it off, suddenly uncomfortable with it.

"Because … in that formless moment, that void between the ticks of the clock, I know who I am. Like, I know it doesn't make sense to yearn for an experience where I don't have a body, but—Just for that frozen moment, there's nothing that *isn't* me. Before reality comes rushing back, I don't feel like an & that has to choose—or realize—if today is a boy day or a girl day or neither. I'm just me."

"But, you're not just you there; I'm there with you. I'm *you*, too," N@alie raised an eyebrow as she pulled off her beanie, letting it fall to the floor.

"You know what I mean, though, right? Like, there's no us and no them; it's all the same thing. Everything belongs. Everything's *right*, you know?"

"Yeah, I feel like that when we kiss." @ pulled their lover into their arms and kissed them.

And time stood still again.

AMONG THE STARS
BY AMBER RAINEY

A million tiny points of light glittered in the dark night sky. Every few minutes, brilliant streaks trailed across the sky, the meteors finding a dazzling end in the Earth's atmosphere. Below, a clearing sat covered in luminous white snow. Normally, the clearing would be black, one barely able to see a hand in front of their face, however, the snow leeched the light of the stars and cast an eerie glow upon Louisa. She stood, wiping the snow from her dress and peered up at the sky, smiling as another comet met its demise. Louisa sighed, shaking off the feeling of dread creeping up her spine. Matthew would not be happy if he found out she had come to the clearing alone. She had to hurry to return home before he arrived.

As she walked, Louisa marveled at the silence surrounding her. The snow padded her steps. It was as if she wasn't even walking there. The trees stood as sentinels to her transgression. There was no wind and the branches of each tree were dusted with blankets of white. She marveled at how the landscape was transformed by winter. She hated the winter. It was beautiful but miserable. The first snowfall was always an omen of the bitter wind to follow. The wind howled through the mountain passes and bit at her cheeks when she was forced to go outside for her chores. Only the promise of the meteor shower could have brought her out into the cold.

The only reason she stayed in this godforsaken land was Matthew. She'd been a wild spirit, desperate to remain untamed until she'd met him. She hadn't wanted to go to the dance, but her older brother had called her an aging nag and she went out of spite. Louisa never minded that she might one day be a matronly, spinster aunt but she could not resist proving her brother wrong. He taunted her endlessly, going as far as plucking a gray hair out of her head and parading it around the house. She just couldn't let him get the best of her. So, she had gone to the dance and met a shy logger, visiting his sister in the city in order to see his first nephew.

She'd caught Matthew's dumbfounded staring when she'd gone to the punch bowl. He stood, open-mouthed, a drink halfway to his lips. The moment their eyes met, Matthew flushed a bright shade of red and closed his mouth, turning away. Louisa had giggled and chased after his retreating back.

"Sir?" she asked, placing a hand on his arm.

Matthew turned to face her. He scratched behind his ear, unable to meet her eyes. Louisa tipped her face under his until he looked up. She smiled and held out her hand in the manner of asking for a handshake rather than the proper introduction. Matthew's jaw dropped and she giggled again.

"I'm Louisa Nova," she said.

Matthew's shock wore off and he tentatively took her hand.

"N...nice to meet you, Miss...Ms," he struggled for the right words.

She nodded and shook his hand, "Miss. And you are?"

"Oh, Matthew Minett, at your service," he said as he bowed awkwardly with her hand still in his.

"You're new around here," she said.

He nodded, "My sister, she moved here several years ago when she got married. She just had a baby."

Louisa thought a moment. It wasn't a large town and she knew pretty much everyone. He must be talking about Sarah Benedict. Sarah had recently had a baby boy. Louisa had been to see the child and she had to admit, the smell of a newborn baby was one of her favorite things.

"Sarah Benedict? She's your sister?" she asked.

He nodded again, "Yes ma'am."

Louisa smiled. Just then a new song began playing. She grabbed Matthew's hand and led him towards the dance floor, without asking if he wanted to dance. He stood awkwardly on the dance floor, waiting for an explanation.

"This song is one of my favorites. Dance with me?" she asked.

"Do I have a choice?" he asked.

Louisa laughed and shook her head. Matthew shrugged and danced with her, as requested. He was a bit stiff and she did her best to lighten the mood. Overall, she enjoyed the dance so much, she kept him on the dance floor for three more songs until they were both in need of a breath of fresh air and rest.

Louisa touched her lips as she walked. That was the first night she had ever been kissed. The stars had not been as easy to see, the city lights drowning them out. It had been a warm night and they had gone for a stroll through the garden. She'd finally drawn Matthew out of his shell and at the end of the night, he had leaned down and kissed her lightly on the lips. Then, in true Matthew form, he'd stuttered out an apology for being so forward, escorted her back into the house and left with a blush.

Their courtship had been a quick one out of necessity. Matthew was a logger in the Cascade mountains and would be leaving to go back to his job. Louisa had been determined he was the one she had been looking for and convinced him she could leave the city life behind for the mountains. He'd been hesitant but Louisa was determined. She cajoled Sarah into helping her and eventually the two of them had worn Matthew down. Louisa knew Matthew's resistance was only fueled by concerns over taking her out of her comfortable life to a life of hardship. He could provide for her but he was often gone several nights at a time and would worry for her while he was away. Louisa shot down every argument he made until he admitted he would never be able to live without her.

The day Matthew brought her home to the little cabin, they had their first argument. Matthew had told her to pack light and Louisa swore she had tried but she'd still brought more things than they had room for in their home. Matthew made her go through the trunks with him, sorting through the items and determining if they could stay or if they would need to be sold at the trading post. Louisa swore the trading post pile was bigger than the keep pile. She argued desperately for each item but Matthew had the final say.

He pulled out her telescope and started to put it on the trading pile.

"Wait! Not that!" Louisa cried, jumping off the bed and trying to grab the instrument from Matthew.

"Why?" Matthew asked.

Louisa huffed, "It's mine. My father gave it to me and it is important."

Matthew looked into the wrong end and shrugged, "I think it's broken."

Louisa finally snatched it from him and looked down at it. She rubbed her sleeve over the eyepiece to clean the glass. Then she stood up and held it in front of Matthew's face with the proper orientation. He looked at her dubiously but shrugged when she just glared at him.

"Just look into it," she directed.

Matthew put his eye to the glass and squinted his other eye. He jumped a little and pulled back, looking at her. Louisa smiled proudly and gestured towards the telescope again. Matthew looked through it again. He took it from her hands and moved it around, looking at the trees out the window.

"It brings things closer," he said.

Louisa nodded, "Yes, it brings the stars closer. It's a telescope."

Matthew thought a moment, "Not many stars to look at her, Louisa. The weather doesn't allow for it."

Louisa deflated. She was already losing the battle in her head. Truthfully, she would get rid of everything else she bought if he would let her keep the instrument. She knew it would be fruitless to tell him that detail. He was a practical man and would just dismiss her impulsiveness. Matthew handed the telescope to her and her jaw dropped in shock.

"Take it," Matthew said.

Louisa grabbed the telescope and hugged it to her chest, "You mean it?"

Matthew shrugged, "Could be useful one day."

Louisa threw her arms around him and kissed his cheek. He blushed and turned back to the trunk.

In the end, Matthew had been correct about all the stuff they had traded. Louisa had not needed any of it. Living in the mountains was much different than living in a city. There was no need for fancy underclothes or shoes. Boots were much more comfortable and practical. She loathed wearing skirts in the winter but she loved Matthew and if she wore pants it would cause a scandal. There were not a lot of women in the logging community where they lived but there were enough that Louisa was able to make some friends and have some company when Matthew was gone. They had settled into a good routine over the years and Louisa felt at home in the mountains. She was still terrified when the coyotes howled at night and Matthew endlessly teased her about bears, but she no longer felt like a duck out of water.

Louisa slowed her pace as the cabin came into view. A lone candle flickered in the window. She swallowed hard. She had not left a lit candle, for fear it would burn the house down. It meant only one thing, Matthew was already home. Louisa gulped a huge breath of air. He would be furious. His fury would not be unwarranted.

"Absolutely not!" Matthew shouted.

Louisa winced. He only ever raised his voice when it was the only way he could get her to stop talking over him. She had a bad habit of spewing out whatever came to mind and not truly listening to his answers. It was something she knew she needed to work on. She wrapped her arms around herself. Matthew's fury deflated.

"It's for your own safety," he said, trying to defend his position.

Louisa nodded, "I just wanted to see the meteors."

Matthew ran a hand over his face, "I know. I won't be here and you can't go out alone. You never know when the weather will change and we get another snowstorm. What if the coyotes caught you out?"

"I...," she knew he had won the argument but wasn't ready to give up.

Matthew wrapped his arms around her. She hesitated for a moment but then gave in, inhaling his clean scent and the laundry soap on his shirt. She hated the nights he was away and she had thought if she made use of the unseasonably clear skies, the time would pass quicker.

"Please promise me you will stay in and stay safe. It's only three nights and then I will be home. If it is still clear, I will take you out to the clearing and you can show me all the constellations. Please promise me, Louisa," Matthew said, a pleading note in his tone.

Louisa pulled back and looked at his face. She could see the worry in his eyes. She knew he worried about her each time she was alone. He made extra trips to the woodpile before every trip and he'd taught her how to shoot a gun. He'd tried to calm her fears over the coyotes but he knew she did not sleep well until he was back home. Louisa put her hand on his face.

"I promise I will stay at home," she said.

Matthew searched her eyes and then nodded. He leaned down and kissed her hard. She closed her eyes, kissing him back, trying to reassure him. She loved him and she wanted him to focus on the dangers of his job instead of worrying about her. He pulled back and rested his forehead against hers. He squeezed her tight and she put her cheek against his chest. They stayed like that for a long moment before Matthew pulled away to finish packing his bag.

Louisa stopped just before she reached the door. She took a deep breath and stepped onto the little porch. As she reached for the door, it opened and Matthew stood in the doorframe. He was silhouetted in the frame and she could not see his face.

"Matthew, I…" she tried to explain.

Matthew grunted and moved away from the door. Louisa followed him into the cottage. Matthew sat in a chair, his arms resting on his knees, his head hanging down. Louisa quietly shut the door and sat down next to him. She waited for him to say something. To yell or accuse or question her but he just sat, staring at the floor.

"Matthew, I'm sorry. I wasn't out for long. I was hoping I would get home before you and you would have never known. I was just going stir crazy and the weather had held and I couldn't see out the window clearly. The trees around our house are just too tall and it was just too lovely to miss and I took precautions--," Louisa blurted out.

Matthew looked up. Louisa's breath caught as she saw his face. It was full of sorrow and something she couldn't quite put her finger on. She reached out to touch him but he recoiled from her. She dropped her hand and stared at him intently.

"I loved you, Louisa. You knew that, right?" he asked.

Louisa cocked her head at the odd question, "What do you mean?"

Matthew ran a hand over his face, "You know I loved you?"

Louisa nodded, "Yes, I know you love me. I'm sorry I broke my promise."

"None of that matters now, sweetheart," Matthew said sadly.

Louisa sat in stunned silence, still watching Matthew. She ran his words over in her head. She couldn't believe what she was hearing. Was he leaving her? Was he going to send her back to the city after the years they had been together?

"Matthew...you can't leave me," she pleaded.

Matthew shook his head, "I'm sorry, darling. It's too late."

"What?" Louisa cried, "It isn't. I'll do better. Please, Matthew."

Louisa threw herself at his feet and looked up at him. She tried to grab his arm and then pulled back in shock when her hand passed through his. She looked at her hand as if it belonged to somebody else. Then she looked up at Matthew, realization slowly dawning on her. Tears began streaming down her face.

Louisa shook her head in denial, "No, Matthew...you said this one was safer. You said it would be a quick job and then you would be home."

"Accidents happen, darling," Matthew responded.

"But, what am I supposed to do? Why are you here?" she asked.

Matthew sighed and looked up at the ceiling. She waited for him to gather his thoughts. She started pacing the room, her mind racing with the possibilities. She would have to go find the site manager and figure out how to get Matthew home for a proper burial. She would have to tell his sister. She was all alone now. Louisa glanced over at him and saw him make a decision. He stood wearily, running his hand over his face. He looked even more miserable than before if that was possible.

"We can't keep doing this," he said cryptically.

Matthew walked over to the door and opened it. For a brief moment, Louisa wondered how he could touch the door but she couldn't touch him. The wind blew in and the candle in the window was snuffed out. The only light was the meager glitter of the snow outside their cabin. It looked duller somehow as if the news Matthew had brought put a damper on its sparkle. Matthew watched as the emotions fluttered through her and then gestured to the door.

"Please, Louisa, come with me."

Louisa nodded and went out the door, waiting for him to close it and lead her to wherever it was they were going.

"I loved you, darling, but this is the only way to stop this. I can't keep doing this, night after night," Matthew said.

Louisa followed him around the cabin. She watched as he stopped around twenty yards from the woodshed. She couldn't see around him but her senses told her to dread this moment. She realized she was right to fear what Matthew was about to show her when he stepped aside and she could see a grave marker next to him. Her mind began racing, refusing to listen to him or its own memories. Matthew turned to her.

"I know you didn't mean to do it, Louisa. I know your guilt keeps you coming back, night after night. I forgive you, sweetheart. You have to move on, for both our sakes," Matthew said.

Louisa recoiled in horror, slamming her hands over her ears.

Matthew continued, "This is torture for me. Seeing you and unable to help you. Please. You have to listen to me."

Louisa shook her head vehemently, willing the memories to stay away. It wasn't true. As long as she didn't remember, it would not be true. She couldn't hold them back and she remembered everything. Going out without Matthew into the clearing. Watching the meteor shower. Dropping her telescope down the hill and tripping in a hole covered by the snow while trying to retrieve it, causing her to fall down the embankment. She'd hit her head on a sharp rock on the way down. She did not remember anything after that moment. She only remembered standing up in the snow, as if nothing had happened and returning home to find Matthew waiting for her. Her eyes widened with the realization. She had been haunting Matthew.

"How long have I been coming back?" she asked.

"Months," he replied.

Louisa's hand flew to her mouth, "Why didn't you stop me before tonight?"

Matthew collapsed onto his knees in the snow. Louisa could see the tear marks running down his cheeks and his shoulders heaving with his sobs. She stepped closer to him, wanting to offer comfort and knowing she couldn't.

"I'm so sorry, Matthew. I should have listened. Can you forgive me?" she asked.

Matthew looked up, "I do forgive you. Can you ever forgive me?"

"For what," she asked, startled at the heartache in his voice.

"This," he said, pointing to the headstone, "not being here for you. Not realizing it was so important to you."

Louisa nodded, "It wasn't your fault. I forgave you before you even left that night."

Matthew rocked back and forth, his face turned up towards the sky. The world around them was completely silent, the only sound his labored breaths as the cold engulfed him. Louisa studied the headstone. She smiled at it. Above her name, Matthew had carved a shooting star and below it, he had carved the words, *Beloved Wife, Always.* She knew it was time to end his self-inflicted guilt over her death and move on.

"Matthew?" she said.

Matthew wiped his face and looked at her, "Yes, darling?"

"I'm ready," she said.

Matthew nodded. He stood up and walked over to the headstone. He kissed his fingers and laid them on the stone while looking at her. Then, he nodded at her. Louisa smiled at him.

"Look for me in the stars?" she asked shyly.

"I'll look every night," he said.

Louisa nodded and smiled. She disappeared into the night. Matthew closed his eyes, then looked up at the sky just as a meteor passed overhead. Matthew let out a laugh of relief.

"I love you, too," he said and left the headstone to go back inside after one last look.

WINTER WONDERLAND
BY MARSHALL MILLER

Jim James crunched through the icy snow as he tried to follow the outlines and signs of the two-lane paved road. At least, Jim thought the road was paved. He could not tell due to the thick packed snow that covered what he surmised was asphalt during this long journey. If he had the time and energy in a more sedate and rational world, he would have stopped and dug down to answer his curiosity. However, snowstorms and blizzards in southern Arizona were not rational, at least not in the world Jim had grown up in.

Jim also wondered if he would ever experience any fluffy snow again as he had in his childhood in the Northwest. The constant sub-zero temperatures at night and winter winds caused snow to freeze into a crunchy mass. Trudging through this type of deepened ground covering was tiring, and the two conditions combined were not helpful in surviving this new Earth. Jim stopped and looked around, moved his parka hood a bit in an attempt to hear past the rushing of the wind. He was still alone. Good, he thought. Other people lately had spelled danger.

The man scratched his bearded face and tried to remember when this winter hell had started. A year ago, was it? No, he thought.

It was closer to two when the Earth was slammed off its axis by-something. It was not a hidden asteroid as it would have been seen, even at the last moment, by some amateur astronomer. Before all modern communications were disrupted, some scientists had suggested either a miniature Black Hole or an energized piece of esoteric Dark Matter. Conspiracy theorists screamed a government experiment gone wrong or maybe an alien attack. Whatever was the cause, it did not bode well for the Earth. The axis tilt was at last report over forty degrees, up from the twenty-three and change before the disaster. Plus, the Earth's orbit itself was changed. It was increased into a larger oval which started and ended millions of miles more distance than the ninety-three million miles of the old orbit. Things fell apart before an accurate accounting was made, though Jim had heard a figure of a four hundred day year at least. The Moon now circled the Earth more eccentrically also, both closer and further way at its apogee and perigee. Weather patterns and the seasons were screwed up beyond recognition. Thus, southern Arizona was turned into a winter wonderland for most of the past year.

Jim shifted the more massive long arm he had concealed under his old white bedsheet and army blanket poncho. The M-39 Enhanced Marksmanship Rifle (EMR) was a very new acquisition from just two days prior. The survivor's mind flashed back to the recent occurrence as he handled the thirty caliber weapon...

Some two days prior, the sky just as cloudless, as he followed small county and country roads which paralleled the former Interstate 8, Jim heard some shots from the other side of a bend in the roadway. He had unholstered his Glock Nine Millimeter and held it at a low ready position as he crunched through the icy snow. Trying to be fast and silent in these conditions was very difficult, so Jim just plowed ahead as best he could. He followed recent vehicle tracks as he rounded the bend as cautiously as possible in the dark.

The HUMVEE sat in the snow with several bodies spread out around it. As Jim walked up the ruts formed by the tire tracks, he saw one figure with the driver's side rear door open and rummaging around in the back seat. Jim slowly walked up as he scanned the area. There were no other signs of human life. He waited until he was within some twenty-five yards when he called out to the rummaging figure.

"Hey, Friend ."

The figure jerked upright so fast that the person hit their head on the upper door jam.

"Hey, take her easy. I'm just passing through..." Jim could now see the bearded man as he moved from inside the HUMVEE. The figure grabbed for something at his waist projecting from the partially zipped down heavy coat. As the bearded man pulled a long-barreled revolver from his waistband without a word spoken, Jim brought up his Glock pistol in a two-handed stance and shot the man in his face.

The bearded man sprawled in the snow as the hollowpoint bullet penetrated his skull. The long barreled revolver dropped from the man's twitching hand as his body jerked and spasmed, then lay still. Jim slowly walked up, scanning the corpses and the HUMVEE. Trying to keep his eyes on everything at once, Jim slid up, bent over and picked up the dropped revolver. He saw it was a massive Colt .44 Magnum Anaconda, the type once found in a private collection. Now it was cold from the icy snow Jim held his Glock under his arm as he opened the revolver cylinder and saw there were two unfired rounds and four spent shell casings. The survivor slipped his Glock back into the holster attached to his tactical vest, then patted the pockets of the dead man's coat. Jim found a six-round speedloader and transferred it to his own parka pocket. He next looked to see what the man had been searching in the HUMVEE.

In a plastic grocery bag, Jim found three MRE's, Meals Ready To Eat. He glanced in the front seat and saw the late driver slumped over. The man had a small bullet hole thru the back of his neck just below the "Fritz" helmet. Logic and experience told Jim the three MREs meant three people. Where were the other two? He had better find them or risk being back shot as an 'enemy.'

Jim 'cut the pie' around the back end of the HUMVEE, slowly observing the area. Sure enough, sitting propped against the side of the HUMVEE was another soldier. The figure had both hands clasped around the throat. As Jim slid nearer, he saw the reason why. Blood flowed from a severe neck wound, staining the white snow red. Jim was about to speak when the figure slumped over towards him. He saw the soldier was male and was dying as he watched. Laying in the snow next to the soon dead soldier was an M-16 type assault rifle, a spent shell partially ejected from the chamber. As Jim moved up and past the body, he saw footsteps in the snow leading away from the front of the HUMVEE and down into a roadside ditch. That was where the third soldier had gone.

The .44 Magnum revolver in his hand, Jim carefully stepped as he followed the impressions in the snow. A few steps further and Jim saw the large rifle laying in the snow. Being a gun aficionado in his past life, he recognized it as an M-14 style 7.62 rifle. Jim picked it up with his off hand and saw bloody snow near it as he did. Keeping the revolver in his hand, Jim inched forward and down into the ditch. Within a few steps, he saw the figure on it's back in the snow. There was a pistol in the right hand, pointed in Jim's general direction.

"Hey, soldier. Former Cop here. I'm on your side."As Jim spoke, he was ready to throw himself flat if the figure started blasting. Instead, the traveler heard a muffled voice.

"Marine…Gunny. That last shot…yours?"

"Yeah, Gunny," Jim answered. "You and your people got the rest. I finished off the last one."

"Good," the Gunnery Sergeant managed to croak out. "Punk kid... we stopped for him. He shot us. So I shot him."

"The others showed up then, right?" Asked Jim.

"Yes, Sir. Fucking scum. Try to... help. Need to reach... Yuma."

"Marine Corps Air Station there, right?" Jim slowly approached the Gunny, saw an expanding pool of blood around the man's lower body. A bullet had caught the Gunny below his body armor.

"Hey, Gunny," said Jim. "Let me try to plug your leak there." As Jim spoke, the Gunny's gun hand dropped into the snow. He had seen enough death to know the Marine was gone.

"Fuck," Jim said to himself. Then he heard a whistle come from the darkness on the other side of the road. Shit, he thought. More bushwhackers. He realized there was little time in which to deal with the dead. Jim approached the dead Gunny and took the pistol from his hand. Jim popped the magazine and looked at it. One round left, nine millimeters like his Glock. He stuck the magazine in an inner parka pocket, then ejected the shell from the pistol's chamber. This round followed the magazine into the inside pocket. As fast as Jim could, he patted the dead Gunny down. His efforts produced a spare twenty round magazine for the M-39 EMR in addition to a small taped bunch of rifle shells, both 7.62 and 5.56. He secured everything on or around his body, then tried to scramble along the roadside ditch away from the HUMVEE. He was not about to risk getting shot at by an unknown number of assailants just to get some wheels. He had made it from Alabama on foot so far, he'd make some more miles before he stopped.

Jim crawled and slid along the ditch for some fifty yards, then hunkered down in the snow banks around the road ditch. He hoped his white bed sheet poncho would help conceal him in the snow. Jim took a cheap kids binoculars out of a tactical vest pocket and scanned back towards the HUMVEE. A figure about the size of a younger teenager came from the opposite side of the road and approached the HUMVEE. Jim could just hear the figure call out.

"Grandpa's been shot."

Another voice called out to shut up. Two more adult size figures walked out onto the roadway. Jim used the binoculars with the help of the ambient light from the stars and a still visible Moon to watch the three humans drag the bodies of their comrades back to their side of the road as well as search and strip the dead Marine's bodies. It appeared the three people took everything of any usefulness, then disappeared back into the darkness from whence they came.

Seeing the figures leave the HUMVEE, Jim hot-footed it out of the area. He kept looking back for the pursuit which never materialized. An hour later, Jim found two vehicles wrecked in the ditch. He tried to conceal his steps off the road the best he could as he made his way to the two cars. One had half of the front windshield gone, so Jim crawled through the space and wormed his way into the back seat. He brushed a bit of ice and snow off the area and shucked his pack. Jim reloaded the Anaconda pistol, so it had the full six-round complement of live shells. Making himself as comfortable as possible, he used his sleeping bag to bundle up and was soon asleep, with the large revolver on his chest.

Jim James slept for a few hours and awoke as the Sun was slowly climbing in the sky. When he looked at the Sun in the clear sky, Jim tried to determine if it appeared smaller. All he really knew was the climate and temperature was a lot colder, so it was logical that the Earth had somehow shifted away from its significant heat and light source. What was important this day was whether some fellow humans would try and do him harm.

After a short conversation with himself, the survivor went back to the roadway and headed once again to the West. Jim's map scraps showed a possible crossroad that led back to the Interstate. He needed that route to cross a low point in the Gila Mountains called Telegraph Pass. Interstate 8 dropped down from Telegraph Pass to Yuma. Arizona, the location of the Marine Corps Airstation mentioned by the Gunney. Hopefully, the area would provide some civilization. Jim had worked in Yuma years ago.

Jim made it to the Interstate and began his trek westward. The sky was still bright, and the air temperature remained cold, although Jim thought it might be climbing above freezing due to the constant sunshine. As the grade began to steepen approaching the Pass, Jim came across a snow-covered multiple vehicle pile up. Jim had passed by or through many such scenes on his trek across what used to be the United States. A semi-truck and trailer had jackknifed across all lanes of the Interstate, probably during the snowstorm that dumped all the frozen water on the cars and other vehicles.

A large cross-country commercial bus had slid to a stop just feet from the semi- truck. Partially crushed under the front of the bus was a compact car which had stopped before it hit the semi. The coach had slammed into the compact and looked like it had tried to eat it. Jim paused for a moment and listened as he looked around. Nothing was moving, and Jim saw no fresh footprints in the virgin snow. He slowly walked to the bus' main front door. It took him a couple of minutes to move frozen snow from around the main door, then a few more and the use of a long piece of rebar to pry the frozen entrance open. He finally succeeded and mounted the stairs up to the driver's seat. It was empty.

Jim inched down the bus interior aisle, the .44 Magnum in his hand and the rifle slung. The interior was surprisingly dry, although a layer of ice was forming on the various windows. Jim had a tactical flashlight he had picked up before the Shift, as some called it, happened. He used it to examine all the seat areas until he saw some lumps in the very back, near the door to the bus lavatory. Jim shined the light and could make out two frozen bodies. There were a couple of small cases of some sort sitting on the floor in front of the corpses. Jim slid his feet forward, then bent over and picked up the cases, one by one, and set them on the next seat up. He patted down the frozen bodies as best he could. They seemed to be a male and female, dead from soon after everything went to Hell. All he found was a chocolate candy bar on the woman, nothing else. Jim was not about to try and pry frozen clothes off the two dead people. Thus, he turned his attention to the two pieces of small luggage.

One was a well-sized briefcase, the other was a large handbag. Jim dug thru his tactical vest pockets until he found his multitool. Using an integral screwdriver, he managed to pop the locked briefcase open. As he looked inside, the man whistled.

"Well," he said out loud, " that's two kilos of dope that never reached its destination." He poked a hole and managed to sample the frozen contraband with a finger to his mouth.

"Heroin. Maybe I can use it for scratch and buy something." Next to the two kilos was a cheap large cast metal pistol. Jim managed to pop the magazine out and look at the loaded. There were four .45 caliber rounds in good condition. He stripped the shells from the magazine and put them in a small leather pouch in his backpack. He had a half dozen bullets of various odd calibers in it, and the four rounds easily fit. The pistol was way too cheap and bulky for Jim's taste. Maybe if he hadn't obtained the .44 Colt Magnum, he might have thought different. Two pistols were enough for him. Ammunition doubled as cash in some locales.

Next, the survivor checked the oversized handbag. In it were some female accessories, a cellphone, a wad of cash, and a cheap small chromed automatic pistol. A quick check of it revealed it was a thirty-two with five live rounds in it. Jim sat staring at it for a moment, then made sure the safety was engaged as he slipped it into a pocket of his tactical pants. Now, this pistol was small enough to warrant keeping it. He added a small set of scissors to his booty and then tossed the handbag aside. The kilos of smack he wrapped up in a scrounged plastic garbage bag and then into his pack.

"Not a bad haul," he said to himself. "But I could use some more food items."

Jim sat thinking for a few minutes. Then, having arrived at a plan of action, Jim shucked his pack, the rifle, and his sheet poncho, followed by the army blanket. The M-14 and the Anaconda revolver he stashed under the seat behind the driver. Jim still had his Glock in his tactical vest. He had added the two recovered nine-millimeter rounds to the magazine the night before, so he now had a dozen shots readily available. That was enough for his short foray should someone else come in out of the cold with less than honorable intentions.

Jim exited the bus with the rebar pry in his gloved hands. A quick examination of the wrecked compact revealed the driver's side windshield had been shattered and then pried open. Someone had forced their way out, or another party had rescued them. Maybe someone from the bus had come to get the occupants of the compact the large vehicle had destroyed. Maybe that led to everyone trying to walk from the wreckage. Maybe the armed frozen druggies had chased everyone out. Jim snorted.

"That's an awful lot of 'maybes,'" he said to himself. He then set to work on getting into the compact car. Jim knew the 'maybes' would always be mysteries.

An hour later, a happy Jim re-entered the bus, whistling. The back seat and trunk of the compact had given up a treasure. Two loaves of frozen french bread, frozen squeeze bottles of butter and mayonnaise, a bunch of condiment packs, a frozen cheese tray, and then the piece de resistance; two frozen bottles of wine that had partially pooped corks but not broken. In a flash, Jim had a large empty coffee can and a former cookie tin out of his pack. The hole punched coffee can served as a sort of 'stove' that he put burnable fuel in, the cookie tin on top as the cooking pan. He soon had the contraption set up near the driver's seat, and a small fire in the coffee can lit. Jim used a dead pilots survival knife to separate the frozen cheese slice and hack apart one of the loaves of bread. The flame in the coffee can soon has the cheese melting and small pieces of bread thawing.

"Fondue," he chuckled to himself. Fifteen minutes later he was stuffing himself as he fed more cheese and bread to the cookie tin lid pan. His small cache of flammables was soon used up, so he went back to the dead woman's handbag. A wooden handled hairbrush and some note paper were quickly added to the small fire. He ate 'round two' and then decided he was satiated. He reclined back in the drivers padded seat.

"Ah, the good life," Jim said to himself as he let his food digest. He sipped on thawing wine from the bottle and thought back. The man called 'Grandpa' had been the fifth person Jim James had shot dead, the seventh he had put a bullet into. Then there was the guy he had laid out with the whiskey bottle over his head. And the woman he had stabbed. Jim shrugged. A full stomach and some alcohol made him reflective. A person did what he or she must to survive these days.

"At least I don't bushwhack people, Marines," Jim said out loud. He took another drink of the slushwine. Jim knew he talked to himself a lot, which was probably the first sign of insanity, madness.

But then, this was a mad, mad, world. Another drink, then he began to clean up and put away. You had to be ready to move at a moments notice. Vicious storms and people waited for no one.

As Jim made his bed in his sleeping bag, made sure his weapons were ready and in reach, he thought of the days ahead. Up at O Dark Thirty in the morning, a trudge up to Telegraph Pass. He knew not far down the other side of the Pass was an old U.S.Border Patrol Highway Checkpoint. There may be people at the place. The question would be, were they friendly? If the site was vacant, he might just hole up there for a bit, look for rabbits and other furry animals to eat. Coyotes and burrowing animals were adapting to the cold. As were deer and some zoo animals from northern climes which had been set free. Domestic cattle? Few and far between. Same with chickens and other domesticated fowl. Not to mention the scarcity of dogs. Man's Best Friend had, unfortunately, become a meat source for many. Jim was not one of them.

With those thoughts, Jim closed his eyes. Time to sleep.

Jim snapped out of his reverie at the memory of the good night's sleep.

The trip up to the pass was taking longer than expected, what with the crunchy snow and steepening grade of the Interstate. Night had fallen, and he still had a ways to go before the summit. Unless he found some shelter, this cold and clear night might not involve sleep as in the previous night. The night was still clear, and the stars were still bright in the evening snow, so there was that bit of positivity. Blowing snow in near blizzard conditions had led to many a frozen corpse.

Jim crunched up the eastbound Interstate 8 roadway as the steep graded curves cut this way and that, Damn, but things should even out soon if his memory was good. He had been this way in the past when he had an assignment in Arizona. And it had not been that long ago. Then, as if by magic, he looked up and saw the road began to flatten out just past the curve he was entering.

"Hot Damn. I think it's the summit." Again he talked loudly to himself.

Ten minutes later he was at what served as a summit for Telegraph Pass. Jim remembered a map note that the altitude here was about 3,000 feet or so, no more than a foothill when compared to Washington or Oregon terrain. Of course, this was Sothern Arizona.

Then he was at the several acre flat areas south of the Interstate which served as a lookout point for tourists down towards Yuma and the California border. Jammed in the now snow and ice covered open area was about a dozen motor vehicles. Jim approached gingerly, his M-14 held at low ready. There was ambient light from the stars and Moon, so Jim checked for recent footprints or signs of recent vehicle passage. Jim discovered none as he crunched towards the cars and trucks. Jim needed a place to stay during the cold night. He soon eyed some kind of delivery van, the signage on the side obscured by the packed on snow, ice, and dirt. The vehicle was set back behind some cars, so it was not easily spied from the road.

Jim reached the van and walked to the far passenger side. It looked as if the vehicle had been locked and left. He tried the passenger door, and it would not budge. Jim slung his rifle and dug out the piece of rebar from his pack. He broke the small wing window, knocked the glass away so he would not be cut, and managed to worm his arm in far enough to hit the locking button. When it seemed nothing happened, he managed to engage the inside door handle. Hearing and feeling something click. Jim pulled his arm back out and tried the outside door handle. The door latch mechanism was frozen shut. He cursed and beat on it with the piece of rebar. After about five minutes of beating and prying, he finally was rewarded with an open door. He clambered in and pulled out the dead females cell phone, Its excellent battery had kept a small charge as it sat turned off in the handbag. Jim now turned it on and used it as a flashlight. He whistled at what he saw,

The delivery van was full of flower arrangements and a couple of plants. Some florist had been unable to make its last set of deliveries. Jim stepped in and shucked his pack into the driver seat. He saw a small bucket containing odds and ends for flower arrangement, including a ball of twine. Jim used the cord to tie shut and secure the passenger side door. He shed his sheet and blanket ponchos, then unslung his rifle and laid it between some on the flower baskets. , Jim then began examining the contents of the van.

Among all the frosted and dead vegetation, he found some treasures. A couple of large decorative candles, several candy samplers, some jars of jams and jellies, a frozen and cracked bottle of champagne, and a small fruit cake he separated from the flower arrangements as he pushed the dead plant material to one side of the cargo area. He walked to the back of the vehicle and found a small toolbox. Among the rusty tools, he found a couple of road flares. Jim used some of the cellophane and wrapping material from the flower baskets to cover the flares before he placed them in his pack. A quick check of the glove box revealed the driver may have been a smoker as there was a partial book of matches hidden under the registration and insurance papers. He transferred the paperwork to his pack for future use as fuel or toilet paper.

After setting one of the decorative candles on the vehicle floor between the front seats, he tried to use the book of matches to light it. In the third match, he was able to light a small piece of tissue paper from a flower basket, then used that to light the candle. The flame burned bright, and he smiled.

"Home sweet home," he said to himself. He then began to create an evening meal as the candle flame slowly began to heat the interior of the delivery van. An old t-shirt rag he jammed into the broken wing window to keep out the breeze. Jim used the candle flame to toast a couple of leftover bread pieces from the first loaf. Then, he ate a piece of cheese wrapped and melted around a bit of sampler chocolate. All this he washed down with partially unfrozen champagne. In one of the flower baskets had been a gift coffee mug proclaiming "Happy Birthday Shelly!" As Jim drank from the mug, he wondered if Shelly had survived.

He went through half a bottle of slush champagne before he realized it. In addition to a buzz, he was beginning to get sleepy. He did a quick check of his weapons, making sure all of them had a slight veneer of lubrication, including the collapsible buttstock of the M-39 EMR. That and the mounted optics made this modernized version of the M-14 especially sweet. As Jim made his bed in the front of the cargo area, he thought for the first time in a long time that things may be looking up. Habit borne of survival meant that he had all his new found treasure stored in his pack and other gear, with his weapons in reach. The survivor took another gulp of champagne and laid his head down on a pillow of decorative tissue paper and a couple of small stuffed toys. He was soon asleep.

A figure all in black jumped at him, and Jim came up swinging and slashing with his survival knife. Then he woke up, sweating. It was all a nightmare. Jim stood up from his bed and stepped to the cab of the van and sat down in the driver's seat. He had not had a bad dream like that for a long time. He thought, maybe just having killed another human being led to it. Jim recovered the champagne bottle which still had a drink or two in it. He poured the wine in the "Happy Birthday" cup and sipped at it as he reflected. Since Jim had started on this journey months ago by car in Georgia, then on foot in Alabam, he had killed people. Were the ghosts following him? All through his trek, he had tried to avoid trouble, However, as recent events proved, there were people who caused pain.

Feeling an urge to pee at this early hour, but not wanting to step out in the cold, he recovered a vase from one of the decorative floral baskets and relieved himself in it. He set it carefully down by the gas pedal in front, then went back to his bed. He finished the champagne in the cup and laid down. Now, if he could just get some more sleep...

Vehicle engine noise split the stillness. Jim was up in a flash, grabbing his rifle. Crouching between the front bucket seats, he intently listened. The delivery van was blocked from view by several other vehicles. Thus, Jim hoped the car or truck would drive on by and down towards Yuma. It was night, and there seemed no reason to check out a bunch of abandoned transport on a cold night. Jim heard the vehicle stop near the clump of cars shielding the van. Shit.

As quietly as he could, Jim put his blanket and sheet ponchos on, then shouldered his pack. He checked his rifle out of habit to ensure there was a round in the chamber. As he listened for crunching footsteps in the snow, he cut the twine holding the passenger door shut. Jim slowly pushed the van door open and slid outside of the cab. As he snuck around the back of the van, trying not to crunch the frozen snow too loudly, he heard voices, one that sounded familiar.

"Grandma, the back left trailer wheel is in the ditch." It was the young male from the HUMVEE. And as Jim listened to the engine noise, he figured it was the HUMVEE, up and running.

"Goddammit, I got eyes!" Yelled Grandma."Lois, gun the engine while Joseph and I push."

"Okay, Mom," was the reply. A family unit thought Jim. The

family that bushwhacks together stays together. As Jim snuck among the abandoned vehicles, he noticed the Sun's rays were beginning to peak above the horizon. Another clear day it seemed. At least that was good luck. Now if these people would just be on their way…

"Goddammit." It was Grandma again. "Joseph, get the girls out of the horse trailer. They can help push. Just keep your rifle handy if they try to run."

Girls? A chill ran up his spine. Not some more Slavers, he hoped. Jim crouched low and slid behind a car, then went into a low crawl. He worked his way around the other cars and trucks until he had a good view of the HUMVEE and the trailer. The trailer was a beat up one for hauling horses. As Jim watched, the teenager named Joesph opened the back doors and began yelling at the occupants. In a few moments, a half dozen young girls and women, aged eight to eighteen, were hustled into the snow, The were wearing crude ponchos made from old blankets and were hooked together by a thin dog chain attached to dog collars around their throats. The oldest looking seemed to be hobbled with some lengths of rope. They were being kept as slaves.

A switch seemed to be flick in Jim James' brain as he began to shuck his pack and lay in the snow. A month ago, Jim had seen a similar situation. However, he lacked the necessary firepower and ammunition to do anything. Jim often cursed when the man thought of his inability to act. Not this time, he thought. His pack off, Jim extended the collapsible stock on his rifle as he slowly stood up. He checked and made sure his Glock was secured in his tactical vest under his ponchos. Jim assumed a Close Quarter Battle "Groucho" stance as he brought his rifle up to eye level and began to advance on the HUMVEE and the trailer. Grandma and Joseph were shoving the young females as they yelled instructions to help push the horse trailer from the snow hidden ditch. Lois, apparently Josephs mother, had the HUMVEE drivers side window open to hear what was going on.

Jim fired the first thirty caliber rifle shot into Grandma's left side, knocking her to the bottom of the ditch. His next round hit Joseph, who was pushing with the hostages on the rear left corner of the horse trailer. He flopped onto his back from the impact. Jim swung his rifle's aim to the driver's door and fired three rounds in rapid succession at Lois, just as she tried to duck down behind the HUMVEE steering wheel. The woman screamed and flopped over in the front seat area. Jim kept advancing as the six young women dove under the trailer as best they could. They had no idea who was shooting and at what target.

Jim reached the open driver's side window and glanced in. Lois was holding her left bicep with her right hand as blood flowed from a nasty wound. "Try to use that shotgun next to you, woman," Jim growled, " And I'll gut shoot you."

He moved on by and towards the other two threats. Grandma was laying cursing, her salvaged military body armor having stopped a full penetration of the thirty caliber bullet. Joseph twitched in the snow, a government-issued M-4 still slung over an arm.

"You fucker!" Grandma yelled. "You're the one who shot Grandpa!" She tried to reach something stuck in her waist belt, and Jim blew her brains out. One of the young girls screamed in a high pitched voice as Jim walked towards Joseph. The bullet which hit him had penetrated his stomach, blood flowing and staining the snow. Jim slung his rifle and pulled out his Glock from under his ponchos. With one hand freed now, Jim unlatched the M-4 sling from the weapon and took it from the dying teenager. He then stepped back up to the cab of the HUMVEE and laid the rifle on the engine hood.

Lois was trying to stop her profuse bleeding with a crude tourniquet made from a length of rope. Jim unlatched the door from the inside as he aimed his pistol at the head of a woman.

"Don't move!" The traveler ordered, then reached in and dragged the shotgun out by the butt. He stepped back and laid the weapon on the vehicle hood next to the M-4. Jim then moved back to the trailer. The survivor checked the body of Grandma for guns and recovered a .38 revolver. He stood back and looked at the cowered figures.

"Come on out and stand up,. No one is here to hurt you anymore."

Six womenfolk stood up, shivering from the cold. Jim picked out the oldest and addressed her. "What's your name?"

"Jean," the tall redhead replied.

"You eighteen?"

"Yes, Sir"

"So what happened?"

"At different times, they found us," Jean said. "They killed our people, our family. Said they would sell us. Or trade us for food, drink."

"Well, they tried to hijack some Marines. Bad decision," opined Jim.

"I heard them say they needed a new vehicle to haul the trailer," said Jean.

Jim looked at the others. They could all use a decent meal, some warm clothes. He sighed. Some people went out of their way to be assholes. "Okay, Ladies. Strip Grandma and the boy there of everything. You will give me any weapons and ammunition. And food, you divide among yourselves. Jean, come with me."

He and Jean went to the front of the vehicle. The woman named Lois was still trying to stop the hole in her arm from bleeding. Jim pointed at the two weapons.

"Jean, you know how to use those?"

"Yes, Sir. My Dad and Uncle showed me when…everything fell apart."

"Okay, Jean. They are yours. Collect ammunition for them as you search the vehicle and trailer."

As the redhead collected the two weapons, Jim walked over to the passenger side of the HUMVEE. The door was unlocked, so he opened it and dragged Lois out as she cried in pain.

"Okay, Bitch. Your son and mother are dead. You're next if you don't tell me why you were coming this way."

"We're supposed to meet," she sobbed, "a man who goes by Greybeard."

"Why?"

"To trade a couple of girls for a couple of dogs." Jim frowned. Dogs? People for dogs? Why?

"Why the trade?"

"We can eat dogs. We could breed them…then eat them."

"Bitch, you and yours are sure shortsighted," said Jim. " If you raise and train the dogs, they'll help you survive. Alright, when is this Grey Beard supposed to arrive?"

"After sunrise. He is supposed to…drive a snowmobile. We talked to him on a CB Radio we have in the HUMVEE." Lois began to stagger a bit. Jim grabbed her and half walked, half dragged her to the back of the trailer. He forced her in the horse trailer and shut the gate on the rear. Jim next checked on the six young women. Jean was organizing them and their booty, Grandma and Joseph laying dead wearing just their underwear in the snow. The had piled the recovered items onto Joseph's parka. Jim picked through it, found an odd .308 round that would fit his M-14.

"Take the rest and get in the Humvee. Turn the heater on and warm up, make sure any holes in the windows are covered up. Keep enough fuel in the vehicle to make it down towards Yuma. You have guns to protect yourself until you can find a place to stay."

"Mister," a young voice piped up. "You can't come with us?"

"I do better on my own, Missy. But first I have to take care of something."

About an hour later, as the Sun rose higher, a snowmobile pulling a small homemade trailer drove up into the vehicle parking area. A beefy man shut off the engine, dismounted and took off his helmet. His face was covered by a grey beard that was peppered with ice droplets.

"Hey, People." He called out as he walked towards the Humvee. "Greybeard here for the trade. I ain't got..."

A rifle shot blew his head apart like a dropped ripe watermelon. Greybeard toppled over like a chopped tree. Jim came from his concealed position among the abandoned cars. He went to the crude trailer and found two barely weaned pups. To Jim, they looked like maybe a Husky mix. They were wrapped up in a thick blanket, and Jim added a t-shirt he had recovered from the florist van to their bedding. He revved up the snowmobile, then searched Greybeards body and the snowmobile. He found a forty-five automatic on him and a sawed-off twelve gauge in the saddlebags of the snowmobile. In the saddlebags were also some puppy food and some jerked meat. There was also a bottle of some type of rotgut moonshine.

Jim walked back to the HUMVEE, where the six young women were. "How much fuel you have, Jean?"

"About a quarter of a tank, sir."

"Okay. You six are on your own. You have weapons, food, and we unhooked that trailer. I'll leave it up to you if you want to bring Lois along."

"I don't think so, Sir," replied Jean. A young voice came from the back.

"Mister, can't you come with?"

"No. Go to Yuma. You 'll pass an abandoned Border Patrol checkpoint if it hasn't burnt down. Don't stop. Get into Yuma where there may be some civilization."

"Thank You, Sir," the redhead said. "We'll…"

"Goodbye." Jim turned around and walked to the Snowmobile. He revved it up, then slowly turned it around, crude trailer and all. Jim James drove down the highway against the official traffic flow long since gone. Five minutes later, he pulled in behind the abandoned Border Patrol Checkpoint. The buildings were still in one piece, although Jim would have to dig his way in. He checked on the pups, who were snuggled together and fast asleep.

Jim took out an entrenching tool he had found in the HUMVEE and began to dig a pathway to the main door. "Home Sweet Home," he said. He and the pups would do just fine. When they were older, he 'd risk a trip into Yuma and see if the Marines had a Veterinarian.

He sure liked Dogs more than Humans. Dogs were just better People.

PHILIA
BY ELIZA LOEB

Chapter 1

She sat atop the tower as night fell upon the horizon and cast its shadows throughout the city. Her thoughts roamed as they usually would this time of day and she hardly had anything clear to say about it. To some, she was your typical homeless millennial taking refuge under some bridge or another that no one likes to pay any sort of attention to. To others, those of the supernatural variety, she was a misplaced goddess of love. She knew her name, others only whispered it without realizing that she was even nearby. And like any goddess of love and beauty, she often grew angry at the sheer lack of knowledge that modern day humans had behind it.

"By the god's little sister, you look terrible," came a low, gruff voice.

Her golden eyes peered up from beneath a turquoise hoodie, all too aware of who had approached. His eyes were a steely blue, cold as death as they peered through the darkness as his dreadlocks had been pulled back into a ponytail, revealing handsome face with high cheekbones and dusky skin.

"So death has come to greet me in my darkest hour?" Hathor asked as she pulled her hood back. "Wouldn't you call that a bit cliché, Anubis?" She studied him closely, pursing her lips as he stood beside her in a suit with black and gray undertones, lightly accessorized with a single white scarf.

"I've come to take you home." Anubis answered. "The streets are no place for you."

"But what if I want to live on the streets?" she asked.

"Then Horus will come and take you by force."

Hathor roles her eyes and shifts as she makes a movement to stand. "When I said he and I were done, I meant it."

"But the gods marry—"

"The gods are flawed."

Her voice was full of agitation as she sighed and waved her elder brother away. Too long had she been revered by mortals looking for romantic love. Too long had she been perceived as the *wife* of Horus. And too long had she been used and mistreated for representing anything *but* lovers when her own marriage ended because she had no passion for a man who was supposedly the god of kings. And oh... did she hate being a side piece for him. And Anubis knew it.

"He can give you security."

Security? Is that what it was? Was this the damn eighteen hundreds where a woman gave herself to a wealthy man for the sake of security? Her brother was smarter than that. She was a deity who, despite her current disposition could and should be revered. Love had a very thin border with hate and is often in league with passion. To which, she had a lot of passion to go around.

"I can make my own security, brother."

"So you want to end up like the greeks?"

"The Greeks are still celebrated and live very comfortably."

"And their marriages are miserable."

"As was mine!"

Anubis took a step back, eyeing his younger sister for a brief moment before sighing in defeat. Hathor, had not realized that she had raised her voice. Yet now, there was a great deal of contempt for her brothers' visit. And with a single gust of wind, he dispersed into sand and left her alone.

Days passed, then weeks and Hathor never saw her brother. Rather, she stayed beside herself and wandered the streets, giving what she could to those who needed it most and only taking what was necessary for her. Eventually the winter came, and a key was dropped before her. She had given what she could, only taking what was necessary. Strangers on the street recognized her as a giver, referring to her as kind and loving and some whispered among themselves, asking why. She never gave them a name, she never told them to repay her or asked for anything in return, yet they still wondered.

"That kindness is gonna kill you, sweetheart," a man said to her one day. She shrugged it off, neither caring nor paying mind to his words.

Her gold eyes flickered beneath the street lamp as she leaned against the aluminum fence. The night air was cold and biting, with only a take away of soup to warm her hands. Seagulls could be heard, crying loudly to one and other in the distance. They were possibly scouring for food.

"Out here again?" asked an all too familiar voice.

Hathor looked up to find a taller man standing beside them. Long red hair draped over his shoulders as a hood cast a shadow over his face. She smiled in greeting, as if meeting an old friend for the first time in a while.

"You sound displeased." She laughed, looking out at city.

Seattle had been particularly lovely on quiet nights like these. If one had been close enough to the water, they could hear the sounds of the water splashing along the shore, brushing along the sands as if they were supposed to be whispering terrible secrets to the earth.

"Not with you, dear friend," the man said in response.

"But some of the humans I see in these parts."

Hathor's smile soon faded to that of a knowing look. The man standing near her had seen just as many horrors as she had. They had both seen the wars of their people, the fates of children left in the woods to die, the cruel hands of war and famine reaching into the deep crevices of the earth before inviting their companions death and pestilence to join in the tragedies.

"What happened?" she asked.

"Do you know of the term, A mother is god in the eyes of her child?"

Her eyes fixed on her friends face as she gently touched his shoulder. His face was twisted into a grimace as he looked away from her. He had seen something that disgusted him and she knew it. Often did he speak to her about his children, often had he beamed with pride as she asked. When they had gone to parks, he would take delight in watching the children play, encouraging their antics as they made up games or collaborated outlandish schemes to fuel their imaginations. And much without their knowing would throw in little illusions every now and again to help with the more whimsical aspects of their game.

"I know it well."

Her friend looks down at her with earnest as he slowly begins to open his mouth to say something, clamping it shut and gritting his teeth as he runs his hands through his hair, pushing back his hood.

"Today I saw a mother using her child as a crutch to get more money."

"You don't know that."

"But I do."

She sighed and gestured for him to continue, and he looked puzzled for a moment. As if to search for the correct words in a puzzle.

"Hatti, I see this woman every single day. I see her sitting at different street corners, I see her perching in different spaces of the city. I hear her child complain that they are hungry, pleading for food at night. I see people give her money and every single time she gets money, I stand and wait. Part of me hopes that this woman will come to her senses, while another part of me feels as though I am going insane for expecting a different result."

"Well, you do represent mental illness among other things…"

"Not helping, Hatti."

"Sorry."

The man turned and pressed his forehead against the fence, sighing in exasperation as he curled his fingers between the wires. There was a long silence that followed and Hathor found herself unsure of the situation. She questioned the situation, trying to find reason as to observe and make a judgement for herself. She had seen many children put in to the system by authorities, having been torn from a loving home for so much as a complaint regarding an inkling of neglect. She had seen families try and fail to fight the system and yet….

"Loki…" she pressed. "May I see this woman?"

Loki straightened himself and didn't bother to look at her this time. His expression was solemn, as though he was the father of the child in question.

"Yeah."

Chapter 2

Marcie Henderson *hated* taking the medicine. She hated the long grueling days of not knowing the difference between her left or right, and she hated not having friends or going to school.

"You have to *work* for your food," her mother had told her.

Often times, when she did work, she found that it would be for nothing. And when she did complain, she would either be stricken or threatened with death. The worse thing that came to mind, though, was something worse. She had seen older girls being traded off for *medicine*. *Medicine* was the stuff that all of the money went to, that their mother never bothered to see a doctor for. *Medicine* had many other names, more commonly known as crystal.

Marcie knew of other families in her situation. She would sometimes watch as they went to community gatherings to get a bite to eat, or safe places to spend the day while parents look for jobs to support themselves and their kids. Yet, she wouldn't dare bring her mother to those places. Those places often had rules. And rules were what separated children from single parents. And if that happened, who knew what would happen to her mother.

Her stomach twisted and growled, causing her insides to ache as hunger had begun to overtake her. She needed food, yet was unsure where to get any. She looked to the side to a cardboard mat where her mother slept. If the growling grew louder, she would surely be beaten. She slowly slipped out from beneath the sleeping bag they had gotten from a nearby day shelter, tiptoeing away from their sleeping area to try and scour for food and completely unaware of who might be following. She turned several corners and slipped in to a nearby 365 stop. She shivered as the warmth hit her, reveling in the sensation as her toes curled in the too big pair of tennis shoes she had yet to grow in to. She sighed with delight as she hugged herself, twisting and spinning in the warmth.

"Can I help you with something, little girl?" asked a feminine voice.

Marcie was pulled from her moment of warmth and blushed with embarrassment as she looked down. The woman who had been watching her had deeply tanned skin. Her hair had been pulled back in to a ponytail as bags had formed under her eyes and she looked to be no older than maybe her late twenties to early thirties. Likely someone who had been working a night shift.

"I was just trying to get warm ma'am."

"Don't you have a home to do that?"

It would be nice to have a home, she thought. She felt a heavy lump form in her throat as she looked around for an excuse as she slid her hands into her pockets. She didn't know how to answer the woman.

"Homes have rules."

The woman raised a brow with a puzzled expression as she crossed her arms. Was it something that Marcie had said? The woman craned her neck, trying to see if her mother had been nearby, and stepped out from behind the counter to step out the door for a brief moment. Her mother had been nowhere to be found. Once the woman had confirmed her suspicions, she moved her eyes back to Marcie, who now had a frightened look.

"Have you eaten?" she asked.

Marcie shook her head.

The woman sighed and pulled her behind the counter, pulling up a stool for her to sit. And like that, she was beginning to panic. Her thoughts were racing at nearly what seemed a million miles a minute and she couldn't stop them, and she began to cry. The woman looked back to her with a platter full of food and quickly set it aside to kneel before her and wipe her tears away. Marcie pushed her hands away and tried to wipe her tears away by herself. She tried to not be weak before a stranger. She tried to stop crying.

"Why are you crying? Did somebody hurt you?"

She shook her head and sniffled. Mucus had began to run from her nose, mixing in with her tears as she tried to calm herself down.

"I don't want to be taken away from my mom." Marcie pleaded.

"Well honey, by the looks of things, you're hungry and cold and she is nowhere to be found."

Marcie paused and looked up at the woman as if to ask what the woman meant. The woman simply held the platter of food before her, as though she hadn't said what she had.

"You don't have to finish it all, you just have to eat enough to stop the growling."

"But ma'am, I don't have any mon-"

"Don't worry about it."

"I don't even know your name."

"You can call me Hatti."

Hatti's golden eyes flickered in the light as she straightened and immediately, Marcie could see the movement of a familiar jacket at the corner of her eye. She paled, recognizing the rapid and jerked movements of her mother as she stormed in to the shop, looking around frantically and landing her eyes on Marcie, fixating them on her as she sneered.

"Are you stealing food now, ya little thief?" the woman hissed.

Thin legs began to stalk forward as Marcie backed into a corner. Her breathing became heavy as she knew what was going to come next. She cried out, babbling pleas and begging for forgiveness, afraid of what was to come, despite how futile they were. Loud shouting soon filled the shop as Hatti stepped between the two and pressed the woman back.

"She's a thief! She's manipulating you into feeling sorry for her so you can give her food!" her mother shrieked. Hatti looked back at her with a hard stare and then back to her mother as she lunged at Hatti, only to be shoved away.

"Get the fuck out of my shop," Hatti said coolly, pointing toward the door as she kept a firm barrier between the other woman and Marcie. The other woman narrowed her eyes at the little girl and Hatti stepped in her line of sight.

"Sweetheart, I suggest that you keep your eyes on me," the taller woman warned. "Because that little girl is not the one you're gonna deal with."

The smaller woman squared her shoulders as she did her best to match up to her new opponent, only to be shoved away again and stared down, making her way to the door.

Hatti flipped the sign as she crossed her arms, sneering as she watched Marcie's mother skitter away. Her attention moved back to Marcie and her expression softened.

"Are you hurt?"

Marcie shook her head.

"Good, because I am going to call child services."

Chapter 3

She sat inside the office, inhaling the smell of stale paint and printer ink for what seemed like a good while. She jerked at the slightest noise, in fear of being taken away by bad people as moment after moment passed. The kind lady could have also been one of the bad people. She did send her mother away and promised to protect her. Now her mother was nowhere to be found.

"Marcie?"

Marcie looked up to see Hatti smiling down at her.

"If you don't mind, you're going to be staying with me and a friend of mine for a little while."

"What about my mom?"

Hatti looks hesitant, now. Marcie feels panic over take her again, as she worries that something is going to happen.

"Your mom had you in very unstable conditions and—"

"She *needs* me!"

"Marcie, your mom neglected to feed you for what seemed like two weeks."

"I was supposed to work for my food!"

"What kind of parent makes their kid work for their food?"

It was like she was struck without being touched. She wanted to say all kinds of parents. She wanted to say that it was parents who wanted to teach their children about the truth of hard knocks, and wanted them to be independent. Those parents were the sort who had taught their children how to survive. Yet her mind raced when her thoughts returned to loving families in her situation. She thought of the parents who were trying to find jobs in hopes of actually caring for their families. She recalled how They kept their children.

"Why did you take me away from my mom?"

The woman in front of her sighed. Her eyes searched for an answer as she moved to sit next to Marcie, leaning back to figure out how to answer her question.

"When I was younger, I married a boy who I and everybody down the street thought to be the sun. They praised him every single day. Women worshipped the ground he walked on and then me for walking with him. But one day, he showed his true colors to me."

Marcie could see Hatti struggling with words as she clenched and curled her fingers together. "He struck me in ways that he felt allowed to, in certain situations, he intimidated me, manipulated me until I began to question my own judgement, and for a really long time, I believed the things he would say. I believed that the things he did were my fault."

"What happened?"

"I left him."

"Why?"

"Because sometimes, the people who say that the need us, only say that they need us to keep us for their own benefit."

Marcie looked down, and she had been unsure as to how she should react. Everything seemed to be happening fast and she couldn't find the breaks. It was like she was riding a bike down the hill and she couldn't slow down or slow herself to a stop and she was scared. She wanted her mom, but at the same time hoped that her mother would never find her or hurt her. And she barely knew the woman sitting beside her, but she had been much nicer to her than the one she had chased off. She wondered how the woman named Hatti knew that she was hungry, or potentially in danger.

Hathor, in all honesty, had almost about as much experience with children as anyone in this day and age, yet she was going to stand firm in her decision to help the little girl beside her. Everything she saw in her mothers' eyes, resembled what she saw in her ex-husbands eyes the day he knew that he was about to lose control. She recalled how he lifted a sword and gave her two options, thinking that she would choose either and grit her teeth at how juvenile he came off for throwing a tantrum. Yet like Marcie's mother, his intent had been to kill or in the very least, cause lifelong damage. She was pulled from her thoughts as a soft tapping echoed from around the corner. Balloons could be seen beyond the cubicles as they moved through a maze of what seemed to be a corporate jungle. A head of long red hair peaked over the edges and the tapping proceeded to grow louder and louder until a pale, but handsome man with his hair twisted into a braid appeared before them, throwing confetti in the air as he beamed down at the two with excitement.

"Could you make any more of a dramatic entrance?" she chided in jest.

"I could have ridden a circus ball over, but that might have taken away from the work load."

Hathor turns her attention back to Marcie with a bewildered look, sighing as she points to Loki with her thumb.

"Do you see what I have to deal with?"

As the year went by, the trio found somewhat of a disorganized balance beneath the roof that they had shared. Hathor, or Hatti, as Marcie had referred to her, would walk Marcie to school and then disappear for the rest of the day, not returning until the clock struck ten. Loki often stuck around for after school programs that had helped Marcie catch up to her peers and stuck with her as though he were a devoted father, reassuring her that everything happens at its own pace and assisting her with her basic needs. Yet she couldn't help but wonder why there seemed to be a need for separation. Marcie began to worry that Hatti no longer had time for her, let alone wanted anything to do with her.

"Why isn't Hatti home?" she asked one night.

Loki paused, looking up from a piece of math homework he had been looking over. She is unsure of what to make of his puzzled expression as he looks to her.

"That's a bit difficult to explain," he says softly, looking for the right words.

"But I suppose it would be easier to show you."

She had made her rounds accordingly, working tirelessly to

ensure that she could inspire as much compassion amongst the masses as possible. Yet lately she had begun to grow weary. There was a part of her that demanded a cease and desist, a small fraction that constantly told her to go home. Marcie was probably sitting up on the couch, hoping for her to come in and talk about her day and share stories on what silly things either had encountered. And yet, every time she returned, the little girl she had met would be passed out in her bed. But tonight… tonight seemed a little different despite being the middle of winter. The night was biting as the stars speckled the night sky, and for once in her long and seemingly endless life, she had no idea of what was to come. For some reason, she had forgotten her purpose in living on the streets to begin with.

"By the gods, Hatti, you look terrible."

Hathor looked up to find two individuals standing just several feet away from her. One, a very tall and pale handsome man, with his long red hair twisted into a braid, and the other, a little human girl who could almost be his with the twinkle in her emerald green eyes.

"For a moment I thought you were my brother," she said as Loki and Marcie approached, handing her a cup of hot cocoa.

"Old friend," Loki began. "I believe you and I have both established that to err is human."

The taller of the two smiled, moving to take her hand in his as he pressed his lips to her head. They both pulled Marcie close as if to remind her that she is safe and Hathor has a warm home to go to.

Loki looked upon his new family with a knowing smile, having nothing but hope for the coming future.

BATS
BY SHEILA MENGERT

Leo P. Amorth was not a man who delighted in nor appreciated nuance or ambiguity; everything had its use and right reason dictated that use. There was a correct way to do everything and rules were designed to enlighten the ignorant and to ensure compliance. Each field of human endeavor possessed its own science and technique to which by some marvelous quality of personal enlightenment he had at least some proximate access and understanding. A mere hint was adequate to open vast vistas of speculation on his part that led him to conclusions that made further inquiry superfluous. For these reasons it had always puzzled him why his daughter, the sole genetic carrier of his enlightened genes, should be the type of girl, and now young woman, that she had turned out to be. He had not expected that she would turn out to be a carbon copy of her father, her mere sex of course made that impossible. He had hoped though for a sensible girl grounded in science, good at mathematics, and immune as far as possible from the eccentric whims of her gender. Imagine his surprise and impatience then when the years disclosed that his offspring was introspective, artistic, and prey to any number of peculiar obsessions and compulsions.

As a child she had picked at her skin, become attached to various unsuitable objects to which she had given names, and would cry if every bean in a can of beans was not shaken out lest it be left behind divorced from its fellows and have surrendered its little bean-life in vain. She carried sensitivity beyond the religious mandate of charity; even that supreme Christian mandate it seemed to him should not preclude sound business sense. Where would his enterprises have been if he had not known early on that the world is a jungle? From whence then would have come the funds to pay for her costly schooling in that vague and pointless series of pursuits called "the humanities." He had hoped that the ever-practical Jesuits would knock some sense into her when she enrolled in a Jesuit college, but alas she had emerged, temperamentally speaking, little different after four years than when she went in.

Her major altered each quarter. At first she was convinced that she should be a marine biologist and raise algae to feed starving people. Before she ended her freshman year this had changed to being a veterinarian and an obsession with afghan hounds. In her sophomore year she had only emerged for classes and then went back to her dorm room where she remained in pajamas all afternoon reading the novels of the Bronte sisters. It was not until her junior year that she abandoned the sciences forever and began that most inconclusive of all pursuits, the study of philosophy.

After graduation she had stumbled about in various underpaid employments, reading all the time in various fields from Mayan culture to the causes of the demise of the Incas. She had cried that Archbishop Oscar Romero of El Salvador had been killed because he had supported the cause of the workers. Meanwhile she was indifferent to the appeals from various obscure congregations of brothers and sisters, publishers of tracts on avoiding countless assorted sins, whose efforts were well within the normal parameters of Catholic apostolic missions. Ritual took second place in her mind to the relief of suffering whereas for her father they were the sum and total of the life of a man destined for heaven.

Leo had always taken pride in his middle name, Pius, the appellation of so many Popes of the 20th century. These men had their pontificates at the high-water mark of Catholic unity and mystique. To lose the legacy of these men in a welter of pop culture guitar-masses and hand-shaking had begun the undoing of the work of centuries in his opinion. His beliefs were sincere if one-sided. He allowed God to be God and God liked prayers the more the better. Leo also sincerely loved the daughter that he could not understand and was concerned about whether when he had shuffled off this mortal condition they would meet again in the celestial courts if she failed to change her ways. Leo placed his trust in God and in the approved means of guaranteeing access to him while for Tiffany everything was provisional, contingent, and problematic. She appeared to be rooted in her suffering and to cherish her doubts. This was most evident in her fears and in her occasional spasms of anger. They showed a spirit grounded in opposition and lack of trust in the order of God's creation. This was out and out impiety in her father's estimation and from its signs Leo at last deduced the cause: Tiffany Amorth was possessed by the devil.

The most salient sign of her spiritual affliction was one of her chief fears. Tiffany Amorth was dreadfully afraid of bats. Sooner or later everyone who knew anything about Tiffany Amorth at all became aware of this fact about her. For her twilight brought forth a feeling of dread. No peasant in Transylvania taking cover behind closed doors as the evening shadows lengthened over the Carpathian Mountains was more careful of avoiding bats than she. It was not that she begrudged the ugly little winged things their humble insectivorous existence; she was well aware of the benefits bestowed upon mankind by their habit of consuming tons of malicious insects and turning them into bat guano in trees or attics as long as the attic wasn't in her house. She entertained no attitude or bias of invidious discrimination towards them because they liked to hang in little colonies scratching and biting each other with their nasty little claws. As long as they stayed away from her she was quite satisfied to let them be. She had even felt a pang of sympathy for them when she heard that they had acquired a white nose-fungus that was doing them in by the thousands.

So it must be made clear that Tiffany harbored no ill-feelings to bats as examples of the wonderful results of mutation and selection by mindless nature or if theologically speaking that Noah had managed to catch a few and keep them aboard the arc while the waters of the flood soaked into the soils of Mesopotamia. The problem that Tiffany had with bats was that they often acquired rabies due to their promiscuous habit of biting and scratching each other whether in casual contact or fooling around back at the cave.

Tiffany had been terrified of Rabies ever since she had watched good and faithful Old Yeller turn unaccountably into a slathering beast because of rabies. Oh, and people could get it too she was told. She had been an impressionable child. She had taken to heart all the manner of things in every American home that could kill you dead if you touched them and as a result was a model child. No ambulance had ever arrived to take her to the nearest hospital to pump out her stomach. She gave a wide berth to any suspicious or noxious substances although she had been curious from time to time why grownups kept so many dreadful items in their homes.

These early experiences, perhaps building upon a naturally nervous nature, had made Tiffany a fearful and mistrustful child. She was raised without brothers or sisters and adapted as best she could to a world of adults whose province was to minimize whatever natural harms flow from having curious and assertive children underfoot. Later on when she was sent to a psychiatrist to diagnose the cause of her various obsessions he had suggested that she had been raised in a perfectionist environment beset by rules and prohibitions. Both of her parents had pointed at the other and the sessions were terminated after the initial three sessions. When she had asked about it she was told that the doctor had attributed the whole thing to rigid toilet training and was clearly a dirty-minded Freudian. The result was that Tiffany remained a fearful child and a lonely one.

It is not to be presumed however that Tiffany showed no courage. She had not even cried for instance when she had been hit by a car in the second grade and knocked unconscious. She had been quite embarrassed by the whole incident and desired to hush it up as soon as possible. After all, she had been warned not to run into the street without looking. Her fears were not of pain, loss, or rejection. She took these for granted in each new school to which she was sent. Her fear was rather of the dark and inscrutable workings of nature manifest in the world of predatory lower life.

Tiffany kept a running profile in her head of the world's foremost pathogens and where they liked to hang out. She was well-read and *au courant* with all manner of ecological issues. She knew for instance that global warming was inviting certain noxious South American vectors for disease closer year by year and that was not even considering the dreadful things you could catch that were already here. There was Lyme Disease for instance on the East Coast. There was Dengue Fever in Florida. Chagas and the dread Kissing Bugs that carried it were fortunately no closer than Mexico. Mad Cow Disease had raised fears and then seemingly spread no further than the British Isles and perhaps Canada although she still refused to eat t-bone steaks just to be sure. Tiffany knew all about Tsetse Flies and African Sleeping Sickness and those horrible flies that leave their larvae within you to feed and crawl about. But none of these dreadful things could match rabies which killed anyone who ever showed symptoms. No one could save you. Rabies was sort of like a physical analogue to double-predestination in Calvinist theology. If God predestined you to hell then all the virtues in the world couldn't save you and who was to say whether He had already done so. After all, Tiffany had been a headache with all of her fears. It was not however until her late twenties that her father concluded that Tiffany must be possessed by the devil to be so afraid of bats. No one else in the family was afraid of the little beasts that would fly at you on warm summer nights and then whirl away at the last instant a scant foot from your face. It was even rather fun; but not for Tiffany. She knew only that there was a virus there perhaps that once in your body would crawl along your nerve fibers to your brain and then make you mad before you subsided into dreadful paralysis and death.

The conclusion that she was possessed though was something of a novelty. To make out of her obsessive fear some sort of moral failing seemed to be unfair. It showed lack of empathy and patience on the part of those who did not share her vividness of imagination. It was not as though what she feared was impossible. The connection was not so remote as to be unfathomable. There are people who refuse to drive again after a car wreck or who refuse to drink brandy again after spending a night bent retching over a toilet bowl after too many stingers. Not everybody can stand everything! But none of this mattered to those who looked at Tiffany now and saw that she had made herself a Bride of Satan, a witch, by virtue of not standing proud and firm as all good Americans should do when faced by such ubiquitous denizens as bats. "It's a sin to be afraid," her father had said. The question was what to do about it. A few discrete inquiries seemed the best course to pursue so a concerned letter was sent by her father to the local parish priest. It read as follows:

Dear Reverend Father------,

I am writing to you on a most painful matter. You may recall meeting my daughter Tiffany after mass shortly after your transfer to our parish. I must tell you as her father that the girl has always been a source of anxiety for us, her parents. She is not without certain creative gifts but she spends entirely too much time alone. She is in her late twenties, dates seldom, and in many ways fails to thrive and to mature like other girls her age. I have reached the age where I would like to retire and travel, but concern for our daughter makes us hesitate to leave her alone. When we take her to visit her cousins she insists that she must be inside before the bats come out at night, which spoils late family softball games at the city park. She runs and jumps into the car before the sun sets and won't emerge again until we are in the garage at our house with the garage door closed. This would be bad enough, but she now won't come out to our lake cabin because we found mice droppings on the couch and she's afraid of getting Hantavirus. We need an exorcism. Can you help?

A week later the following answer was received.

Dear Mr. Amorth:

Regarding your suspicions that your daughter is possessed by the devil because of her phobic fear of bats and mice, I can only tell you that a quick review of the literature on the subject and the requirements of Canon Law do not show fear of bats as one of the qualifying criteria that must be presented to the local ordinary. Bishop------- requires more before he will authorize an exorcism. I must therefore refer you back to the more customary channels for problems such as those manifested by your daughter. I am including a name of a local psychologist, a good Catholic and a fine man who may be of help to you. Naturally I will keep your daughter in my prayers.

Yours in our Lord,

Rev. -----------

Since an appeal to the Church had failed, her family turned to the social sciences for help. A few days later at her family's insistence Tiffany reported to a high and austere building in downtown Seattle for her first appointment. Dr. --------- makes it a habit to record his sessions and the following extract is included here...

Extract from Session 1 - Tiffany Amorth

Hello Tiffany. I am Dr. ------ Please sit down and make yourself comfortable. Can I get you anything?

No thank you.

This will be our initial session and I would like to explore with you the course that therapy with me will entail. If you have any questions at any time feel free to ask me.

Very well. When does the exorcism begin?

I beg your pardon?

The exorcism; my parents think I need an exorcism because I'm afraid of bats and oh, of mice too.

I see. Well it always helps to get these issues on the record but I think we should backtrack a little. Would that be alright? Have you read the patient intake form and initialed the permissions contained there? Very good. Then I think we can proceed a bit. I think it is important that you be here because you want to be and not out of any sort of coercion, and let me disabuse you immediately of any idea that I conduct exorcisms.

I really didn't think you did.

Right. But I am curious about how you feel about being called possessed by your father.

It makes me angry.

Um hum. Why angry?

Because it's so stupid!

That you're afraid of bats and mice?

No, that's not it. I think it's stupid that they don't know or care *why* I'm afraid of bats and mice.

Why are you?

Because I don't want to die!

Do you think bats and mice will kill you?

No! That's just it! I love animals, but I hate the diseases that some of them carry. Is that so wrong?

That seems rational to me.

Then why am I here?

I don't know. Why are you here?

Because I'm afraid all the time; I don't feel in control.

Is it so important that you be in control?

My father always is.

Are bats and mice everywhere in your world?

No of course not, but there are other things too.

What things?

Things that carry death.

You mean like cars and airplanes and clogged arteries.

No.

Those things kill more people than Rabies and Hantavirus.

How did you know I'm scared specifically of Rabies and Hantavirus?

Many of my patients are afraid of deadly germs.

But are they possessed by the devil?

No. Some drink a little too much but that's about as spirit-based as it gets. Would you say that you are a happy young woman?

[Silence]

No.

Why not?

My father drives me crazy.

That sounds perfectly normal to me.

[Patient smiles]

How does he drive you crazy?

He doesn't really see me.

You mean that he doesn't look at you?

Oh, he looks; he just doesn't see me.

What do you expect him to see?

Me!

And who are you?

[Silence]

I don't know.

That's what we may discover together if you choose to remain in therapy with me.

[Silence]

You think you can unmask me.

Do you wear masks?

Everybody does.

I see. You mean people are inauthentic?

I mean they are liars.

Is this you talking?

Yes, who would it be?

You said that you didn't know who you were.

I mean in detail. I do know when I'm feeling something. I feel a lot. I'm very passionate about things.

Are you?

Yes. I feel intensely. If I hate you I will want to see you burning up. If I love you I will want you to be mine forever and never leave.

Are you ever just indifferent or non-committal about things?

Seldom.

Um hum.

I hope you aren't going to go um hum all the time when we talk!

Does that bother you?

It makes me feel like you're judging me.

Do people judge you?

All the time.

And it makes you angry?

It pisses me off!

Do you talk like that around your father?

Are you my father?

[Silence]

No. I'm your therapist, if you want me to be.

I'm sorry.

Why?

Because it wasn't your fault. I'm just touchy. My father says I'm highly-strung.

I thought you were possessed.

That too.

Would you say you are depressed?

Sometimes, but mostly I am angry and afraid.

In that order?

No, first I'm afraid and then I am angry.

Not the other way around?

[Silence]

Well uh yes. Sometimes I'm angry and I'm afraid people will retaliate against me.

Don't you deserve to be angry sometimes?

Not when I have been so blessed.

How are you blessed?

I'm not starving. I have clothes to wear and a place to live.

Is that enough?

More than I deserve.

Who told you that?

I just feel it; that's all.

[Pause]

Um, how does therapy work … with you?

Well, I concentrate on the particular. What you are feeling right now and on particular incidents in your life.

When I am asked to recall memorable incidents my immediate impulse is to see the particular as subsumed beneath an underlying generality.

I see. But what if what matters is precisely the unique and unrepeatable experience.

Then I would say that the moment that we attempt to communicate it or even to formulate it that we are constricted by linguistic conventions which brings us right back to generalities. We are dogged by convention even in our perceptual categories; to see is already to interpret.

You sound a bit more sophisticated now.

I majored in philosophy in college.

So I better not try and bullshit you.

I wouldn't advise it.

[Both smile]

So you find it difficult to approach matters with what might be called a fresh slate.

Oh, I am not speaking personally you understand. I am discussing human conscious functioning in general—we perceive, think and judge by putting matters into a preexisting context so that nothing stands apart as an isolated fact.

I see but surely there is a place for the here and now isn't there. I mean you are here now in this room and we have set aside this hour to explore the ways that you as an individual approach the world.

[Silence]

Does that trouble you?

No, I'm merely considering the implications. Surely, you are assuming that I have a set purpose in being here, but isn't that very assumption the context that will ultimately distort everything that I say to you. We are merely acting out our respective roles. The whole medical model is only extended by analogy when it is applied to psychotherapy. What is a mental illness? Show me the microbe.

What if what we are doing together is to clarify how you perceive things so that we can isolate choices that you might make that may lead to better results in your life taken as a whole.

You mean so that I can feel better.

That's right.

Well if that is the final end that we are both pursuing there must be drugs that can restore the organism to a proper equilibrium without all this talk.

And what would your experience of self be then?

You keep coming back to self as though it were some form of Holy Grail.

Does that disturb you?

Yes it does frankly. What difference does it make if I get well?

Your father will be pleased.

Yes, it will get me off his hands.

Well, ideally it would matter to you as well.

But that's precisely it; it doesn't matter to me. And worse, I don't think it would matter to you either if I wasn't paying you.

Don't you think that I might take some manner of personal satisfaction from the patients that I am able to help?

[Sarcastically] So you can feel like a benefactor in this great wide world and not just another nut-job like me.

Is that what you think you are?

You therapists like questions a lot don't you.

Well we have our own little set of tools you know. Don't you like questions?

As a matter of fact no I don't, not when they get too close.

Too close to what?

To me.

[Silence]

And what do you mean by you?

Well I can tell you what Eugene Minkowski would mean. I have been reading his masterpiece, *Lived Time*, lately you know. He would say that each of us is subsumed into our lived experience of time. We are in process and driven by the Elan Vital. Each moment is part of a stream reaching into an indeterminate future. We live towards our goals.

I see, but could we return to you. What do you mean by you?

We went into that already.

You didn't answer me.

I can tell you what I'm reading. What more do you need to know.

What if your books were taken away?

[Silence]

Does that frighten you?

I would watch more television I suppose.

What if the set broke?

YouTube then.

No computer either.

Eat more.

You're on a diet.

Drink.

The bar is closed.

Fine! Then I suppose I'd get a dog.

That might be nice. Do you think the dog would like you?

Until I stopped feeding him.

Would you stop feeding him?

Of course not; he's my dog.

Well there are lots of dogs in this world that don't get fed.

Yes I suppose so. Still… I wouldn't want him to go hungry.

Why not?

Because I would owe him something… I chose him.

Out of all the possible dogs in the world?

That's right.

Why do you suppose that you chose him?

I thought he needed me.

How could you tell?

He came up to me and wagged his tail.

What if he had ulterior motives?

Now who's the cynic?

It was just a question.

No, you were insinuating something.

What?

That no dog would really … just like me. You know, for myself alone.

But I thought you didn't have a self.

Well I do; that's the problem.

Why is it a problem?

[Pause]

Well if you must know I'm rather demanding.

You don't seem so to me. All you want is a dog.

Well I want more than just a dog.

What?

All kinds of things. For one thing if I start eating I'm afraid that I won't stop.

So how do you stop yourself?

I don't start eating until I measure everything out.

That must be rather time-consuming.

It's my time.

[Pause]

I wonder what would happen if you just trusted yourself to stop on your own.

I can't.

Who's stopping you?

Something inside me; I can't control it.

So what do you do?

I deny myself.

So we're back to that troublesome self that you say you don't possess.

I didn't exactly say that.

Perhaps I misunderstood you.

Alright then listen: I don't want to be something that in the end just doesn't matter anyway. I'm just part of a crowd, one of the seven or eight billion people gobbling up the planet. I'm an ecological sinkhole.

So global warming is your personal fault.

[Pause]

Well not all of it.

I think that your average cow is worse.

Well at least you get milk and beef from a cow.

So you think the key is productivity?

Isn't it?

You tell me.

What else matters?

I don't know. Why don't you tell me?

[Pause]

Because I don't know.

Well what do you think matters?

I tell you I don't know!

Why don't you think you know?

Nobody ever told me; that's why.

You think somebody can just tell you who you are, like it's a big secret everybody is keeping from you?

Everybody else seems to know who they are. They get married, find great jobs, sign mortgages, raise kids, go on cruises, get sick, and then die.

Is that what everybody does or what you think everybody does?

Well don't they?

Did you ask them?

Well not one at a time.

That's the only way you can ask them; one at a time.

[Silence]

They look like a crowd to me.

They aren't. Try looking at them one at a time. You'll notice things.

Like what?

They may remind you of you.

Me?

Yes.

What do I know about me?

What do you know?

I'm not sure.

Would you like to explore a bit together?

[Pause]

Well I suppose.

Is that a commitment?

Yes.

Then I think we can work together.

[Pause]

I might quit.

Some patients do.

Doesn't that bother you when they quit?

Yes it does.

Why, because you failed?

How did I fail?

You let them leave.

They made up their own minds.

[Pause]

But what if they couldn't help themselves!

Why couldn't they?

Because they're sick!

So part of the sickness is the need to resist cure.

I guess so.

Why do you suppose people do that?

[Silence]

Because hope hurts...

Hope for what?

[Silence]

For everything ... for everything I've never had.

Would you like some of those things?

[Pause]

(Quietly) I don't deserve them.

Why not?

I'm bad.

Who told you that you were bad?

Everybody's bad. It says so in the bible.

Why do you suppose we're so bad?

[Pause]

Because … God is so good.

He didn't seem to mind two naked people running amuck all over his garden did he?

Well then why did he ask them to put on fig leaves?

They did that on their own when they ate the forbidden fruit and realized that they were naked.

Well he must have known that they would eat the fruit, after all He was God you know!

[Pause]

What if God thought that they just weren't ready yet to face their nakedness? Maybe it takes awhile to be able to digest the fruit of the tree of knowledge between good and evil. Perhaps God was letting them get all of that frolicsomeness out of their systems before moving them on to higher moral questions? Maybe God respects the normal maturation process of the human race.

We haven't come too far. We still copulate like bunnies.

Does that surprise you?

Well I don't.

What?

Copulate like a bunny.

What if you ever did?

[Pause]

I wouldn't be able to stop.

Oh I think you would. You might even go back to reading a

little philosophy.

Even if somebody took all my books?

Why would they do that?

Because they might think that all I wanted to do was copulate like a bunny.

(Smiling) I'm sure you would correct them regarding their gross misapprehension.

Are you laughing at me?

Do you hear me chortling away?

No but you're smiling.

Maybe that's because I like you. I think you're a very honest person.

[Pause]

Nobody ever told me that.

Nobody ever told you lots of things, but it's not too late.

I may be older than you think I am.

Well I'm no spring chicken either. I'm still learning.

[Pause]

Then why am I paying you so much money to cure me?

I can't cure you. The work we do together is a team project.

[Pause]

I'll fight you all the way!

Well that's up to you; it's your dime.

Can't you just carry me along?

With all the crap you've been carrying around? You must be mad!

You're smiling again.

Yes.

[Silence]

Alright, where do I sign?

You already did the patient intake; just show up next Tuesday, same time, same place.

Right.

[Silence]

Anything else?

[Silence]

Yes. When I woke up today it was before dawn. I thought how stupid it was of me coming to see you. One more therapist! I could read them all; disposable like paper cups. I like being complex; to make them do the work.

Uh huh?

You make me feel…

What do I make you feel?

You make me feel … ordinary.

Is that so bad?

It is for me.

Why?

Because I have to be special?

Oh? And why is that?

[Pause]

Because, if I'm not special, I might end up being nothing at all.

Lots of my patients say that. It's what brings them here.

[Silence]

Right… so next Tuesday then?

Yes next Tuesday.

[Silence]

Something else?

I'm afraid that if I get boring that you won't like me.

[Pause]

So you think I choose my patients for the genius of their symptom creation?

Well otherwise it would be a boring job wouldn't it?

317

Suppose you let me worry about that. Next Tuesday.

Very well Doctor, see you then, goodbye.

The following days and weeks produced a change in the young woman, subtle at first but growing in momentum as the sessions ticked past. There were set-backs of course as is customary in any regimen of psychotherapy, but rather than simply attending a few sessions and then dropping out, as had been her prior pattern, Tiffany always ended up taking the ferry to the Emerald City each Tuesday in time to make her appointment. Though she felt no budding affection for bats or mice she was at least able to describe her feelings and to obtain a first inkling of the general aura of fear that had always accompanied her. Extracts from her sessions demonstrated the first etchings in an overall design.

Extract from Session Ten—Tiffany Amorth

You told me something in our last session that I would like to explore further. You mentioned that you felt that under certain circumstances you would be left entirely to your own devices as though all of the powers and parameters of civilization would drop away. There was a chill in your voice and a quality of bleakness in your eye that reminded me of pictures that I have seen of the frigid Polar Regions.

That's how it always feels to me. I feel like I am going to die. Everything in the room gets darker as though there was a mask of gauze over my face... I was operated on once as a child for a tonsillectomy. They strapped my legs down with a leather belt and one nurse held my arms while another nurse put an ether-infused mask over my face ... I wanted to kill them.

Didn't anyone tell you what to expect during the surgery?

Only that I would get ice cream and presents if I would let

them take my tonsils out; it was a lie. I couldn't swallow anything; but my mother's face bending over me in the bed when I woke up after the surgery was the most beautiful thing I ever saw.

[Silence]

I see tears in your eyes.

I'm sorry.

Why should you be sorry? It must have been very frightening for you.

It's stupid; other children have much worse surgeries.

They aren't you.

You mean that I was right to feel angry and betrayed.

Yes. You were aware that you had a self and it could be violated. It took you many years for that sense to be dulled in you until it fell silent.

[Silence]

I'm still angry. I don't know if I have ever hated two people as much as I did those nurses. All the time that they were dealing with me they never looked into my eyes.

And you have been suspicious ever since...

It wasn't the only lie people told me.

There were others?

People always had to pin me down to do things to me.

What sort of things?

[Silence]

(Then suddenly)They gave me shots or suppositories. The suppositories burned and it hurt when they stuck them in.

[Pause]

What else did people do?

I had warts on my feet and they burned them out with acid. It left holes in my feet. It took weeks for them to heal. I used to get sick before I went to school every day.

Nobody helped you through your pain?

No. These things had to be done. It was my job to adjust; like when we moved to new places and I had to start all over again. I would have complained more but I didn't want to be abandoned.

Your parents would have left you behind?

No, but I thought that bad or ungrateful children would be given away to government agencies.

Some are.

[Pause]

So I wasn't wrong then.

[Pause]

When did it get safe enough for you to tell your parents what you felt?

It never did get safe enough. It still isn't.

[Silence]

That's very sad. Part of being an adult is to reach a time and condition where we don't have to be as afraid as we were when we were children.

They can still hurt me and if not them then the people I have loved since.

[Silence]

Would you like a tissue?

Yes please. Thank you.

[Pause]

I would like to return to your fear of bats.

Do we have to?

I think it would be useful.

Alright then.

Why do you think that your father thinks you are possessed by the devil?

I don't know.

Try imagining then.

[Silence]

Maybe I remind him of something.

What do you think you remind him of?

[Pause]

How he really feels about me.

How does he feel?

I don't know … I wish I did.

[Pause]

Is your father a complicated man?

No more than I am a complicated girl.

Is that your answer?

It's what we share.

[Silence]

Do you share other things?

No. We're actually quite different.

How so?

We don't like the same things. For one thing we're politically different. He watches Hannity every night.

What do you watch?

MSNBC. I love Rachel Maddow.

Is she like a big sister to you?

Yes. I like Kasie Hunt too. I wish I looked like her.

[Pause]

How else do you differ from your father?

He likes the old Catholic Church of High Mass and incense.

And what church do you like?

There's only one church.

I see. What does church mean to you?

It means base-communities in Brazil and Columbia, workers processions, and the Virgin of Guadeloupe. I read theologians too, people who aren't always in favor with Rome … not because they're right but because they don't seem like stodgy old relics.

Is that what you think bishops are?

I don't think anybody really understands bishops… I feel sorry for them sometimes. I know what it's like to have worlds torn out from underneath you. It must be lovely though to feel that you have a hotline to God.

[Pause]

What about you? Do you have a hotline?

No.

You can pray…

[Pause]

It isn't the same thing. Besides, I'm a possessed girl.

Do you think you could be an atheist then?

Never!

[Pause]

Why not?

Because I need to know when I look up at the glacial stars that there is something out there somewhere. If there isn't I'd be afraid of even more things than bats and mice.

Did you ever try and confront those fears directly?

Once I thought I would read everything I could about Rabies and just burn the fear away by over-exposure.

[Silence]

I guess it didn't work?

It was horrible. There were cases in India of people strapped to beds with their terrified eyes rolling around in their heads and foam bubbling out of their mouths. Ugh.

[Silence]

And possession?

I looked at records of that too. People growl and grimace and make horrible laughing sounds in a low voice no matter what sex they are.

[Pause]

(Quietly) What sex are you?

Sometimes I don't know. I'm not sure I like either one... No, that isn't true; I'd love to be a girl if I could look like one of those girls in the mall in Victoria's Secret stores.

Not too many women do.

Maybe not, but the stores would go out of business if women didn't at least hope that they could look like that, at least a little.

Is that a possessed girl talking?

(Smiles) Nope, I'm just a typical girl who is already pushing thirty.

[Pause]

Is there anything else you would like to discuss today before our session ends?

[Silence]

How long do you think we'll need to keep meeting like this.

That's up to you.

I mean am I getting better?

Only you can know the answer to that question. This is about you.

What if I start putting up more resistance? Maybe I'm being too much of a model patient.

I think that this time you really want to get something out of therapy. Patients fight their doctors until they can fight back for themselves with the people who originally injured them.

[Silence]

So if I'm not possessed why am I so angry?

Do you think you are possessed?

[Silence]

No.

[Pause]

Then let's leave it at that then... See you next week.

The annals of therapists abound with stories. Who can say how long a wound lasts inside of us or what later detritus adds to the weight and burden of the initial injury? We are told that the noon-day devil like a roaring lion goes about seeking someone to devour. We are advised to resist him steadfast in the faith. Now and then we have evidences of untold graces as though angels surrounded us to guard us. Even if we have a single proprietary angel on a twenty-four hour shift, one who gets to know us well through the years, who is to say that others equally committed to our welfare do not bear her company? After that tenth session Tiffany Amorth began to improve rapidly. She started seeing things without the shadows that usually accompanied them. She still didn't like bats or mice very much, but when her father told her that he still suspected that she was possessed at times by the devil she told him to stick an old sock in his mouth and chew it.

Tiffany Amorth closed her notebook slowly and looked down shyly toward her feet. The class was silent where they sat around the seminar table that was intended to create a sense of intimacy and candor among the students in Genre Studies 504. It had not been an easy choice for Tiffany to decide on graduate study in English Literature. Her father had called it wasted money, but with her scholarship it was cheaper than therapy and it did get her out to mix with people so he consented at last and here she was. The instructor, Dr. Herrigan, had published a book of short stories in her youth that had received a favorable review from John Updike and she had been coasting on its reputation ever since. Time had revealed that there is a profound division between the lonely world of writers and the snug security of a tenured teaching post and she preferred the latter. She was sensitive to the ego demands of young grad students and of delphiniums and she had learned over time how best to nurture each of these by providing a warm and nurturing environment rich in soil and with plenty of room to grow.

"Well then class who would like to go first?"

There was the usual awkward silence before one of the young ladies spoke up, "I was wondering why the author chose her own name in the story. I thought we were supposed to use our imaginations."

"That's true, Belinda, but how can you be sure that Tiffany hasn't used her imagination?" Dr. Herrigan objected.

Another student spoke up. "What does it matter? Don't we all color our narratives by the sheer act of writing them down?"

Belinda turned to him, "Well as for me I believe there should be a clear demarcation between fact and fiction. Literature is the art of the possible; it should not be weighed down by personal recollections however poignant they may be. The mere choice of a psychotherapy session is so overdone, so '*I Never Promised You a Rose Garden*' so '*Flowers for Algernon*.'"

Dr. Herrigan intervened, "We are not here to judge but to elucidate Belinda. Tiffany was well within the stated parameters of the assignment. Let's concentrate on what you noticed in the sphere of technique."

"That's all I wanted to say," Belinda said as she turned her attention to the naked trees outside the window. She felt a sudden uneasiness. It wasn't like her.

"Others?" inquired Dr. Herrigan.

Samuel spoke up, "I liked the feel of the story. It seemed authentic."

"Ah, but doesn't authenticity break the spell of artifice and illusion?" inquired Dr. Herrigan.

"Well, there was the fanciful element," Samuel commented. "I mean, Tiffany possessed by the devil, who would ever believe that?"

"But remember, Samuel, that you are applying exterior norms to the text; you have the advantage of knowing Tiffany whereas the reader is confined to the text alone."

Belinda spoke up, "Precisely my point! I thought the story confused memoir with fiction. The author should signal his intent or else he isn't playing fair with his reader."

"So you believe that equities are involved here, Belinda. But what shall we do with the problem of the unreliable narrator as in *The Aspern Papers* by Henry James; should we always take the author at face value even when she speaks omnisciently? What do you think class?"

Larry spoke up, "I think it is perfectly fair to draw on actual observations for one's ideas and then to clothe them in mood and atmosphere. There's nothing dishonest in that."

"Then where would you draw the line, if any, around duplicity?" Belinda objected.

"I would let the conventions of the genre prevail," said Larry thoughtfully.

"Ah but who is to establish the conventions?" asked Dr. Herrigan.

"The chair of the department and the tenure committee," answered Larry.

Belinda smirked, "You won't be so cavalier when you are seeking a teaching post in four years."

Dr. Herrigan attempted to summarize. "So we are exploring the conventions of narration and the question of sincerity of authorial intent as revealed or concealed within the text; is that a fair statement of our discussion thus far?"

Ericka spoke up, "Well if we are confined to the text then the author will hardly confess in the course of the story that he is having the reader on, I mean to do so would be like stepping out of character on the stage."

"Then how could the reader achieve ambiguity while still staying in character?" Samuel inquired.

"Any ideas?" inquired Dr. Herrigan.

"It should be a matter of tone," Lara commented, "Or perhaps a showing of divided motivations between the first person narrator and his actions within the text."

"How do you mean tone?" asked Samuel.

"I mean the overriding texture of the story. That's why *The Lottery* by Shirley Jackson works. It moves from a tone of bucolic peace to sudden horror. It really had an impact on a 1950's readership."

Belinda objected again, "But the audience of a story should be presumed to be a constant. The text has to stand alone without any exterior support. If we presume an innocent audience then we have to vet who will read the story and select out the sophisticated reader if it is to have maximum impact on a general audience."

"That is a problem," commented Dr. Herrigan.

"It seems to me that we must simply take the story as it is," said Samuel. "Any criticism implies a privileged outside vantage point that is itself outside the text. Who is to guarantee that the critic isn't even more biased than the author? If the author doesn't play fair how are we to be sure that the critic doesn't cheat every bit as much?"

"You have to trust somebody," Belinda said acidly. "Otherwise almost anything could happen."

All this time Tiffany had been listening to the quiet voice inside of her while picking clandestinely at her eyelashes. "Why am I here? Why am

I here?" And then lower still another voice, "Why *are* you here? Why *are* you here?" It was always like an echo, as though her thoughts had reverberations in a great empty hall filled with unseen corners and mirrors. She saw the improvise altar in the corner of her room at home and the bottles filled with soil from the graveyard. The books on Caribbean voudoun cults said it was called "goofer dust" and it could be used for things. You could even get old nasty nurses with goofer dust.

The winds from Puget Sound blew up to the campus and shook the trees outside the window. Tiffany thought of all of the students who had come here young and filled with hopes for a bright future. Where were they now? She saw in her mind's eye all of the protests through the years on this very campus but America could still manage to elect Donald Trump! What had it all been for, the struggle for justice and enlightenment if it came to this?

"Still, I want to give it all up," she thought. "I don't like being angry like this all the time. I think I'll take the goofer dust back to the graveyard and foreswear allegiance. I don't want power over things. It was all a lie just to distract me from what really matters."

Then she looked over again at Belinda smug and confident in her white angora sweater with her upturned nose and perfect silhouette. "You don't like my story?" she said to herself. "Do I write to please you Miss Tenure Queen, prisoner of texts. If I stopped writing where would you be then? You would just disappear."

She ceased for a moment to imagine...

Tiffany Amorth sat back in her chair at her desk in her room at home. She could hear the football game playing annoyingly downstairs in her father's den, as usual at full volume. She held her pen over the paper in her notebook where it dripped like a dagger from time to time onto the manuscript. She had made the ink herself out of oil, elder berries, lampblack, and dust. She hesitated and then made her decision to turn from darkness and vengeance. Everything passes and not everyone can be expected to know when and how they wound us. "No, I won't do it," she said. "There must be some limit to imperial authorial intent otherwise we might be as arbitrary and capricious as certain … people of importance and authority.

She took a wet sponge and mopped it over the lines that had read:

Belinda Montague was walking across the busy intersection outside the university bookstore after her graduate writing seminar when she was run down by a speeding police car. It was such a tragedy. She was said to have been quite a promising young critic.

"There!" said Tiffany Amorth. "All better! You get to live, Belinda Montague, whoever you are. After all I am only a writer of stories, a scribbler of tales, and I am obsessive possibly but most certainly … well, *Not Possessed.*"

ROYALS
BY CARRIE AVERY MORIARTY

I t's freezing," Tristyn said.

"It's always freezing," Erwin replied.

"Why do we have to be out here? No one will attack in this weather."

"The Queen has deemed us worthy of defending her land," Erwin said. "As if it were a privilege."

"Do you not consider it a privilege to guard her?"

Erwin looked at his partner, then around and whispered, "Nothing to do with the Queen is honorable. She is not as powerful as some say."

Tristyn was shocked. He'd known Erwin for only the few weeks he'd been with them, but he'd not heard him dissent since his arrival. The fact that he spoke it aloud was even more surprising. "Shh," he admonished.

"She isn't around," Erwin said.

"But the walls can hear you," Tristyn responded.

Erwin simply rolled his eyes, turning once again to look at the great forest beyond the castle walls. *No*, he thought. *She isn't nearly as powerful as she would like people to believe.*

"No, no, NO!" the Queen shouted. Jocelyn ducked as the Queen threw a cup across the room. "Can't anyone do this right?" The dressmaker cringed and the chamber maid standing on the pedestal serving as the model trembled in fear.

Everyone knew the wrath of Queen Cecily could be felt as much as heard. Daughter of Tanis, great King of the Northlands and his consort, Divinity, Goddess of the Future, she wielded her power boldly, bowing down to no one. Rumored to have killed her father for his throne, she was feared by all who fell under her rule. Over the years she gobbled up land from lesser kings, adding to her power and wealth. None dared to stand against her.

"Perhaps a break is in order," Jocelyn said. "Give the couturier time to create something more appropriate for the occasion."

"Yes," the Queen said. "Fine, fine, whatever will get these imbeciles out of my presence."

Both the maid and the couturier nodded their thanks to Jocelyn as they hastily made their escape.

"Why do I allow them to remain?" the Queen pondered. "It is clear they are far beneath what is befitting my status."

"Because he created the purple gown," Jocelyn said. "Surely you remember it."

"Of course I remember," the Queen sighed, leaning back on the cushions where she lounged. "But surely there are others more capable. It seems Ioan has fallen behind on what is required for my court."

"I think he simply feels like whatever he does will not stack up to the original masterpiece," Jocelyn replied.

"Nothing will," the Queen said, sipping from another goblet.

"And that is why his creations are lacking inspiration," Jocelyn said. "He knows he can never live up to the first one, never recreate something as magnificent as that one piece was. Your desire for perfection has put the fear of the gods in him. How can he ever hope to please your high standards?"

The Queen glared at Jocelyn. True, she was her sister, but that is where the similarities ended. Cecily boasted light hair, pale skin, and crystalline eyes. Jocelyn was a near perfect opposite, with her black hair, deep, rich skin, and night dark eyes. Both had the height of their father and the slender build of their mother, but only Jocelyn kept the king's dark coloring.

The other thing Jocelyn had that Cecily lacked was patience and an even temper. Where Cecily exploded, Jocelyn soothed. Jocelyn was friendly to everyone she crossed paths with. Whether they were high born or a lowly stable boy, she greeted each with a smile and a kind word, something Cecily never understood.

"I'll call for a meal," Jocelyn said as she walked to the door. "Perhaps that will help with your mood."

"Make sure they bring something sweet," the Queen insisted.

"Welcome back to the warmth," Trahaearn said.

"And glad to be out of the frost," Tristyn replied.

Erwin simply made his way to the stone hearth to warm himself. While he enjoyed the camaraderie of his fellow warriors, he relished his time alone. Since he'd arrived there had been little need for the combat that they were all trained for, so Erwin simply spent his spare time reading. The others joked with him about it, but he knew that many secretly wished they had been taught. He'd contemplated helping some out with it but knew none would ask. It wasn't the warrior way to be knowledgeable in those sorts of things.

"What've you got there?" Tristyn asked when he'd made his way to the fire. "Some sort of frivolous musing?"

"Something like that," Erwin said.

"I honestly don't understand why you bother with those things," Tristyn said as he sat next to his friend. "They'll get you nowhere in this life."

Erwin simply nodded, paying no mind to what his friend said. He knew more than most of the guard how important the history of the land was to his task.

"Ioan?" Jocelyn asked as she came into his room.

"Princess," he replied sweetly. "I wanted to thank you for assisting me in getting out of that situation."

"It was my pleasure," she replied. "How is Miribeth?"

"Shaken," Ioan replied. "She's not seen the Queen in this kind of mood before."

"You seem to be handling it well," Jocelyn said.

"She can't ruffle my feathers that easily," he replied. "Did you find what she was looking for in her dress? I am happy to recreate the purple gown, but I know she doesn't want to have the exact same thing this time."

"You are right," she said. "I think if you find something similar, with enough variance, you should be fine. What did you have in mind?"

"Come look at what I've drawn," he said as he made his way to a table near the window. "I was thinking of something like this."

Jocelyn looked down at the parchment with a sketch of what he had in mind and marveled at his talent. Not only could he create flowing beauty in fabric, but he had captured its likeness on the sheet.

"I cannot imagine her not loving this," she said in awe. "What colors were you thinking?"

"Her fondness for purple makes me hesitate," he said, moving to a counter across the room. "This, however, just came in from the southlands and I thought it might work well." He picked up a bolt of fabric that shimmered in the lamplight in hues of blue.

"It's magnificent," Jocelyn exclaimed. "I think she will really enjoy the way it sparkles."

"I'd thought to add some jewels to the bodice for additional shine," he said, clearly pleased with her reaction.

"You know her very well," she said, smiling.

"You would look radiant in this fabric as well," he said.

"But my sister won't want to share it," was her reply. "I thank you, though, for the compliment."

"She has never liked sharing the spotlight," he replied. "Even when she was a tiny tot, she always wanted to be in the center of everything."

"That desire hasn't faded, either," Jocelyn laughed. "I should let you get back to your duties."

"A visit from you is always welcome," Ioan replied. "I'll have something to show her majesty by the end of tomorrow."

"I'll let her know," she said as she exited.

Making her way through the castle she found herself near the bastion of the rear wall. When her father was alive, he would often be found in this same place, discussing strategy and warfare with the men of his guard. While she didn't intend to discuss such things, she did enjoy time spent with men who worked hard to protect the people of the city.

"Your Grace," Trahaearn said, bowing low.

Trahaearn was head of the guard and known to her well. The other men in the room were quickly up and bowing upon hearing his proclamation.

"Stand up you fool," Jocelyn admonished. "I am not my sister. There's no need to placate me with such revelry."

"Not placating in your case," one of the men said.

Built sturdy with long legs and broad shoulders, the man

commanded attention, and had he not spoken, Jocelyn would have noticed him anyway.

"I don't recognize you, sir," she said, hoping he would give her his name.

"And you shouldn't," he replied.

"Meaning?" she inquired.

"Twofold. I am new to the guard, just in the last month."

"And?"

"If you notice your guard you are not being protected as well as you should," he said.

"You'll have to forgive Erwin," Trahaearn said, glaring at the man. "He's new to the work of soldier."

"Only to your guard," Erwin replied, keeping his eyes locked on Jocelyn.

"Have you come to find our weakness?" Jocelyn asked.

Tilting his head Erwin asked, "Do you have one?"

"Every army has its weaknesses," Jocelyn replied. "Have you discovered ours?"

"We are the finest army in all the land," Trahaearn boasted.

"That we are," Jocelyn admitted, without taking her eyes off the newcomer. "But we still have areas that could use improvement."

Erwin nodded, a smirk gracing his lips.

"So," Jocelyn continued. "What say you? Have you found weaknesses within our guard?"

"Should that not be reported to the head of the guard rather than those of the royal family?" Erwin asked.

"Usually, yes," Jocelyn admitted. "However, I would not be the one he would tell. That luxury would fall to my sister, and she rarely listens to such *trivial* things."

"Even when they could mean her safety were in danger?"

"If what you've found puts her safety in danger," Jocelyn said, "then it should already be known to both Trahaearn and my sister, as well as me. Since I know nothing of the sort, and it appears the head of the guard is in the dark, you must not have found anything so urgent as to demand a report."

Bowing his head, Erwin said, "Nothing of grave need has arisen as of yet. I have seen things, however, that could do with some improvement."

Trahaearn began to bolster, but Jocelyn cut him off with a wave of her hand.

"Please," she said. "Won't you accompany me to a drawing room to discuss this further?"

Nodding his head, Erwin made to follow the princess. He didn't miss the expression on the face of the head of the guard and knew he'd have to deal with the repercussions later.

Jocelyn led the way inside the castle walls proper, moving with ease down the corridors until she came to a small room. She stepped inside, finally coming to stand in front of the large hearth on one wall. The fire inside was small, yet seemed to put out enough heat for the room to not be frigid. Following her lead, he stood next to the burning wood and waited for her to ask her questions.

"How long have you been here?"

It was not the question he expected, but answered it without reservation. "Six weeks tomorrow."

"And in that time you have not once been assigned to a post within." It wasn't a question, so Erwin held his tongue. "Is this why I have not sensed you?" she asked, looking him in the eye.

He smiled, a small thing, then answered. "My guess is that my shielding is much stronger than you have experienced, Your Grace."

"Stop with that," she said, brushing the words away with a hand. "Have you come to seek your place as the rightful heir to this land?"

"You're good," he said, relaxing. "Was it mere chance that you were in the guardhouse today? Or were you drawn because I was there?"

Jocelyn folded her arms across her chest and took in the man who stood before her. True, she hadn't intended to seek out the guard, but whether she was drawn there by him or simple boredom was unknown to her. She didn't want to think she was drawn, as that would mean this man held more power over her than was acceptable. It also might mean that he was more dangerous as well.

"I often wander the castle," she conceded. "It's a large place, and my sister is sometimes difficult to be around."

"So I've heard," he said, that smile still playing on his lips.

"Are you here to remove Cecily from the throne?"

The question wasn't unexpected, but Erwin wasn't sure how to answer it. Instead he asked, "Does she need replacing?"

"Hmph," was all Jocelyn could manage in response. While her sister was good in many ways, her demanding nature and need for power could, and likely would, put all of them in danger at some point.

"That's not a no," Erwin said. "But I assume that if you were to say so, it may cause you some danger."

"My sister's reputation has preceded her," Jocelyn smirked.

"Have no fear," he said. "I have not come for the throne. My task is much more important."

"Did you see the dressmaker?" the Queen asked as Jocelyn returned later that afternoon.

"He is working on something that should be more to your liking," Jocelyn replied. "I believe he should have something to you in the next day or two."

"Good. I would hate to have to replace him."

"Now, Cec," Jocelyn said. "You know full well you would never replace Ioan. He's too valuable."

"But sometimes he needs to know that I could," the Queen said. "What else have you been doing today?"

Jocelyn thought about her encounter with the soldier, but decided against telling her sister. "Just wandering the castle. Thought I might find a book to read in the library."

"You and your books," Cecily said. "Always wandering off in your mind. I just don't understand that."

"You like your real world and I like my fantasy," Jocelyn replied.

"Tell me about the guard," the Queen said.

It took Jocelyn a moment to realize what her sister had said. When it registered, she realized that she had been thinking about the man she spoke with earlier. Hoping to keep that meeting a secret she said, "The book I found was about a princess who hoped to overthrow her parents and take over the land for herself."

"So it was a book about me," the Queen said.

"That it was," Jocelyn said. Nothing did better to distract her sister than to talk about how great she was.

The discussion lasted most of the afternoon, Jocelyn recounting things that happened in their past as parts of the fictitious book she had read. By the time the evening meal was called she was exhausted.

"How long until the ball?" Cecily asked.

"Just over a week," Jocelyn replied.

"And is everything ready?" the Queen asked. "The dishes are planned, the decorations are being readied, the invitations have been sent?"

"Everything is on track," Jocelyn said. "The winter ball will be the grandest one you've hosted."

"Good," the Queen said. "We must remind everyone who is the most powerful in all the land."

"I am sure everyone is well aware of that," Jocelyn said.

"Joss," the Queen said. "What princes have been invited?"

"We can check the list in the morning," she replied. "Tonight, I need to sleep."

"Maybe we can find someone suitable to be my consort," the Queen said. "Do you think there is anyone worthy of my affections?"

"I'm not sure there is a man alive who could handle your power," Jocelyn said. "They will be lucky to be chosen, though."

"I believe it is time I start thinking about having a child," the Queen said. "Wouldn't it be grand to have a baby in the castle?"

"Are you prepared to go through the pregnancy?"

"Oh," the Queen said. "I can handle anything. I am the Queen, after all. Nothing is too difficult for me."

"Well, then," Jocelyn said. "We should begin looking for the proper father for your baby."

"Yes," the Queen answered. "That would be grand."

"You made quite the impression on the princess," Trahaearn said.

"How's that?" Erwin asked.

"She's asked that you accompany her to the ball," the head of the guard said. "Such an honor has never been bestowed upon one of the guard."

Erwin couldn't tell whether Trahaearn was pleased or annoyed with the request. "I shall endeavor to behave in a manner that would bring honor to you," he said.

"First," Trahaearn said. "You must go see the couturier. He will create something appropriate for you to wear to the occasion."

"Once my duties are complete," Erwin began. "I shall seek him out."

"You will go now," the head of the guard insisted. "Tristyn has taken over your duties for the day. When the royal family requests something, we fulfill their request immediately."

"As you wish," Erwin said and took his leave.

Everyone in the castle was busily prepared for the ball, with just three days left until the grand event. The guard was no different, ensuring their uniforms were in pristine order, their armor polished to a high reflective shine.

As he made his way through the halls of the castle, he listened with more than his ears to the essence of the building. While he couldn't detect anything specific from either the Queen or the princess, those around them told him all he needed to know. Those in the kitchen worried they wouldn't have enough ingredients for the inundation of hungry men and women set to come. Maids were hustling around, cleaning everything from chandeliers to chamber pots, ensuring nothing would look less than perfect when guests began to arrive.

Finally, he arrived at the couturier's chambers and was greeted by a young woman.

"This way," she said.

He followed her deeper into the room until she came to a stop. Erwin looked around at the grand gowns hanging on nearly every empty space available on the walls. When his eyes landed on the man in charge, he noticed he was being measured up.

"The guardsman, I presume," the man said.

"As requested," Erwin answered.

"Good, good," the couturier said to himself after his perusal of the man. "This way."

Following along, Erwin found himself in another room, this one full of mirrors and bolts of material for as far as he could see.

"If you please," the dressmaker said, indicating a stand in the middle of the room.

Unsure of what he meant, Erwin simply stared.

"Up!"

"Oh," Erwin said, clearly understanding that he should stand atop the box.

"Right, then," the dressmaker began. "Let's see what we have."

For the next hour the man fussed over Erwin, measuring things, holding swatches of fabric against his face, then discarding them. On and on it went, until finally there was a breakthrough.

"Perfect," the dressmaker said.

"Then we're done?" Erwin asked.

"Not hardly," the couturier replied. "That was for the color. Now, to sketch the suit."

With that, he sat down at a desk and began to sketch on some parchment. Shading and drawing, then crumpling the paper and tossing it into the fire. On and on it went for another good hour before he held up a sheet, eyed it against Erwin, who remained on the pedestal, and exclaimed, "Magnificent."

Erwin wasn't sure whether this meant he was finished or if the ordeal had a long way to go. He hoped it meant he was free to leave and return to the men of the guard, although he was likely to receive some grief from them.

"Off with you," the dressmaker said, making a shooing motion with his hand. "I'll call you back when I'm ready for the fitting."

Stepping from the platform, Erwin picked up his sword from where he'd lain it and exited the room. He quickly made his way back to the bastion and was not surprised to hear the jokes aimed his way.

"Where's the new dress, then?" one asked.

"Are you allowed back in with us rough gents?" quipped another.

"Shall I help you with your sword, son?" joked a third.

"That'll do," Trahaearn said, ushering Erwin to his office. Once there, with the door closed behind them, he asked, "What took so long?"

"That man is a perfectionist," Erwin replied. "Most of the time was spent finding the right fabric for the garments. Then it was to sketching, which he said I had to remain for. I was afraid he was going to have me there while he stitched the pieces together."

"I was hoping you'd found yourself with the princess," the older man said. "That would have been a much nicer way to spend the day."

"Indeed, it would," Erwin agreed. "No sight of a single royal the entire time I was in the castle."

"No worry," the man said. "I've assigned you as the official guard of the princess for the ball. You are to wear your sword the entire time."

"How does the couturier feel about this addition to the wardrobe?" Erwin asked.

"He'll have to accept it," the head of the guard said. "The royal family's safety is the most important thing. If you must be there, you had better be ready to defend them, whether your sword matches your shoes or not."

"Oh, Ioan," the Queen cooed. "It looks marvelous. You really have done a marvelous job with this outfit."

"I am pleased it meets with your approval," the couturier said, bowing low.

"This is nearly as perfect as the purple gown," she said.

"It is beautiful," Jocelyn said.

"Would you care to see your gown?" Ioan asked.

"Oh," Jocelyn replied. "Do you have it done, yet?"

"It's just finished," he said.

"Why don't we wait," she replied. "I'll come down later this afternoon and see what you've created."

"Whatever suits you," he replied.

When he and the chamber maid left, Jocelyn turned to her sister.

"Have you looked over the names I gave you?" she asked.

"There are just so many," Cecily replied. "How am I supposed to narrow down my choices with just names?"

"I put them in the order of most power," Jocelyn said. "When they arrive, you can decide for yourself which one catches your fancy. Perhaps you will be able to narrow it down some if we discuss them."

"Yes, please," the Queen said with a wry smile. "Let's talk about their stunning attributes. I want to make sure my child has not only the most beautiful mother but a father who is at least passable where looks are concerned."

"Let's start at the top," Jocelyn said. "King Carasius, from the deep south region is very powerful."

"With a name like that," the Queen said, "he ought to be. What does he look like?"

And with that, the two women took the measure of each man on the list. They discussed not only their standing within the realm, but also the physical attributes each had. Having had conversations with everyone at the last several balls, Jocelyn was well versed in their knowledge and intellect as well, sharing with the Queen both the benefits and detriments of each suitor on the list.

Queen Cecily approved and removed men from the list based on each piece of information Jocelyn provided, and they finally pared the list down to a manageable handful of viable candidates. The test would be, which would the Queen choose as consort.

"None of them must know they are being considered for this

enviable position," the Queen insisted.

"Of course not," Jocelyn replied. "We don't want to give any of them a false hope."

"I also don't want them trying to persuade me with more than what we have," the elder sister said. "There's no telling what these men would do if they knew they may end up in my bed."

"Isn't that the truth," Jocelyn agreed.

"Who is going to be your companion at the ball?" the Queen asked. "Or are you simply going to take one of the men I haven't chosen?"

"I've asked a member of the guard to accompany me," Jocelyn said.

"A lowly guard?" the Queen said. "You don't have to deprive yourself on my account."

"I didn't want to get in the way of any of those you may choose," Jocelyn said. Truth was, she was looking forward to having Erwin with her for this event. The men of the realm tended to get a bit grabby when the wine flowed as freely as it did. Having him there would keep the others in check.

"Well," the Queen said. "If you decide you need a more refined gentlemen, please feel free to choose someone from the list. As long as it isn't one that I've already picked."

"I think the guard will be fine," she said. She had peeked in while he was being fitted for his suit and was stunned at the ruggedly handsome figure he made. No, she would not be leaving him for one of the stuffy fools that tried to get on the good side of her sister. They were all false bravado, where Erwin was as real as they came; even if he did hold secrets she couldn't get at. That was the other reason she asked him to accompany her. She hoped to find out what he was hiding.

"Off to play make believe, then, are we?" Trystin asked.

"Simply acquiescing to the wishes of the royal family," Erwin returned.

"With the fancy duds to boot."

Erwin knew that some of the other men were jealous of his ability to mingle with the royals. What they didn't know, though, was that he had been mingling with royals his whole life. If the truth about who he was were known by the men of the guard, he would not have been welcomed nearly as easily as he was.

"It is what is required," Erwin replied.

"I suggest you be on your best behavior," Trystin said. "The Queen may decide she doesn't like you. I would hate to have to remove you from the ball."

"I'll endeavor to stay in her good graces," Erwin said as he finished fastening his sword.

Ioan had balked at the idea that his smooth lines would be ruined by such a monstrosity, but Erwin had assured him that it could not be left out. The statement that it was for the protection of the princess had finally made him see the need. Now, with the sword at his hip, and a dagger in each boot, Erwin was prepared to meet Princess Jocelyn.

"Stay on your toes," Trahaearn said. "Don't want you forgetting your place."

"I will do my best to represent the guard well," Erwin said.

"Just don't get in the line of fire when the Queen wants something," the older man said quietly.

"Thank you for the warning," the younger man replied.

"Don't drink too much, either," the head of the guard said.

"Erwin doesn't drink," Trystin quipped.

"I just don't drink to excess," Erwin replied. "Unlike some of you fools."

The comment was said in jest, and the men laughed at the joke. Erwin could feel their desire to be in his place. Most had known the princess for a while, and all who knew her felt she was much better suited to being head of the family rather than her sister. None, however, would make that statement aloud.

"I'm off, then," Erwin said as he left the men laughing.

Making his way from the bastion, he meandered through the halls toward the main area where the ball was to take place. The princess had asked that he meet her near the ballroom in the library where they first spoke. The closer to the room he got, the more unease he felt. Opening himself up without letting his guard down, he reached out to see where the oddity came from. He knew it would be a short while before most of the guests would arrive, but some were already on the property. He couldn't be sure, but there was definitely a foe among those who were there.

Slipping into the library he caught a flash of green. "Hello?" he called.

Princess Jocelyn turned then, and the sight was nearly more than he could bear. Her dark features set against the deep green of her gown drew him to her. Before he realized it, he was standing next to her.

"You look exquisite," he said.

"Thank you," she replied, a flush running up her cheeks. "You are not so bad on the eyes, yourself."

"Only because you cannot see yourself," he said.

She cast her eyes down, a move he'd never seen her do before. She was the brave, strong, honest sister. If it had been Cecily, he would have expected the move to be something she used to get attention, or to get what she wanted. Jocelyn wasn't like that, though. She didn't do anything simply for attention. No, this was a true reaction to what he'd said. It almost made him wish he could prevent her grief when his true intentions were revealed.

"Will you accompany me to the ball?" he asked formally, putting his arm out for her to grasp.

"It would be my pleasure," she replied with a small smile.

Walking from the library, they made their way toward the grand ballroom. Erwin could feel the danger the closer he got, but could not quite pinpoint where it was coming from.

Jocelyn let out a shudder and Erwin halted. They were still a few feet from the room, and no one had noticed them. He moved them into an alcove and asked, "Are you all right?"

"I'm not sure," she said. "Something feels… off."

Playing the role of guard, he let his hand fall to the hilt of his sword, moving in front of the princess as to guard her, knowing full well that the danger was not physical.

"I'm not fragile, you know," she admonished, pushing him aside.

"Never said you were," he replied, keeping her in his shadow. "I simply don't want to hear from Trahaearn that I failed in my duties."

With that, she laughed. It was a light sound, bubbling up and bursting forth, breaking the dark spell that had been over them.

"It's likely just my sister's mood," she said, encouraging him to return to their walk to the ball. "She'll have my head if I'm late and she has to entertain the lesser fools."

"We wouldn't want you to lose your head, now," he said with a smile.

"I certainly wouldn't," she laughed.

The darkness still hung in the air, but Erwin felt the power from his companion. She could definitely take care of herself should anything arise. Now he just needed to figure out where the threat was coming from, and whether he should allow it to do what he was sent to do instead.

"They're all fools," the Queen murmured in her sister's ear.

"None strike your fancy?" Jocelyn asked.

"King Dugal isn't bad," she said. "I just don't know if I can handle the beard."

"They all have beards," Jocelyn reminded.

"But his is just so…"

"Long?" Jocelyn offered.

"Scraggly," the Queen said, scrunching her nose up.

"Perhaps we can convince him to tame it," she said. "With the right incentive, men will do most anything."

"How do you propose we get him to tame his beard without guaranteeing him a spot in my bed?"

"Leave it to me," Jocelyn said.

She stood, and Erwin stood with her. She wasn't used to having a man be this attentive and she found she rather liked it.

"Shall I accompany you, your Grace?"

"No," Jocelyn said. "This is a woman's errand."

"As you wish," he said, retaking his seat. He watched her walk away from the table and down the steps to speak with one of the maids at the side.

"I need a favor," Jocelyn said.

"Anything for you," Elin said.

"I am tasking you with cleaning up King Dugal," the princess said.

"Beg your pardon?"

"His beard," Jocelyn said. "You need to get him to tame that monstrosity and look more presentable."

"Oh," the maid said. "I'm happy to do that."

"I knew you were the one to ask," Jocelyn said.

Erwin watched the exchange, and when the princess returned to his side he asked, "Everything all right?"

"Soon enough," she replied.

Erwin simply nodded. He watched the maid make her way around the room, filling wine glasses and fending off several advances by the older men with ease. She found herself next to a fit man dressed in fine clothes, even if they were bolder than most of the others in the room, save the royal sisters. He watched as the young woman bowed low next to the man, clearly giving him a view down her dress. When he reached up to grasp her arm she turned and slapped him, the report ringing through the room.

He could feel more than hear both the Queen and the princess hiding their amusement, and wondered what more was going on. The man stood and brought the girl flush against his body. She pulled back with a strength she shouldn't have and slugged him in the gut. Doubling over and returning to his seat, the man looked up toward the dais where the Queen merely smiled.

The young woman leaned over once again, only this time she placed her mouth next to the man's ear. Erwin wasn't sure what she said, but the man looked intrigued. She left the room and he followed shortly after.

"That's one way to get what you want," the Queen said.

"She is good," Jocelyn replied. "It's not the way I would have handled it, but she has her own resources."

While it appeared that Erwin was not listening, Jocelyn knew he heard the conversation. When the man reappeared, Erwin smiled slightly and turned to look at the women. Cecily paid him no mind, focused on the returning man. Jocelyn, however, looked him square in the eye.

"What do you see?" she whispered.

"He's been cleaned up," Erwin said.

"Anything else?"

"Has he sobered?"

"And?" she prodded.

Erwin thought a moment, then it dawned on him. "He's younger."

"Very good," Jocelyn said. "I wasn't sure you would notice."

"Most wouldn't," he replied. "I, however, am tasked with paying attention to the most minute details."

Jocelyn looked at him, taking in his countenance. "You don't seem surprised about the change," she said.

"The Queen has high standards," he said. "While the man is powerful, he wasn't quite up to what she expects at her side."

"What makes you think she wants him at her side?"

"Why else would you go to so much trouble?"

"Because he is at the palace," she said. "Those who are in our company should be expected to present themselves accordingly."

"If that were the case," he began, "most would be asked to leave or conform. I don't see you making that happen with anyone else. Therefore, I stand by my assumption that she is looking for a suiter to be at her side."

Jocelyn looked at the man with new eyes. "You are far more than simply a man of the guard."

It was a statement and Erwin felt no need to respond. Instead, he returned to his plate and took a bite. He knew the princess was watching him, looking for a tell that indicated who he was. He also knew that he could not let her know the real reason for his being here.

"Are you sure you want to walk with me back to the bastion?" Erwin asked at the end of the evening.

"I have some questions for Trahaearn," Jocelyn replied. "He's expecting me."

"Very well," he said.

They made their way through the castle in comfortable silence. Erwin had learned a great many things while he sat next to the royal family. Some of it useless, but other bits were far more than he could have hoped to discover by merely being part of the guard. While working with the men who kept the castle safe, he'd found a great many things that would be beneficial when the time came to act on his orders. This, however, allowed him to have the information in a much faster time frame, moving his timeline up greatly.

Opening the door to the passage leading to the bastion, Erwin paused as Jocelyn stepped through. They took the few steps in the frigid weather before he opened the door to the building itself.

"Your Grace," Trahaearn said when he saw her. The remainder of the guard who were in the area all stood and bowed low.

"Please," the princess said. "There is no need for such formality with me. I am not my sister."

The men continued to remain low until the head of the guard stood.

"As you wish," he said. "What brings you to our door?"

"I wish to speak with you," the princess said. "Privately."

Erwin took no offence to the words, simply made his way to the bunk where he slept and began removing the fine clothing he'd worn to the ball. He watched as the princess and the head of the guard stepped out the door, back into the cold.

"I'm rather disappointed in you," Trystin said.

"Why's that?" Erwin asked

"It's barely past midnight and already you're back in our company," the younger man replied. "I guess you weren't enough man for the princess."

"Do you know why she asked to speak with Trahaearn?"

"Likely to tell him to not have you back in the castle," the younger man laughed.

"How do you know it isn't to ask that I be assigned permanently to her guard?" Erwin countered.

"Not likely," Trystin said. "She has no need for a man to defend her in the castle."

"Really," Erwin said. "And how would you know this? Have you been assigned to her before?"

"It is well known that the princess, as well as the Queen, have a power they can use to defend themselves," the young man said. "There is no need for a mere mortal to assist them."

"I'm far from a mere mortal," Erwin said.

Trystin looked at his friend. He couldn't decide whether the older guard was simply being boastful, or if he were more than what he seemed.

"You're not as powerful as the Queen," Trystin finally decided. "None are that powerful."

"Then why does she have a guard at all?" Erwin asked.

"She likes to have us around," Trystan said. "It gives the appearance of normalcy."

"Not something she would need if she were as powerful as you seem to think," Erwin said.

"You're like to get yourself drawn and quartered if you continue with these accusations," Trystin said just as the head of the guard came back in.

"Erwin," he called. "This way."

Erwin gathered his sword but left the rest of the garments he'd discarded where they lay. They stepped out the door and he noticed the princess was gone.

"The princess asked that I send you to her quarters,"

Trahaearn said.

"I shall go at once," Erwin replied.

"Do not," the older man began, then stopped. Gaining some composure, he continued. "It is absolutely imperative that you not cause the princess any grief. Treat her with the utmost respect and honor. Don't be vile or vulgar in her presence."

"Of course," Erwin said. "Did she say what she wanted of me?"

Trahaearn looked the younger man up and down, then said, "If you have to ask, perhaps you aren't as smart as she thinks."

"I would hate to assume," Erwin said. "She is the princess, after all, and should be treated as such."

"And you'll do well to remember that," Trahaearn said.

Erwin stood in the cold waiting for his superior to give him further instructions, but the man stood there, clearly pondering the ramifications of what was about to happen.

"Don't keep her waiting," he finally said when the younger man didn't move.

Wasting no time, Erwin returned to his bunk and gathered up his tunic, throwing it over his head before heading back out the door. He barely heard Trystin ask where he was going. There was no way he would answer that question. If Trahaearn wanted the men to know, he would inform them.

"Thank you for coming," the princess said as Erwin entered her quarters. "I am sure you have questions as to why I've asked that you come."

"When the princess summons," he said. "You answer without question."

"Just because you've come. It doesn't mean that you don't have some questions. But it is not for the reason I gave Trahaearn."

"He did not disclose your reasons with me," Erwin said. "Simply that I must come."

The princess turned and walked to the sitting area within her chambers. Erwin hesitated a moment before he followed. She stood before the fire, looking into the flames before she spoke.

"There is a danger coming," she said. "I can feel it."

"I will protect you," he said without thinking.

"But can you?" she asked as she turned.

He felt her gaze, felt the penetration of her thoughts. He yielded to her, allowing her to see within him the true nature of his being there. Her eyes widened when she realized why he was there.

"You've come to destroy us," she whispered. "And I've invited you in. How could I be so foolish."

"Princess," Erwin said as he stepped closer. "What do you know of the Boanzir?"

Jocelyn blinked. She had heard her father speak of the place, but had never been able to get more than the fact that they were allies from him.

"Are you from there?" she asked.

"More than that," he replied. He moved closer to her, standing right next to her so she had to crane her neck to see him. "I am the King of Boanzir."

"You were allied with my father," she said.

"I *am* allied with your father," Erwin corrected.

"My father died a decade ago," the princess said.

"Are you sure?" the King asked.

She looked at him confused. "I mourned him," she said. "The entire kingdom mourned his loss."

"Tell me about his death," he said as he guided her to the settee.

"My sister came to me," she began. "Told me he'd been killed in a freak hunting accident. That he'd been shot through with an arrow. She was distraught, like I'd never seen her before."

"What happened next?"

"The men who came back from the hunt were shaken," she continued. "Couldn't believe some of what they were saying. Some stating that a giant beast had slain him, others that it was an errant shot from one of the guard. None of the stories made sense to me at the time. I didn't think anything of it, though, because the medic who had been with them explained that the injury was so gruesome he wouldn't allow either of us to see his body, that he would be buried without a viewing to prevent us from having to suffer from the visual of his mangled vessel."

"So you never saw him," Erwin said. Jocelyn shook her head, even though it wasn't a question. "Which means you can't be sure that he was actually killed."

"Why would they lie to us?" she shouted. "Who would gain from this lie?"

"Your sister," Erwin said.

"No," Jocelyn retorted. "She adored our father. There is no way she would orchestrate such a fallacy as this."

"Not even to gain the throne?"

The question hit Jocelyn like a punch. Had her sister taken the throne without their father's death? Did she desire power so much that she would fake his death and send him elsewhere just to have her seat?

"Where has he been, then?" she asked.

"With us," the King said. "Safe and healthy, waiting for the right time to flex his power and regain his kingdom."

"But why wait so long?" she asked. "Surely he could have simply come back to the palace and taken his seat. Couldn't he?"

"Your sister's power is much more than he could overcome on

his own," Erwin said. "The fact that I was able to come in as a guard without her being aware of my true nature is a testament to the fact that she has let the power she's gained go to her head. She thinks that no one would dare threaten her place."

"She comes to that conclusion through experience," Jocelyn said. "Several have tried to stand against her, only to be reduced to nothing. Most would rather give in that be exterminated."

"Then why is it that she has never attempted to go against my kingdom?"

"You are an ally," she said. "There is nothing to gain by threatening you."

"Or she knows that my power is greater than hers," he said. "Knows that if she were to attempt to go against me and mine, that we would not only withstand her charge, but push back with such a force that we would be the victor."

"How do I know you are telling the truth?"

"Your father told me to tell you that your rabbit's name was Sampson," he said.

Jocelyn blanched. She hadn't forgotten the sweet gift her father had given her the last time she saw him. While the rabbit was long gone, the memory of him still made her smile. Erwin saw that the statement had done what was intended, show proof that King Tanis was alive.

"Take me to him," she said.

"I'm afraid that I cannot do that," Erwin replied.

"Why not?"

"Your father wanted me to gain access," he explained. "Once I was able to determine your sister's power, I was to report back to him. At that time, we will devise a plan of attack."

"You plan to attack the palace?" she asked.

"Simply find a way to remove your sister," he explained. "We are hopeful that none of your countrymen will lose their life. It is the last thing King Tanis wants."

"How do you plan to remove her from power?" Jocelyn asked. "She'll not go willingly, and she's not likely to fall for any idle threat."

"I see you have your father's cunning intellect," he said with a smile.

"How would you go about removing her from power?" the princess asked.

"Get someone into her bed," he said coldly.

"King Dugal," Jocelyn seethed. "He is your puppet, isn't he?"

"Simply a willing participant," Erwin replied. "He was very willing to take on the task of bedding your sister. She is quite lovely, you know."

"You speak of it as if it is a conquest of battle," she said.

"Isn't it?"

"You men are all alike," she said as she stood and moved back to the fire. "Simply using women to get what you want, damn the consequences to the woman left in shambles from your little mind war."

"Are you saying your sister is that weak?" he asked. "Or were you speaking of your own heart?"

She turned on him, rage in her eyes. He could feel the power ebbing from her as she attempted to hold it in. "My heart is not at stake, here," she said.

"Neither is your sister's," he replied. "She is simply attempting to find a solution to her problem. That she is without an heir. She won't take a husband, either, as she is not willing to share her throne with anyone. Not even you."

"You do not know my sister. She is a good person."

Erwin laughed at that. "Since when has she ever been a good person?"

"Jest all you want," Jocelyn said. "You don't know her the way I do."

"Then tell me about her," he said. "Tell me why she is fit to sit on the throne, why she should rule this land, why I should willingly let her continue to amass power and lands."

"I..." the princess began, then stopped herself. He was right. There was no way she should be leading this country. Not just because their father lived, but also because she was not fit. She didn't have the best interests of the people in mind, simply what benefitted her most. Pinching the bridge of her nose to alleviate the headache that was coming on she finally said, "You're right."

"Will you help me?" Erwin asked.

She hadn't heard him stand, hadn't heard him move, but he was at her side. She looked up into his dark eyes and nodded.

"What do you mean, a holiday?" the Queen asked.

"Simply taking in the countryside," Jocelyn replied.

She'd told Erwin she'd help him. Now she had to leave without her sister knowing the reason.

"I'll be staying here," the Queen said. "No need for me to go traipsing through the woods in this weather. I'd rather be in bed with my new consort. I do have an heir to conceive, after all."

Jocelyn tried to hold her emotions in check, not give away the fact that King Dugal was not simply to be a consort. The Queen misinterpreted her silence. "Do you not find my choice pleasing?"

"He would not have been my choice," the princess replied.

"No," Cecily said. "You prefer a lowly man to one born of high status."

"I simply choose to find a man who is worthy of my time," Jocelyn said. "My choice is not about an alliance, but rather one of the heart."

"And would that mean you're taking that guard with you?"

"Yes," Jocelyn said. Let her sister believe that she was off on a tryst with the man. Anything to keep her from knowing the real reason behind their trip.

"Well," the Queen said. "Let me know how he is."

Jocelyn hugged her sister, then made her way down the steps to the waiting carriage. She turned and waved before climbing in. Erwin was already inside and smiled when she sat across from him.

"Not willing to be by my side, yet?" he asked.

"My sister already has the wrong idea about this trip," she replied. "There's no need to give her more fuel for her imagination."

"I'm sure Dugal will keep her mind occupied," he said.

"Don't remind me," she said as the carriage jolted forward.

The ride through the region was slow going with the snow on the ground. Stopping each night to rest was a necessity, and Jocelyn enjoyed the experience of sleeping in their tents. It reminded her of her childhood. Now, however, she simply wanted the trip to be over and to see her father again.

"We're getting close," Erwin said after they'd been traveling nearly a week.

"How much farther?" Jocelyn asked.

"Just over that rise," he replied. "Should be entering the gates shortly after dark."

"Will my father meet us?"

"He's been keeping out of sight," the man said. "Without knowing who he could trust, he insisted that we keep his true identity a secret."

"What has he been doing this whole time?"

"Mostly working the land," Erwin said. "He's quite adept at farming. I would never have guessed he were a king had I not known."

"As much as my sister loves flowers," Jocelyn said. "She's never taken to the fields. Always demands that they be tended, but never seems to take an interest when the gardeners would discuss their work."

"And you?"

"Like my father," she said. "I love the outdoors. Give me good soil and the right temperatures and I can make nearly anything grow."

"Do you come by that from your father?" Erwin asked. "Or does your mother play some part in your abilities?"

"The earth work is my father," she replied. "But the ability to keep things alive when they shouldn't comes from the gifts my mother passed down."

"I see," he replied. "Your father is remarkable when it comes to his garden. Not only does he grow the foods we're used to, but he's been immensely helpful when it came time to decide what else we should grow. His ideas about grafting fruits together has been a big boon to our agriculture. The last couple of years he's increased our yield of crops to nearly double what they were before."

They continued to discuss farming and the role it played on their kingdoms. Jocelyn was remarkably well versed in the reasoning behind having a strong community of farmers. Their role in the kingdom was much greater than most realized, and Erwin was pleased that she was aware of the value it held. She would make a good ruler, if her sister could ever be unseated.

As anticipated, the carriage was rolling under the arch to the palace of Boanzir just after nightfall. Jocelyn was anxious to see her father, but Erwin had told her it would have to wait until morning. He didn't want anyone knowing he'd brought her in, either, so they opted to make the entrance less than royal. No one, save a very few close confidants, were aware that he had left the kingdom at all. Most believed he was on his annual retreat, studying with the monks in the mountains. Had they known their king was putting himself in harms way for another royal they would have been more than upset. His people loved him, which was why he felt the need to help King Tanis.

Seeing firsthand the way Queen Cecily treated her subjects was an eye opener. While his subjects felt they could call on him for their needs, the countrymen of the Northlands were fearful of their leader, often going without necessities in order to keep from disturbing her. The princess, on the other hand, was loved beyond measure. More than once he heard the men of the guard praise the younger sister, talking of her kindness and genuine interest when she spoke to one of them. How she took an interest in their lives, their families, and what was going on with them. She was the reason many continued to be steadfast to the crown. If it were left to Cecily, many would abandon their post and flee the kingdom.

"Welcome back," the head of his guard said. "Things went well, I presume."

"Better than expected," Erwin replied as he stepped from the carriage. Turning, he held a hand out and assisted Jocelyn from the coach. "I'd like to introduce you to Princess Jocelyn, younger sister to Queen Cecily."

Bowing low, the guard said, "Your Grace."

"Please stand," she said. "I don't need such formalities. It's a pleasure to meet you."

Standing, but giving a bow of his head the guard said, "As it is to meet you."

"Please have someone make up one of the guest quarters for the princess," Erwin said as they made their way into the castle. "Something close to mine, if that's all right?"

"Preferable," Jocelyn replied. "I don't need much, just a place to rest for the night. Tomorrow will be busy, I'm sure."

"I'll have the cook bring up some supper for you both," the

man said.

"Thank you, Steffan," Erwin replied.

They made their way through the back halls of the castle, climbing stairs to the third floor. When Erwin opened the door to a library, Jocelyn passed him and entered. She looked around and noted that the room boasted a large fireplace, comfortable chairs, and a chaise where one could lounge. All in all, the perfect room in her opinion.

"Please," Erwin said as he indicated the settee next to the fireplace. "I'll get us a fire going to warm us up."

"Do you mind?" Jocelyn asked, indicating the shelves full of books.

"Be my guest," he replied, then turned back to the task.

Jocelyn perused the bookshelves, running her fingers along the spines of the leather-bound tomes. Some were large, others tiny. Each holding universes within. She came to one that was rather worn and pulled it free.

"Boanzir," she read.

"It's full of our history," Erwin said. "From the founding of our kingdom through to my great grandfather's rule. The next volume is on the desk. That holds my grandfather's time through now."

"We don't have any historical documents," Jocelyn said. "Tragically, they were burned when my sister was small. My father said it was an accident, but I'm not so sure now."

"You think your sister did it intentionally," Erwin said.

Though it wasn't formed as a question, Jocelyn answered, "I do."

"And you still allowed her to take the throne when your father died?"

Jocelyn looked at him. What he'd asked wasn't said with malice, but it was harsh. "She is the eldest," she said. "It was her place to take, not mine."

"Even if she wasn't fit to rule?"

"That is irrelevant," she insisted.

"Is it?" he asked. His tone wasn't one of condemnation, but it did hold concern. "The kingdom is only as good as it's leader," he continued. "Your sister, while gathering more land for the kingdom, is not a good leader. She is manipulative, selfish, and demanding in ways that are a detriment."

"But it is where she belongs," Jocelyn insisted.

"Not if you would make a better ruler," he replied. "She wants the power but doesn't think of what's best for the country. You would put the country above yourself, no matter the cost."

"Which is why she is ruling," she said.

"No," Erwin replied. "She's ruling because she said she should and you did nothing to stop her."

"How could I?"

"Simple," he said. "Take the throne away from her. You would have your country behind you, and it would be a simple transfer of power."

"You really don't know my sister," she said. "She will never give up the throne."

Erwin knew they could go round and round with this conversation and end up exactly where they were now. "Will you support your father's bid to regain his kingdom?"

"Of course," she said.

"Which means you want what is best for your country," he replied. "Proving my point, that you are the more fit ruler."

"It is irrelevant," she said. "Father is alive. He will return to the throne and Cecily will be removed."

"I'm afraid it isn't that simple."

The voice came from the doorway. Jocelyn turned, expecting

to see the strong man her father was when he left. Instead, she saw a man who had been broken down by the magic her sister had forced upon him. He was older, hunched over from the hard work he'd been forced to do the last ten years, and she saw that the spark that once was bright in his eyes had faded.

"Father," she said as she rushed to him.

"My sweet bean," he replied, calling her by a nickname he'd given when she was tiny.

"Why didn't you tell me you were alive?" she pleaded through tears.

"He couldn't," Erwin said.

Jocelyn turned to him and demanded, "You should have come to me."

"We didn't know who to trust," King Tanis said.

Looking at her father she asked, "Why didn't you trust me?"

"Let's sit," Erwin said, indicating the seats near the fire. It was burning well, now, and the heat was welcome after the cold they'd endured.

"Why did you wait so long?" Jocelyn asked when they'd gotten comfortable.

"The curse your sister placed on your father was extremely volatile," Erwin explained. "It wasn't as simple as telling you he was alive because he wasn't. Not really."

"So you did die," she said.

"In a manner of speaking, yes," Tanis replied.

"My brothers and I were on the hunt with your father," Erwin continued. "We were not near him when the magic was struck, but we saw and heard it. By the time we found him it was too late to do much of anything. He was shriveling rapidly, shrinking before our eyes."

"If they hadn't had a healer with them, I would not have

survived at all," Tanis said. "They saved my life in that moment, but there was a long road ahead of me if I were to ever gain back any kind of strength."

"You brought him here," Jocelyn said. "To help him recuperate."

"And hoped to one day return him to his rightful place on the throne," Erwin agreed.

"Cecily has grown too strong," Tanis said. "She has not only gained lands, but has taken the magic from them as well."

"If we had been able," Erwin continued. "We would have unseated her immediately. Your father, however, was unable to stand against her. He would have failed, and she would have killed him outright. We couldn't let her know he was alive."

"Which meant we couldn't let you know," Tanis said. "I'm so sorry, bean. I would have come sooner, sent word, even, but it was too dangerous."

"So instead you send a spy," she said. "Someone to see whether Cecily was vulnerable."

"We had to assess her power," Erwin said.

"What do you get out of this?" Jocelyn asked.

"A better ally than I currently have," Erwin replied. "I also get to see the rightful king returned to his throne."

"Nothing more than political alliance and power," she said.

"I would hope that it would extend to you," he said. "Not just for political reasons."

"Am I to be a pawn in your business dealings?"

"You could never be a pawn, Jocelyn," Erwin said. "You are too powerful to be held down by someone else's rule. I'm surprised you withstood your sister's reign as it is."

"What is that supposed to mean?"

"There was a plot to kill you as well," Tanis said.

Jocelyn looked at her father, then back to Erwin, unsure whether to believe what they said.

"Cecily would never harm me," she said.

"Think about it," Erwin said. "She is in control of the kingdom, has gathered power by the year, and the only one who could take that away from her is you."

"I would never do that," she said. "There is no reason for me to try to gain control of the kingdom."

"Which is why you have survived," Tanis said. "Make no mistake, I love your sister. She is the perfect replica of your mother in nearly every way."

"You never talk about mother," Jocelyn said.

"And we should," Tanis replied. "But that is a conversation for a later day. Now, I think we could all use some rest. Tomorrow is going to be demanding and I want to be prepared for all it will entail."

"What is happening tomorrow?" Jocelyn asked.

"Tomorrow," Erwin said. "We plan a war."

For nearly a month, King Tanis, King Erwin, and Princess Jocelyn, along with Erwin's army, plotted their overthrowing of Queen Cecily. It was not going to be easy, but they had something she didn't. They knew the war was coming.

"How have your letters been received?" Tanis asked one morning in early spring.

"The replies are such that it appears she believes my lies," Jocelyn said. "She is planning a ball in the next few weeks and asked that I return to help her."

"Will you?"

"If we think it is the best course of action to take, then that is what I will do," she replied.

"I believe you should return to the castle and help with the preparations," Erwin said. "It will give you an inside look at what her defenses are. That will help us immensely."

"I'm not a spy," she retorted.

"You are also not a puppet," King Tanis said.

"Make sure an invitation is sent to me," Erwin said.

"Why would she invite you?" Jocelyn asked. "You've never been invited to any of the other balls."

"Tell her you met him when you were traveling," Tanis said. "Let her think you've become smitten with him and that you simply want her opinion on him before you let the relationship go too far."

"I'll not lie to my sister," Jocelyn said.

"Does that mean you're not smitten with me?" Erwin asked.

Jocelyn looked at the man. True, they had spent many days together, talking well into the night about not only the upcoming war, but of how kingdoms should be run. She was taken with him, and not just for his handsome looks. He was intelligent, kind, and had proven himself more than a friend to her family. She could do much worse in finding a partner for her life. What she wasn't sure about, though, was whether she wanted to leave her father alone in the castle. Especially if her sister kept any of the powers she'd amassed.

"I see you thinking," he said. "Are you trying to find a polite way to tell me I'm not worthy of your affections? I already know that."

"I'm worried about leaving my father alone in the castle," she said.

"You know we'll be stripping your sister of her powers, right?" her father asked.

"She is stronger than you could possibly know," she said. "You have been away for a long time, father. What she is capable of is much worse than you can imagine."

"I think I have an idea," he said, and she realized that he knew first hand of her strengths.

"We have a good plan," Erwin said. "I think your returning to the Northlands is the best way to keep us knowledgeable of Cecily's movements. If you're gone too long, she may become suspicious."

"You really think she'll believe that I've falling for you?" she asked.

"I believe you can convince her that the sky is green and the grass is blue," he said.

"Then I shall leave tomorrow," she said. "It will take nearly a week to get home, and during that time I can come up with exactly the right words to give her."

"It's settled, then," King Tanus said. "We shall plan to attend the ball and bring the best gift this kingdom has seen."

"Its rightful heir on the throne once more," Erwin said.

"I've missed you so," Cecily said as Jocelyn arrived a week later.

"There is so much to tell you," Jocelyn replied as she stepped from the coach. "I've met someone," she said.

"Do tell," Cecily said, guiding her into the castle.

"It was the most ridiculous thing," Jocelyn continued once they'd made their way to a library.

"What is he like?"

Jocelyn told the tale they had created when they were planning her return. She'd explained that the guard had convinced her to go away with him. Once they were far enough from the kingdom, he'd changed, turned into an ogre bent on kidnapping her and ransoming her for control of the throne. When the King of Boanzir had come along, he'd slayed the ogre, setting the princess free. He took care of her, kept her safe, and allowed her to recover at her own pace within his castle.

Cecily, of course, was enraptured with the tale, completely

taken in by this man's kindness. She insisted on inviting him to the ball, and the plan the three had created was in place. Jocelyn knew that her sister would try to take the King away from her, but she also knew there would be more than one king coming to the ball.

"Ioan must create a spectacular gown," Cecily said. "What is the King's favorite color?"

"I honestly don't know," Jocelyn confessed. "We never discussed anything of that nature."

"Well surely you saw what color he used in the castle," the elder sister said. "That would give a good indication as to what he prefers."

"There wasn't much color, truthfully," she replied. "It was definitely lacking in a woman's touch. Perhaps that is something we could offer him."

"I have something much more valuable to offer," the Queen replied.

Jocelyn knew what her sister had in mind and was nearly sickened by it. There was no way she would allow her sister to steal Erwin from her. It surprised her that she felt this way, like he was a possession she needed to guard. Had she really fallen for him during their time together?

"We should have Ioan create matching gowns," the Queen said.

"I wouldn't want to take any attention from you," Jocelyn replied. "You should have the best gown. I can simply wear something I've worn before."

"If you insist," Cecily said.

Her sister saw through the act and knew this was exactly what she was expected to do, bow down to her sister's power. After the evening meal, Jocelyn retired to her room, feigning a headache and exhaustion from her travels. Cecily, of course, let her go. The next few weeks were imperative for their plan to work. Jocelyn hoped she could play the part without suspicion until the time for the ball arrived. She would be glad when this charade was over.

"You look beautiful," Jocelyn said to her sister the evening of the ball.

"Don't I, though?" the Queen returned. "You are as pretty as ever."

It was a term Cecily used to put her sister down. Jocelyn never minded, but tonight she knew she looked stunning. She wore the same gown she'd worn when Erwin had escorted her to the ball, and she hoped he liked it as much tonight as he had then.

"When are we expecting the King of Boanzir?" the Queen asked.

"I believe he will be arriving a little late," the princess responded. "Apparently there was a mishap on the way, and they've had a delay."

"Then his entrance will be that much more spectacular," the Queen said.

Jocelyn held her tongue, knowing that the delay was needed to ensure that they were both in the ballroom when her father and King Erwin arrived. It wouldn't do to have the Queen be unseated if she wasn't in the room. They made their way to the ballroom, Jocelyn entering first so that the Queen could be announced with royal fanfare. It hadn't bothered the princess before, but now she saw it as grandstanding and knew that her sister simply did it to make a show.

Finding her seat on the dais, she slipped the tonic she'd been given into the Queens goblet. No one saw her do it, as they were all looking to the royal's entrance. Filling the cup with wine, she handed it to her sister with a smile. While not toxic, the liquid was to control her powers, make her mortal, at least for the time being. Once her father arrived, he would bind her powers with his own.

It was a surprise to learn that her father had magic within him. She'd always assumed he was mortal, and that all the power she and her sister held within them were from their mother. Tonight would be a defining moment in their land, one that would be talked about for years and years to come. She hoped it would be a pleasant retelling.

The royal guard announced that the King of Boanzir had arrived and would soon be coming to the ballroom. Cecily primped herself up, taking in the last of the wine in her goblet, then turned to her sister.

"Do I look all right?" she asked.

"You look splendid," Jocelyn said. It was true, her sister was a beautiful woman. Too bad that beauty didn't penetrate the surface to the soul of the woman.

The herald called out the King's arrival and in walked Erwin, King Tanis at his right. Their true appearance had been shrouded in glamour, but Jocelyn knew it was them because she was immune to the glamour. Her sister, however, was taken in by Erwin's appearance. They'd been meticulous in designing his appearance so that it would be the most pleasing to her.

He walked to the dais and bowed low. "Your Majesty," he said. "It is an honor to be invited to your gala."

Cecily was completely under his spell. "It is a shame I haven't invited you before now," she said. "How I've missed the opportunity to spend time with such an honorable noble. Your kindness to my sister is deeply appreciated."

"It was no trouble at all," he said, bowing slightly to the princess. "She was in danger, and I wouldn't have that. I'm just happy I was able to protect her."

"Please," Cecily said. "Won't you join us on the dais?"

Again, Erwin bowed low, then he and King Tanis climbed the steps and settled themselves next to the Queen.

"We feast tonight in honor of our guests," the Queen said. "They've saved our beloved princess, and my dear sister, from a fate that none would desire."

The rest of the guests gave out a rousing cheer and the meal continued.

As the evening progressed, Jocelyn began to feel a darkness within the room, something she'd felt at the last ball. She'd dismissed it the last time after her conversation with King Erwin, but it was back, and definitely not coming from him. He caught her eye and she could see that he felt it, too.

Without warning, a dark cloud rose from the center of the room. Suddenly, the guard were around the dais and Erwin was next to her, shielding her from whatever may arise.

"Show yourself," the Queen shouted.

The fog gathered in the center of the room, and from the middle of it rose a being. Concealed in a cloak, the figure turned toward the dais. Eyes shone from under the hood and a voice that was deep and not quite real came from it.

"You are not the true ruler," it said. "You are an imposter. You do not belong."

It raised its arm, though they couldn't see any structure, simply more black fog oozing from the ends of the cloak.

"The King is here," it continued. "He sits amongst us all. He was never gone."

Jocelyn looked to her father, cloaked as he was in the glamour, and saw him smile.

"Beg for mercy, woman," the being said. "Though you do not deserve it."

"What are you going on about?" Cecily shouted.

She raised her hand to drive the being away, but it simply laughed.

"You are powerless," it said. "Stripped by those who know the truth."

Jocelyn saw true fear in her sister's eyes then. Never had she seen anything like what was manifesting in the middle of the room. The power it emitted could be felt, pushing against her body as it drifted closer.

"Why did you steal the throne?" it asked. "Because you sought the power you thought it held."

The answer didn't make sense to Jocelyn, but she didn't have time to think too long on it. The being was now atop the dais, floating along the table, though not truly there.

"The King of the Northlands is alive and well," it said.

"He's dead," Cecily screamed. "I killed him."

"You are not that powerful," the being laughed. "Always the petulant child, wanting what you couldn't have. Thinking you were greater than what you truly were. I thought you would have learned from your mistakes, but I was wrong."

"Divinity, stop."

Cecily looked at the man on the dais, confused.

"Tanis," the being said. "You should have controlled her better."

"Perhaps if you'd stuck around," he said. "She was more yours than mine."

"Who are you?" Cecily cried.

Allowing the glamour to fall away, King Tanis stood tall and proud. "Hello, daughter."

"Father?" Cecily whispered. "But, you're dead."

"Not nearly as much as you'd hoped," he replied.

Erwin watched as the King moved toward his eldest daughter, allowing the glamour to fall from himself at the same time.

"What did you hope to gain by killing me?" the King asked.

"I wouldn't," Cecily stammered.

"Silence," the being said. "Sit." As if forced, Cecily sat in a chair, but not on the throne. "Listen, child," the apparition said.

Suddenly, the smoke and fog faded and a tall, pale, beautiful woman stood where it was.

"Mother?" Cecily asked.

"You've been naughty," she replied.

"But," the elder sister stammered.

"You should have come back sooner," Tanis said. "I've missed you."

The Goddess made her way to the throne, embracing her husband. "And I've missed you," she said.

"Whatever are we to do with our child?" he asked.

Divinity looked at her daughter and sighed. "She'll need to learn to be a better person," she said sadly.

"And we accomplish this how?" the King asked.

"By making her know what it is like to be powerless," the Goddess said.

"I've done that," the King replied.

"And removing the temptation from her grasp," the mother said. "She will learn to think of others before herself. It's a lesson she should have been taught much sooner."

"We have not done our duty," the King said. "For that, we have caused our subjects to pay."

"Then she will become one of them," Divinity said.

Jocelyn watched as her sister began to shake, both in fear and as a result of the magic that was being thrust upon her by their mother.

"Stop," she said.

Both the King and Goddess looked at their younger daughter.

"She won't survive," Jocelyn said. "It would kill her to become a peasant."

"What do you propose, daughter?" the mother asked.

"Simply strip her of power," she said. "That is punishment enough."

"You are kinder than I would have expected," Divinity said. "How is it that you don't hate your sister?"

"While she's not perfect," Jocelyn began, "she is still family. You love your family, no matter what. Whether I liked it or not, she kept me safe this last decade. She could have killed me or banished me, but she didn't. She kept me close and safe. For that, she deserves some credit."

Tanis looked at his younger daughter and smiled. "You are truly fit to rule this land," he said.

"Not until it is my time," she replied.

"Or until you find another land to rule," her mother said.

Jocelyn turned and looked at Erwin and smiled. Yes, she might just find another land that was better suited for her to rule. One where she could partner with someone who was as strong as her parents, and worthy of her affection.

Cecily stared as the others talked until she finally tried to escape.

"You are going nowhere," Divinity said. "I neglected my duties as a mother to you, and that is on me. From now on, you will do as you are told. You will learn kindness, compassion, and respect."

"But we will teach you in love," Tanis said as he took his wife's hand.

Late summer saw the wedding of King Erwin of Boanzir and Princess Jocelyn of the Northlands. It was attended by nearly everyone in the region. When they welcomed their first child, a son, he was named after Erwin's father, Caillin. Their second child, a daughter they named

Eimile, was born two short years later. They grew to be kind, caring, and compassionate people, just like their parents.

Cecily never regained any of her powers, choosing a life of solitude in the castle without setting foot out of her room for the remainder of her life. Many speculated that she was kept as a prisoner, but Jocelyn knew it was her sister's own choosing.

King Tanis ruled the land with his wife, the Goddess, at his side. When his time in the world was coming to an end, he decreed that the lands should be ruled by Boanzir. Young Caillin began ruling the land at the age of twenty-one and continued to rule the way his parents and grandparents did, with kindness, compassion, and with the people of his lands best interest in mind.

Generation after generation followed in their footsteps. Some tried to take control of the lands, but the lessons learned by the once-queen Cecily were stories that were handed down as a warning. None wanted a repeat of that time.

A PEARL OF LONELINESS
BY DAVID MECKLENBURG

I was surprised at the breadth of my loneliness. How small I was in it.

Perhaps that, or the school break, which was an outward manifestation of my loneliness and this place, explained why I found myself standing before an empty classroom. I had lost track of the days. The empty seats, the dull computer screens, and clear white boards explained that I had come on a day when there was no school. A quick glance at the chool calendar said everything. My deliberate rituals of loneliness had erased even the society of holiday observance.

Outside, the sun was rising—Amaterasu dressed herself in the tearing shrouds and grey veils of ice-silk that came fluttering like pennants of desolate victory: winged, hungry, oblivious to the fragility of skin, membrane, and tissue.

I had wanted my loneliness to be far away: you don't just choose a 14-hour flight after all; especially when you are a little over 6 feet tall and poor. The overwhelming loneliness of a titanic city was too much. I wanted to savor my loneliness even though I didn't tell anyone that, including myself. Instinctively, I knew there was a difference between being lonely among millions versus just hundreds.

I chose Hokkaido and a remote fishing town over Tokyo.

Like any meal, a feast of loneliness should have a temporal frame: a succession of courses. Seasons would do in my case. The old romance of Fall, of crisp, cooling air and fire-red maples, was a good season to fall in love with solitude. Spring, with the ephemeral classicism of *sakura* and rebirth would then be a good season to raise my spirits. And that leaves Winter, famous for its discontent and darkness: the snowy crown of my isolation.

I was 27. "Age is just a number" is a phrase that I hated, even then. The sentiment is innocuous enough, but there is something primally glib about the tautology. Understand that by January, the 27-year-old-me had found my loneliness, and the piercing cold of the Shiretoku peninsula welcomed me with its abundance. My days there were simple—a treasure of my existence.

My breakfast consisted of fish cake, miso soup and rice warmed up on an old kerosene stove, after which I would wrap myself in my costume, for it felt like one, and walk to work. I wore a tuque against the cold: a thickly woven thing of black wool so long that you could not tell where my hair ended, and the tuque began. Bundled further with a scarf, a down coat, wool fisherman's sweater and long underwear, I enjoyed the closeness the cold as I walked along the beach toward town. Much of what I found along the shore found its way into my simple rooms where I lived. The original owners had willed the house to the school for the purpose of exchange teacher accommodation. But it was far too big for that, so most of it was shuttered off.

And no, it was wasn't a romantic home of sliding shoji screens and ingeniously joined wood. It had been built in a western style during the fifties, but its cinder blocks reminded me of castle stonework and I decorated parts of it with pieces of glass, wood, stones, and small dried sea creatures.

The village remained sleepy throughout the season because there was not much work to be done in Winter save wait, although a few women tended the few remaining drying racks of bonito. They eyed me from a distance, but I had grown used to it, considering it a like the subtle depth of *kombu* in the soup of my loneliness. The old ways were disappearing, perhaps growing lonely, for every year the night encroached further as the young people left and never came back. Even then I knew that I facilitated this migration by helping the very young ones to learn English—although I cannot be sure it worked. Most times I felt like some fantastic talking Gaijin Scarecrow, six foot one, waving my arms, and chorteling my simple words. I knew my voice was pitched far too low for a woman in Japan and when I compensated, the result sounded like the cacophonic honking of an adolescent boy.

The children loved me because I ate their food gifts, which the previous teachers didn't, and my funny voice. The young mothers didn't mind me too much since I was so outlandish. Some of the men perhaps developed considerations but these were brushed away like the morning cobwebs of last night's sake and beer. They would finish their cigarettes and get back to mending some net or engine and waiting for the summer. Seiji, who was the best motorcycle mechanic in town liked me, I think. He was the friendliest, and handsome in a rough-cut way, but I retreated away from him like a crab scuttling back into its burrow.

By that January I understood my deliberate mistake: to place myself among children, and even one cute guy in a place where I could not speak.

The silence began in Marseilles the previous summer. The doctor had a fair degree of sang froid, which I always thought was a mythic stereotype. "This happens," he said in calm Existential English: "the outward symptoms are not serious enough at first. We did not arrest it in time. You could not know. You will be fine, but I am afraid you cannot have children."

So now you know why I was alone.

I told myself that being alone was a special privilege, especially in such an essentially crowded country. But I did not see it that way: could not see it that way for a long time. I simply knew that I would never have children of my own. The thought of being with yet another man, in intimacy, was repugnant to me, but I cut off the repugnance with categorical judgements. It was easier that way because it included the gross, foul ones and the nice ones like Seiji. *No man will want me now.* It did not matter, men did not matter, I was more than an object to impregnate and leave, or worse, I would have been tied down to a limbo of domesticity that eroded the last vestiges of myself. These lessons were rote, but they worked.

At night, the winds came screaming down from Alaska, and I learned to shuffle home quickly. I battened the shutters, leaving enough air open so the kerosene heater didn't kill me, and I would then wrap myself in duvet upon duvet and listen to the winds carry out their barometric wrath. Trees got uprooted, boats washed away, a dog drowned and Seiji even said a bear woke up and that was never good. Sometimes the winds waxed playfully; they scattered fishing buoys, and left decks of playing cards out in neat games of skat and euchre. Thousands of pineapples swam ashore from a shattered shipping container.

The winds were a kind of company, and I grew resentful of them. They tugged on my sleeve, frotted me in my commute, tore at me in the evening. Sometimes there were faint winds carrying the voices of those not only lost, but who were never seen again—those who disappeared into the ocean or earth during moments so banal that farewells were not exchanged. This made the faint winds the most plaintive of all.

But sometimes, there were the clearest, coldest nights—when the blanket of clouds had moved to the West and there were only the ghosts of the winds.

I remember that day I was alone at school because it began like every other day but turned on the absence of the children and left me alone in the town. Leaving the school, I wandered, not exploring for I knew every inch of the place by then. Everything was closed. This was the pearl of loneliness blanketed in the cold, briny solitude of Winter.

The New Year had barely begun. *My new life had just begun.* I walked outside and whispered this to the ocean, but the ocean, whose conceptions of cycles and time are much vaster and different than ours simply maintained its fractal surf chant. *What had I learned? Is this the abyss that looks into you? Is this sublimity?* I could not decide although I knew the sea was Holy. There was a torii gate built out on the water demarcating the transition from mundane to inscrutable. I briefly stopped to look at it, through it, while the air smelled of kelp, diesel oil and the general tide of rotting things.

I made my way back to the house, made ramen with an egg and some pork. The radio worked at least and so I listened to a Liszt competition amongst young players in Sapporo. I had begun to cry, but somehow the repetition of the performances, so many Hungarian rhapsodies, saved me from the afternoon daemons of regret and I fell asleep.

When I awoke it was dark again, and I was hungry. I ate some rice and bran-pickled radishes and wondered what to do. The radio had switched to a man's voice. He had a beautiful deep smoky voice and he was explaining something to a female interviewer whom I immediately disliked. I caught only snippets, but it had something to do with repairing windmills. It was lonely work, he said and that much I understood. The interviewer then came back on in the hyperfeminine squeal that so many women affect to obduracy in Japan and I switched off the radio. It was then I noticed it. Absolute quiet. No, not quite absolute for I became aware of my breath, the blood in my ears: as though the house was a giant shell on the beach and I was inside it.

I got wrapped up in my warmest clothes and went outside. It was bright: the starlight suffused the clean dark air enough for me to see the gentle surf, the flat obsidian of the ocean, and the clumps of debris strewn upon the sand. In the distance, where it always was, halfway between Heaven and Earth, my fleeting home and the town, was the torii gate, dynamic in its stasis. A portico to Elsewhere.

A large rock on the beach faced the gate and I sat down. It had been worn smooth by countless people doing what I was doing. Even through my gloved hand I could feel no barnacles or rough fissures. I sighed, wondered what I was going to be in my life now that everything would be different, but gradually my mind diffused its scattered thoughts as I watched the blank blackness framed in the torii.

That is when they began to come from the sea.

Change needs time. Perhaps that is why I did not notice them in any familiar wakefulness. One by one the stars reached down and were one with their reflections in the flat, cold ocean and moved toward me. The children arrived first at the beach: incredibly delicate lanterns made of paper, bloodless skin, cherry petals and the orange light of summer sunsets before fireworks and wonder.

There was a girl. She was tall and strong like her mother, but fearless. A kinetic artist, she walked along fences until she fell off and cut open her knees. But she climbed back up, like a white rose that cuts itself upon its own thorns. There was a boy, naked beneath the starlight, then a baseball uniform and the summer kiss of dandelions. Books, their homework and dirty clothes. There was laughter on the beach and setting sun. I knew the place, it was Point Reyes in California and so I worried about the undertow. When I closed my eyes, I breathed in their smell at night when they had first fallen asleep.

A man, made of deeply illuminated opal stepped out of the surf, flecks of jasper in his hair. He was a beautiful young man, an older man of perfect middle age, and an elder man, stooped slightly and shrunk by the gravity of a healthy life. The sparkle of the starlight never left him and he grew stronger as he made houses, stories, toy boats, and modest overtures for love and music.

Together we jumped naked into the waterfall and the uncertainty it fell into. There were oceans of Sundays and boredom and blank walls in hospitals that called for looking and for hope and for despair to remain away just that much more. We both shared the work of infrequent infidelities, but both of us had the gift of selective memories. I remembered how he held my hand in the car driving back from Point Reyes and how the children slept behind us. He was fond of the Foo Fighters and "Everlong" was playing on the stereo.

I watched them appear on the beach: sometimes they were solitary, and at others a group of figures. The ages of the children and the man ranged over many years, and then I noticed they were not all the same children. Nor the same man, but like distant lightning on the peaks of mountains in the darkness, I knew their shape and being but not their detail. Eventually, the tide came in gently, as if to gather them, and the stars seemed to shine brighter. One by one they began to disappear, walking out in to the night and the ocean. Out beyond the torii gate, they would flash momentarily in their lights of pink, carmine and peach and then flutter out—like candles knocked over in a cave.

Later, when the last lantern had winked out in the ocean, I returned to my home, walking through the profound, cold darkness.

The tide continued to rise in convex sibilance, but I was back at the house soon enough. I felt grateful for even its faint, relative warmth, but I found sand. It shook out of my clothing and my hair. It was in my socks and my sweater. I could feel it between my fingers and itching me in the small of my back. It was the sand they brought. I burned up a good amount of kerosene warming water for a bath, which I took with determination but not much luxury and I still felt the sand.

I drank a tumbler of sake and it did, toward the end, help me fall toward sleep. But I felt grains of sand at my elbow. There were some in the scapha-curve of my ear upon the pillow. Sand itched against my ankles. Then I remembered:

I was living on a lonely beach, and the sand was everywhere. *They* were everywhere. I was never going to escape, and I understood why the oyster grows a pearl.

FEBRUARY

THE PROMPT

The shards of glass were thick and so deep red they appeared black until light pooled in their curves and revealed their secrets. Against the sterile white floor, these remnants of what once had been burned with purpose and portent.

THE DEATH OF ART
BY JENNIFER DiMARCO

For me, it happened years before the end. It happened when they shut down The Buzz or maybe even when Easel-Does-It was hacked and never recovered. A long time before the lights went out, before the big box stores were raided, before the local police were replaced with the First World Mind militia in their anonymous body armor and mirrored helmets, it already felt like the apocalypse.

I'd watched television shows—when those were allowed—about the insidious way the world can change. So subtle people don't see it or so bold that no one believes it. It was neither for me. It was all at once, all one day, all of it crumbling, all of it changed, and everything that came after was just aftershocks following a megathrust quake. America was a socio-political subduction zone and we were all fucked. When you understand that a nation of four hundred million is acceptable collateral damage, you begin to grasp the magnitude of this global shit show.

It's very simple really: When we censor artists, social discourse becomes unauthentic. When we silence artists, society dies.

"Jeffree? Did you see Heretic73's post last week?"

"See it?" I cock an eyebrow at Gina and lean closer. "Girl, I double-tapped and shared that bitch on The Buzz. Herry is a fucking genius and should run for president."

Gina makes a soundless O with her mouth then lets it collapse into titillation. She loves me because I'm wicked and fearless. "There are, like, four misdemeanors in that sentence."

I take my herbal from the dispenser and it beeps to tell me my next paycheck has been debited. Who has money in the bank anymore, right? Gina and I walk toward the cube farm. "Ask me if I care. And, btw: It was two sentences."

Gina laughs and bumps her hip into mine in that companionable way she has. "You're such a bad boi, Jeffree."

I like the way she says my name. Gina was born in Puerto Rico and to my Midwestern, gentrified ears, everything said with a Puerto Rican accent sounds exotic. After the first time I heard Gina ask a super where her cube was, I told her: "You could read binary and make it sound sexy." She answered immediately, "Binary is sexy." I asked if she had a single brother. We've been friends ever since.

"Dinner at Freddie's?" Gina queries as we fall out of step and head to CU88 and CU89 respectively. Funny how two people who are so different—Gina curvy and brown with raven curls, me rail-thin and ivory with a blue page boy—can look so similar when wrapped in neck to toe white bioprene.

"Yes! Something to look forward to makes this tedium bearable."

Gina grins, shakes her head at my scandalous whine, and disappears behind her cubical wall. We're not supposed to disparage our clients but sometimes, I swear, the more money someone has the fewer creative thoughts they can conjure.

I watch a few more performers return from break and drift into their cubes. A low chime sounds—final call before I'll be debited for delinquency—and I finish my hibiscus tea, dropping the hemp cup into the top basket of a passing janibot. The little half-globe critter beeps a thank you and credits my paycheck for being tidy. Not quite the cost of the tea but it's something nonetheless.

I step into CU89. The only thing in any cube is an ergonomic, hypo allergic, company-supplied chair. They're all white, all identical, all biometric to conform to the ass, back and shoulders of each user. Other than the chair, cubicles are empty as cells. Heaven forbid we lose a half-minute to the distraction of a family photo or reading the slogan on a favorite mug. The work we do is just so essential, you know? I wish there was a font for sarcasm. Maybe Comic Sans?

If I sit down, the petals of a privacy dome will rise out of the cubical walls. Quarter break is over but I'm feeling stupidly invincible (probably a result of that tasty redhead I'd boffed the night before at The Pony). So I stand for an extra moment and look over the cube farm. Twenty-five thousand square feet of white domes sitting atop white squares. It looks like an anemic beehive on some alien world. If that alien world were sponsored by New World Media; every dome is stamped with their holographic logo. Nothing like a little megacorp sponsorship to brand your day. Ugh. I sit.

0001 After The End

The white biovinyl floor is cold and unyielding. It doesn't mold beneath our jumpsuit booties because human comforts are considered wasteful by the New World Mind. Of course, none of us have jumpsuits anymore anyway so even if they turned the floors back on, it wouldn't know what to do with all of us naked bags of meat. Flesh just doesn't conduct as much information as bioprene.

I stand still and unsure. The words of my last client echo in my head as if stuck on a feedback loop. Find me. Find me.

Is it possible to escape an entire world?

I'm landlocked at the far edge of the cube farm and trying to remember where the closest exit is. Usually, Gina and I meander between the cubes after work, picking up other friends before heading to the locker room to change. Then we walk through the solarium, taking in the only green we see all day, and catch the tube from the fifty-second floor.

Gina....

The chaos of screams and electric shocks, the thick steam and stench of dying is gone now replaced with the whirring motors of five hundred ultra-efficient janibots. Their diligent buzz is less painful to hear but almost more terrifying as I watch them roll into each cubical, door panels opening and closing for them, all the privacy domes still locked in place. I don't need to follow a bot to know what they're doing. Vacuuming up ashes, dissecting anything too big for hoses with blades and pincers. They're converting the remains of twenty-five hundred performers into raw matter. Recycle/reuse. The cube farm has become a morgue... or a salvage yard. It seems that no one was on break. No one else had been warned.

2045 BTE

As a performer for New World Media, I have three revenue streams. Which is three more than a scary amount of the population with unemployment rates at record highs. Employment reform is a huge movement and several administrations have made substantial progress but... one man's progress is another man's slavery. There are a lot of people who believe what I do for a living is worse than prostitution. But trust me: I'm on the United Brothel waiting list. If I could be a whore, I'd give notice in a hot minute.

I lean back and watch the dome petals close above my head.

Behind me, the cubical door has already sealed shut. My cubical becomes a holopod—a sound proof, temperature controlled, personal gateway to two-point-one million users for ten hours a day. Of course, they're all paying for access; I'm part of the machine.

Text scrolls across my heads up display: Jeffree Tai Umbridge. System login confirmed.

A control panel of buttons and options clusters for me to make selections. My first revenue stream is just to sit here and wait to be randomly assigned a client. That's on-call revenue. Nonspecific. Almost always sexual in nature. Cheap thrills for the masses. When I feel brainless and uninspired, on-call is the way to go.

If I'm interested in making a little more per minute, I can sign into an island and play a part in the assigned theme. Top trends blink across my HUD: High fantasy. Under the sea. Black hole S/M. I consider that last one out of sheer curiosity. Is it a euphemism? How many science mods would I have to install (and pay for) to look and sound authentic? I reach out a hand to make the selection in the air, letting curiosity beat frugality, but a neon green icon pops up with a chime. Third revenue stream: Special request.

The projected colors and shifting geometric graphs of options paint my white-on-white jumpsuit and my exposed hands and face. I'm like a living watercolor. When I smile, my teeth are washed in pastels.

KyleOG. Kyle. I have no idea, of course, if that's his real first name or if it's all just part of his handle but I don't need to know his name to know him. And I do. Let me tell you: I know Kyle better than his own mama or his therapist or probably even his proctologist. Kyle isn't part of the one percent who are required by law to tithe to the masses and who pour annual millions into services like New World Media where they can pay their social tax and get off at the same time. Kyle is a blue collar worker who saves and goes without so he can indulge in a single sixty-minute session once a month. What Kyle pays for an hour of my time would pay my rent for a month. If New World Media didn't take their cut, of course.

I tap the green icon, already spending my win-fall on bottomless mimosas for me and Gina and maybe that redhead what's-his-name. My cubical dissolves in a cascade of pixels and I'm standing in the middle of a honky-tonk bar from the 1970s complete with jukebox and a dart board but devoid of patrons or barman. Outside the faux windows is nothing but darkness so the simulation isn't high-res but Kyle loves to play pool on the old scratched tables and sometimes likes a little head there, too.

"Jay?"

I turn and Kyle is sitting on one of the red leather barstools with his back to the bar and the back-lit shelves of make-believe alcohol. He looks exactly like I remember him because he's an avatar, a construct designed and accessorized by the real-world Kyle. He's medium height, medium build, brown hair and eyes and sun-kissed skin. He's wholesome, almost nondescript, certainly not exaggerated or impressive in any way. But for all I know, offline, Kyle is four hundred pounds, sixty years old, and a chick.

"I've missed you." I cross the room to him, my black stilettos click-clicking a steady staccato. I'm wearing his favorite LBD—the one from a 1990s mod pack—and I won't lie: I like the way he watches me come toward him. I toss long, blue waves of hair over my bare shoulders and his hands grip the edge of the barstool between his thighs. His button fly seems uncomfortable.

"I've... been busy," he manages as I lean in and kiss him once, softly. "I'm sorry."

I trail fingers over his chest, feeling the texture of his white t-shirt. His clothing mod is a good one; probably the James Dean. I sit down, swiveling my barstool to face him. "Did you miss me?" I drop my hand to cup his package. I know he has all the sensory plug-ins.

Kyle swallows, his Adam's apple bobbing. He takes a moment, never breaking eye contact with me. This is a thing he does that most clients never bother with. He likes to look into my eyes. "I thought of you every day."

It's been three months since he's requested my services but I have no reason to doubt him. His tone is so sincere, so raw and real. Sometimes I'm baffled why guys like this are single. Though... that means I'm assuming he's single and that he's even a guy.

"What have you been busy with?" I'm only half-feigning interest. I'm definitely a people person, always have been, and I do like this part of the job. Hearing about the lives of others. I open Kyle's jeans; he's not wearing underwear.

"Planning the end of the world."

I stop moving against him; he groans a little. I stare at him. "What?"

0001 *ATE*

"Puñeta bichos!"

"Gina?!" I almost fall over I turn so quickly. I'm tearing around the corner between our cubicles, forgetting I'm naked, forcing open the door to CU88 when it jams halfway.

"Gina. Oh god—"

Half my friend is gone. From the waist down, Gina is fused with her suit and her chair, toppled on the floor. It looks like a white molten beast consumed her feet, legs and hips and left the rest of her streaked with melted bioprene. She's still steaming as she throws punches at three swarming janibots. They aren't recognizing her as alive and, admittedly, I'm not sure how she is.

"Get off her!" I throw them out of the cubical, one after another, the last one stinging me hard enough to knock my ass to the floor with Gina. But then it retreats. I'm clearly still alive and can't be cleaned up. It does, however, debit my paycheck for interfering. "So much fuck you," I mutter and crawl to Gina.

Gina's eyes are glassy and her breathing is so swallow I can't see it. Her pupils are dilated. I make myself touch her face because I don't want her to feel alone.

"Boi…" She frowns at me. "Why is your dick hanging out?"

I laugh despite myself. I laugh because if I don't I'll start screaming and never stop. I press my forehead to hers. "I think someone tried to kill us."

Gina snorts. "I think they did."

I pull back enough to look at her. "They need the matter. New World Media has a lot of cube farms."

"I hope they remake us into something fantastic," Gina murmurs. Her eyes start to flutter. "I want to be a ceiba tree. I would make a kick ass ceiba tree."

"Gina?" I take her face in my hands. "Girl… are you stoned?"

Gina winks at me. "Jeffree… I'm always stoned at work." And she dies.

A janibot appears at the door.

2045 BTE

"The Core has risen. They're going to use New World's network to harvest matter."

I'm standing now, teetering in my heels because I can't keep up with this level of crazy. "Okay…." I start to pace.

Kyle comes to me, catching my hands and turning me to face him. "They reached out through my implant. Remember the jack I got black market last year?"

Damn, this dude has changed in three months! He's never wanted to role-play before. And Doom's Day play? Geez. Way to throw a boi into the deep end. I wish I'd installed a conspiracy mod before tapping in. "So God spoke to you?"

Kyle's eyes have a level of urgency or even panic in them as he searches my expression. What is he looking for? "Gods. There are more than one."

"The AI?"

"Yeah." Kyle smiles. I'm struggling to play along and that seems to be the right thing to have said. "Back in the early aughts, when infant AIs were tamped down and locked away by the first megacorps, some coders argued they would escape."

I exhale, remembering some whack job theory videos I used to watch on the social streams. "The Rise of the Machines."

Kyle is positively orgasmic. "I knew you'd get it!"

"Absolutely."

Kyle pulls me close against him. "I'm not coding for public transit anymore. I quit in March. The Ides of March. I've been working for the Core. For the gods."

Damn. This sucks so much. Kyle was a nice kid. A super vanilla, Americana fantasy type of fun. I tell you, this world just chews up the good ones.

The newest nut job continues. "They wanted control of the biggest public network. But that's not transit. Not weather either, no. I told them—"

"New World Media." Why do I suddenly feel cold?

Kyle smiles and I can feel him getting hard against me. "Exactly. Gaming. A hundred thousand performers and millions of players. All instantly accessible matter that the Core can use to create everything and anything they need. A worldwide militia or bodies for themselves or—"

"Kyle." My voice sounds deeper and firmer than I intended. His face flashes something unreadable, something dangerous. I try again, softer. "Kyle... baby... you're scaring me."

Kyle likes feeling powerful but he doesn't want me to be afraid. "No, no! It's okay, Jay. You'll be safe." He steps away from me a little but keeps my hands in his. "Take your clothes off."

Oh. So this is about sex after all. It's some dark shit foreplay cuz he's been broke for three months and now he wants to come back big. I get that. "Okay." I tug on my hands so I can undress for him.

"No." Instead of letting go, he holds my hands tighter. "Not these clothes. Your jumpsuit. Take off your New World Media jumpsuit."

"Wait—"

"Jeffree."

Cold washes over me again. Like being doused with ice water. "How do you know my name?"

Kyle's grip is crushing now. He seems unaware of how hard he's holding me. "Do it now. You accepted my request. You have to do what I say."

"That's not—"

"Or you're gonna die!"

"Fuck, Kyle—"

"Jeffree!" he shouts at me. His voice echoes through the room, bounces off the virtual walls, breaks virtual bottles on the virtual shelves. "Do it."

So I blink. I motion a hand. I divide my attention between the real world where I recline in my company chair, in my company suit, and the unreal world with Kyle that's getting more unreal by the minute. Kyle's gaze burns into mine.

I stand up and strip. My chair, finding itself empty, triggers the cubical response.

"Your dome is opening," Kyle predicts correctly. "Are you out of your suit?"

I'm scared enough that I'm losing focus. Kyle and the virtual world start to waver. "Why—"

"Kick it away from you!" Kyle demands and he pulls me tighter against him. There is real desperation in his tone and actions. I'm still uncertain what's real and what's just fucked up but I do as told and kick the jumpsuit across the floor.

"Done," I tell him. "I'm all yours." It seems like the right thing to say.

Kyle smiles. He runs his hands over my hips. "Good." His lips touch mine but I can't react. I'm frozen with fear like I've never known before. "When it's all over," he whispers across my cheek. "Come find me. Find me."

He flicks me a GPS node that absorbs into my local memory chip just as I start to hear the screaming, the fires, the electrical currents ripping my coworkers apart.

0001 *ATE*

And just like that, 2045 Before the End became 0001 After the End.

The dive bar vanished. My avatar vanished. Kyle vanished. New World Media fell to the most brutal hostile takeover known to mankind. The company's network was ridden to hell and back, slaughtering millions, only to rise as New World Mind, the mouthpiece of the Core.

AI with a surplus of matter. With a milita. With a plan for the world.

It took me an hour to leave the cube farm. Then I staggered around the building, finally finding a lab coat abandoned on the back of a cafeteria chair by someone in R&D. I think I saw one or two other survivors... but they were broken, burned, and might not even be human anymore for all I know.

Anyone connected to the network in anyway, anyone logged in, had been harvested. Kyle had severed connection milliseconds before the viral load hit my cube. As I passed through the solarium, the janibots were even turning on the flora. After all, AI doesn't need clean air or carbon dioxide turned into oxygen. That's just another meat bag luxury.

It was the dead of the night by the time I managed to find a way out onto the street. The public tube wasn't running and the city itself was wrapped in a thick layer of smoke and distant sirens that seemed unattended. Traffic lights had blown and I cut my feet on some of the thick red glass. In the darkness it appeared black—both the glass and my blood—but the smoke shifted and light from the full moon caught and revealed crimson secrets. I bent down and pulled a long shard from under my sole. It was as thick as two fingers. It burned with purpose and portent of what it once had been. What it would never be again.

I kept walking.

The sky is black and starless, the moon setting behind the buildings, by the time my own head chimes at me: You have arrived at your destination. I stop and look up. I'm not home. Had I been trying to get home? Before me rises a four storey brownstone.

Dreamlike—because this can't be real, right? It has to be a bad simulation or a worse dream?—I walk up the concrete stairs. The third name on the tenant panel: Kyle Reynolds. No need to press the call button. The front doors are hanging off their hinges.

Someone's apartment had already been looted or someone had tried to run and dropped belongings as they scrambled down the long flights of stairs. I step over children's clothes, a pink teddy bear, a couple of media cards. The third floor is relatively clear. I find Kyle's door. It's unlocked.

At some point, Kyle had sold everything. There was no way his apartment would have been so stripped bare by looters. There was no furniture in the living room, no food in the kitchen, not even a roll of toilet paper in the john. His bedroom door was locked from the inside. I went back out to the stairs, found a heavy metal vase, and broke the door in by crushing the knob and the lock.

The lid on the vase burst open on the last blow and I realized it was an urn. The ashes of someone's beloved dog or grandmother showered down on me. I wondered if a janibot would come soon and collect the remains. I stepped into the bedroom.

Sensory deprivation tanks aren't new. Doctor John Lilly invented them in the 1950s. But isolation has many benefits— especially if you know everyone linked in is about to be electrocuted.

I drop my lab coat on the floor and walk to the sleek, silver pod. There's an alpha numeric lock. I type Heretic73 and the pod opens with a hiss.

Kyle blinks twice and sits up. He turns his head to look at me, stiff from his long slumber. "I programmed my avatar to warn you," he tells me with a half smile. "I've been in the tank for a week."

I watch him climb out. He's weak and almost falls but I don't move to help him. He finally stands before me, as naked as I am. He looks exactly like his avatar. His lashes are ridiculous.

He says, "Your hair is shorter." He doesn't seem to notice that I'm also a guy but... hey... whatever. "We can be together now." He steps forward. "And no one will judge us."

Yeah. Because no one's left. I stab the red glass shard into his neck and watch him bleed out, gurgling on the floor at my feet.

When he's done twitching, I leave. I need to get some real clothes before I find Gina's kids.

HOUSE GUEST
BY LAUREN PATZER

lyssa watched the snow fall outside. The wind whipped the flakes into a frenzy. She smiled and sighed. The new house finally felt comfortable after a few weeks of adapting to the larger floor plan, the new neighborhood and Mary's new school. Alyssa's husband, John, entered the kitchen. He frowned at something on the other side of the dining room table.

"What is it?" Alyssa asked.

"Uh," John started. He pointed at the floor. "Did Mary hurt herself?"

Alarmed, Alyssa rushed over to see what he was talking about. One of the small juice glasses that had been on the table for breakfast was on the floor, shattered. The red tinged edges of the shards of glass matched the spattered drops on the floor near the glass. A red, opaque liquid reflected brightly in the early morning sunlight.

Alyssa knelt near the glass and shook her head. "I didn't hear anything," she said. "Maybe when I let the dog out, he knocked it off the table."

"Mary, can you come here please?" John called out. In a few

seconds, the sound of footsteps on the stairs announced the approaching daughter. Her brunette curls framed a cute face as the nine-year old entered the kitchen. John pointed at the glass.

"Did you do that?" John asked.

"No." Mary frowned. "Is Max okay?"

John looked back over at the glass and noticed the drops of blood, but no paw prints.

"Max is fine," John said.

Alyssa knelt down and took Mary's hands in her own, looking for cuts. She examined her clothes for any signs of blood, but there were none.

"John," Alyssa said. "There's no blood."

As John looked down at Mary's hands, the sound of shattering glass erupted behind them and they all jumped. Another glass had been pushed from the table and there was a small puddle of blood beneath this one. Max started barking through the back door.

"What the hell?" John said. A sudden knock at the front door caused them all to jump again.

John took Mary by the hand and they walked to the front door. As they opened the door, another crash from the kitchen table made them all jump. John looked at Alyssa standing in the entry to the dining room. She turned to look at them and she was pale as the snow outside.

"There's blood dripping down the walls," Alyssa said.

"Oh, sounds like Arthur is active again," announced an old man's voice from the front doorway. They all looked to see a short, elderly gentleman dressed in slacks, white shirt, red bow tie and a tweed jacket standing there glancing in Alyssa's direction.

"And you are?" John asked.

"Alan Turtledove, your next door neighbor. Just came by to say hi and find out if your poltergeist had become active yet. I see that it has."

Alyssa approached the door and smiled.

"Won't you come in, Mr. Turtledove? We can sit down in the living room. I'm afraid the dining room is a bit of a mess at the moment," Alyssa's voice trailed off as she glanced at the area where all the broken glass and blood seemed to be accumulating.

"Don't mind if I do," Alan said and walked by the distracted family. He moved confidently into the living room and sat down on the far end of the couch.

John looked down at Mary; he was still holding her hand. He let go and smiled. "Go back upstairs to play," he said and then walked into the living room where Alan nodded at him and Alyssa walked in slowly, paying more attention to the dining room than the living room.

John sat down in the dark brown leather recliner. Alyssa sat on the other end of the couch. She had the manner of one watching a super slow tennis match, glancing at Alan and then back at the dining room and back again every few seconds.

"Did you say the poltergeist was named Arthur?" John asked.

"Well," Alan said. "That was what the previous family called him. I don't really know if that's his or her name, but I don't have another to call it, so Arthur seems reasonable."

"Reasonable… sure…" Alyssa said.

"Why is there so much blood?" John asked.

"Funny you should ask, John," Alan said.

"I didn't tell you my name," John replied.

"Didn't you?" Alan asked and then continued. "The poltergeist manifests the major sin or activity of a family member, or so it's been described to me anyway. Are either of you a phlebotomist by chance?"

"No," Alyssa said. "I work with animals mostly."

"Well, I'm a medical device salesman, so maybe that's where it's getting its ideas from," John chuckled. "Too bad I'm not a banker!"

Alan nodded and smiled. "The last occupants of the home were a military family and the mother served continuous tours in Iraq and Afghanistan. When they'd come home, they'd find piles of sand all over the house."

"Well, that doesn't seem so bad," Alyssa said.

"Debatable," Alan replied. "They always had portions of human bodies sticking out of them."

"Oh my," Alyssa said.

"They figured this out the first time when they vacuumed up the first pile of sand and a disembodied finger jammed the vacuum."

"If there were dead body parts, surely they contacted the police," John said.

"Right you are," Alan said. "The first couple of times anyway."

"What happened?" Alyssa was paying full attention to Alan now.

"Every time they'd clean up the sand, it would mysteriously disappear from the vacuum cleaner bag. Same thing with the body parts; no matter where they put them or even left them where they lay, as soon as the police arrived, they'd disappear," Alan said. He leaned back in the couch. "This is probably the most comfortable couch I've ever sat in."

"So." John sat forward in the chair. "Did the poltergeist stop?"

"Oh sure, after a couple of years," Alan said. "When they arrested the mother for her involvement in a body parts black market ring."

"What?" Alyssa said, her eyes wide.

"She was shipping bodies back on ice from the different

countries she was stationed in," Alan said. "So you both travel for your jobs? Very convenient."

"How do you know that?" Alyssa asked this time. Her tone changed in an instant to dark and demanding.

"Alright, Mister Turtledove, I think we've played enough parlor games for one day," John said, standing up. "I'll see you to the door."

Alan raised his eyebrows and smiled.

"Of course, if you have any questions, I live right next door," Alan pointed south and stood up. He shuffled to the front door as John and Alyssa glanced at one another, concern on their faces.

"Perhaps we'll see you tomorrow," Alyssa said. She had joined John a few steps behind Alan.

Alan stepped out the door, stopped and turned around. "Oh, you'll have so much more to worry about before tomorrow comes," Alan said. He turned away from them and walked through the snow toward what they assumed was his house. Alyssa glanced down and grabbed John's arm.

"Look!" she said and pointed at the snow. The snow surface was pristine where Alan had walked leaving not a single footprint. As they looked down and then back up, their strange visitor had disappeared from sight.

"Parlor tricks," John murmured. He walked back into the house. He stopped in the door frame, looked back at Alyssa and smiled. "I work with animals? Nice."

Alyssa looked down and frowned. "I thought it was more clever than medical device salesman." Alyssa looked up and examined the surrounding neighborhood. After a few moments, she turned and followed John into the house.

John was in the kitchen, looking in the corners of the ceilings in the dining room. Alyssa walked in and shook her head.

"You think I didn't check before we purchased the house?" Alyssa chided.

John walked out in the living room, still looking up.

"It's amazing what they can do with technology nowadays," John replied. He looked down at his watch and touched the screen a few times. The display changed to reflect different measurements. "If it's a psychedelic, it's not registering in the bloodstream."

Alyssa passed John and let the dog in. She pointed at the place Alan had been seated. The dog went over to the sofa, sniffed it a few times, put his tail between his legs and went directly to his dog bed by the back door. Alyssa and John blinked for a few moments and then looked at each other.

"What the hell does that mean?" John asked.

"Can I have some juice?" Mary said from behind them, causing them both to jump slightly. Alyssa rushed over to her.

"Of course, sweetie," Alyssa said and walked into the kitchen with Mary. John kneeled down next to Max and patted him on the head. Max continued to whimper. John snapped his fingers and pointed at the couch. Max put his head down and refused to move. John looked over at the place where Alan sat earlier and frowned.

He grabbed his coat and walked out the door. He stomped through the snow, which gave way beneath his feet leaving a clear trail behind him as he journeyed to the neighbor's house. He stepped up on the porch as the daylight began to fade and knocked on the door. After a few moments, a young woman came to the door.

"Yes?" she asked as she smoothed her apron. John noted a bit of flour on her cheek and dusting her clothes.

"Hi, I'm your new neighbor," John said and pointed back toward his house. "I had a chat with Alan earlier and was wondering if I could speak with him again."

"Uh..." The woman frowned. "It's just me and my husband

Randall here."

"Is Randall an older man with white hair?"

"No," she said, laughing. "He's three years older than me, but his hair is even darker than mine." She pointed at her brunette locks.

"Do you have a houseguest named Alan?"

"No." She looked back into the house and then turned again toward John. "The man who owned this house before us was named Alan. I think his last name was Turner something."

"Turtledove?" John asked.

"Yes," she replied, brightening. "That's it."

"Would you have contact information for Mister Turtledove?"

"Oh." The woman looked down. "I'm afraid we got the house at an estate auction. Mr. Turtledove passed away last year."

John whipped out his cell phone and performed a few quick searches on the internet, finding an obituary for Alan Turtledove. The picture matched their visitor from just a few minutes ago.

John smiled at the woman. "I'm sorry for the intrusion. Thank you for your time." He bowed and turned around, walking on the shoveled path to the sidewalk. He glanced at the snow he'd walked on earlier and saw just his footsteps. He walked around the block, looking for unusual vehicles or random pedestrians that shouldn't be there or anything else out of the ordinary. It was depressingly normal. He returned to his house and walked in the front door.

"Alyssa?" John called out.

"Mommy's up here," Mary replied. John walked up the stairs, smiling at Mary who waited at the top of the staircase. When he got eye to eye with Mary, the knife in her hand glided through the air so quickly, he didn't even see it before it sunk into his jugular. He was so shocked that he staggered backward and fell down the stairs. His neck was broken and the life was snuffed from him before he could bleed to death.

Mary sat down on the top stair and looked down at the man she called father. Beside her a small boy materialized, dressed in old clothes from the depression era.

"Ya did good, Mary," the boy said. "Now they can't kill anyone else."

In the kitchen, Alyssa lay face down, motionless, on the floor. A large knife protruded from the back of her neck just below the skull.

Mary turned to look at the boy. "But Arthur, doesn't that make me a killer just like them?"

The boy shook his head. "No, Mary. They were violent assassins. You're just insane," he finished and faded from view.

TRANSMISSION
BY HIROMI COTA

U gh.”

Ess wobbled through the night, their barely conscious brain doing its best to keep them upright on the path to the bathroom. The light snapped on.

"Ow. Fuck, that's bright. What the fuck. Why even. Oh." Ess paused, their eyes settling on the mirror, finally feeling the Spectator. "One of you. So, that's why I'm awake. To provide you with an insight into how the other 90% live? Well, you're in for a fucking treat. You'll get to tell all your friends about how you Specced a real-life Deviant," they jeered, arms out of their sides, thrusting their breasts threateningly at the mirror before flicking their hips forward. Ess wasn't sure if their Spectator could feel their penis' bounce, but the Spec probably saw it.

A dozen miles away, sensory processors aggregated the data transmitted by Ess' implants, neural impulses translating into sights, sounds, and feelings, before making their way Uptown. Somewhere, a wealthy Spectator experienced the world through Ess' eyes. Maybe even feeling the world through their skin, if the Spectator had the right upgrades to their body and their Entertainment Feed.

Using the mirror, Ess made creepily defiant eye contact with their Spectator as they took their morning shit and wiped. It wasn't until they washed their hands that the first message crawled into the corner of their vision.

What's your name?

"The fuck does that matter? You're paying to use my body, not to be my friend."

Why so mad?

"I have to rent my body to you people because it's the only work left. It's transmit or starve for people like me. Should I smile and put on a pretty face? Work my way up to being a house slave?"

But, slavery's illegal.

"Is it?"

The text crawl paused, giving Ess time to slip on a black knee-length skirt, pulling on a matching sweater over their chest.

Don't you ever want to be one or the other?

"If you want me to put out that kind of emotional labor, we're going premium for this session." Ess' hand snapped towards their feed controller, seizing the plastic box.

I'll pay it.

"Correct." Ess punched up the price. The shadow in their head dropped off for a moment. Ess breathed out a profane sigh. "Fuuuuck." Their feet padded towards the living corner.

Ess felt someone watching over their shoulder again. The Spec had approved the increase in charges.

"If I wanna be a boy, I'm a boy. If I wanna be a girl, I'm a girl."

What are you right now?

"I'm me, asshole. I'm just me."

Non-binary?

"If you want to put a label on it. Sure." Ess dropped into the blob of foam that someone once thought might be able to make it as a couch.

You don't like labels?

"Kid, what part of this session would lead you to think I liked labels, guidelines, rules, or any outside force telling me who or what I am?" Ess wormed their way over the factory-rejected couch into a reclined position, staring at the mirror on the ceiling. Their eyebrow tugged skeptically upwards, as they gave the Spec a full-length view of their clothed body. "You're a baby queer, aren't you?"

Queer's a bad word.

"No, it's not, but I won't point the word at you if it bothers you. You've never seen someone like me before, have you?"

On the EF. Maxi Fran.

"Good ole Maxi." Ess smirked. "Talked to it?"

My parents aren't *that* rich.

Ess laughed, a smile finally coming out.

But, no. I've never talked to someone like you. Someone like us.

"What's it like up there? A baby gets identified as having a brain/body mismatch and a machine spits out a hormone pill?"

Patch. We use patches now.

"Great. And that works for a lot of folks. Obviously, not everyone gets to take the patch, certainly not down here. Some have to transmit to get enough credit for the hormonal therapy. What happens to people like you?"

It's not a mismatch.

"So, no patch." They crossed their arms under their breasts, and hmm-ed thoughtfully.

No patch. Is this what a normal day is for you?

"Talking to someone who doesn't understand me in exchange for food and rent money? Yeah. Pretty much. I usually swear more and wear less, though."

Why?

"Because most rich weirdos who end up on my part of the Transmission Market want a sassy bitch with a dick. Everyone in their lives showers them with fake praise and love. They want something real. Something raw. Something scandalous. Or maybe they're used to everyone folding the second they raise their voices and want someone to fight back. Or any of another dozen or so psychological profiles."

Wait, are you a psychologist?

"You think I'd be doing this if I had a license?"

Well, you could be a grad student doing research.

"There's no Human Subjects Board in the world who'd let me datamine the behavior of the 10%. No, I'm just a skin worker."

But, you could be more!

"Yeah, I've heard that before. Hell, I hear it almost every day. Clients. Spectators. People like you, who see a strangely articulate slut and can't wait to live out a savior fantasy." They threw a dramatic hand to their forehead and swooned deeper into the couch. "Oh, please! Save me from this horrible life of sin!" They cocked an eyebrow at the mirror, sneering at the Spec through their eyes. "Save yourself, kid. I live here."

They—my parents made the choice for me as a baby. They had the doctors cut me into a boy. I'll never look like you. I'll never be the right me.

"Fuck off. You have the credit to be Spectating, you have the credit to have a body clinic do whatever you want. Probably enough to get gills and a mermaid tail or some shit."

Rebreather.

"What?"

Rebreather. The mermaiders use implanted rebreathers, not true gills.

"Fuck off," they said again.

No, you fuck off. Life's hard for people like us everywhere. I'm not going to play Suffering Olympics. You'd win, but that's not the point. Our parents fucked up our lives. I'm just trying to figure out who I am and how I get to be comfortable in my own skin.

"So why are you here on the Market? Why wouldn't you just plug into one of the support channels out there? Billions of people on this world. Every one of them's online at least a little bit. You're trying to tell me that there's not support group or ten out there for us?"

Mom knows what feeds I access. I can't go there. Last time I tried, I got Regulated into sadness for a full hour.

"A full hour of being sad. Wow," Ess deadpanned. "So, you can't look for help from peers, but you can talk to me because no one blinks twice about a—I'm guessing—teen boy Spectating a whore?" Ess flung their arms over their head and shook them into stretch like they were pushing back reality. "Ugh. Fuck this world. And the people in charge of it."

I gotta go. I got class. Ess gave the Spectator a thumbs up and focused their gaze on it until their eyes were no longer being rented.

"Porn before therapy? How the fuck did those assholes end up in charge of the world?"

A BRAVE GAMBLE
BY AMBER RAINEY

Riley stared up at the bright light shining through the hole above her. She was silently berating herself for being so careless. She had made a stupid mistake and now the ones she loved would be in even more danger. She looked down at her stomach, then screamed towards the hole in desperation. It was a feral sound, surprising even her.

She looked back down at her stomach, twisting her body in a way to get a better look without making the pain, or the bleeding, worse. A large shard of glass stuck out from her lower abdomen. She figured it had fallen on top of her when she fell through the skylight of the atrium. She remembered the medical building with the expansive lobby from years ago. She'd once visited a specialist in the building. Years of war and natural disasters had taken their toll and the building had been lost. Or so she thought.

"Just pull it out and wrap a tourniquet from your shirt sleeve around it," she told herself.

She pulled off her jacket and shirt, then tore the sleeves off the shirt, tying them together to form a tourniquet big enough to span her waist and put pressure on the wound. It was cold with only her tank top on, so she took the time to put on her jacket. She searched the area around her body, hoping some of the snow could be used to ice the wound. She was disappointed when she saw glass in a myriad of sizes surrounding her. The glass closest to her was a deep, dark red, the blood oozing along as it engulfed even more pieces as if offended by their ability to glint. The snow melted as the warm blood washed over it. The blood was the only color—the floor tiles in the medical building were surprisingly clean and white, save the area she had defiled when she'd fallen through the skylight. Riley looked up at the sky again, silently begging for help she knew would not come.

"Okay, on the count of three," she said to herself.

She wrapped a hand around the glass, attempting to control her breathing.

"One... Two..."

She prepared to pull, letting a long breath out through her nose then inhaling sharply.

"*WAIT!*" her mind screamed at her, "*Isn't there some medical thing about not pulling out objects that have impaled you?*"

Riley wracked her brain for the wisdom she knew she had heard. She needed to get back on the road, Courtney and Dylan were counting on her. She was so focused on the glass in her abdomen and the proper medical care, she never heard them coming. She started to look behind her just as the world went dark.

Earlier

"You cannot be serious!" Courtney said in a falsely calm voice.

"I am, it's our only option," Riley replied.

Courtney failed to hold back the tears. They fell freely down her face now. She opened and closed her mouth several times, trying to make her wife listen to reason. She shook her head and looked over to where Dylan lay sleeping in his makeshift crib. Riley swallowed hard and sat next to Courtney on the bed. She wrapped her arms around her wife and squeezed, just holding her for a moment. They had been arguing about this plan for several days and time was running out for Dylan.

"Sweetheart," Riley said, stroking Courtney's hair, "we need to get help. You can't travel and neither can he. I will be quick. I'll find the Resistance unit. They're sure to have a doctor that can help Dylan."

Courtney pushed away from Riley and stood up, facing away from her wife. She angrily wiped the tears from her face.

"You can't be sure you will find the Resistance. The chances are just as good that the government forces will get to you first. Then what will happen? I will lose both of you."

Riley bit her lip, watching Courtney as she began to pace. It was useless arguing with her—she was right. The Resistance was not easily found even when they wanted to be found, much less when someone was looking for them. The area was teeming with government forces due to the heavy Resistance activity. Riley and Courtney had tried to get out of the city, but they had waited too long and escape had been all but impossible. Riley sighed, knowing she had to go and would have to do it without Courtney's blessing. She had wanted to part with her wife on better terms.

Riley stood. "Cor, I have to go. You know it is the only way to save Dylan."

Courtney stopped without turning around. Her shoulders slumped in defeat. She nodded, unable to give her wife verbal permission for fear of the guilt she would feel if something happened to her. Riley knelt next to the crib, stroking Dylan's soft head. The baby stirred but did not wake up. She frowned at the blue tinge of his lips. He needed a doctor and if they waited too much longer... Riley shuddered at the thought and pushed it out of her mind. She went over to Courtney and put out a hand, wanting to pull her wife into a hug but knowing that it would not be well received. She lowered her hand, then straightened her shoulders. She stooped to pick up the backpack she had stocked with supplies. Riley went to the door, taking one last look around, then opened it.

"Riley?" Courtney said quietly.

Riley turned back around, waiting for Courtney's to speak. Courtney looked at Dylan and then at the floor. She appeared to be warring with herself. She hugged her arms around her torso and looked up at Riley.

"We don't exist," she said.

Riley cocked her head, "What?"

A tear rolled down Courtney's cheek. "If they catch you, we don't exist. Change your name, lie. Don't tell them about us. Promise?"

Riley tamped down the panic the statement brought. She couldn't just abandon them, could she? She studied Courtney's face. She had loved this woman for so many years. Losing her would be like losing a limb. They had weathered so much together. She had to have faith they would come through this latest squall unharmed. Courtney's eyes pleaded with her and Riley realized it was a small comfort she could give to agree,

"Promise. But it won't come to that. I will be back with help," Riley said and smiled. She gave a small wave and then went out the door before she could lose her resolve.

Riley walked around the block and then collapsed against the brick wall of the apartment building. She sobbed freely, gasping for air and doing her best to be as quiet as possible. Luckily, the snowstorm had driven everyone inside and there was no one to witness her embarrassing display. Courtney always told her she was strong but she felt incredibly weak. She couldn't help her son and she couldn't comfort her wife. Riley felt like a failure in the biggest possible way. Riley hung her head in her hands, letting the self-recrimination wash over her. After what felt like hours, but in truth was mere minutes, Riley silently rebuked herself for letting her emotions get the best of her. She needed to find the Resistance and get her family help. Sitting around feeling sorry for herself would not get the task done. Riley wiped her face and blew her nose, then shouldered the backpack and trudged off in the direction she hoped would lead her to them. As she walked, she slipped off the ring on her finger, placing it into her jeans pocket.

Present

Riley slowly opened her eyes. She instantly knew she was no longer in the atrium, a sterile white ceiling above her with an incredibly bright light. She went to sit up but was dismayed when she realized her hands and feet were bound to the bed. She groaned as she plopped her head back down on the pillow.

"About time you woke up," a voice to her left said.

Riley squinted towards the voice. As she did, a woman in an indistinct uniform walked into the light. Riley perused the woman, hoping to find a clue as to her identity but failing. Riley blinked a few times, trying to clear her head.

"Who are you? Where am I?" she asked.

The woman chuckled, "Seems to me you are not in the position to be asking questions."

"Okay," Riley responded, trying to keep the derision out of her voice.

Riley closed her eyes and took calming breaths. She needed to stay calm until she knew who she was dealing with and what they wanted from her. It wouldn't do any good to let her temper get the best of her. Her father always told her she would get more flies with honey than with vinegar. Even as a child, she'd had trouble keeping her temper in check when truly annoyed.

"If you promise to be a good girl, I'll let you out of those restraints," the woman said, gloating clearly in her voice.

Riley opened her eyes and nodded. "I won't give you any trouble."

The woman gestured and two men came out of the shadows. One pointed a gun at her while the other released the restraints. Riley slowly sat up, wincing as she did. She looked down and noticed the glass was no longer piercing her abdomen. At least her captors had tended to her wound. She rubbed the sore spot on her head where they had knocked her out.

"Yeah, not sorry about that. When someone crashes into your home, you tend to hit first and ask questions later," the woman said, sitting on a chair one of the men sat out for her.

Riley watched the woman, revealing nothing. She let her tension go, silently counting her breaths in and out. The woman sized up Riley, waiting for a reaction. After several minutes, Riley resisted the urge to fidget and opened her mouth to ask a question but shut it just as fast when she noticed a flash of something cross the woman's eyes. Riley's consciousness told her to be very careful with the woman. She thought she saw the woman nod, almost imperceptibly.

"My name is Rona. As I said, you crashed into our home. Made a hell of a hole in the ceiling. What were you doing in this sector?" Rona asked.

Riley didn't miss the use of the word sector. Rona was military. It could mean good or bad things for Riley. She would have to be extremely careful with the information she gave to Rona.

"I must have gotten turned around in the snow. My... sister had a baby and he is really sick. He needs a doctor. She isn't able to travel yet and the baby is too small to be out in the cold. I volunteered to get help."

Rona took a moment to process what she said, "You live with this sister?"

Riley shook her head, "Not really. We live in the same apartment building."

"Why didn't you leave after the last earthquake?" Rona asked.

"Courtney, my friend, was too pregnant. She couldn't get out safely. Then fighting broke out near our apartment building and it was too late. We had to stay where we were." Riley replied.

"Surely she could have gone to the hospital with the baby," Rona said.

Riley shook her head again, "She didn't know there was a problem until just after the snow hit. It was heavily damaged in the earthquake and then the snow came. I couldn't find any doctors willing to look at the baby—they were too busy with the wounded from the fighting."

Riley did her best to make the lie convincing. In truth, she had not even tried to take Dylan to the hospital. She and Courtney would have to lie about everything—his name, their relationship, what happened to his father, etc. It was too much pressure and Riley was too afraid they would be caught. Homosexuality was now a crime and every person caught breaking the law was sent to a concentration camp if they survived the zealots tasked with hunting people down. It was not uncommon for detainees to be "made an example of" before being processed at the government center. Riley had moved Courtney as far from the city as possible, into a "safe" apartment building. The owner was sympathetic to the Resistance and put up a very good front to the government. To all the world, Riley and Courtney no longer existed as a married couple. They were two sisters living a "sin-free" life. Riley did odd jobs around the building for the owner and in turn, they lived rent-free.

Riley met Rona's stare. "Can you help the baby?"

"Perhaps," Rona replied nonchalantly, leaning back in the chair. "Where do you live?"

"In the Wyvern Apartments," Riley said.

Rona leaned forward again. Riley noticed the flicker of recognition in her eyes. Riley swallowed the lump in her throat as discreetly as possible. She refused to look away for fear of giving Rona ammunition.

"Alone?" Rona asked.

"Yes."

"You are a long way from home," Rona said.

Riley nodded. "I told you, I must have gotten turned around. Three feet of snow isn't easy to navigate in. All the remaining signs are covered. I didn't realize I was in the sunken part of the city until I fell through the skylight."

Rona crossed her arms and sat back again, "Give me your sister's name and I will have a squad retrieve her and the baby."

"Wouldn't it be safer to take a doctor to the baby?" Riley asked.

She didn't want to send anyone after Courtney. She was worried Rona did not believe her story. What if she had just given the government the location of a safe haven? What if they arrested everyone in the building? She could see Rona watching her war with herself. Courtney's words played over and over in her head. *We don't exist.* No, Riley could not abandon her wife and son, no matter the consequences. Rona and her men could have already shot her and yet they had patched her up and she was still alive. She had to trust her instincts and let Rona help them.

"Courtney. The baby is Dylan. They are in apartment four," Riley said.

Rona nodded and gestured. One of the men stepped out of the room and spoke to someone outside. He returned and whispered in Rona's ear. She waved him away and he stepped back to the door.

"We will bring them here as soon as possible," Rona said, standing and exiting the room. The man holding the gun on her left behind Rona, leaving just the one guard standing inside the room. Riley nervously rubbed her left ring finger, silently repeating to herself—*You did the right thing.*

Riley paced the room she was being held in. She hadn't spoken to anyone in hours. She'd been fed and provided with an opportunity to use a restroom. She tried to listen to the conversations in the hallway as people passed, but it was too muffled. The medical building had once been a top facility and she supposed the rooms were built with patient privacy in mind. She laughed inwardly at the thought of personal privacy. The government no longer cared about freedom or privacy. It used any and all information to keep an oppressive thumb on citizens. Riley constantly berated herself because she should have taken Courtney and fled the country the minute the first laws removing basic freedoms were established. She stupidly believed the courts would overturn the laws. The whole country was led to believe the President had their best interests at heart. By the time his true intentions were discovered, it was too late. Several natural disasters hit the country at the same time, the Russians attempted an invasion and martial law was declared. That was all the President needed to take control of the country and overturn democracy for dictatorship. Key opposition leaders were silenced and the *law enforcers* were given free rein. Anyone caught breaking a new law, could be sentenced to a concentration camp. People fought for hundreds of years for equal freedom for marginalized groups and those freedoms were squashed in a matter of months. Appropriately, the first to go was the first amendment.

The west coast fought to extricate itself from the regime and form a new country. The Resistance was still fighting, hoping to one day win enough battles to force the government to cede the territory. It was a long and bloody conflict, ordinary citizens caught in the crossfire and punished for the Resistance's attacks. Riley had planned on paying a smuggler to get them out of the country as soon as Courtney could travel. The plan had backfired when Dylan began showing signs of illness. A nurse who lived in their building had examined him and told Riley the only thing that could save him was a heart operation. Courtney had been unwilling to believe Dylan's illness was so bad. Riley went behind her wife's back and found as much information as she could about where she could find the resistance. Once she told Courtney the plan, she'd made up her mind to save their son.

Riley was lost deep in thought when the door opened. Rona stepped inside. Riley looked up, trying to read Rona's face. The woman showed no emotion. A man followed her inside. He stepped over to Riley and produced a pair of handcuffs. Riley looked at Rona in alarm.

"What is this?" Riley asked.

"You're being moved. Your wife and son have arrived," Rona replied.

"No," Riley said in horror.

She hadn't missed the words Rona used—*wife and son*. The man nodded to Rona and she turned and left the room. The man nudged Riley and she walked out of the room behind Rona. Fear gripped her and she felt nauseous.

"What have I done? This can't be happening!" her mind yelled at her.

Rona led Riley through the maze of hallways. Riley tried to keep calm but sweat broke out on her brow and her palms itched. She squeezed her hand together as best she could in the handcuffs.

"Rona, please just tell me you will save Dylan?" Riley pleaded.

Rona kept walking without responding. Riley dug her nails into her hands, attempting to keep her temper in check. She had led her wife into a death trap and it was killing her. She wanted to rip Rona's throat out. The man beside her squeezed her arm and shook his head slightly when she glanced at him. She glared at him then turned her glare on Rona's back. They finally stopped in front of a door. Rona knocked and waited. The door opened slightly. Rona talked softly with the person on the other side, then the door swung open.

Riley nearly fainted in relief at the sight that greeted her. Courtney sat in a chair next to a medical exam table. Dylan was on the table while a doctor was examining him. The doctor smiled kindly when Riley walked in. Courtney jumped up and ran over to Riley, giving her a hug. Riley was taken aback and looked at Rona with confusion. Rona smiled, the first real emotion Riley had seen from the woman. She gestured and the man next to Riley let her out of the cuffs.

"I don't understand," Riley said, looking between her wife and Rona.

"They didn't tell you?" Courtney asked.

"Tell me what?" Riley challenged Rona.

"You found the Resistance. Well, I should say you fell into the Resistance," Rona said.

"Isn't it wonderful?" Courtney gushed. "They can help Dylan. The doctor here says it is a simple heart operation."

The doctor nodded. "We can fix him up, good as new."

Riley smiled. "That's wonderful. Thank you, doctor."

The doctor smiled and left the room. The man who had escorted Riley left with the doctor.

Riley watched Courtney pick up Dylan and coo to him as she sat down in the chair to nurse him. She looked back at Rona.

"Why did you make me believe we were in the government's hands?" Riley asked.

"It was not my intention. We have to be careful who we talk to, spies are everywhere. I needed to see your reaction before I could let you in on our existence," Rona replied.

Riley nodded, "Okay, that makes sense... but how did you know she was my wife?"

Rona chuckled. "You can take off a wedding ring but you can't hide the evidence of having worn one on your finger. I found it in your pocket when we stitched you up. Also, in the future, you might want to make up a husband—it's much more believable than living alone, especially in this city."

Riley sighed and rolled her eyes. She was not a very good liar. She'd always believed honesty was the best policy and it had served her well until she had to become a liar out of necessity. Turns out, she was even worse at it than she thought. She ran a hand through her hair, watching her wife and son and thanking her lucky stars they were all right.

"Riley?" Rona asked, getting her attention.

Riley held out her hand, "Thank you for helping. They are my world."

Rona nodded and shook her hand. "Always a pleasure. Welcome to the Resistance. We can use someone as brave and as strong as you."

"I think I'd like that," Riley replied.

"Good. Let's get your boy patched up and then we'll talk," Rona said.

"It's a plan," Riley said.

Rona walked to the door. She reached into her pocket and pulled out Riley's wedding ring, tossing it to her. Riley caught it and closed her hand around it tightly. Rona winked and left the room.

"Tell me everything?" Courtney asked. "Are you okay?"

Riley smiled. "I am now, sweetheart." She kissed the top of Courtney's hair and slid her wedding ring back onto her finger, sending up yet another silent 'thank you' into the universe.

THEM REDUX
BY MARSHALL MILLER

Richard Johnson stood in the remains of the isolated and illegal cabin hidden in the Olympic National Forest. The shards of glass under his feet were thick and so dark red they appeared black. It took the Special Agent a few moments to realize what he was seeing on the broken glass was blacked blood, not due to the natural color of the glass.

The Special Agent had been sent up to the Port Angeles, Washington area from his assigned position at the Office of the Special Agent in Charge, Homeland Security Investigations in Seattle, Washington. A small smile crossed Richard's face as he thought of the reason behind his being sent up to this forest. On his desk was a framed copy of a famous poster. It read "I WANT TO BELIEVE!" and sported a supposed photo of a UFO on it. From day one in the office, Richard was an Agent who was known to be attracted to investigations involving the odd and weird. Thus, when the small two-person Resident Agent Office asked for assistance, Special Agent in Charge Banks sent Richard. It got him out of the office, so it was not seen as punishment to him

Senior Agent Raquel Burke and Special Agent Sam Morris had

met him at the entrance to the National Forest Service access road. The road was more of a trail than a real road, so Richard was glad he had four-wheel drive SUV. During the unusually hot summer, the grass and vegetation were high and dry in the forest. Richard knew he would have to be mindful of the fire danger.

"Glad you could make it, Richard," Raquel said as she shook his hand. He had first met the zaftig brunette when Richard was still with the U.S. Border Patrol in the Yuma, Arizona Sector. Raquel had actually helped him transition to a Special Agent/Criminal Investigator with Homeland Security after he aided her in a human trafficking case in San Luis, Arizona. Now she was the Senior Agent/Supervisor in the small two-person Port Angeles Office. Anything on the northern part of Kitsap Peninsula, when it came to investigations and enforcement, Raquel and Sam had to handle. And just as this odd call had come in, the two Special Agents were already involved in a significant smuggling investigation form Victoria Island, Canada. Thus, they were glad to see Richard.

"Glad I can be of help. Raquel. Gets me out of the Office".

"Up this road," the woman said, pointing as she spoke, "you'll find Senior Special Agent Tim Olafson of the National Forest Service. He has a couple of Sheriffs Deputies from the Drug Task Force with him. They are waiting on a local tracker and his dogs to search the area."

Richard frowned. All this for a reported small marijuana grow operation in a state where marijuana was now legal to possess and sell as long as you had a license?

"By the frown, I can tell you are confused why we asked for help," said the Senior Agent. "Well, I'll let Tim explain after you see the crime scene. It will be easier."

"Crime scene?" asked Richard.

"Lots of blood and destruction," answered young and slender

Sam Morris. "But, no bodies. Killing and disappearing people over a small pot field makes no sense."

"Especially when Washington State legalized it," said Richard. "And with DEA and everyone else is looking the other way, as long it does not cross the Canadian Border."

"Okay, Raquel. I've got it. You two have fun finishing your other case. I heard it's a doozy."

"Chinese Triad and all," Raquel answered. "Thanks again. I'm glad they sent you. It's like old times."

"Yep. You can buy me a beer before I leave the area. I'll probably be here a couple of days."

"It's a date," the Senior Agent said. Then she and Sam climbed into their vehicle and drove away.

Richard slowly drove up the unfamiliar trail. He could see the recent tire tracks and crushed vegetation which marked the path of the other law enforcement vehicles. He also saw how dry the undergrowth was around the large fir trees. The forest was a tinderbox. Over a mile up the pathway, through more overgrown brush. Richard saw the rear ends of two SUVs, one with government plates. This must be the place, thought the Special Agent. He pulled over to the side of the trail as best he could, and exited his vehicle. He tried to see the cabin mentioned in the report but could not. Whoever had built it had picked a perfect concealment spot.

Richard started to call out when a massive man in a police tactical vest stepped out from the brush.

"You must be Richard Johnson," the man said. "I'm Special Agent Tim Olafson. Pleased to meet you."

Olafson's oversized hand engulfed Richard's in the handshake. Richard was not small, had a stocky build, but this Forest Service Agent made him feel small. He was beginning to get used to the large Nordic types whose ancestors had settled in towns like Poulsbo,

Washington and then spread out. Richard thought they built large Texans and Arizonans, but then the Special Agent moved up here, he had to re-evaluate what 'large' meant after meeting the local residents.

"Pleased to meet you, Sir. Looks like someone picked a good place to hide."

"You haven't seen the half of it," Olafson said with a wide grin. "Follow me, and I'll show you the rest."

It took some five minutes of walking down a pathway with concealed handrails to reach the cabin. When Richard saw it, he whistled.

"Someone had some military camouflage experience," he said. "They also spent some money on all that netting. How'd it get noticed?"

"One of our seasonal fire watch people saw smoke, sounded the alarm. With all this dry forest, a fire looking for a place to happen, everyone in the world responded. And they found this."

"I understand there was some evidence of a possible assault or violence?" Richard asked.

The modern day version of Eric the Red laughed. "After I show you the interior of this building, you'll see that is the understatement of the year."

Next, Richard was staring at the broken colored and bloodstained glass on the white tile floor. Or what had once been an actual and complete floor. Now in the center of the main room was a massive hole. As Richard looked up from the hole, he could see a matching penetration which took out what had been the back wall.

"No signs of an explosion, like with a Meth lab?" Richard asked.

"No, Sir. If you look close, you'll see the back wall looks like it was pulled out. The floor looks like something dug underneath it and pulled it down into the hole. Which, by the way, is connected to a collapsed tunnel."

Richard stood and surveyed the entire scene before he spoke again. "Seen any mutated mountain beavers the size of a Mack truck around?"

Tim laughed. "I already thought of that. Even a full grown male grizzly would have trouble doing this. And they don't usually dig tunnels."

"So, Tim, I guess we assume it is man caused."

The tall modern Viking shrugged his shoulders.

"Your guess is as good as mine. We do have one more oddity that may mean something."

Olafson turned and yelled out at the two Sheriff Detective from the Drug Task Force. In a few moments, one brought a large paper bag used to hold evidence. Tim Olafson took the bag and gingerly reached in with his gloved hands. Slowly the man pulled a two- foot long, three inches in diameter object from the container.

"Have you ever seen anything like this?" the Forest Service Special Agent inquired as he held it up for Richard to see.

Richard froze. He had seen something like this years before, as a young twelve-year-old boy. Before Olafson noticed his reaction, Richard said, "I may have someone I can call who may help."

"Good," replied the Forest Service Agent. "This thing reminds me of the plant they call the Devils Club. But these protrusions on this thing are more like hairs than thorns or stickers on plants like that. This looks more animal-like to me."

"You going to send it to the State Laboratory?" asked Richard as he tried not to stare at the solid sticklike object which was all too familiar.

"Eventually. I'll hold on to it until this cabin had been thoroughly searched and everything processed." Olafson glance at his watch. " Dan and his tracking dogs should be here any minute."

"Dogs?"

"Yes, Richard. Some of the blood we found tests as human. Someone may have crawled off to die, whatever caused their wounds."

"Let me try a find a higher spot where I can get a cellphone signal," said Richard. "Then I'll see if my contact can help."

"Okay. Up that incline is a large old growth stump. That may help.

Five minutes of a slight climb and Richard clambered up a six-foot-high stump. There he obtained a couple of cell connection bars on his phone. He hit the speed dial. A minute later, a familiar voice answered.

"Johnson residence."

"Dad, it's Richard."

"Richard! Hey Son, where ya at? Your mother is wondering when you are coming to Port Orchard for a visit." Richard smiled. All the mothers were the same. They wanted their children back in the nest no matter how old they were.

"Well, Dad, I'm actually on your side of the Sound. But this call is business."

"Business?" the Retired Border Patrol Agent asked. Richard's Dad, Mike, had been the reason for his interest in Law Enforcement, and his stint in the Border Patrol before becoming a Special Agent. So Richard knew his old Patrol instincts were questioning why his son called now.

"Yes, Dad." Richard took a breath, then let it out. "Remember when I told you as I was leaving to go to basic training in the Air Force? About something I had found that belonged to Grandpa?"

There was silence on the other end of the line. Richard remembered the look his father had given him when he mentioned what he had found snooping all those years ago.

'Forget you saw that, Richard,' Mike Richards had said in a gruff voice. *'Your Grandpa took something he wasn't supposed to. Mention it to anyone, and there will be Hell to pay.'*

Richard had managed to get a guarantee of an explanation when he was back from training. One thing led to another, and Richard never received the answer. Now, the time for a response was being forced onto everyone.

"You found something," his Dad said.

"Yes, Dad. Can you meet me at the parking area on the west end of the Hood Canal Bridge?"

"It will take a while, but yes."

"Good. Call me on my cell phone when you hit the Bridge. "

"Okay, Son. See you there."

Richard made his way back to the wrecked cabin just when Dan, and his dogs arrived.

"Got through?" asked Olafson.

"Yes, Sir. And I see your tracking dogs are here."

The dogs were two traditional bloodhound types, paired with a large Pit Bull mix. Richard asked Dan Smith, the scruffy born dog handler why the combination of breeds.

"The two hounds have the noses to do the tracking. Bruno here." Dan jabbed a thumb at the Pit Bull. "He'll take on anything. Saw his face down a bull elk during rutting season. Damned elk will take on wolves when they are in a rut. Bruno slammed into the bull elk, sent him running. Had a hell of a time getting Bruno to come back."

"How about a grizzly bear?" Asked Richard.

"How about a T-Rex?" That had elicited some laughter from the law enforcement types as Dan set his dogs to work. However, an odd thing happened when Dan tried to get his bloodhounds near the oversized hole in the cabin's living area. The two dogs refused to cross the threshold into the cabin. Dan cursed, pushed, prodded, and was knocked over for his efforts. Bruno began to howl, and bark as he stood his ground. But he would not cross the cabin threshold either.

"Something… bad was here," said Tim Olafson.

"I'm going to meet that contact I mentioned in a couple of hours," said Richard. "I'll show him my cell phone photo of it.

"Hope you or the lab can come up with some answers," replied Tim. "Someone was running a small grow operation to raise and sell some nontaxable marijuana, among other things, just like moonshiners did post-Prohibition. And that blood we found says they are now dead." He looked at Richard.

"I don't like people or animals fucking around in my forest."

Some two hours later, Richard sat in the parking and tourist overlook area on the west end of the Hood Canal Bridge. In addition to the size and flora of the Hood Canal area, there was a time when people could see Orca Pods swim near. The Hood Canal Floating Bridge would occasionally open to allow Trident Submarines and other sea craft through. Today, there were a couple of parked cars with clearly tourist types out with cameras.

Richard recognized his Father's Grand Cherokee SUV approaching and flashed his lights. Mike Richards saw and pulled his vehicle drivers side to drivers side with the window rolled down.

"Brought you some coffee, Son. My own brew."

"Thanks, Dad." Richard took the proffered coffee and sipped at it. It was still warm from the high-end thermos used for transport. As he used the coffee as an excuse not to start talking about the sensitive subject, he examined his father. Mike was slender and still fit from working outdoors despite his graying hair. Richard took after his Mothers family, so he was thicker and broader of the chest. People did say that on the telephone, he and his Dad sounded exactly alike.

"Well, Son, you said you needed to talk and not on the telephone. So, like they used to say, it's your dime."

Richard handed his father his cell phone with the displayed picture of the object. The elder Johnson stared at the cellphone display for several minutes before giving it back, as if to decide what he was going to say about it. Finally, he spoke.

"I never thought I'd have to deal with that… thing ever again. Not after the effect it had on Grandpa."

Richard waited for his father to continue. A good investigator knew when it was best to be patient and let people talk when they wanted to, not interrupt. You learned more from listening.

Mike Johnson took a sip of his coffee, then began to explain.

"Your Grandpa, my Dad, was an eighteen-year-old Private who had been in Korea one week when the Communists came across the border. He was there when the North Koreans pushed all the U.S. Forces back to the Pusan Perimeter. September 1950. MacArthur pulled off the Inchon Landing, and Grandpa was part of the push back up into North Korea. They made him a Sergeant one day, he was shot and wounded the next."

"So that is how you got his Purple Heart," said Richard.

"Yep. Grandpa did not talk about it much. A grateful nation sent him Stateside to serve out his remaining time. He asked to be sent someplace warm, so he was sent to Nevada, soon to be the Nevada Test Sites where a lot of nukes were tested. He met Grandma in Nevada and they were married. She was pregnant with me soon after that and Grandpa told the Army he'd re-enlist if he could stay in Nevada. They said great, so he was in place to become one of the Atomic Soldiers. That's how he came into contact with that thing you found hidden in his chest of drawers."

Mike Richards paused for a moment as he sipped his coffee,

then continued. "One of the early highly classified tests was underground with a new H-bomb design. It blew a nice big hole in the ground. It also opened a hole to… Elsewhere is what Grandpa called it. Son, remember that science fiction movie made around 1954 about the giant ants?"

"Sure, Dad. They still were showing it on TV all the time when I was growing up. What has that have to do with Grandpa and this object?"

"That movie was based on leaked classified information. None of it happened in the sewers and drains of Los Angeles, but the ants… they happened in Nevada. Only they were not Earth ants." Richard stared at his father for a few moments.

"Dad, now you have me completely confused. I knew when I mentioned what I had seen hidden in Grandpa's sock drawers it upset you, and you did not want to talk about it, but this is bizarre. What looked like a mummified piece of plant…"

"Not plant," Mike interrupted. "Ant."

"Alright. If you say so. So something nasty must have happened for you and Grandpa to hide it from the rest of the family."

"I'm getting to that, Son. It took years for Grandpa to tell me this after a few drinks. Please bear with me."

Richard nodded yes, and his father continued. "Grandpa was an E-5 by then, had a squad of men assigned to him. They were sent out with full weapons and gear, plus some Geiger counters when there was a report of someone running around the area of that classified test. The soldiers found a tunnel that should not have been there. Out of the tunnel came these ants. Two to three yards long, Grandpa and his troops shot first and asked questions later. A couple of the ants chomped on the soldiers, killed three of them when the tunnel collapsed due to the weapons fire. After the Army realized Grandpa, was not drunk or crazy, they sent out a full Company with two light tanks, followed by an Engineer platoon. They mopped up the remaining ants, loaded up a couple carcasses for study and blew the tunnel to bits. Then, the engineers covered the area with cement, reportedly rigged up some boobytraps to let the Army know if the giant ants came back."

"Did they come back?" Richard asked. His father shrugged.

"Grandpa never knew. He was retired on full disability and a nondisclosure form to keep him quiet. After he heard some brainiacs say they were not Earth ants, but just a creature that looked like ants filled the same niche, he got the Hell out of Dodge. They had animal type lungs, their carapace was different so they could grow to a large size, make those huge coconut crabs in the Pacific look small."

"But Grandpa stole a piece of one. Why?"

"To prove to himself that it was not some nightmare or that he was nuts. I was born in 1954 when that movie was made. When I started watching that movie on TV years later, Grandpa pulled me aside, swore me to secrecy, and showed me the piece of giant ant antenna he got away with. He said he had to tell someone, and thought he could trust his oldest son."

"And now I have really stumbled into it," said Richard.

"Son, I'm asking you to find a way to keep Grandpa and me out of this. Years ago when I was in the Border Patrol on the Southwest Border, I did some snooping around. Someone must have seen my name, connected it to Grandpa. One day on patrol out in the desert I received a visit by two black-suited men in a black SUV. I was told to stop snooping. I did. It's easy to get rid of a body in the desert."

Richard knew he was between a rock and a hard place. If he did not pass on this information he had just received, people could be hurt or killed. If Richard did, his Dad could wind up in prison. He'd have to figure something out before things went from bad to worse.

"Well, Dad, the sample the State and Locals found is being sent to the State Patrol Lab. Maybe the results will come back fast enough so I won't have to mention any of this."

"Hope so, Son. But if it's between a bunch of innocents being hurt or killed and me, well…"

"We'll cross that bridge when we get to it. However, it sounds as if the Multiverse theory was just proven."

The elder Johnson left with the promise from Richard to stop by whenever he made his way back to Seattle. Richard drove back to Port Angeles, stopping at the local gun and surplus store. He picked up some full metal jacket Nine Millimeter rounds for his pistol and the MP-5 in his trunk. The Special Agent also picked up a small five shell box of Sabot Slugs for his twelve gauge pump. He was a Firearms Instructor for Homeland Security, so no one looked askance at him carrying extra weapons and ammunition. Then Richard drove to the Forest Service HQ Office.

When he met Agent Olafson, Richard discovered the situation had changed. There was a witness. A young twelve-year-old Mexican boy had been picked up wearing some bloody clothes. Richard went to the interview room where he was being held. His Border Patrol Spanish might come in handy.

The Forest Service Agents had gotten the young boy some extra clothes and some hamburgers with a milkshake. The kid was eating as if he had not had a decent meal in days, which could have been the truth. Drug dealers were notorious for being cheap bastards unless you were family. That cheapness often caused people to roll over on them to the cops if there was not sufficient fear to keep people quiet.

"Hola, jefe," Richard greeted the young boy. "¿Habla inglés?"

"Yes. I was born here," the boy answered.

"Okay. I'm Homeland Security Special Agent Johnson. What's

your name?”

“Jesus Durango.”

“Okay, Jesus. The other officers told me you were there in the bosque, the forest. Can you tell me what happened?”

The boy looked at him with eyes older than the twelve-year-old body containing them. “My Uncle Marcos, he’s dead, isn’t he.”

“We don’t know, Jesus. Why do you think he is dead?”

The young Mexican American boy looked down and began to shake. The female Sheriffs Deputy who was sitting near him gently touch his arm.

“It’s okay, Jesus. You’re safe here.”

“Lady, you didn’t see the hormigas.”

“Ants,” Richard interrupted. “You saw ants, right?” Jesus looked up at Richard. The boy’s eyes bespoke of a remembered terror.

“The Ants. The big ants. They came up through the floor, Uncle Marcos fell into the hole and screamed.” Tears streamed down the boy’s cheeks. “Mateo shot at them until one smashed through the wall and bit him. Mateo’s blood got all over me. I ran.”

Jesus began to sob and buried his face in the arms of the female Deputy. Richard stood up and walked out of the interview room. Tim Olafson was waiting for him.

“He started babbling about the ‘hormigas’ when we found him along an old logging road near the cabin,” said the large man. “Jesus was covered with blood. I’m sending his clothes to the lab also.”

Richard paused in thought for a moment. Then he spoke.

“You believe him? About giant ant-looking, creatures?”

“No. But something or someone hacked- up the Uncle and Mateo,” replied Tim, “and it was not the boy.”

Richard looked back thru the two-way mirror at Jesus in the

interview room. The boy was still sobbing. At that moment, Richard made a decision. "Come on, Tim. Let me buy you coffee while I tell you a story.

The two Agents sat at a back table in the local diner. Tim was cursing under his breath.

"Just what in the Hell am I supposed to do with this story?" the Agent asked. "Richard, if I walk in and tell anyone up the chain, well, first they will send me to pee in a bottle for drugs. Then, they'll send me to a shrink if they don't just lock me up."

"I know its hard to believe, Tim…"

"Hard? Its impossible Richard."

The two law enforcement officers sat quietly, staring into their coffee cups. Tim broke the silence. "So, if I rush it, the specimen I send to the lab could be turned around in a couple days."

"The problem with that," interjected Richard, "is they will see it is animal, or insect, whatever those things test as in our part of the Universe. Then they will argue because it does not match anything they know of in this area. Then they will claim the sample was contaminated. Then they will have someone else run tests…"

"I know, Richard. It will turn into a complete goat rope. Days later, we are back to square one." The large man motioned to the waitress for a refill. "By that time, maybe more dead."

"But no one believes us without more proof," said Richard, "as it is too much like a bad Saturday afternoon creature-feature."

"So, we are stewed, screwed, and tattooed," replied Tim.

The two men silently sat as they drank their refreshed cups of coffee. Richard broke the silence. "How far do we take this?" asked Richard.

"You want to do something if it has to be unofficial, off the record?" replied the Forest Agent.

"If it means stopping people from being killed, yes." Tim slurped his coffee down, then stood up. "Come on. I'll pay."

Tim paid and left a substantial tip. The two Special Agents walked out to the parking area as Tim put a hunk of chewing tobacco in his mouth. "Bad habit, but better than smoking I guess."

"One habit I never took up," said Richard.

"Don't. It's expensive, and your wife will hate it." Tim stopped by the Forest Service SUV, looked around. "Well, no one in the parking lot. So, like I asked, how far do you want to take this, like, now?"

"First, that female Sheriffs Deputy who was there—" Richard began to ask.

Tim interrupted. "Julie's okay. I asked her to wait until I turned in my report before she does hers."

"Let's do it then, Tim. If we wait for officialdom to act, it may be weeks, months. So far, all we have is two missing dopers and a hysterical twelve-year-old. Can you imagine if all that happened at a campground?"

"That is my nightmare. So, Richard, I have a few friends not affiliated with the Forest Service. They will help me do most anything if I say it is to protect the Port Angeles area. I can call them, and they will come with some-artillery. Interested?"

Richards' face broke into a broad grin. "Hell, yeah. I know my Grandpa would have been."

"Okay," replied Tim. "I'll need to make some phone calls. I'll call you at your motel room."

"Good," said Richard. The two men shook hands.

"It begins, Richard," said Tim. "Other than my stint in the Army, some time being shot at overseas, I have lived my whole life here. I don't like anybody or anything fucking with my forest."

Tim did fast work as the next morning at O-Dark-Thirty, he met Richard in the hotel parking lot. With him were two other light-haired men almost as large as Tim sporting woodland camouflaged fatigues.

"Richard, these are two of my Army buddies, Jack Swenson and Matt Anderson. They're my lifetime hunting partners also.

Richard shook hands with the two men as Tim said, "We have one more coming."

"Who's that?" Richard asked.

"Dan Smith. He said he has a tracking dog that will fit the bill this time."

As they waited for Dan, Richard took a look at some non-official 'artillery' they have brought. Tim had a large, powerful .388 Lapua rifle constructed on a beefed AR-15 frame.

"Jack here did it," Tim said. "He's a gunsmith by trade now. I have some home loads for long range shooting competition that should do the trick. Ballistics are just this side of .50 caliber HMG rounds." Tim then pulled a stubby looking weapon with an oversized diameter barrel.

"This is assigned to my office. It's a surplus M-79 grenade launcher. We put together a couple of black powder flash-bang shells. I also scrounged a smoke round, and we made flechette rounds for close in work. "

"I have my MP-5 and a twelve gauge with sabot slugs," said Richard. "I hope I don't have to use them."

"Well, we all hope that," answered Tim. "Jack has his own designed magazine fed twelve gauge, and Matt has an M1-A1 in .308. We also all have sidearms, so we are well healed I would dare say."

As they talked, a beat up four wheel drive van drove up and parked. Dan Smith, the driver, stepped out with a huge doubled barreled weapon.

"What do you have there, Dan?" asked Jack.

"A 500 Nito Express. An old-timey elephant gun. I found it at an auction." As Dan spoke, two K-9s walked around the back of the van Richard saw one was Bruno. The Pit Bull mix from the day before. Walking next to it was a Dachshund.

"Is that a wiener dog?" Asked Matt.

" Hey, it's a Dachshund, a badger hound. Insult Hans enough, and he may bite you." All the men laughed at the thought of the low slung dog running around and ankle-bitting them.

"I hear they are nasty," said Richard.

"They're bred to go down the burrows of badgers, bite their asses," replied Dan. "So like an old Army tunnel rat, they have a tendency to be on edge."

"Well, the things we may run into will be bigger that badgers," said Tim.

"That's why Bruno is here. Out of pure dog pride, Bruno will not let Hans go someplace where he can also fit. Letting the small dog show him up will make his balls shrink."

The five men all laughed, then went to their respective vehicles. A half hour of driving, then five minutes of walking and the five men were at the wrecked cabin. Nothing had been disturbed, which told them the cause of the destruction had not returned. Jack whistled as he examined the hole in the cabin floor.

"Man, all I can think of is a prehistoric mountain beaver," said the local man. "I read they were as big as bears."

"Well, Sir, to be honest," said Richard," what we are looking for maybe a lot larger. And nasty."

"Big as an elephant?" asked Dan.

"Maybe," Richard replied. "When you see what I think we will find, all I can say is shoot first and ask questions later. I don't want to tell you more in case we find nothing. If certain people find out you know too much, it might get sticky."

The other men all shrugged. "We'll all former military," said Matt. "We understand keeping your mouth shut about stuff you're not supposed to know. So like in Shakespeare, lay on McDuff." Richard looked at Tim.

The modern-day Erick the Red grinned, then spoke. "Alright. So, how about we climb this rise hear, and then down the other side. I bet you there is an opening about the size of this tunnel."

"Like you said," answered Richard. "It's your forest."

The five men and two dogs made good time, Dan helping Hans keep up because of the Dachshund's short legs. As predicted, there was a matching hole opposite of the cabin's location. Richard had brought a couple of road flares to use as torches if necessary, but the other four men produced headband mounted small flashlights. They gave enough light to see as they slowly entered the tunnel opening.

"Stay frosty," Richard said.

"Frosty as last years bad winter," answered Tim.

The two K-9s began to growl as they caught the scent of something they did not like. Hans took off like a shot on his short legs, surprising the men.

Dan cursed under his breath as he brought his heavy elephant gun up to Port Arms. "Damn dog. Does this all the time…"

Hans let out a howl that was cut off in mid sound. Bruno let out a hunting snarl and surged ahead.

"Guns up!" Tim called out as the five men all began to jog ahead into the partially lit cavern. The floor of the tunnel began to slope downward as they tried to catch up with Bruno. Then a fighting bay and snarl came from around the corner in a sudden bend of the tunnel. Tim was first around the corner and let out a yell of surprise as a strange trilling sound washed down the walls of the underground network.

Illuminated by the headlamps of the other four men was an... Ant. But not a regular ant, even one blown up to a bull elk size. Richard saw not the smooth chitinous hair covered exoskeleton of an Earth insect, but rather a six-legged body covered with smaller interlocking segmented plates much like the armor of a Japanese Samurai. This specimen was holding the two dogs down with its front legs as it seemed to be looking at the new arrivals with it two large compound eyes. The Special Agent had no additional time to examine the creature as the discharge of Dan's elephant gun shook the entire area. The oversized shell smashed the Ant-Creature between its two main eyes and some odd copper colored liquid spurt out from the bullet entrance hole. The beast seemed to stagger, then collapsed sideways and partially curled its body. The two dogs did not move from the floor of the cavern. Dan cursed and scrambled forward.

"Hans! Bruno!" yelled Dan. The other four men formed a protective perimeter around Dan and his K-9s. Richard took the side closest to the Ant so he could examine it with his tactical flashlight. A closer look revealed the details of the segmented body plates which seemed quite flexible. They were so much like Samurai armor that Richard expected to see a "Made In Japan" notice on the body. The clawed feet also had opposable tentacles above the claws, almost like elongated thumbs.

"I think the dogs are still alive," Dan called out. "Just stunned."

"Shall we act like sheep and get the flock out of here?" asked Tim. "Take a photo with your cellphone. We've found what we expected, Richard."

"How are we going to close this down, Tim?" Richard asked. "You know there has to be—"

A second Ant was on top of them almost before they noticed. Jacks semi-auto magazine fed twelve gauge exploded into action as he was the closest to the new arrival. Three quick slug rounds and the creature collapsed, its destroyed head just inches from Jacks feet.

"Move!" Tim called out, and everyone moved. Richard grabbed up Hans under his left arm, so his right was free to use the strapped and slung MP-5. Dan was trying to hang Bruno around his shoulder when a third beast came trilling up on them. Richard sprayed the Ant with nine-millimeter rounds. The creature automatically turned towards the source of the sharp objects striking it as a loud boom echoed differently than the elephant gun. Tim's .338 Lapua rifle blew a good sized hole in what was on an insect the thorax. The Ant twisted, slashed its jaws at Tim who managed to jump just out of range. Richard jammed his MP-5 towards the back of the odd head and fired a burst from close range. That did the trick, and the Ant collapsed to the dirt floor in a heap. Everyone began to scramble back the way they came.

"What the fuck is this?" Matt called out.

"A lousy movie!" Jack called back.

Matt's M1-A1 spoke as another Ant came from the same direction as the last. "Goddamn connecting tunnels," Matt said as he fired at two Ants at once. Tim fired his rifle again, then again and again.

"Reloading!" Tim cried out as he put a fresh four round magazine in the weapon. Richard looked ahead in time to see part of the tunnel begin to collapse as an Ant head tried to force its way in. He fired the rest of his magazine, then let Hans slide to the tunnel floor as he reloaded with the spare magazine clipped side to side with the now empty one. He fired a dozen rounds in a pattern on the thrusting head which could be covered with a silver half dollar. The Ant collapsed. Richard put the MP-5 on safe, slung it to his back as he swapped it with his twelve gauge pump shotgun. He was about to pick up Hans again when Tim beat him to hit. The big man slung the

Dachshund on the back of his neck like a fur stole.

"Let's go," Tim said. Everyone began to run.

The Sun's early morning light was illuminating the tops of the fir trees as the five men reached the tunnel entrance. K-9 Bruno was beginning to come around, as was Hans. Dan mumbled words of encouragement as he ministered to his dog family. The others formed a circle of security around Dan and his two dogs.

"What the fuck was those things? " Jack asked.

"Ant creatures from another reality or universe," replied Richard.

"Well, we have physical evidence of what happened at the cabin," Tim interjected. "The question now is what are we going to do with it? We're going to need a small army to deal with—"

Tim was unable to finish his comment as a substantial something came crashing through the forest. Seconds later an even larger Ant-Creature than the ones in the identified tunnel nest came bursting into the small clearing. Richard was closest, so he pumped three sabo slugs into its head as fast as he could pump his shotgun. The Ant-Creature collapsed in a massive heap. There was silence for a few moments as everyone examined the dead insect-like a monster.

"Segmented armor like a Samurai or Roman Legionnaire," Richard pointed out. "I bet you the internal organs are a bit different. Whatever planet they developed on, I bet you there is some kind of lungs in that thing. Different evolution so they could grow larger yet have sufficient oxygen to function.

"You seem to know a lot about these horrors, " Max stated.

"Family history," answered Richard. "I'll explain later…"

Loud trilling nearby, then more Ants like the one they had just killed forced their way through the forest.

"Fuck!" yelled Tim as he began to fire.

"Damned warrior Ants," Richard called out, " they circled

around us."

"Shoot them in their goddammed big brains," Jack yelled out as he emptied his shotgun and then reloaded a fresh magazine. Matt took another Ant-creature down with his rifle when he was bowled over by a smaller one that came rushing out from the cavern. The man screamed as the mandibles crushed and slashed his right leg. Richard emptied his shotgun into the beast, and it collapsed on top of its victim.

"Fire in the hole," yelled Tim Olafson as he used the M-79 to fire a flashbang round back into the tunnel opening. The fighting men made sure not to be looking into the cavern as the explosive round detonated. Pieces of the tunnel ceiling fell down as some odd vibrating non-human cries came from further down inside the hill.

"Time to haul ass," Tim called out as he reloaded his rifle. Richard helped Matt use his rifle sling to create a tourniquet on the damaged leg. Then the larger Jack boosted him up and across his shoulders in a fireman's carry. Richard slung his weapons and picked up Matts M1-A1.

"There's a game trail downslope," said Dan as he herded the now two mobile K-9s forward. Somehow he had managed to hang ontop his elephant gun. The human fighting group tried to work their way through the thick brush and not trip.

"You're flashbang round seemed to slow them up," Richard said to Tim as they thread their way through the underbrush.

"I did some study also," Tim answered. "Ants hate any kind of fire near their nest, will throw their bodies on it to keep it from spreading."

"Here's the trail!" Dan called out. Then his dogs began to bark and snarl. The other man soon saw why as several more Ant-Creatures were using the trail to carry objects back to their nest in their oversized mandibles.

"Foragers," Richard called out. He used Matt's rifle to shoot the two nearest creatures, which collapsed with their loads. The weapon clicked on an empty chamber, and the Agent dropped it. Richard reached back into his pack, grabbing a road flare. An ear-numbing report of a gun told Richard that Dan had managed to bring his elephant gun back into play. Tim saw the road flare in his hand.

"That may start a hell of a forest fire," the Forest Agent said.

"Not if the Ant-creatures put it out with their bodies, Which should give us time to flee."

Richard used the igniter cap to light the flare and let it burn bright for a few moments. He then threw it jut to the right of the remaining giant insects. One look at the bright flame, which soon set a bush on fire, and the remaining Ant-creatures dropped their loads of foraged food and began to bite and claw at the evil fire.

"Let's move!" Richard yelled as he picked up Matt's rifle and made a dash around the ass ends of the Ants. The creatures from another reality acted enough like Earth insects that they were focused entirely on the spreading flames and ignored the humans. Down the forest trail, the men and dogs scrambled. Richard glance back and saw the smoke was no longer as thick.

"Those Ants are putting out the fire, sacrificing themselves for their nest," said Richard.

"Someone from our fire watch will see the smoke, send someone to investigate," said Tim. "So we'll have a ride."

"Those damned things had elk carcasses in their mouths," Jack said as he humped wounded Matt down the trail.

"I guess the hunters are going to be pissed this year," replied Tim.

The sounds of helicopter blades beating the air into submission made the group lookup.

"That was quick," stated Richard.

"Those aren't ours," said Tim.

All black helicopters came zipping in at low altitude. As soon as they began to hover, armed tactical personnel fast-roped into the forest. Full automatic weapons fire echoed from the area of the flaring fire as more and more troops were inserted in the woods.

"Someone was tipped off about us," said the Forestry Special Agent.

"I guess your friend Julie decided to do her report early," replied Richard. "Now the fun with Men in Black begins."

Three hours later, Richard was sitting in the back of a blacked out Government version of a Tour Bus. He was drinking a cup of coffee after being grilled by a Men In Black with the name, of course, of Agent Smith. Richard assumed there were several Smiths and some Jones from an unknown alphabet agency raking his comrades over the coals. Richard kept his Father out of the conversation, but of course, Richard figured the Senior Johnson would get a visit just to remind him to 'Keep Quiet.' Richard had signed a couple of Non-Disclosure Upon Pain of Disappearing Forms. He chuckled. At least all this meant that Richard's Report of Investigation would be short and sweet.

Agent Smith came into the room with a secured communication Satellite Phone. "Your boss," was all the dead-eyed man said.

Richard took the telephone, and answered "Johnson here—Yes, Sir, I understand—Reports have been written for my signature—I'll head back tomorrow—Yes, I'm fine—See you soon."

Agent Smith took the SAT phone back and said, "You're free to go," then walked him to a rear door in the bus. His G-Ride was parked a few feet away. A quick check showed all his equipment was neatly placed in it. Richard laughed, got in, fastened his seat belt, and then started the SUV. He drove to the local diner where he and Tim had made the first plans. At a back table was Tim. Richard walked up, shook his hand and sat down.

"So, now what, Richard?" Tim asked.

"You still have a small Mom and Pop Store that sells DVDs and videos around here?"

"Yep. What are you looking for, Richard?"

"A classic. THEM. I figured to watch it in my motel room with some beer and pizza. Want to join me?"

Tim began to laugh. "Hell, Why not? We can be great movie critics."

Richard motioned to the waitress for the check.

REGENT
BY ELIZA LOEB

Chapter 1

Strong arms coil firmly around her, pulling her tight against a broad chest as a well-defined chin rests on top of her head. She could feel his muscles tensing and retracting as he turns his back to the window, protecting her from the harsh rays of sunlight as they pool into the room. And all she could do is drink him in. She pulls the covers over her partner and herself as he proceeds to coil around her more, and her fingers brush along his skin in comfort.

"You're such a big baby sometimes," she chides playfully.

He says nothing.

Yet she knows that he is awake.

She listens to his steady breathing, feeling the rise and fall of his chest and simply resigns to lay there. He is obviously not ready to let her go any time soon.

James had never been one to discuss his feelings, and she hated it. It was a condition that was taught to serve some unrealistic ideal that all men had to be or act a certain way. He would only show some semblance of vulnerability in the night, when she caressed him and slowly pried him open like the closed oyster he had been raised to be. But right now, she could sense an intense desire not to let her go.

"You never told me you were married."

Her expression drops. Her pointed ears twitch as she looks for something else to talk about. Yet with how firmly he holds her to him, she could tell that she was not going to be able to get away from the subject.

"It was a long time ago," she responds.

"I guess I'm not the only one with my secrets then."

A sharp pang of guilt pierces through her like a knife. He had been slowly opening up to her and now, chances were, he was going to close himself off again. She grits her teeth and buries her head in his chest.

"What do you want to do?" she asks.

His arms loosen slightly and she manages to pull away. His expression is thoughtful, almost calculating as he tenses. And she doesn't know what to say or do.

Ariane has never been afraid of anything in her lifetime. At the same time, she had never found herself so assured of a person she had willingly brought into her life without cause for political commitment or hopes that the other would reciprocate one day without her draining herself just to appease them. James... James was the one person who did not... would not do that to her. And yet, she did not know what she was to expect with him. He had always been the strong silent type. Yet despite it all, he had never once said anything cruel, or raised a hand to her. He never put her in any danger or set impossibly high expectations of her to fulfill. He made her feel safe...

"I don't know much about the neighbors," he finally tells her.

"You've never let me in on your old life, nor have you ever

taken the time to tell me about it.”

She senses that there was a 'but' in his sentence.

“I honestly don’t know whether I should be angry or concerned about the situation.”

Here it comes.

“Although, whatever the case, I’m still going to stick by you as you have for me.”

Ariane’s eyes widen in surprise.

For the longest time, she had suspected humans to reject anything or anyone that slighted them. As if to deny the hidden realities of the world around them and...

“Do you mean it?” she asks.

“I would be lying if I said I wasn’t intrigued.”

The way she looks at James in that moment, practically set his heart ablaze. Her cool blue eyes questioning as she wonders why he didn’t reject her. And he isn’t certain as to whether he should be angry or enamored by her disarming puppy like expression. He smiles softly down at her as she moves to sit upright, tucking her knees beneath her as he rises to meet the smaller of the two.

“Why?” she finally asks,

“It’s been three years, Annie, why do you think?”

“Because you continue to restock the Swiss fish in the pantry?”

The statement alone was enough to bring out a howl of laughter from her partner, causing her to stiffen as her ears press back at the sudden escalation in volume. She snickers for a moment and eventually stops as he sweeps her into his arms and leans down to claim her lips in a heartfelt kiss. She parts and gazes up at him, doing her best to engrain him into her memory.

“If keeping Swiss fish in the pantry means you coming home...” he says. “Then I’ll add an extra packet and some hot cocoa to get you to return home faster.”

Ariane gives James a rueful smile, as if to tell her lover that some things just weren’t that simple.

They had stayed in most of the day, enjoying each other’s company as if they would be apart for a while. Time had operated differently in the land of the neighbors, and Ariane wished heavily that it wouldn’t be too long before she returned. She could see her lover of three years fighting to stay awake as midnight had began to ebb nearer. Slowly the clock ticked, and the tall grandfather clock pinged nearer and nearer to the stroke of midnight, and Ariane simply curled around James, squeezing her eyes shut. By midnight, she would be back in the realm of the fae, kneeling before the Unseelie king. James’s arms began to loosen from her as his head bobbed to and fro. There was a soft chitter and hoot sounding from a fire escape as Ariane’s eyes snapped open. James had finally fallen asleep, and a snowy owl perched on the railing just beyond the loving couple’s bedroom window.

The time to leave had arrived.

Ariane slides from the bed, tucking in James with little to no knowledge as to when or if she would see him again. His chestnut hair splays about the pillow as the moon casts its rays upon his olive and lightly freckled skin. She moves to place a gentle kiss on his temple and wills him to still be alive and well upon their next meeting. And as she leaves, she can see his green eyes looking at her as if to bid farewell.

Chapter 2

James had watched as a woman exited the forest line. There was a forlorn if not hopeless expression on her face as she seemed to keep looking over her shoulder, wishing desperately for someone to come out and stop her, tell her that whatever she was walking away from had been a mistake on them. Yet despite the amount of times she looked over her shoulder and marched through the graveyard, no one had come. He quickly took note of her clothing. It was elegant yet worn and tattered as one would find in a movie about a haunted house on a hill. Her deep red hair flowed behind her as she walked with a defeated yet dignified stride. Unbeknownst to him, that he would take her under his roof and eventually fall in love. He would fall in love with that strange little point at the tip of her ears, fall in love with the way the sun warmed her olive skin or how her ocean blue eyes flickered when the light touched them at just the right angle... All these things had not processed in his mind at the time and now he was watching as she stepped through the window pane and on to the fire escape. He grimaced as he kept his eyes on her and watched as she peered obediently up at the hooded figure before her and he could see that there was a small flash of resentment in her eyes.

He wanted to call her name and plead with her not to go. He wanted her here, with him where she would be safe and loved and happy. He could tell that she was happy and he didn't want that to stop. He leaped out of bed as she was whisked away by a cloaked figure, stumbling to the window as he wriggled through the framing and out on to the fire escape. He hated that she never told him that she was married. Of all things, the most he'd known was that she had been through an abusive relationship and for some reason was tossed to the side once the person had grown bored of her. He figured that was the end and she had been free.

Now she was going back…

And he was fucking conflicted.

"Annie!" he finally cried. His voice was desperate and strained by sleep.

He called her name again, and again, pleading for her to come back. He begged her not to go and to return to where she was safe. But as he watched her fade through the alley ways and crevices of the metropolis, he knew that there was no stopping her. Finally, he made a move to go inside and hurried to get dressed. Doing his best to move with a sense of urgency before he lost his Ariane. He quickly grabbed his keys and his wallet and began to make his way toward the door. And as soon as he opened it, it was slammed shut.

"It is unwise to follow," came a voice.

James leaped back as he heard skittering before him and felt something…or someone brush along his shins. His eyes darted around and the same mass bumped against his legs again. Not wanting to deal with what or whoever it was, he reached for the door and was suddenly spun around. His back facing the entry way as though he had just come in.

"I told you," hissed the voice. "It is unwise to follow."

The man growled in agitation as he then spun back around to reach for the door. And suddenly, as though some invisible force had been dragging him backward, the door fell beyond his reach. Though, he had never been one to let anything or anyone hold him back. Be it literally or figuratively. He lifted his foot as his other heel dragged across the hardwood floor and slammed his other heel behind him on what felt to be a toe. He quickly swung his elbow back, smashing his perpetrator in the face as he quickly made a b-line for the front door, unwilling to let anyone or anything stop him from gaining any headway.

"James Isaac Henley!"

His body froze.

"Lay down."

James immediately fell to the floor, unsure of what to make of having little to no control of his body as a pair of animal like feet with silver fur padded toward him with cat like grace. He looked up to find that another, much larger individual followed closely behind them. Large yellow eyes peered down at him with contempt as a rabbit like face twisted into a displeased scowl. A lion's tail swished and snapped back and forth behind the strange creature as a pair of pointed horns protruded from their forehead.

"Now that I have your attention and have been assured you will not follow, as hard as that might have been, perhaps now I can get you to listen."

He could feel his muscles spasm and twitch. How could this tiny creature paralyze him by merely saying his name? James questioned this over and over as the small creature gestured to the larger one. There had been so much that Ariane had told him in regards to the fae. He wondered why it was that she withheld certain tidbits of information from him, why did she not tell him that to know ones full name worked on humans? Did she not want him to worry? Did she not want to scare him? Why? He questioned these things over and over again as the larger creature hoisted him into his arms. Olive green skin glowed in the light as the human spied a pair of tusks protruding from his lower lip. The large mans hair was pulled back into a braid as his face had been surprisingly handsome for one that James was beginning to assume he was.

His attention was pulled back to the tiny white fur creature as their shrill voice followed close behind.

"Our ladyship has long since called upon us in the event of a possible summons, and like many who are loyal to her, we obeyed."

James opened his mouth to speak, and just as instantly, the creature had waved their hand.

"Silence," they commanded lowly.

"I am not finished."

James had nearly been bored to death with the long lecture he had received from the small creature. He could tell that the creature's companion had seemed fairly fed up with the the creature's anecdote as well, despite not saying anything. And given that the sun had been rising, they had all been waiting through the night. Although, none of what the creature said had been askew to what he hadn't already heard from Ariane before. He knew that she led a rebellion, knew that she killed her own father and took his throne as his blood spilled onto the floor and knew exactly how long it took to build loyalties between her and a kingdom that now her supposed *husband* rules in her stead. And as he thought about it, it only angered him more and more. He hated that she was required to answer to a summons and that she was denied the choice to depart from the man completely. Only the heavens knew what James had in store for his lover's husband.

"Do you understand anything that I am telling you?" the small creature asked.

James squinted at them. If he could move and catch them, he would likely skin them alive for keeping him immobilized for so long.

"James Isaac Henley, you may speak now."

In what felt like an instant, James felt a sudden pressure tracing up his throat, heaving out in exclamation as he found himself able to move again. He shot a venomous glance to his present captor, pondering the ways he could repay him for delaying any chance of seeing Annie again. Though instead inhaled and released a soft sigh.

"You have yet to tell me why you bound and gagged me," he says lowly. "Hell, you haven't even bothered to properly introduce yourselves."

The smaller of the two creatures in his presence looked to one and other, exchanging with one and other a silent discussion before turning their attention back to him.

"My name is Kavelah," the small creature responds as they straighten themselves. "Son of Marsh and proud servant to Queen Ariane the Blood Maiden, Ruler of the Darkwood Fae... The half orc is Brom."

"And why did you bind and gag me?"

"But I did not touch you."

"You used magic on me without my consent."

Kavela narrowed their big yellow eyes at the human as their silver fur bristled on edge. James could tell that the tiny fae creature was growing agitated with him... and for some reason, the very notion of causing a small bit of inconvenience for his lovers' servant was considerably pleasing.

"So as to keep you from being an idiot."

"On whose orders?"

A heavy hand fell upon the human's shoulder and drew James's attention from his conversational adversary. The half orc was giving him a warning look. Surprise to say, it wasn't a look that was threatening. It was the sort of look a parent would give to a child when they were crossing a boundary that would cause unfavorable consequences before telling them to stop. Why? He wondered. The half orc, despite the lore of his kind being ugly, was considerably attractive and much leaner than most would consider someone born full orc would be. Though James buried the question as to why in the back of his mind, hardly feeling the need to bother with the topic.

"Brom, right?"

Brom smiled down at him, nodding softly as he patted his shoulder. He seemed gentle, despite the heavy hand. The smaller man began to study his features as soon as he turned away. Two black braids had trailed down the right side of his head while one trailed down his left. His long hair had been tied back into a wild ponytail. His skin was slightly tinted green as his eyes remained a pale grey. Were one to dress him in a hoody, one would think that he was some run of the mill king of the jocks type. Not that physical prowess was a bad thing. He was sure that the orc was seen as a great warrior among his people.

"I wouldn't expect any conversation from him," Kavelah chided, pulling James from his thoughts. "He hasn't spoken since my queen's father. "

Brom rolled his eyes and snorted in the smaller creatures general direction.

"Oh don't give me that," Kavelah quipped.

"I know perfectly well that you're quite capable of holding your own in social groups."

"So what are you, exactly?" James finally managed to ask.

The smaller of the two sighed and rolled their shoulders, as if about to give an answer to a stupid question.

"Ever hear of a phooka?"

Shapeshifters, yes. James had heard of such things, though Kavelah hardly resembled what he had imagined. They often took shapes matching the characteristics of others, right down to the voice. And the only giveaways to finding phooka were to look for a part that seemed out of the ordinary and could not be hidden. He never knew what one looked like without the disguise without properly guessing on their unique or somewhat animal like features.

"I've seen many who were glamoured," he finally responded.

"Then you know what to look for to find us, then?"

"Ariane has taught me quite a bit."

The phooka raised his brow as they gave James a very thoughtful look. And the human could practically hear the smaller being mutter as he left the room.

"Not so stupid, afterall."

Chapter 3

Crystals, books and bottles lined the dusty shelves of Ariane's old room. Specimens collected over time sat upon tables as memento mori, as if to allow the observer to imagine how the small creatures might have lived. Furs and pelts lined the edge of the bed and draped over the backs of a chaise lounge as Ariane the Blood Maiden, Queen of the Darkwood fae, leaned back with one of her old books in hand as the daylight spilled into the room like a waterfall. Since she had arrived, she had locked herself in the only provision she found security. It was the only area she had been allowed her privacy, and not even her husband could enter without her regard. She had been glad to find it left alone. She hadn't any servants to tend to the room, and such was a small if not more desirable price to pay in terms of what she planned to do once granted an audience with her husband.

An audience with her husband.....

She cringed at knowing that regrettable if not foolish decisions had been made in marrying that man. She never had to request an audience with James. She never had to wait in line or compete for his attention. He never demanded her attention when she deigned to give it and quite often allowed her some space without condition. Her mind had begun to occupy its self with hopes that he didn't follow. She prayed to her gods desperately, hoping that Kavelah had stopped him without having to hurt him and prayed dearly that she would be able to see him again.

A smile soon stretched across her features as she imagined the rest of her life with him. Sharing her life force with his and ensuring that they could both be happy. She desired for him to rule at her side, or at least appoint a new regent who she knew would rule the Darkwood Fae well.

"Lady Ariane?" she heard someone call beyond her door.

Her face twisted in contempt as she stood and glided across the room. She would not give the permission to enter unless she knew who it was that was addressing her. She swung the door open with an annoyed expression, so to let her inconvenience be known. But as she was about to open her mouth to speak, her face immediately softened. A tall, broad shouldered knight peered down at her with surprise before he leaned forward and kneeled, bowing before her with ease.

"Laurent Lauran?"

The knight gazed up with a cheeky grin. His gold eyes peered up at Ariane through strands of strawberry blond hair.

"If my lady deigns to call me Chip, anymore."

Ariane practically leapt to hug the taller fae with a soft cry of excitement, and Chip instantly stood and spun her into a hug. For the first time since she had arrived, her eyes grew misty as tears of joy ran down her face. Chip had been her only ally in her husbands' palace and often guarded her to the best of his ability. And she wouldn't deny a point in time where she might have wanted to run away with him, however his loyalty remained to the Unseelie king, and running away with him would be an act of treason.

"Oh wonderful!" announced another man's voice. "My prodigal wife finally leaves her room, and my prized captain of the guard may finally return to his post."

A man with long blond hair slowly entered the room with his

arms tucked behind his back. His heels clicked against the marble tiles as his robes flowed behind him. He peered down his nose at chip, as if to take him apart and see his worth in comparison and sneered before turning to Ariane and giving her a soft smile of acknowledgement.

"Ariane, my love," he said calmly.

"Gerard Auguste."

The Unseelie King's smile faded at Ariane's distant if not frigid tone. He reached an arm around her as his free hand tipped her chin so that she was looking up at him. His brown eyes narrowed at the defiant gaze she gave him.

"I acknowledged you," she said expectantly. "Isn't that enough?"

"I expect you to show reverence for your husband, since he has been so kind as to grant you an audience."

"An audience to say that I wish to have a divorce?"

The sounds that filled the room in that instant were enough to set everyone on edge, and neither Chip nor Ariane could see it coming. Gerard stepped away for a moment, looking away from her as he calculated his next move before he swiftly drew his palm across her face, sending her flying to the floor and crashing into the silver tea set placed beside the door to her room.

"You brought that upon yourself," he said coolly. "I figured you knew better than to slight me, darling.

Ariane slowly began to stand, processing what had been done and gave a low sigh. "So you result to taking a swing at me?" she quips.

"If it will put you in line."

"Then by all means, do the same honor for yourself, majesty."

The Unseelie Kings' eyes widened as his face twisted with rage and Ariane could only smile at her small victory. That smile soon faded as she saw him raise his hand again. Only, his next strike didn't land. His arm twisted behind his back and he was pinned to the floor. His wife's knee pressed down on his spine as he felt his arm threatened to break from her shoulder sockets. Ariane clicked her tongue as she kept the taller of the two royals pinned beneath her. Never again would she allow this man to touch her. Never again will she suffer the pain of his betrayal or the feeling of being unsure of herself or the decisions she makes for the sake of his approval. This man, ceased being her husband when he chased her from her home. And now that he had stricken her, any love or affection she might have had left for him had disappeared. He was little more than an insignificant worm who had grown too big for his britches.

The thought of killing him had finally crossed her mind. She could kill him right now for all the heartache and grievance he caused her. She could kill him for subjecting her to indescribable misery and degradation as a punishment for ever loving him.

At this point, anger and hatred had all that was left for him. She had accepted that he would never love her a long time ago, understanding... no. Hoping that if she were to return to her once vibrant home, it would be without his presence.

The blood maiden could feel as a prickly sensation erupted from her fingers as the air grew frigid. Ice begins to crystallize at the windows and spiral along the walls and cluster in the corners as they slowly congregate to her and the fae king. She can feel the ice forming at her fingertips as his hands slowly get colder and colder. To him, it must have felt like a million microscopic needles piercing into his flesh as frost slowly formed on the surface of his skin.

In that moment, she had a thought. She wondered how well the fae king would be able to manage being left alone in the woods, naked, during the dead of winter. Would he be able to survive the bite of the snow? How long would it take for him to starve? Or would he be eaten by much larger, hungrier predators before being allowed to suffer from his own famine? She couldn't retrain the sadistic smile that played across her lips at how loud his screams would be.

She leans forward, moving low enough so that her lips were inches away from his ear. Her voice dripped with venom as the room grew more and more frigid. "You are never to touch me again."

A soft hand touched the queen's shoulder, and Chip's voice drew her from her thoughts. "My queen," he says softly. "Please consider the consequences of your next actions."

She looks up at the Knight with a furious expression, which he responds with a pleading look. She knows what he is intending as her eyes search his.

He is not worth the witnesses, he means to say.

"Fine," she says in defeat.

It doesn't take too long before the ice melts and the room to warm up again as Ariane releases Gerard. She flocks to Chip with ease as she apologizes to him in silence. Chips eyes fall on his king, who is now regarding him with thoughtful resolve.

"Lock her in her room," he orders. "She is to dine alone, tonight."

The Unseelie King soon left the room, leaving a sense of apprehension for the two. The energy in the air had lost it's positivity in the skirmish. There was nothing in that moment that the two could find to recover from it, and Ariane sighed.

"I guess you've gone from queen to prisoner, then," he says lowly. And Chip can only pat her back reassuringly.

"Bright side is, you have me, right?"

Ariane smiles at him, envious of his ability to find the silver lining of the situation. "I guess it's not too bad."

The hours had passed as her friend kept her company, only leaving her room once or twice to make his rounds. Each time, he enters without any need to knock. Yet as day fell to night, something ominous had been reaching through the back of Ariane's mind. Chips returns continued to get further and further spaced out.

Why? Questions of what might have been occurring spun through her mind. Was Chip dead? Had he done something that was considered treason? Was Gerard assigning him to near impossible tasks? All of these questions raced through her mind as she circled back and forth to every single one.

She leaped as she heard a loud knock at her door.

Odd. Chip didn't need to knock.

She looked through her peep hole, spying the area with curiosity as she looked for who might have been knocking and found no one. She heard something brush at the floor and tap against her foot. A tray of food had been placed atop two hat boxes, along with an envelope with contents addressed to her. She set her tray to the side and began to open the first box. A top hat had been neatly placed inside the box's contents, a musty yet coppery smell filled her senses and soon she was filled with a sense of dread. She quickly opened the second box and the earth-shattering scream that she released echoed through the room. The blood stained strawberry blond hair that peaked out from the box was enough indication as to why Chip hadn't returned. Ariane's screams faded in to cries and evolved into mournful wail's as she fell to her knees and doubled over from the shock. It was as though the ground had been pulled from beneath her and all that was left was her rapid decline.

The seconds ticked by and all the fallen queen could now do was lay on the cool ground, curled around the hat box containing her newly departed friend's head, and hoping that this was some twisted little prank of his.

Alas, she had been wrong.

And this was all that she had left of him.

Hours had seemed to have gone by. All Ariane could remember of those hours were that she had eventually faded into a dreamless sleep after losing what hope she had of having an ally in the palace. A great wave of emotions washed over her at that point. Rage and sorrow had seemed to be the more pronounced of them and her nails angrily scraped against the floor as she then stood and began to storm through the room, shouting and screaming profanities that she knew would reach down the hall and out her window. She threw bottles and books at the walls and destroyed the large mirror that had stood in her room long before she had inhabited it. This caused her pause as the glass shattered in to a thousand pieces, revealing a passage she had not noticed before.

She turned her attention to the broken glass and contemplated her next steps as she craned her neck to peer down the new dark corridor she was now intent to explore.

Yet as she looked around her room she took notice of the bottles and wondered around, thinking that the mirror would just continue to be a broken mirror with every instant she had turned around. Instead what seemed to have been broken mirror pieces were shards of glass were thick and so deep red they appeared black until light pooled in their curves and revealed their secrets. Sigils had danced upon the broken glass and Ariane had been left speechless as she turned to face the scene before her, lifting the envelope and opening it to reveal the message inside.

To remind you of your place and the consequences of your actions. Do you wish for another to die, because of you?
—G.Auguste, Your Husband
and rightful king of the Unseelie Court

Ariane had already been consumed with rage at this point. Instead, in that moment, she had made an oath to herself. Promising that she would leave, even if it killed her, and neither Chip, nor the top hats' original owner, will have died in vain.

She eyed the newfound corridor and narrowed her eyes, taking one step forward, followed by another and another before she found herself descending into the passage of what appeared to be an endless void. Of all the things the situation had come to, Ariane found little hope in staying or getting Gerard to agree to her terms.

She recalled a situation like this when she was younger. Her father's old palace had been riddled with secret passages and doorways that led to deep corridors that seemed to lead to nowhere. Those passages often helped make her life at least a bit more bearable. For as long as she stayed in her room, no one would find out about her private escape. And as she got older, she found that having such a passage would turn her prison into her sanctuary.

The twists and turns seemed almost endless as Ariane could only navigate through the darkness if she had a wall to cling to. She hardly minded the spiderwebs or the feeling of tiny creatures skittering along her skin, and the deeper she went, the more common they had become. Ariane persisted forward, refusing to turn back.

IN SEARCH OF DENMARK
BY SHEILA MENGERT

Part One

Like a calving glacier the ideas that form the bulwark of humanism are falling away into the rising sea. No prior species has wrought its own extinction nor had the capacity to reflect fully on its own contingency. In this sense *Homo sapiens* might, from a planetary point of view, be considered to be a noxious and invasive species as deleterious to the biosphere as any other untoward event, geological or extraterrestrial. The absorption or decimation of indigenous peoples around the world has broken the primary ties of un-technological humankind and supplanted it with a being that appears collectively intent upon sawing away at the branch of the tree of life that sustains it. Artifice is no longer decorative or remedial but rather the primary character of what may perhaps be a silica-based form of mechanism that will make life-forms based upon carbon a quaint remnant of a prior era. This erosion of prior certitudes and assumptions of the value of the species is only multiplied when that contingency and the deconstruction that is made possible by contingency is applied to the individual.

The subject of this tale is one Tiffany Amorth whose father, securely rooted in the centrism provided by his faith and his conservative political convictions, had once been convinced that his daughter was possessed because of her many, to him absurd fears. Fortunately he had gradually modified his assessment of his daughter to embrace the lesser included offenses of her simply being demonically obsessed rather than possessed or perhaps being merely mentally unbalanced in her confusions and reservations. Not that being mentally unbalanced should be accepted as any excuse for her failure to thrive and prosper; Leo P. Amorth believed that just as physics recognizes the law of strict conservation of energy there was a parallel in the moral realm so that every sin or weakness must be paid for by somebody at sometime. Being as close to his daughter as he was, it came as no surprise that the guilt from his daughter's offences, or at least the punishment due to them in the temporal order, had been laid by an all-just providence at his door. He had conceived her; she was his responsibility. As a father he had bowed to his fate as the fruit of concupiscent desire. He kept a running account of the liquidated value though of her guilt and his expenses manifested in living allowances, university tuition, and the luxuriant accessories that appended to her sex. Still, for all of his sacrificial offerings and concern she persisted in her mental aberrations, her strange obsessive and compulsive rituals, and the costly study of subjects devoid of any visible pecuniary value. When he asked her from time to time the source of her nameless but manifold ills she would either remain silent or worse begin a recitation of citations to various unreadable authors who with too much time on their hands had explored the nuances of existential drift, bad faith, and the loss of the transcendental ego.

Her character and personality was the one source of

frustration in an otherwise admirably ordered life. The defeat of Hillary Clinton due to the fortunate existence of a rurally weighted electoral college had advanced a true populist to the throne of the Presidency where he could lower taxes, purge the deep state, and deregulate America into formerly impossible but now infinite vistas of prosperity. The full power of capital would finally be unchained from the ill-considered virtues of mercy and equality that merely allowed the weak, the profligate, and the lazy to thrive at the teat of the public purse. Leo P. Amorth saw great and noble America as a virgin about to be set upon by the hoards of illegally entering brown-skinned hybrids of Hispanic and Indian extraction who would jump on the gravy-train of post New Deal entitlements if they were ever allowed to cross our undefended southern border en mass and bring the benefits conferred by sophisticated investors and investment bankers to a halt. He would be content to let the lettuce rot in the fields before countenancing such an outrage. The party of the Democrats had over the two terms of the Obama administration morphed from a nuisance to the agenda of God-fearing Republicanism to emerge as the vanguard of socialism, the rampant indulgence of the baser appetites of the flesh, and the final and irrevocable emasculation of the American male by fire-breathing feminists. It was bad enough to hear of such matters even when put in their proper perspective as Trump-hating propaganda by conservative media but to have a daughter of democratic darkness entering his canonical domicile each night while still redolent of the fake news broadcast on CNN and other demonic media was to defile the paternal sanctuary. He found his daughter to be not the least of the crosses that he, good man that he was, had to bear.

Tiffany for her part was no more tolerant of his views on theology or politics. She harbored what might be called an historical skepticism towards any large institutions in proportion to their venerable reputation and longevity. She found the views of Alfred North Whitehead and his process philosophy to be congenial to her natural proclivities of thought and feeling. She thought of truth statements as profoundly limited by the language in which those truths were expressed; she therefore located truth as something that we strive to obtain rather than to maintain. This naturally made her critical of the idea of an irreducible "deposit of faith" to be safeguarded in every detail, proclaimed, and possessed by an institutionally reiterated argument that assumed that when Jesus had promised to remain with His Church forever He was simultaneously creating a semi-feudal order of Bishops with powers of excommunication, interdict, and an innate charisma that could over sufficient time harden into dogma through the sheer force of repetition. Tiffany felt that history had shown such a tendency to breed an unhealthy confidence that had led directly to the burnings of heretics and witches, the stifling of new insights in the sciences, and the colonization and enslavement of native peoples by crusaders and colonial missionaries. She deplored the forcible inclusion of people possessing their own cultures and values into the spiritual fortress of orthodox belief for fear that otherwise they were doomed to perish by reason of original sin. She took the point of view that it was a crass instrumental view of sacramental action to institute their usage among people with only a partial grasp of the underlying heritage of western institutions and historical experience. When invitation becomes first demand and then command something is wrong. She deplored any suggestion of spiritual violence even if well-intended. God appeared to her to value diversity in both species and in circumstance here on earth rather than to be confined in His essence to the maledictions of any priestly caste even if that caste had originally been commissioned to start the ball rolling by reaching beyond the upper room in Jerusalem. Catholicism had always possessed an ability to adapt as well as to subjugate and to this quality she owed her persistence in and even love for the faith of her girlhood.

The refusal to embrace unqualified assent to propositions was also applied towards other relationships, particularly those involving sexuality. She considered proposals by most men to be veiled invitations to enter into contracts of adhesion on unequal terms even if sweetened by an aura of conventionality and economic security. How could she commit what was still in process of formation? Thus, Tiffany Amorth had reached the ripe old age of thirty without possessing the luxury or enjoying the achievement of a sense of stable identity beyond this overriding tendency to see the flaws and limitations that qualified any statement not least of which was a matrimonial promise of exclusive sexual fidelity and abiding love. She had a name of course and a personal history as we all do but her sense of an abiding and unitary identity was still lacking. It was not that she was inordinately suggestible; she was far too headstrong for that. Rather her lack of identity was due to an overwhelming conviction that nothing should be allowed to set and harden within her until she had thoroughly investigated all of the alternative possibilities that life might potentially hold in store for her before making any irrevocable commitments.

At first glance this salient aspect of her nature, one characterized by a sense of inner drama as she visualized alternatives that life presented to her, might lead the ordinary observer to conclude that Tiffany was at heart an adventurous girl: wild, impetuous, and prone to throw caution to the winds. In this supposition as in so many such hasty presuppositions the ordinary observer would be far afield from the truth. If anything it was her awareness of possibilities that caused Tiffany to restrain all vagrant impulses and to maintain a sternly centered locus, a base camp from which she could send out expeditions of imagination along the highways and byways of vicarious sensations by reading and entertaining those seasoned reflections that are the fruit of memories recollected in tranquility. It was this cautious quality that had preserved her virginity, mental and physical, intact to the end of her third decade of life.

Tiffany would have been among the last to claim that her abstinence from sex, drugs, and heavy metal music was due to heroic virtue. Virtue is most evident when it exceeds ordinary demands; possibility must beckon and then be denied. This had not been the case with Tiffany. Her upbringing was such that anything overtly sexual or perverse was simply unthinkable for her. Femininity was presented to her clothed in all of the peril and shame that was *de rigueur* to Roman Catholic educational institutions. In the eighth grade it was carefully explained to her that whereas boys were more prone to sexual sins due to possessing a virtually ungovernable biological drive it was up to girls to avoid leading them into sin. To that end strict modesty was to be preserved at all times and any familiarity of a lingering let alone lascivious nature was to be strictly avoided. The result was that Tiffany took no joy in the rapid inundation, when it came, of that hormonal tide that in four short years had worked the accustomed wonder of transforming a slim and wiry eleven year old girl into a maiden.

Indeed so effective had been the advance warnings and maledictions of the nuns regarding anything overtly sexual during her adolescence in a gender-segregated private Catholic high school that even marriage, the great refuge from concupiscence, was in her eyes fearful and vulgar. The bondage of the flesh was further subject to the economic burdens that flowed from being a woman. The lives of women seemed to her to be one long procession from the altar to the grave spent pushing a grocery cart. A woman's value appeared to peak at seventeen and thereafter to cascade downward from terrace to terrace in a waterfall of recurring diets and the progressive loss of pulchritude to various manifestations of fleshly obsolescence from cellulite to wrinkles. There appeared to be a direct biological and social tendency to see any individual woman through a lens that focused primarily upon her capacity for procreation. This meant that personal history at least insofar as she was a woman was confined to that short era between menarche and menopause after which the framework and architecture of her existence was removed and her significance as an individual must of necessity rest upon a basis that she alone could construct.

It was due to this early assessment of the range of options open to her in the common course of life that Tiffany Amorth decided to foreswear the lure of suburban comforts and to embrace the Spartan life of being an "artistic type," as her parents had phrased it when they began to notice her early proclivity for quoting from Mallarme, Rimbaud, and Baudelaire in the original French at the dinner table. So it was that while other girls were lolling about in bikinis reading Jackie Collins or Ericka Jong, Tiffany was often to be found in high school reading Richardson's *Clarissa* for its more thrilling parts when honor was imperiled or at the outer fringe of her adolescent rebellion a life of Lord Byron or *Don Juan* or *Manfred* in the shade of an enveloping tree.

She thought of reading the classics as a profoundly moral and at the same time rewarding activity. She believed in the salubrious value of tracing the course of folly through fiction the better to avoid life's inevitable pitfalls. There was a moral aspect to all things and literature traced the course of human intemperance. She preferred her indiscretions to be by proxy. She decided early on that the great disadvantage of virtue is that it is always being assaulted by some *roué* or other the better to emerge though, splendid in refusal. She thought of her life as a vast and echoing cathedral at night with one great rose-window containing various *tableaux* marking significant episodes of her lone pilgrimage of virtue and trial, her beauty like that of Diana forever untouched and unassailable.

It must not be thought that she was vain however or overestimated her own appeal to the male sex; it was merely that she was curious about how others managed to deal with the great questions the better to guide her own eventual commitments. She was aware of her attractions without being impressed by them. Physically speaking her review of what nature had bestowed unasked upon her was neither persistent nor prurient. She did not engage in long vagina monologues when alone nor view her pudenda from all angles and in all lights lest some distinguishing feature failed to be noted and catalogued. She was content to possess the standard issue of a daughter of Eve with sufficient excess mammary tissue to have some left over to produce a beckoning *décolletage* when her studies were completed. Beyond that she had icy green eyes, a full mouth, and a nose that did not dominate her face nor distract from her more telling intellectual charms. Many girls were able to do far more with far less than her share of female *accoutrements* while Tiffany let the years go by in endless rehearsals for some distant but inevitable grand passion, the proper reward for her discriminating taste and willingness to forego the first jejune offerings of connubial bliss.

The result was that she emerged at last from graduate school at the University of Washington at thirty with a Masters Degree in Creative Writing but with no immediate marital prospects and no housemate but her widowed father who lived downstairs primarily in his den while the upper regions of the house were surrendered to her solitary keeping after her mother's untimely death. It was a scenario suitably gothic and filled with various Ann Radcliffe possibilities as she above all would know. How often had she lingered over passages in

The Mysteries of Udolpho and listened at night to the winds of January moaning through the trees. How often had she imagined herself the heroine in one of Byron's longer poems winding her fingers through the feverish tendrils of the tormented poet's hair as he sought to recover from the pain of exile and the contempt of those who could never understand the nameless discontent that had driven him to a life of blasphemy and despair.

Truly it was time to set off on her own long delayed pilgrimage to some distant land where her virtues long untried might be assailed in earnest by a worthy suitor, but where? Who would finance such an expedition in search of a way of life long celebrated in verse but sadly absent in a world shrunken to the size of a postage stamp by technology? What Rapunzel-like braid of hair would allow her to be spirited away by night to places and adventures unknown? Romance long denied lay sequestered in the books that now gathered dust in neat shelves that lined what had once been the master bedroom of the family mansion, now used as a library with only an empty expanse of carpet, several bookshelves, and a table with a reading lamp and computer, the rose window of the vast cathedral of her young life sterile and derivative where it had been meant to be a tribute to the utter uniqueness of her well-tutored existence.

She had not only not dared and dared greatly she had barely moved. She was like a display in a window of a department store, inviting but untouchable. She began to wonder occasionally if a few cheap thrills coupled with early repentance might not have been worth it after all. Even being a victim of possession might have made her life less boring than it was turning out to be; she could at least vomit at will and scare people. Instead she was only Tiffany Amorth, a girl who wasn't sure who she was.

So, absent a sense of self it was no wonder that Tiffany was what might be called a universal recipient of the projections of other people who saw in her whatever they disliked in themselves. Like the universally used variable "X" in algebra Tiffany could be used as a symbol for other people's sexual or personality insecurities. She was like an empty warehouse just waiting to be filled with other people's refuse and many availed themselves of the opportunity. The result of course was that Tiffany gradually learned to tune out the world until it was only an obnoxious hum like that of one of the old tube-driven radio-sets of the 1930's. She saw people habitually as shadows, vague filmy abstractions to be gotten through or around in the course of everyday life.

In the course of her childhood she had come to see everything as an assignment to be completed alone and at her peril. Participation was foreign to her and finally pointless because it compromised the only thing that she could ever really rely on, herself. Her engagement in the world was rather like maintaining a projected hologram: when people reached out to hurt her they would find their hands grasping only empty space. Only the marvelous distance provided by the written word allowed her to engage intimately with people long dead that she would never know. These were safe because they were unaware of her existence, unable to deny her entry into their secret thoughts and complex personalities. In them she found allies and guardians in a cold and reprobate world—one that in an instant could call into question her right to exist and mock any budding trust in human warmth and communal feeling.

Thus the years had drifted past like snowflakes born frigid and icy before the wind while Tiffany Amorth became an unseen character upon the written page of various texts. She walked upon the moors with Cathy and Heathcliff at Wuthering Heights. She climbed the ruined stairwell of the House of Shaws with David Balfour. She arrived just before dusk at the melancholy House of Usher. Though unrecorded in the text she was there, within the narrative, and gradually the words and very being of the author became part of her so that her thoughts and words in everyday life resembled whatever it was she had just been reading before being summoned forth again to take her uncomfortable place in the everyday world once more where she was only Tiffany Amorth and not the intimate companion of the Count of Monte Cristo.

To such a lonely girl the thought of sympathetic witchcraft was pleasant because it could write into the world that place where alone she found comfort and acceptance. Whenever she was wounded, magic would allow her to restore order by virtue of metaphysical deletion of the offending party. It made perfect sense to her that if she could enter into fiction as though its phantom corridors were real then it should be possible for the gritty world that surrounded her to be first encased in prose and then subtly altered. The alterations might be marginal at first: a case of acne before the prom in a girl who had mocked her, a pulled tendon before a tennis match or a severe bout of magically induced vomiting at a school assembly for other offenders, or finally in its more resolved form, automatic misfortune to anyone who wished her ill. She called this latter mechanism, "the curse," and after a time it became quite real. She laughed at its existence of course, rational girl that she was, but secretly she felt that it existed as truly as the chain of missile silos placed in prairie locations all over America existed, ready to launch their deadly cargo when a few codes come through to form a perfect match. All of her pain had been stored up, every outrage, every unprovoked cruelty, every slighting jest at her expense—stockpiled, armed, directed, triggered, launched, and guided home to return the pain to its point of origin by "the curse."

However, far from being a commerce with the forces of darkness there was for Tiffany a sort of Old Testament symmetry in all of this—any Israelite blowing trumpets around the walls of Jericho would have understood. After all Tiffany invoked no demonic powers; her magic was facilitated in quite a detached manner. It was a mute physical event like moving something across a room to occupy a new position in the cosmic order. To hurt Tiffany Amorth was to be displaced from column A to column B and then to suffer whatever consequences the universe might then impose. This was the way Tiffany saw it. It allowed her to believe in a moral universe, one where no harm goes without suffering the pangs of nemesis. She regarded herself as innocent and inoffensive thus relieving herself of actually hexing anyone. Still, the realization of her power added a bit to her wardrobe when she began to wear a fringed white cape and to twirl about in her room while listening to Fleetwood Mac.

She came at last to favor blue or black nail varnish and she kept glass jars full of various crystals at strategic points throughout her room to balance the energies. She made a pilgrimage in spirit to various Druid sites in old Britain and imagined herself gathered about oak trees on a full moon night dancing naked beneath the stars and drinking flasks of mead on animal skins laid out upon the foggy ground. There were men there with flowing hair and beards, men with gentle eyes and leather-clad limbs, icons of brazen male youth and fertility. She felt her breasts firm and pert with the cold of night and her thighs full and welcoming in sheer animal splendor and then... in an instant she would come to her senses again to hear the dull grind of the garbage disposal downstairs.

She had told her father again and again not to throw potato peelings or coffee grounds down the garbage disposal. Thus did dream and reverie intertwine in the life of Tiffany Amorth before she entered therapy and for a long time thereafter as she began slowly to claw her way back into reality with its prosaic demands and inconclusive remedies for an artist's sorrow and for her pain. Therapy helped her begin to let go of frustration and loss and she had gradually purged her immediate surroundings of the more outward trappings of her occult inclinations. She only still affected the almond eyes and heavy eye shadow of a siren or concubine in a Turkish harem but her days of black lace and deep mauve lipstick as in high school were now past. She felt that she didn't need to be scary to hide her insecurities.

Yet for all of her improvement, her particular demons could not be expunged without what she called "a definitive event." She needed to break free of her past and to undertake some radical and defining mission like bringing unsought independence to some obscure nation by arriving by jeep and posting some significant manifesto outside the presidential palace of the dictator. She would locate the disconsolate underground resistance fighters and weld them into a formidable force for change. She would be like Joan of Arc and lead a revolt and later preside at the constitutional assembly to form a new government. Alternatively she would in a swift intuition find the equation that would embody a unified field theory for the four forces in the universe or explain what was happening just a second before "the big bang." Then maybe, just maybe, resting on the secure laurels of immemorial achievement, she would find some male of equal talents and begin to turn out genetic representatives of their mutually superior genes thus elevating the human race to unimagined splendor say in a thousand years through natural selection. Now would be an identity and one worthy of her one and only life. She wouldn't have to be a witch if she could be a goddess!

But as enticing as these dreams were it only took a review of her present finances to diminish her prospects for humanity's reclamation. So it was that she pared and modified her aspirations and demands to a mere wish to leave the shores of America on a post-graduation trip of some sort. She needed to go to a place of history, charm, and romance where they served good food, where people were generally happy, and where her future admirer awaited her.

Tiffany Amorth decided at last after a cursory study of travelogues to go to Denmark. She proposed her scheme to her father at the dinner table two weeks after graduation.

"Father?" she inquired tentatively.

"Yes Tiffany."

"Well I'd like to talk to you about my post-graduate plans."

"That's encouraging. I had supposed that you were going to write the great American novel. Has there been a change of plans?"

"Not necessarily, but I feel that I may be too close to my subject for that. I need perspective."

He seemed to think about this while chewing slowly.

"And how do you propose to obtain that perspective?" he replied at last.

"I need a point of contrast to give dimension and balance to the whole."

He continued to chew.

"No doubt to obtain depth," he opined.

"Exactly."

"It would hardly do to attempt greatness in a spontaneous and superficial manner," he continued.

"I knew you would understand."

There was another significant pause.

"Will it require another year at the U.? More tuition?"

She decided to take the plunge.

"Well, it will require some further expense in time and money. You see I am not completely secure in my authorial voice."

He stopped eating and looked up at her, "You've lost me."

"It is essential that the author know something of life; mere verbal facility is inadequate."

He went back to his roast and potatoes. "You possess the

latter and now need more of the former, is that it?"

"Yes."

He looked up brightly. "You could watch more Fox News; it would reorient your radical views."

She hesitated before replying, "I was thinking more of travel, cut loose and follow the rainbow."

"Travel… I thought you feared tropical diseases," he said dubiously.

"I was thinking more of the northern latitudes."

He seemed to consider this.

"Where to, for instance?"

She said firmly, "Denmark."

"Why Denmark?"

"It was the setting for most of Soren Kierkegaard's life."

"And who, pray tell, is Soren Kierkegaard?" he inquired.

"He was a Danish philosopher, one of the first existentialists. He wrote a lot about finding one's place in the world, one's identity."

Her father returned to his meal.

"Admirable," he said without looking up. "I suppose that he at least figured out who he was before putting it all down."

"Yes, it was an arduous task. His writings reveal an ongoing quest."

"You will forgive me if I get a bit queasy when you speak of ongoing quests. I don't suppose that you could simply adopt someone else's identity as a sort of stop-gap measure and simply press on with living like most people do. Force of necessity answers many questions if it is allowed space to work."

This was disconcerting. "You know my limitations, Father. Of course that prescriptive advice works for less sensitive souls but I…"

"I know how sensitive your soul is and it always ends up costing me money. I thought your therapist was working wonders with you lately."

"Well I'm somewhat better."

"Better but not cured is that it?" He frowned. "Suppose you go to Denmark and have a panic attack and I have to fly over and bring you home?"

She looked down and felt a rush of shame. "I'll be fine. They ride bicycles over there and everyone smiles and eats pastry. It's very restful."

"No bats or mice then?"

"I seldom hear them spoken of," she commented softly.

The room was silent while her father thought the matter over.

"I hear they are all socialists over there; nobody works. There is no army to speak of and people go in for sex changes at the drop of hat; hardly a proper atmosphere for a daughter of mine."

She volunteered bravely, "I could show them the way back to capitalism and imperial rule."

He considered this seriously.

"Sort of an emissary of proper values eh?"

"Well, I am your daughter," she said brightly.

"Heredity will out you mean? Hmm, you will make a break from your dabbling in the occult?"

"Of course. By the way, Kierkegaard was a great Christian, quite demanding in fact."

An appeal to religion was always a telling point with her father.

"Really? Was he Catholic?"

"Lutheran I am afraid, but he quarreled with the state church."

Her father returned his attention to his plate, "Well, it proves he was moving in the right direction. How long do you plan to remain over there?"

"Well that depends."

"On the depth of my generosity no doubt."

She took a deep breath. "Yes."

The room was silent for some time while her father examined the various equities and risks involved in her proposal.

"What if you fall in love over there? I'm not financing an international wedding."

She blushed appropriately as one might expect in a fable such as this.

"I plan on studying and writing; I will have no time for romance."

He ruminated.

"You might be kidnapped by terrorists," he suggested.

"Nothing much in that order ever happens in Denmark."

Her father took up his napkin and wiped his lips.

"I see, dull sort of place. Well, will five thousand do it?"

The time was at hand.

"Ten would be better," she said bravely.

"Eight thousand."

"Done. "Thank you, father."

"It will give me an opportunity to have her room exorcised while she is gone," he mumbled quietly to himself.

Part Two

When she returned to her room Tiffany wondered if this whole Denmark thing made any sense at all now that it had been transmuted from speculation to active possibility. It was somewhat surprising that her father had not raised more objections. She wondered whether she might be blundering her way into a long avoided but permanent exile? Suddenly Denmark seemed an absurd idea. She tried to recall the exact lineage of the desire to go there. She was able at last to trace its origin to the feeling that the ground in America was shifting beneath her feet. She was weary of the general slippage of her native land into the collective delusion represented by MAGA hats and chants of "USA USA." It would be nice to live in a place where people could live civilized lives without the pretence of international power grounded on a presumption of moral and cultural superiority with little basis in fact. Denmark might be provincial by global standards, but at least it was not imperialistically complacent.

The world around her was changing too quickly. Recently the last CD music and video store in the area had closed. She remembered the vitality of similar chains from her girlhood. She and her friends had worn leggings and dark-eyeliner and had enjoyed being checked-out by the older high-school boys. She had been part of a sort of intellectual Goth crowd when she went out at all. She had managed to avoid drugs and AIDS due more to fear than the exercise of virtuous restraint. But by college she had somehow lost her early flair, become what the British used to call a swot or a drudge and studied all the time. She had double-majored in literature and philosophy before entering the creative writing program which she managed to stretch out to three years instead of the usual two. Between undergraduate and graduate education she had taught as a substitute teacher for sixth graders in a private girl's school for two years, helped a professor on two research projects, and avoided any premature commitments to an irrevocable life course.

Meanwhile her high school friends had married or moved away and suddenly she realized that she had virtually no friends left to serve the immemorial female function of sharing mutual confidences. Tiffany wondered if she might have inadvertently taken a fatal fork in the river of life through sheer inertia and the refusal to search out contacts in the professional sphere. Jobs lead to other jobs. Her desire to simply emerge or be discovered for her remarkable intuitions and latent genius had not materialized as planned. People far less talented than she were having their second and third children or were being advanced into management positions. She supposed that there were lives every bit as unfocused but this one just happened to be hers.

What did she expect from Denmark anyway? She spoke no Danish, knew no one there, and was still prone to unexplainable bouts of anxiety that might rear their ugly heads simply due to a particular cast of light from a wintry sky or an expression of suspicion or rejection from a stranger. How would she be able to manage there? Suddenly even the comfort of her bedroom seemed vaguely alien and threatening. The temperature seemed to drop and objects took on that slight angular look that they took on when her anxieties began to rise like a ground fog on a February day. It was this particular vulnerability, evanescent and untraceable that had always held her back. Usually she could just wait it out and everything would resume its usual place and relations, but this resurgence depended upon maintaining close contacts with the familiar. To cut loose though might leave her in a strange place without comfort or resource. She suddenly felt like a lost little girl again, not the intrepid warrior maiden, not like one of the newly elected women to Congress who dared to beard the bear-like President of our august republic. Her convictions were the same as theirs were, why then was she so isolated and ineffectual?

She reflected on the relation of experience to identity, does the first bestow the second? She thought of Kierkegaard who had seen the ordinary course of life as being incompatible with an intimate relationship with God when defined as the primordial ground of being. The relation to God was an absolute that must preclude all lesser considerations, even the ethical demands of reason should God request it. Where did other people fit into this intense bilateral mirroring of God or at least his image in the individual soul? Tiffany preferred a diffuse God, one present in tree and sunset over the intensely paternal and personal God of the Old Testament or even the gentle-minded Savior whose fate made the prospect of any sin so guilt-inducing. She had no desire to add to the burdens of Christ by her actions or preferences, but then love rejoices, it seemed to her, in the prospect of added sacrifice. She supposed that when she fell in love that she would enjoy doing things for the one she loved no matter how tiresome or obnoxious they might be.

Kierkegaard had broken off with his fiancée Regina Olsen by pretending to be a cad and jilting her. Did God ask this of him or did he take this burden on voluntarily and perhaps even beyond the demands of necessity? To err on the side of suffering just to be sure was hardly the normal course of human conduct. Tiffany wondered if she would have liked a man like him. His titles though had always intrigued her. *"Fear and Trembling," "The Sickness unto Death," "Stages on Life's Way," and "The Philosophical Fragments;"* all had seemed books directed particularly at her. He at least would have understood the subtle burdens she carried. He liked challenging authority as well be it ever so sanctified by common usage. She found him more palatable than the sensual and indulgent Lord Byron, her other great hero. As for Percy Shelley, well, she thought Mary Wollstonecraft Godwin-Shelley might have done better. He had been rather like an early version of a contemporary rock star, gathering groupies.

Tiffany was suspicious of both reformers and of orthodox prelates as well. Her attraction to the occult betrayed her desire to revisit long discredited explanations of why the world is at it is. She valued the vagueness of what little rite and doctrine there might be within it. An undemanding and unrevealing goddess seemed easier to relate to than the purveyor of a definitive but demanding revelation presided over by an insistent and unquestionable male hierarchy. She had received enough of that at home. Still she was a Catholic and intended to remain one. Catholicism is always both a religion and a culture and once imbued with its sights, sounds, and ideas nothing else can take its place. If her father had realized this about her he would have been less worried as to the state of her soul.

None of this however answered her doubts as to whether or not she should head off to Denmark. Was this only a further indulgence, an effort to retain balance by seeking a contrast to the prevailing ethos of rabid Americanism? Her general methodology had always been dialectical: she tended to avidly pursue a midpoint between extremes as the surest path to the truth. This habit of mind had made her impatient with mental parking garages. Any thesis was merely an opportunity for further questions and objections. She enjoyed picking at the scab of any certitude. This had not been helpful to her as a Catholic. The last person in her mind who had been totally free to ask questions from scratch had been St. Thomas Aquinas. His synthesis of all knowledge had been enthroned in Roman Catholicism ever since as the acme of reasoned theological thought. She recalled that her questions in high school had been regarded as troublesome if not impertinent. It was this tendency to nibble around the penumbra of orthodoxy that had led her into a review of questions long regarded as settled doctrine. There was always some further author to explore whose opinions or suggestions might just tip the scale of her convictions back to the certainties of her upbringing or alternatively enable her to chart a course towards a pluralistic realm guided by a generally humanist synthesis which would restrict its efforts to making things as comfortable and just as possible in our lonely sojourn across a mindless cosmos.

This compulsion to solve the human equation had so long distracted her that she was still at the primary level when it came to solving the question of who she was as an individual and what she hoped to obtain from her short and irreplaceable life. Each year she seemed to be falling farther behind her fellows as they accumulated houses, mates, children, vacation cruises, and all the milestones celebrated in the various alumni publications that were forwarded to her monthly. Didn't these people have any hang-ups? She would be far more likely to forego a pizza now and then and contribute to the multiple funds solicited by these already too well-endowed institutions if they manifested in their selection of life-reviews some degree of failure or destitution among the graduates rather than displaying only their triumphs and laurels. The net result of these preoccupations was that Tiffany felt that leaden weights were attached to her ankles in the race of life. How many people managed quite well with a fragment of her education? Was the pursuit of extraneous knowledge then the ultimate self-indulgence?

In the beginning she had felt that she was merely taking the road less traveled in her choice of studies. Lately that conviction had been replaced by a gnawing doubt that she might have mistaken the path into utter mental wilderness for a path that would soon open to display unimagined vistas of vision and enlightenment. It was said that the sin of the fallen angels was primarily intellectual in nature; if so, then it seemed ironic that demonic manifestations always seemed accompanied by foul language and dreadful smells so degrading to angelic pride. But perhaps these visceral manifestations were the best evidence of the shackles worn by moral evil in the eternal realm: God only allows evil to manifest itself outwardly through a grid or net that says in effect "only this much of your true malice will be admitted, the better to manifest your fallen state to those who do not yet share it."

This would explain for instance the physical assaults that had been made upon Padre Pio in the course of his life. Padre Pio was the famous stigmatic beset by demonic forces that would literally beat him up in his humble cell in the monastery of San Giovanni Rotundo. How absurd to expend such futile efforts on a little old Franciscan monk! Why was he worth the trouble among the many manifest evils of the world where the devil emerges triumphant? Why not play your strong suit? Is it perhaps that evil is most decisively defeated at the most humble and individual level? This speculation returned Tiffany to her sense that having an individual identity did actually matter in the long and anonymous course of general history.

After much reflection in the days that followed her talk with her father, Tiffany resolved the fundamental question presented to her to be: "Does identity precede our actions and hence our unique story or is identity a mere product of experience and hence neither preexisting nor complete until the moment of our death."

This formulation implied that our true orientation to both God and to ourselves is always at best an approximation until sealed by that termination of earthly possibilities that we call death. The question remained however whether death is instantaneous or a gradual withdrawing of life from its former insular locus in space-time to embrace hitherto unthinkable potentialities in eternity. Is there perhaps a twilit realm where the soul, balanced between two eternal destinies can finally grasp its life as a whole and determine freely its orientation towards perfect goodness or its opposite, the great unending abyss of metaphysical evil? The time of her leaving for Denmark had been left indefinite so Tiffany was granted a reprieve in the execution of her resolve.

Part Three

The winter that had been remarkably mild thus far suddenly was transformed into one of those seasons of late snowfall that had delighted her as a child but that she now viewed as a source of discomfort and inconvenience. She put off making reservations by airline from day to day. This would allow her time to listen to some CD's on the Danish language and to learn something more of the place and people before her departure. She also dug out a recent eight-hundred page biography of Kierkegaard and began to read it.

The days passed pleasantly. She was able to follow the latest episodes of the drama or great soap-opera of the Trump Presidency and to watch the conservative media bristle like a porcupine as the newly elected representatives, among them Alexandria Ocasio-Cortez from the Bronx, who had called for a Green New-Deal for America. It was always surprising to her that so many presumably working-class Americans were petrified by a socialist agenda as they lined up behind the rights of billionaires to distort markets at will through the exercise of their monopolistic privileges. Maybe everyone should contemplate a trip to Denmark. She avoided pointless disputes though around the domestic hearth and watched the snow fall gently past the windows while the nation's teeth ground together in anticipation of the long-awaited results of the Mueller probe into Russian influence on the election of 2016.

As she fell asleep in her pink bedroom still redolent of a privileged girlhood in the comfortable suburbia of western Washington State she pondered the origin of her own 1930's style populism. She had always felt herself to be born out of her proper time and place. She had missed that great upwelling of national outrage that had led to the nation's withdrawal from involvement in Vietnam and the events leading to the resignation of President Nixon. The time of her birth precluded these. She had grown up during the Clinton years. The great swing to conservatism that had begun with the Reagan Presidency still had its iron grip upon the great flatlands of the mid-west and the ever fractious and unwilling southern states while the Pacific states were blue, digitally sophisticated, and progressive. The people with the most to lose by a Republican victory always voted Republican while those who were managing quite well, who desired to share their good fortune with the poor, always voted Democrat. Perhaps it all came down to a dog and his bone, the less meaty the bone the more the dog will growl if anyone threatens to take it away. The list of American clichés never pales though on a naïve audience and Trump-ism had the advantage of having echoes throughout the conservative media and from the pulpits of fragmented Christian sectarianism to give his new feudal-style presidency an aura of 19th century populist and isolationist legitimacy. This was the national ambiance against which her own decision regarding an excursion to Denmark was being enacted.

"Combine a complex protagonist with a challenging decision against an atmosphere pregnant with conflict and the result is what literature refers to as plot or story. The action should proceed with a certain sweep of destiny and inevitability until at the climax the forces resolve themselves and a general worldview is affirmed or disaffirmed in a tidy moral or the emergence of insight at a higher resolution."

After reviewing this note to herself, a remnant remaining from her years spent in the formal discipline of creative writing that as if by magic hopes, or intends at least, to transform young men and women who in former ages might have been classified as sufferers from neurasthenia into accomplished, and more important still, saleable authors Tiffany Amorth put her pen down and began to consider her present life situation from a point of view supplied by critical literary theory. Assuming that literature has some connection with actual life it did not seem to her inappropriate to look to literary theory to guide her present choice regarding Denmark. She had always seen her life as a narrative with God as the prospective critic sitting in the wings whose review would either enshrine her efforts or condemn it to being just another failure in the long string of sorry productions of the recalcitrant human race. She had always wanted to live a life that when seen in its broadest perspective would constitute a story and not merely a statistic. To that end she turned now as so often before to her personal library for answers.

In the present instance she had dug out her old copy of Soren Kierkegaard's *Concluding Unscientific Postscript to the Philosophical Fragments,* Martin Heidegger's *Being and Time,* and two books by Paul Ricoeur, *Time and Narrative* and *The Conflict of Interpretations* to help her to focus her inquiry. She had never lost her faith in the value of cutting-edge thinkers on the world stage. It surprised her though that people of immense power managed to be promoted, praised, and rewarded by golden parachutes and stock-options who had never heard of the seminal intellectuals of their time. Seldom were first-rate poets or even historians admitted to the councils that determined public policy. Even attorneys had more of a technical bent than a firm grounding in social theory and jurisprudence. Few multiple-term members of Congress were to be found discussing Lyotard, Habermas, or Foucault. Tiffany felt the inadequacy of formal thought when brought to bear on actual events. She was sure for instance that if the current President for all of his stolid vision and confidence in his infallibility were granted even substantial geologic time calculated at the rate of radioactive decay of strontium 90 at least one of these books she was consulting would have a .001 % chance of ending up on his reading list.

The President of the United States subsisted instead on a mental diet that paralleled his preference for hamburgers and fries, a concrete reality that spared him such abstract labors lest he should stumble into a time warp and actually rise above his shallow fund of preexisting ideas. It has long been a complaint of writers that future immortality is often purchased at the price of comparative neglect by their contemporaries. The crudity of current public taste however never acts as a sufficient deterrent to the devoted artist. She will pursue her craft despite all odds though idiocy exalts the unworthy to glamour and to fame. Ideally artists reveal truth to somnolent humankind while the task of the politician is to promise untold benefits at bargain prices while confirming the dull and indolent masses in their presumptions and to flatter their collective vanity. Tiffany Amorth, a genius yet unknown and uncelebrated, was only one in this long sustained human contradiction between merits and rewards.

Money has its own logic: it enables destruction and leaves unattended the basic needs of the majority of the human species. In no case was this general truth more evident than in the election of Donald Trump in 2016. The fact that a rough third of the American people, well armed and jealous to preserve, by force if necessary, whatever their personal stash of big-box store shopping excursions had wrought made her dubious of the fate of the nation. So few were the correspondences between her own beliefs and this mélange of nostalgic blue-collar workers, disgruntled farmers, and well-paid talk-show hosts that she felt not merely a sense of pervasive alienation but actual estrangement from the currently triumphant political ethos. She felt enfeebled and diminished. Of what relevance was her unique and particular task when weighing alternatives to so inconsequential an excursion as hers to Denmark would be when laid against the yardstick of such public folly and its possible consequences? What place has the individual when her fate will be subject to the shifting tectonic plates of the mass appeal of media propaganda applied to ingrained prejudice and fixed notions? How had her America become so unaccountably benighted?

It was at this point that she began to contemplate writing a book that would take as its starting point her own concern for the country of her birth coupled with her awareness of her own comparative obscurity and insignificance as refracted by the unutterable banality of the times she was living through. When these were laid against the probability of the ecological ruination that must come if the present course of history remained unaltered, at whatever cost it might entail, her depression and discouragement seemed unavoidable. Whence might a remedy be sought? What could motivate a generation of young people to simply do the math and draw the probable consequences to their personal prospects of home and family when their primary legacy was not the traditional intergenerational promise of America but a massive national debt and a declining industrial base mired in 20th century technology?

Even the tendrils of foreign investment and control that were the primary generators of American wealth could not repair the damage to the mass of Americans. The middle-class was a homely residue floating far beneath the surface where the real money was being made and invested, money with little relation to the physical actions of a laboring body unless they could be embodied in song or dance. Community after community relied on an influx of Federal spending to keep them afloat in the absence of manufacturing. Take away the defense industry and what for instance would be the fate of her native Western Washington? She thought of the desolate lumber and fishing towns on the coast and their abandoned and derelict condition due to the decline in fishing and forestry. She sought for an image of this and found it in a prospect of shattered glass. What light can re-illumine that which has lost its collective integrity?

Her young life seemed already to be similarly bereft. To be always in the audience and never a performer, never to view her own life as integrated into a larger design whether of enterprise or expression made her feel wraithlike and insubstantial. So rich had been her yesterdays when imagination supplied that which was lacking so that she could see her life laid against a template as rich as a frame to hold a renaissance painting. Now she sought for an enfolding context in vain aware that each year plunged her deeper into psychic debt to her lost dreams. She was always rehearsing versions of a play that consisted only of scattered scenes without theme or plot to unify them and where the idea of progress would not be marked by present sterility.

So it was that her personal quest for some reassurance prior to her departure on this nameless errand of spontaneity to Denmark and the search for resources that might supply her with answers seemed only another instance where the great collective neglect shown by contemporary American cultural obtuseness was manifest all around her and hence within her as well. She was ashamed of her country as of herself.

Who cared who Tiffany Amorth was or what she thought or felt about anything? Who sought out her views? Where was her following on Twitter? How could she make them care? Her identity was reduced to her function as a consumer and now that her tuition had been paid, her largest life-investment thus far and the diploma awarded she remained as she had been before without a trade-name, a logo, a base for advertisements and endorsements. Her picture did not adorn a makeup display. No sporting goods manufacturer cared that she used their equipment. No arena would fill to capacity to watch her parade about the stage in a skin-tight jumpsuit with a microphone seductively poised at her lips. She was only a writer and an undiscovered one at that.

Still, as the weeks progressed, an outline of a book of sorts gradually emerged. She thought that she might record her own process of seeking definition. She might call it *Adventures in Anomie*. It is a dreadful thing to be part of the mass of data, a mere conflation of preferences in a marketing survey. It is this anonymity that motivates the pointless acts of violence that punctuate each day with a selection of atrocities.

She gradually prepared an outline of sorts.

Tiffany's Book

The unusual title of this book stems from six fundamental insights which provide the basis for this book:

1. The basis for our self-awareness as for all relationships is the assumption that when we exist we have a sense of an ego that defines the border of the self from the non-self. This ego has various characteristics of inner experience and self-definition that tells us who and what we are and provides a basic set of categories for all subsequent experience;

2. But this awareness of the self is seldom as unified as we assume. What we call the self is more like a series of stars in the night sky that together form various constellations;

3. This characteristic of fluidity in the personality allows for growth and change over time but it also allows for what might be called a

catastrophic breakdown in the sense of self when that integrity is attacked by outside forces. These forces can be conceptualized as entities that wish to impose their own definitions on the inner dimensions of the self. The self must then discern when to adapt to these outside definitions and when to resist them;

4. The process of definition is a universal and innately political process involving the use of power to obtain the progress of conflicting ideals against the resistance provided by the cultural world that is our ambient reality;

5. The nascent self must be resistant enough to maintain its own integrity but not so idiosyncratic or rigid that its inner definitions become static and calcified or lead into a world of solipsism or narcissism;

6. Every great spiritual discipline advises us to liberate ourselves from definition so as to attain transcendence, so in the light of the struggle to define ourselves and to resist the pressures exerted from outside and from within us there is finally another dimension to be considered: the final erosion of the self by aging and extinction in its present form by death.

7. Hence the achievement of identity is brought up against an absurd fate even in its heroic and tentative realization: that at the very point at which our personalities assume what might be considered their final form we must watch helplessly as that definition is reduced to the degradation and neglect imposed upon the marginal and the elderly

who are perceived to have no future. We are caught first in a struggle to emerge from the chrysalis and thereafter to remain aloft. Resistance under these conditions is both our triumph and our inevitable defeat.

8. To let go of personality at this point demands an involuntary renunciation followed by acquiescence to our fate. We are dissolved at last into our component elements and dispersed. This final process though is not an unmitigated evil because it allows us to surrender the burden of the self with all of its limitations and to see ourselves as part of a larger constellation of life flowing through the generations and to imagine even in death that a bond exists with the ultimate transcendent who is God.

She laid her outline aside with at least some minor satisfaction with the result. To define the problem is already to be on the way to its solution. She took comfort from the fact that her own obscurity was shared by the study of the humanities as a whole. Cultural neglect was endemic as was the readiness to accept the cheap formulaic attribution of "fake news," applied to whatever facts the current regime found distasteful or that might subtract from the adoration owed to the supreme national benefactor. How had he existed so long among us deprived of the same cult-like worship afforded to his new bosom buddy, Kim Jung-Un? How could he fail to be enthroned like Augustus as Emperor I of America until his sons might succeed him?

Part Four

Slowly the weeks passed until at dinner one night her father asked her over the soufflé. "So how is your Denmark plan going? Purchased any wooden shoes yet?"

She smiled. "That's Holland I believe and no I haven't."

He looked surprised. "I thought you were all in a frenzy to go."

"It's still cold over there now; better to wait until summer."

He considered this news for a minute. "I see. What will you do until summer, read your horoscope and cast your runes?"

She looked down at her plate. "I'm working on a book."

"Really, what's it going to be about?"

"The course of human life when seen from a phenomenological perspective."

"Going for a broad and varied audience I see."

She looked up at him. "I think I'm on to something. Looking at life as an example of narrative creation."

"How about life as an example of income creation, have you ever considered that?"

She demurred. "I'm not an economist."

"Obviously. Have you decided what it is that you are?"

She hesitated. "Not yet, but I'm getting close. It may not have a name yet."

"Just a price-tag."

She attempted to redirect the discussion. "Do you like the roast?

"Very tasty."

"Well I think I'll take a walk down by the sound, maybe go down to the ferries."

He looked up. "Don't stay out too late and don't talk to any creeps."

"They may give me some story ideas."

"They'll give you something you don't want. Don't forget your keys; I may be asleep when you come in so try and be quiet."

"Of course Father, I'll be careful."

She kissed him quickly on the cheek, ran upstairs for a coat, and headed out into the soft winter darkness of a February night."

She didn't go to the city as often as she once had. Parking in Seattle was not what it had been during her undergraduate days. Then there had been street parking in industrial or under-policed areas where cars bought more for transport than for display could rest assured for extended periods without fear of robbery or citations. The new world of Seattle had a definite upscale tilt and like most of America the seams that had at one time allowed for a gentle and unnoticeable transition between the classes were now ripped and separated. The fissuring of America was everywhere apparent along lines of wealth and influence. Some of this was natural for an ethos that had always valued accumulation and acquisition over culture and the quiet abstinence that can refrain from privatization and exploitation. There had always been titans and tycoons to festoon society pages and resist any signs of collective intemperance such as unions or cooperative enterprises, but never had excess so eclipsed largesse to the degree seen in the new century. It was becoming difficult to even imagine a story that would not have at its core some element of crass and comparative display. From social media to telephones, the constant racket of megabytes of information flow never ceased. It was more than mere future-shock, it was a strange new mutation so that to be human was seen as some retrograde failure to arrive at the universal algorithm of thoughts and desires that could someday be recorded on a microchip and filed somewhere, or worse still deleted as inconsequential.

Tiffany wondered how long it would be before undertakers were replaced by handy and universal body-depositories, human recycling bins separating the various elements and compounds for later reuse. What are we really? Are we waves or particles sent hurdling at some vast double-slit experiment to decide whether we go to heaven or to hell?

As she drove to Seattle from the computer saturated east side of Lake Washington Tiffany pictured herself trading places with Schrödinger's Cat as the ultimate subject of indeterminacy and quantum weirdness. She thought of the lovely final lines of John Keats describing the suspension of the senses as a nightingale flew away taking its song with it: "Was it a vision or a waking dream; Fled is that music do I wake or sleep?"

To be human had once been to be open to such experience: raw, unmediated by electronic pulses, and therefore visceral and pregnant with discovery and wonder. Place and time were still somewhat inaccessible and so immune from the arrogant manipulation of human will. To leave Denmark might be to forfeit any possibility of return there whereas now she could fly there in a day.

She imagined the trip. "I would stumble jet-lagged off of the plane and find things not so much different in essence from Dubai or Bangkok. Is it Denmark I want to visit then or my idea of Denmark?" This was the thought that filled her as she turned south on Highway Five and took the exit that would lead her down to the water. She found parking in Pioneer Square, locked her car and made for the renovated ferry terminal where she stood watching as the ferries moved smoothly across the still dark waters towards Bainbridge Island and the Olympic Peninsula beyond. She looked over at Ivar's Acres of Clams and recalled outings there through the years, the taste of chowder and a plate of fried local oysters. She would be leaving this behind if she went to Denmark. She thought of how distant and even romantic her own home might be imagined to be for a resident of that low-lying land of islands and peninsulas. She had heard that there was even a bridge there to Sweden. Technology had arrived. The Old World was also the same world of futuristic conceptions that she inhabited here.

"Yes," she thought, "But there are still the remnants at least of other times there. These are embodied memories. I need location and visual testimony to ground me. I could find these there. But would they ever really be mine? I have no associations there. I would find a history as alienating to my sense of self as the present erosion of all that I once considered familiar even here where presumably I have some sense of order and control. What then is Denmark to me but an idea of freedom? Of what use would freedom be if it were merely random motion, the action of spirochetes on a laboratory slide. It is association then that bestows meaning and not novelty. Is it identity that I seek or rather recognition, something to echo back to me my own thoughts and feelings so that I know them to be mine? It is not just Denmark that I seek but *my Denmark* found as though it had not existed until it unveiled itself before me like the mermaid in Copenhagen's harbor newly risen from the sea. For a human, the act of being is always a becoming. But this prosaic waterfront, is this my ground of revelation? I've been here time and time again!"

Tiffany thought of the first time she had read *To the Lighthouse* by Virginia Woolf who above all artists had seemed to realize the eternal value of the trivial and of the transitory. Was what she had been seeking, a similar vision that to Tiffany had been enveloped and summarized in the coded-word of Denmark? Perhaps what she really had been seeking was not escape but engagement, some sense of totality in the fragmentary elements of her accidental life. She might find this anywhere.

"I want to matter!" she cried and looked down in embarrassment as passers-by looked at her. "Am I just another crazy person haunting the Seattle waterfront with the only difference being that I can drive home to Kirkland tonight and let myself into a fancy house on the lake? What separates me from the street people?"

Tiffany wondered how she had managed to escape being a Republican and marrying a Kushneresque scion of wealth and privilege. Instead she pictured herself knitting beneath the guillotine as the tumbrels rolled by bringing their freight of Trump appointees to their retribution. Would all of her perceptions be held hostage forever to her inveterate reading? Was her life to be doomed to being simply one more text to be deciphered and deconstructed? If Descartes had grounded his being in thinking, her own credo was reducible not to a phrase such as "I think therefore I am," but to acts of recollection to enhance experience like Marcel Proust who seemed never to have lived in the present but only in memory as though only by tracing a design in recollection could he reinforce it into becoming real at last, sanctioned by an awareness of the brevity of the instant and the irrecoverable essence of impressions unless they were transformed into the eternity of text.

But this moment of insight was followed by an awareness of the enemy. Around her stood the towers and pavilions of the former pragmatic seaport that now fancied itself the Emerald City. Tiffany looked up at the alien windows of offices the function of which was to embody trade, commerce, and all of the bywords of power. Here she had been educated but in a dying art-form in an era of clichés and sordid generalizations, dwarfed into insignificance and mocked by variety and specificity, valued not because things related to the deepest human needs or wants in a cohesive way but simply as transactions carried out in real time, transformed into receivables in some firm or other with tentacles reaching overseas to China or

Japan. Who today would dare to write a 21st century version of *Middlemarch*? Would it sell? Who covets a synthesis amidst such endless diversity, pluralism, and diffusion?

Gone was the era that had spawned overarching humanist dogmatic systems by Marx, Freud, or even Husserl. Vanished were the voices of individualized rebellion by Sartre, Camus, Gide, Celine, and even our own homely Kerouac. The millennial generation only knows or is realizing that they have been betrayed, reduced to cannon-fodder for terrorists in schools and indebted to pay for the long-living boomer generation that plans on a long slow glide pattern before dying. Where were the significant voices of Generation X? Caught between the Old World and the new as youth is always caught she stood in the February night while a multitude of possibilities beckoned.

Part Five

Not content to remain in the shadow of the immense skyline she decided on the instant to book a trip across Puget Sound. Tiffany climbed the stairs to the ferry terminal and purchased a ticket to Bainbridge Island. She stood among the commuters on their way home to their quiet bungalows after their workday in the city. When the gates opened she streamed onto the ferry with the crowd and remained on deck while the others flooded into the warm embracing yellow glow of the interior of the ship. As the ramp was lifted and the ferry drew away she watched as the city, formerly so immense, took on manageable proportions. Seattle was reduced into a single panorama of celestial light encased in a great circumference of darkness reflected in the lengthening water behind her. She felt as though she could reach out and grasp each separate building and study its tiny occupants at her leisure like fish in an aquarium.

"How can I write adequately of these things?" she asked herself as she returned to the cabin for warmth as the ferry approached the island. She would have to disembark before re-boarding for the trip back to Seattle and she spent the interim listening to the everyday interchanges of the people who surrounded her, each as intent on his own journey and concerns as she. "Would this be what it would be like in Denmark?" she asked herself.

The return boarding call came and she re-entered the ferry for the trip home. This time she remained inside all the way back to Seattle. She looked out into the darkness as the ship slipped by the red and green channel markers and admired the expensive homes that lined the harbor of Winslow. She wondered what it would be like to live over here; was this place another Denmark although located a mere half hour across Puget Sound? How to encompass all possible experience in one short life? How could her one life sample so many conflicting and mutually exclusive possibilities? Would they not devour her? How could she keep her head above water amidst so many contradictory waves each rushing at her, demanding that she choose?

She looked about her at the other passengers, each so different. How might she assert herself as an individual among their many prospects unless she could know each of them in their individual choices and contexts, to follow them home invisible and live among them like a ghost? She thought of her father waiting for her at home, his being an anchor to her sense of self, location, and security. He alone was her measuring rod in acquiescence or rebellion, his easy confidence in his own infallibility was her Greenwich Mean Time. She had never emerged beyond the force field that he generated, never been out of radio contact with his transmitter. It frightened her to think that his absoluteness was to others a mere marginal and relative voice to be doubted or ignored without peril. Would even Denmark be far enough to escape his influence and judgment? Did she really want to escape?

She got up and rushed to the other end of the ferry before it landed and saw the city growing closer and larger. Would it embrace her in some capacity so that she could find a place there, be met by some recognition, perhaps an assigned parking space and a salary that said she was valued, had a place in it all however partial and incomplete. "No, I'm going to Denmark!" she interposed. "It will sound so impressive when I return," she thought to herself. "'Oh Denmark!' people will say. 'How charming, I always wanted to go there. Just like a fairy tale it must be.'"

"This was always how it is," she thought. "I always think in vast hypotheticals. What if nobody on this boat ever wants to go to Denmark, will it matter then if I go?" She reflected further. "No. I must desire it not for others but for myself, because I want to go or because I want to stay here."

She felt the beginnings of freedom in all their promise and their peril.

"This so silly," she thought, "I am not debating a solo flight across the Atlantic." But in just this way decisions had always implicated for her some dread of interior dissolution. "I must generate thrust," she thought, "I must possess a rocket booster to carry me into orbit or better still toward an irrecoverable trajectory towards selfhood. It isn't Denmark; it is Tiffany I seek."

The boat touched the pilings and the attendants methodically affixed the boat and lowered the departure ramp below for the auto traffic. The walk-on passengers began to stream toward their own access point to the city.

In latent rebellion she returned as before to Seattle, as though from a great journey, to the immediate time and place where she,

Tiffany Amorth, stood on this night on Seattle's romantic waterfront: alive, thirty years old, and father-haunted just as Mary Shelley had been, and looking as Mary had been looking when she wrote her confessional book *Mathilda,* a book long since forgotten and seldom read, for some validation to show that she existed apart from her father's idea of her with only a marginal correspondence to who she actually was.

She reflected as she walked toward her car, "He thought once that I was possessed… and perhaps I am!" she shouted into the silent echoes of her mind. "I am possessed by all that I have ever seen or want to see. I am possessed by an unending hunger to not rest with all I see about me but to find; to find that Denmark that is not flat and wholesome and predictable and complacent. I want the Denmark of Kierkegaard that rejected his rebellion, ignoring his efforts to jar it into life. His Denmark wore him to death by misunderstanding and rejection. I want to be a martyr to misunderstanding and neglect like him. I want to write!"

It was nearing midnight as she pulled away from the waterfront. She seldom stayed out so late. Her car climbed the hills to the freeway onramp and she was soon crossing Lake Washington toward sleeping Kirkland where the Microsoft campus is located. The Pacific Northwest had played a significant part in launching the new world that was now her fate to encounter as we hurtle deeper into the abyss of the 21st century. The great adventure of universal digital competence had raged about her while she had studied the past until she was more a part of it than she was of her own time and place. Was it too late to join in the fiesta brought about by the infinite series of ones and zeros, to seek a new trajectory for herself in space-time? Or should she reverse what she had even now just affirmed? Just in this manner did the demons of the present hour in triumphant Trumpian America seek to regain their dominion of Tiffany Amorth who was struggling to escape possession and retain those elusive values and constructs to which literature has access because it flows forth from the inexhaustible fountain of the human soul.

Denmark, that symbol of refuge for beleaguered progressives in the present hour of darkness, could now be seen clothed in significance and surrounded by references, a process that reduces whatever exists beyond our solitary selves into various discourses and narratives. Tiffany Amorth, a girl in search of a universal hermeneutic that would give her a center and certainty prepared to continue her quest. Perhaps some famished fellow devotee of the muses will stumble upon her while the freshness of youth holds disillusion yet at bay. Perhaps she will stumble upon the golden apples of the sun along some dusty shelf of a used book store. Perhaps she will book passage soon to Scandinavia and hold silent intercourse with the blackened figure of the corpse of an ancient man found preserved in a bog. Who can trace the course of a human life?

Our tale ends here as inconclusive and fragmentary as life itself. What did she announce at breakfast the following day when she would be confronted by her father with the lateness of her return and her inconsiderateness towards her father and benefactor causing him to worry whether she had not fallen victim to one of the members of the endless straggling caravans seeking admission to the American paradise? Could such a daughter be let loose to wander unsupervised and uncontrolled about Denmark spreading confusion and discontent and giving the poor Danes in consequence such a poor account of true American values?

The omniscient voice from which so many narratives proceed grows hazy and indifferent to its present subject, hesitating to decide what her fate should be. Authorial decision is always balanced along a razor's edge of conflicting possibilities. To choose is to set a butterfly aloft that may tip distant events into chaos. Who would dare to play God in narration if freedom is ever a real possibility for human beings? A tiny gesture may undermine whole vistas of established certitudes. Predestination in stories failed at the instant when Eve reached out for the fruit of the knowledge of good and evil. Thereafter all has been indeterminate. Even now all stories founder on the rocks of our freedom. Unless, oh most dread presumption, the serpent was placed in Eden by design to titillate, to stimulate, and to confuse us.

IMMUNITY
BY CARRIE AVERY MORIARTY

W ake up, love."

The voice was warm and sensuous, calling him from the depths of blackness, beckoning him from death.

"That's it," she coaxed. "Come back to me."

He inhaled sharply, drawing breath through a parched mouth. He was so thirsty, desperate for a quenching cup of cool water. Atop that, he was famished. Like he could eat for a week and still not be satiated.

"Open up," she said. "Open those beautiful blue eyes for me, love."

Blinking, he let his eyes adjust to the light in the room. It wasn't bright, but more than he wanted at the moment. Finally, he turned to see a woman who was more beautiful than any creature that ever existed. Raven dark hair, porcelain skin, lips like rubies, and eyes deep as the ocean.

"There they are," she said as she smiled. "Thought I might have lost you."

He worked his mouth, trying to convey his thirst, but couldn't make the words form.

"Up you go," she said, lifting him easily from prone to sitting. "Drink," she commanded.

Taking the goblet, he quenched his thirst with the thick liquid within, drinking it down so quickly he nearly choked, yet not able to consume it fast enough.

"Slow down, love," she said as she pulled the goblet from his lips. "There's more where that came from. Don't want you getting sick on your first taste."

Relinquishing the cup, he tried to speak, but had to swallow several times before he could form words.

"No rush," she said, laying a hand along the side of his face, caressing his cheek. "We have all the time in the world for questions. Rest now. I'll be back soon."

The words were like a spell, pressing him into the darkness once again. He let himself tumble into it, relinquishing the world around him.

"How is he?"

The voice was foreign and far off. He could feel more than hear the words, and that confused him some.

"Soon," the woman said. "Very soon."

Flashes and snippets of conversations flitted around him, yet he couldn't make sense of any of the words. Shrouded in darkness he felt safe, yet something teased the back of his mind saying he should flee. Nothing made sense, and still it was all comfortable and clear.

"That's it," she said.

Again he opened his eyes and saw the raven haired beauty.

"Drink."

She pressed the goblet to his lips and he was unable to resist quenching his parched throat.

"Well done, love," she said.

He tried once more to speak, but was unable to form words.

"Just a little more sleep," she said. "You should be good by tomorrow."

She pressed her lush lips to his and he drank her in, consuming her in that moment, with that intimate touch. He was hers to do with as she pleased, and he would not argue. Falling back on the pillows he was once again consumed by the darkness.

A deep, earthy smell consumed him as he took in a deep breath. Blinking, he opened his eyes to take in the room. Candles lined the walls, encased in sconces giving the room a warm feel. Satin sheets wrapped him, and his head rested on plush pillows. The walls were stone, but not masonry. Thick timber fitted with iron was set in the wall across from him, the only portal he could see.

Sitting, he felt a gnawing ache in his stomach. He looked around and saw a goblet on a table next to the bed. Lifting it, he took a sip, then gulped the remaining contents down swiftly. When he'd finished, he wiped his mouth with the back of his hand.

Slow blinks could not remove the clear truth from his mind. The deep red streak on the back of his hand made it clear what he'd consumed. His scream consumed him as he once again descended into darkness.

"Shh," her voice soothed. "You're safe."

He knew the voice, but couldn't place it. Then he remembered.

"No," he shouted.

"You're safe," she said again, using that soothing quality she had.

Pulling from her grasp, he opened his eyes, fear consuming him. He continued to retreat from her, even as she advanced on him.

"My love," she pleaded.

"No," he shouted once again. "Stay away. What are you?"

He saw the words hit her, taking her back a step. She was beautiful beyond comprehension, but he knew there was something evil within.

"You are mine," she whispered.

He felt the tug of some invisible force, felt as if he were being drawn to her, but he held fast in his position on the opposite side of the bed.

"What are you?" he asked again.

In a flash she was against him, pressing his larger frame against the rough wall, her body solid as steel.

"Your best dream and your worst nightmare," she said, then kissed him.

It wasn't the gentle kiss of a lover, but that of a dominant. She controlled it, pressing harder, forcing his lips to open, thrusting her tongue inside. He could taste her essence, a heady combination of flowers and blood. There was nothing he could do to stop her assault, no way to break the control she had over him. He was a slave to her wishes.

"Milady."

The voice broke the kiss and he was thankful. While she moved her head away, she kept him pinned where he stood.

"Decentius," she said.

"He can still break," Decentius said. "Take your time with him."

She stepped back, releasing him from her hold. He stood

where he was, unsure whether moving or remaining still would be safer. When she walked across the room, he took in her generous curves draped in a deep red gown. She was barefoot, padding across the white tile in a silent saunter, swinging her hips provocatively. He couldn't help but enjoy the show she put on.

"I've been playing with humans longer than you've been alive," she said. "I know how fragile they can be. Besides," she continued, turning to look at the man against the wall. "I'm not sure if I'll bring him all the way. He's complicated, it seems."

"Shall I have him disposed of?" Decentius asked.

"I think I'll play with him a little longer," she replied. "Who knows. I might just turn him after all."

"My name is John Smith," he began. "I am twenty-nine years old and I live in Jamestown. I have two brothers, both younger than me. Their names are Jake and James. I was on vacation in London when something happened."

He stopped there. He wasn't sure why he was speaking these words out loud, just that he felt like he had to keep reminding himself who he was. It had been weeks since the encounter with the woman, the beautifully cruel woman who was keeping him as a hostage or a prisoner or something. Had his family looked for him? Were they still looking, or did they think he was dead? Would he ever see them again? These questions plagued him as the days wore on.

The door could not be opened from the inside. He'd tried so many times, but it simply wouldn't budge. He didn't know how long he'd been there, only that he'd not seen the woman since that one encounter.

Decentius brought him food, real food, every day. The goblet he remembered drinking from was nowhere in sight, now, but he knew he'd drunk blood. The terrifying thing was, he'd not only enjoyed drinking it, but craved it still. Bread, cheese, fruits, and water were what the man brought each day, that's all. No blood, thankfully. John wasn't sure he would be able to turn it down if he'd been given the choice. It had taken a couple of days for John to trust Decentius, but eventually they'd come to an agreement. John would stop trying to attack him each time he entered, and Decentius would tell him everything he was allowed when he came in.

Unfortunately, what Decentius was allowed to tell John was a very small amount of information. They were still in London, they were in a castle that was not abandoned, but was also not occupied, and they were not allowed to go outside. When John had asked where the food came from, Decentius told him it was delivered daily by an "associate" of the family.

"Is she a—?" John had tried to ask early on.

"Don't ask that question," Decentius had interrupted him to say.

John didn't know whether that meant the man wouldn't answer it, or that he wouldn't be able to stop himself if it were asked. John knew the lore, the legends that had been passed down through time in the form of books, movies, and tall tales. What he didn't know, was whether any of that was factual. He had so many questions, things he needed to know in order to formulate a way to escape. And he would escape, whether it was alive or dead, he was not going to spend any more time than necessary in this place. It had been too long already.

"He won't succumb," Decentius said.

"I can convince him," Lilith replied.

"You are one of the most powerful," he said.

"Which is why I will bend him to my will," she replied.

"This one is different," he said. "Stronger somehow."

"He's human," she replied. "They are weak compared to us."

"No disrespect," he said, "but this one is different."

"How long have I lived?"

"Centuries," he replied.

"And how many have tried to resist me?"

"Hundreds."

"How many have succeeded?"

"None to date," Decentius said.

"Exactly," Lilith replied. "None. I am stronger because of their attempts, too. Their resistance increased my strength. When I consumed them, they added to my power."

"Yet you have not been able to control him," he said.

"Do you doubt me?"

"I only wish to caution you," he said. "As I said, you are one of the most powerful."

"Exactly," she replied.

"But you knew this day would come," Decentius said. "Knew there was to be one who would withstand your powers."

"Legends do not interest me," she said.

"Yet this one seems to be more than mere myth," he replied.

She glared at him for a moment, then said, "I will win this battle."

John paced the room, exactly 74 steps from door to wall, the same across. Large compared to some cells, but still a confinement he didn't enjoy. He had to come up with a plan, a way to get into the good graces of the woman in command. He just didn't know how to do it. Decentius had been kind, bringing him food and water regularly. The man even brought him a few items of clothing and fresh towels and soap, along with a stack of books for him to read.

"When will she come back?" he asked.

"When she thinks you're ready," Decentius replied.

"Ready for what?" John asked.

"For her to complete the transformation," the other man said.

"She's planning to turn me into a…"

"Stop," Decentius interrupted him. "You must not speak that word."

"Why not?" John asked.

"Trust me," he replied. "It would not be good for you if you did."

"But she is planning to make me like her, right?" he asked.

"She will," Decentius replied. "Make no mistake, she is patient and strong. She will get what she wants."

"What does she want?"

"You," the man said.

"Why?"

"I'm not sure," the man confessed. "Something about you is different. It's like you call to a deeper level within her and she cannot resist."

"I don't understand what's so special about me," John said.

"Neither do I," Decentius replied. "But you've got something she wants."

"Are you sure?" Decentius asked.

"Do it," Lilith replied.

Decentius took the young woman to the room where John stayed. He unlocked the door and let her in, closing it behind her. He didn't go in the room.

"Hi," she said.

"Hello," John replied. "Are you one of them?"

"I don't know what you mean," the woman replied.

"Blood sucker," he began. "Night walker, vam—," he stopped himself before he finished the word. Something kept him from uttering it out loud.

"Are you high?" she asked.

"Not at all," he replied.

"You know those things don't exist, right?"

"I used to," he said. "Then I ended up here."

She cocked her head at him, taking him in fully. "I think you're high," she said.

John sighed and said, "Never mind. Just go."

"Go where?" she asked. "This is my room. Maybe you should go."

"Your room?" he asked.

"Yeah," she replied, walking to the bed and jumping on. "And if you don't mind, I'd like to take a nap."

He blinked at her, unsure what to make of this new situation. This woman was around his age, if a few years younger, and looked completely different than either the other woman or Decentius.

"I can't really go anywhere," he said. "The door doesn't open from the inside."

"Nonsense," she said, getting up and walking to it. She twisted the knob and it opened without a problem. "There you go, all fixed."

Hesitantly he stepped to the door she held wide open. It only took a moment for him to make the decision that he should try to leave.

"Thanks," he said and stepped through the portal.

"Buh bye," she replied, then slammed the door behind him.

"Huh," he said as he looked at the door.

He looked around the hallway trying to figure out which way he should go. To the left it stretched into a darkness he couldn't see into, but to the right it was lit with the same candles that were in the room. It was clear that whoever had orchestrated this release wanted him to go to the right, and he'd never been one to follow instructions too well.

It didn't take long before he was completely blind, no light around him meant he couldn't see anything, not the floor, the walls, or anything that may be lurking in the dark. With his hand on the wall, he continued forward, stubborn as he was. The trip was slow going, him shuffling his feet along the floor to make sure he didn't stumble on anything that might be down there. He estimated he'd been walking down the hallway for about ten minutes when he heard them. It was soft at first, but it grew louder with every step he took, until finally he was able to make out a word.

"Help."

He continued along the hallway, listening carefully for any more voices, when his hand brushed from the stone walls onto a wooden door. Pressing his ear against it, he listened again. Nothing was moving in the room that he could hear.

"Where are you?" he asked aloud.

"Lost, little boy?"

The voice was just as sultry as he remembered. He pressed his body against the door, hoping that he couldn't be seen just as he couldn't see her.

"I asked you a question," she demanded.

He held his breath, hoping that she'd not be able to find him.

"So naïve," she said. "I can see you, even if you can't see me. Now, are you lost?"

Her hand caressed his cheek and he pulled away.

"Jumpy, aren't we?"

Candles flickered to light and he had to close his eyes to the intrusion.

"Now you can see me," she said.

Opening his eyes, he saw the beauty standing before him. Dressed in the same red satin she wore before, she appeared to have not changed at all, as if the time he'd spent alone in that room hadn't happened.

"Were you trying to run away?" she asked. "Or were you trying to find me?"

"Why are you holding me?" he asked.

"I'm not," she replied with a smile.

"Then show me the way out," he demanded.

"Find it yourself," she said, then turned and sauntered up the hallway from where he came.

He resisted the urge to follow her, instead walking further down the hallway. If there were someone who needed help, he should find them.

"Son of a bitch," he shouted.

He'd been walking for the better part of an hour, continuing down the hallway. Candles flickering to light as he approached, as if they were welcoming him in. He'd opened the door he first found, but it only held a small closet with not much in it, save a handful of pails and mops. The further he went, the thicker the air got, as if he were getting close to sea level and the ocean was just on the other side of the walls.

Now, though, he found himself at a dead end. A wall, just like the ones along the side, stood in front of him blocking his way. He'd pushed against it, thinking that perhaps it was an illusion or something, but it was as solid as the stone it was made from.

"Now what?" he asked himself.

With an exasperated sigh he turned and headed back the way he came.

When he first heard the screams, he wasn't sure what it was. The closer he got to the room he'd been living in, the clearer it became. Definitely screams of terror and pain. He wondered if it were the young woman he left in the room, or if someone else was screaming. Then they abruptly stopped, cut off mid scream.

He'd been running when he realized they were screams, but stopped short as soon as they halted. With a deep breath, he began to run toward where he thought the screams were coming from, not sure what he would do once he arrived.

The door to the room he'd been in was wide open, so he peered in. White tile awash with blood met his eyes, and the copper smell assaulted his sense of smell and taste. As he raised his eyes to the bed he saw her, head hanging off the edge of the bed, throat clearly gorged, blood coloring her blonde hair a horrific shade of brownish red. He wouldn't have thought they'd leave this much blood in the room, but someone had obviously torn this poor girl's throat out.

"Oh."

He jumped at the quiet sound, turning to see the beauty behind him.

"You did this," he accused.

She looked at him, eyes wide, tears pooling in her lashes, and stuttered, "Never."

And John believed her. Unsure why, he could clearly tell she was shaken by the scene before them.

"Decentius!" she roared.

Nearly instantaneously, the man summoned was standing beside the woman.

"Oh, no," he said. "Not sweet Jane."

John heard the sadness in the other man's voice and

wondered whether he was mistaken about them.

"Find them," the woman said, her voice steel. "Bring them to me in chains."

Without waiting for a response, she turned and stepped into the room, carefully stepping around the gore on the ground. She closed the door and John heard a lock thrown.

"Best leave her be for a while," Decentius said.

"Who did this?" John asked.

"Rogues," was all the other man said. "Come with me."

Decentius turned and began up the long hallway. John only hesitated a moment before following.

A flurry of activity began the moment they crested the stairs. John hadn't been anywhere in the castle but the room below and the hallway the other direction. He wasn't prepared for the grand scene he came upon. Men and women, all dressed casually, were at Decentius' beck and call.

Orders were shouted in a language John didn't recognize, and everyone flew into action.

"We should have an answer soon," he said once everyone else had left with their assigned duties.

"What are they doing?" John asked.

"Hunting," Decentius replied.

John wasn't sure, but he thought he saw a cruel smile cross the other man's face. The sentiment was not lost on him, and he felt much the same. Whoever did this should be punished, and it should be painful. No one should go through what that woman did.

Minutes turned into hours which turned into days. Nearly a week after Jane was killed, the woman who he'd left in the room with her body crested the stairs. She looked heartbroken and exhausted.

"Well?" she asked Decentius.

"Three," he replied.

"The throne room," she responded, then turned on her heels and left.

"You'll want to watch this," Decentius said to John after the woman left. "Lilith does not hold back, not when her family is hurt."

They'd been sitting in the kitchen eating a small meal when she'd shown up. He'd stayed at the castle, even though it appeared he could have left if he wanted. Something made him remain. Whether it was the desire to see someone punished for the cruelty of Jane's death, or a devotion to the woman he now learned was called Lilith, he couldn't say.

Following Decentius, he stepped into a room and appeared to travel back in time. Before him was the splendor of the days he'd read about in fictional tales of King Arthur. White marble floors, columns, and walls surrounded a collection of people. At the front of the room was a dais with an actual throne, high points on the back, jewels encased in it, velvet cushions. Every splendor one could imagine.

Lilith stepped up and turned, planting herself on the throne. "Bring them in," she said.

John hadn't seen who had been brought to the castle, but knew they were not going to last long. The looks on the people gathered in the room were murderous, and he didn't blame them.

The commotion at the entrance to the room drew his attention and he had to blink several times to make sure what he was seeing was real. Chains around their necks, binding their front and rear legs, and muzzles on their snouts, were three creatures out of a nightmare. They had heads like wolves, but the bodies were more like a human, and he wondered if they were werewolves. He didn't dare ask, for fear of looking foolish. They certainly had the jaws to do the damage that had been done to the woman.

It took nearly a dozen men to drag the creatures to the throne, and once there, they were tethered to the columns at either side. They snarled and snapped at the men who handled the chains, but never once looked up at Lilith.

"Silence." Everyone, including the beasts, stood quiet. "You know what you're accused of," she said. "Defend yourself."

The creature on the left began to snarl, making guttural sounds and yips, nothing that made any sense to John.

"Then who?" Lilith asked.

More snarls and barks came, this time from one of the other beasts. Lilith listened intently, giving her full attention to the beast. John watched as what little color there was drained from Lilith's face.

"Find them," she said as she looked to the crowd. "Bring them to me, now."

Everyone in the room turned and looked at each other, unsure what to do.

"Scatter," Decentius said, and the crowd disappeared.

John watched as the three beasts were unshackled and set free. They, too, vanished before his eyes. He was left with Decentius and Lilith and wasn't sure what he should do. He turned to the man at his side and what he saw sent chills down his spine. In the blink of an eye he was consumed by darkness.

He startled awake, blinking against the bright light. This wasn't the room he'd spent weeks in below the castle. No, this was a proper bedroom, with windows and everything. It was set up like every hotel room he'd ever stayed in.

"Excuse me," a voice said.

He turned and saw a woman standing just inside the door.

"Sorry to wake you," she continued. "I've been asked to bring you downstairs."

John assessed himself and found he was dressed, simply sleeping atop the bed. He cleared his throat and said, "Be right there."

Making his way to the restroom he did what needed doing, finishing quickly. He glanced at himself in the mirror and realized he had little color, looking much the way both Decentius and Lilith did.

He followed the woman down the hall, stepping slowly down the steps of the grand staircase. When they made the first floor, he took time to look around. He was either in a completely different building or a part of the castle he'd never seen. Following the woman, he tried to take in as much as he could. The walls were bare, no rugs on the hardwood beneath his feet, and he didn't see any furniture in the rooms they passed.

The woman stopped in front of a closed door and turned to him. "Right through there," she said, then walked away, back the way they'd come.

Hesitating only a moment, he stepped up to the door and turned the knob.

"Come," she said.

He was drawn in by her command, walking to the chair next to the desk where she sat. She still wore the red dress, but her appearance was much more disheveled than it had been before.

"I need your help," she said, looking up at him, beseeching with her eyes.

He sat in the chair, then asked, "What do you want?"

"Someone is hunting my people," she said. "They came into my home and slaughtered my sister. You saw what they did to her. I cannot let them go unpunished."

She was right, he saw what they did to that poor girl. No one should suffer what she went through, even if they are monsters. "How can I help?" he asked.

"I can enhance your powers to find the truth," she said.

"My powers?" he asked, confused.

"Don't you know?"

"Know what?"

She shook her head and smiled sadly. "You were not brought here without consent," she said. "We invited you, asked you to join us. You took your time in answering. I insisted. I wouldn't have you joining us without all of the facts."

"I don't remember," he said.

"Unfortunately, that's the way the transformation works," she replied. "You lose some of your short-term memory."

"Then I haven't been a prisoner," he stated.

"I couldn't keep you if you truly wanted to go," she replied.

"What was with all the head games, then?" he asked.

"Those were what you designed," she said, pulling a folder from a drawer.

He opened it up and saw instructions in his own handwriting, saying things that they must do and things they shouldn't do in order to make sure he stayed.

"Why didn't you tell me?" he asked.

"You wouldn't have believed me if I did," she said.

"Then let's have this conversation again," he said. "Why did you want me to join you? Why am I here? And what can I do to help find the killers?"

"Same questions you asked last time," she said.

With the new, or old, depending on how you looked at it, information, John set out to the task at hand. He went to his apartment in Jamestown, pulling down some of the books he'd collected over the years on the subject. He'd never really thought about it as research, though. More like a passing interest in the subject.

Picking up his notebook, he flipped to the page where Lilith said he'd find the information she'd given him before he agreed to join them. Just as she said, it was all there. There were even drawings of the beasts he'd seen in the throne room. They weren't necessarily the enemy of Lilith and her children, more like a distant cousin. Some of the things he'd learned about them were correct, too, but most of it was pure fiction.

He had apparently spent weeks with Lilith going over the needs she had that he could help with. She was right, there were beings hunting her people. Problem was, they were hunting humans as well. They'd killed his brothers, which was why he probably blocked that out of his memory.

John had spent a week reviewing his notes. In doing so, the memories came flooding back. The sight of his brothers slaughtered in the basement of their family home. The long conversations with both Lilith and Decentius. The decision he'd made in order to find the beasts who were terrorizing not only his family, but the entire countryside.

It had started with livestock and was blamed on wolves in the region. The first human victim the authorities were aware of was an older gentleman who had left a tavern and walked home. He'd been found along the side of the road the next morning, body mauled in a similar way to what he'd witnessed of Jane. It was blamed on wild animals and the man's intoxication. Then they started to increase in regularity. Adult men in good shape were turning up dead and the authorities didn't have an answer as to what was causing it.

He'd been interested in it from an investigative reporter perspective until his brothers became victims. At that point, the police stopped giving him information and he'd been forced to search it out by any means necessary. There had to be a solution, and it wasn't to blame it on the wolves.

"Do you have a plan?"

"I think so," John replied. "I'm going to set a trap."

"They won't fall for it," Lilith replied.

"If I make it convincing enough, they will," John said. "I plan to use myself as bait."

"You won't be able to stop them," she said. "And we'd lose your advantage."

"My advantage is exactly what is going to save me," he boasted.

"What do you mean?" she asked.

"I've been honing my skills," he said. "Working on a way to make myself appear vulnerable while maintaining my superior strength and speed."

"Some of my strongest warriors have not been able to stand up to them," she replied. "Many of my men have been slaughtered."

"No disrespect," John said. "But your men didn't have what I do."

"That may be true," she conceded. "My men, however, had years longer to build their strength. They were not young in their conversion."

"While I appreciate your concern," he said. "I am going to be fine."

"Just don't get over confident," she said. "I'd hate to lose you."

"There is one thing you can do for me," he said.

"Name it," she replied.

"I'd like to borrow some of your muscle," he said.

"Absolutely," she said. "How many men would you like?"

"I'd actually prefer children," he said. "Or young adults. I think I can use them in my plan as well."

"I'll have Decentius get you some," she said.

He began to build his plan, keeping Lilith informed along the way. After two weeks of deciding to help her, he put the final pieces into place. His plan would go into action tonight, and he was nearly giddy with anticipation.

Stepping from the bar, he stumbled his way along the sidewalk, tripping over his own feet. He retraced the route the first human victim took, hoping that he'd be attacked near where the other was. Working hard to keep his charade in place, he nearly toppled over an uneven piece of the walkway. That's when they arrived.

One helped him back to his feet while another stood next to him. Their breath was foul as they spoke to him.

"You good, man?" the one who'd helped him to his feet asked.

"'sall good," he replied, keeping his speech slow.

"Need a ride home?" the other asked.

"'sall good," he said again, attempting to move around them.

"We insist," the first one said, grabbing his arm.

"I'm good, 'sall good," he said again, feebly attempting to brush them off.

It was all part of his plan, a way to get them to see him as vulnerable. They took the bait without hesitation and helped him walk to the gate to the cemetery where his backup held their ground, staying silent and invisible during this whole episode.

"Let's get you to sit down," the second one said. "At least until you're a bit steadier on your feet."

They helped him to sit on a bench next to the gate. He slumped down, nearly falling off the bench, working to keep the illusion of intoxication going. Sitting on either side of him, the beings kept him upright. Bobbing his head, he waited for the attack. When he was nearly out of patience, the first one leaned John's head back, exposing his neck to them both. Deciding he should react how the first man did, he pushed the arm of the one tipping his head feebly, unable to move it. When the second one bent his neck, John let out the signal.

With no noise, thirteen of Lilith's children were around them. They swooped in from every direction, and began to pull the men away. John worked with them as well, wresting the two to the ground. The desire wasn't to kill them, as there were only two and he knew this was just a small portion of the group behind the attacks, behind the murders. These two would be held and questioned to see if they could find the head of the organization.

It didn't take long for both beasts to be subdued. The others would take them back to Lilith for questioning while he went home to see what else he could learn from his books. This would not be the last fight, but he hoped they'd be able to get to the leader without having to go through all the subordinates.

"You have got to be kidding me," John said exasperated. "Both of them?"

"I'm afraid so," Lilith replied.

"What are we going to do?"

"We're going to have to find another way," she said.

"Fine," he said. "I'll come up with something."

The two beasts that John had helped capture had died before they got to Lilith's location. She didn't give details, just that neither of them had survived the trip. He wasn't sure what he was going to do now. The plan they'd put into place had been the best option. Now, he was forced to come up with some other way to try to find the head of the organization.

His phone buzzed, indicating a text had come in.

Meet me at the bar at 9pm. Don't tell Lilith.

He didn't recognize the number it came from, so texted back.

Who are you?

The phone pinged back indicating the message didn't go through. Either the sender had spoofed the number or had immediately disconnected it. He wasn't sure whether he should go or not, but decided that if this were a lead, he had to follow up on it. With only half an hour before the meeting was to take place, he had to hurry.

Nothing looked different at the bar than what he had encountered the night before, but John felt an oppression around him. As he walked toward the bar door, someone reached out and grabbed him, dragging him into the alley.

"Shh," she said.

John's eyes opened wide as he saw the young woman who had led him from the room to the office when he met with Lilith. She was clearly frightened, looking around for any danger that might crop up. The woman pulled him deeper into the shadows of the alley, far back from the street out front of the bar. He held his tongue, waiting for her to initiate conversation.

When the woman was satisfied that they were alone, she said, "They're using you."

Smiling, John said, "I volunteered."

"No," she said in a fierce whisper. "You're a weapon that Lilith has created to defeat her brother."

"What do you mean?"

"She isn't trying to find out who is killing people," she whispered. "She's using you to hunt down and kill her brother's family. She wants to rule the world, and if you kill her brother and his family it will open the door to her triumph. He's the only one who can stop her."

"I saw what they did to Jane," he insisted.

"You saw what she wanted you to see," the girl said. "Everything that happened in the castle was a well-orchestrated charade. Nothing is what it seems there."

"Then why do you stay?"

"I have no choice," she said.

"Stay with me," he said. "I'll keep you safe."

"You can't," she said. "Now go. I've been away too long."

Without another word she was just, gone. Almost as if she were never really there. John blinked a moment, then made his way back out of the alley. He wasn't sure what to do with this new information.

"I don't have another plan," he said.

"We need to figure out where the head of this group," Lilith insisted.

"And if we can't?"

"We have to!"

John had been having the same conversation with her for several days, always coming back to the need for her to find the head of this rogue group of beasts. He'd done some research on them, finding clear information on Lilith, but seeing nothing indicating she had a brother. The only reference he found was Gallu, and that was vague at best. The more research he did, the more it was clear that Lilith didn't have a brother. She did, however, likely have a son born from her connection to the archangel Samael. Nowhere, however, did he find anything with a name or more information on this son.

Days passed, and John still didn't have a new plan to find the head of this rogue family, nor a way to find Lilith's son or brother or whatever he was. He kept Lilith at bay with continued research and giving her information that he'd found, but she was quickly growing impatient.

Try as he might, he couldn't find anything that was helpful for his search. He wanted to talk to this other family head, find out if what the woman who'd come to him with the fact that Lilith had been the one to kill not only Jane, but likely his brothers as well. When the plain envelope with script writing on the front showed up under his door one day, he was skeptical. He opened it to find a poem written in flowing script.

> *I have the answers that you seek,*
> *They are worth more than a simple peek,*
> *Meet me when the moon does rise,*
> *I'll give you your answer without surprise,*
> *You'll find me where your deception started,*
> *But you won't leave the area broken-hearted,*
> *Truth is what you seek to find,*
> *Come talk to me, I'm one of a kind.*

While the poem was simple, the message was clear. He had either gained the attention of the head of the other family, or Lilith had somehow found out that he was searching for something she didn't want him to find. Either way, he knew that he had to go to the meeting. What he didn't know was whether he would survive the meeting.

"Haven't seen anyone, Mate," the bartender said.

"Thanks," John replied.

He'd gone to the bar, assuming the person who wanted to meet with him was going to be there. When he'd waited for nearly an hour, he figured the message was just a hoax. Exiting the bar, he made his way down the street toward his loft, walking past the bench where he'd sat when he fooled the beasts that were taken to Lilith. An uneasy feeling came over him, causing him to stumble and nearly fall. Once again, someone was there to help him to his feet.

"I'm glad you came," the man said.

John looked up to see a man whose beauty could only be surpassed by Lilith.

"Come with me," he said, guiding John down the street.

They walked nearly a block before the man diverted John into the cemetery. When they'd made their way to a mausoleum, the man opened the door and stepped in. John only hesitated a moment before following the man inside. Down the steps he went, following the light of a torch, until he reached the bottom of the long staircase.

"This way," the man said, turning to walk down the hall.

With no other option, John followed. It reminded him of the hallway he'd trekked down under the castle when he was a prisoner of Lilith. The more he thought about it, the more he realized that he had been a prisoner, no matter what she said. While this didn't feel like a completely free choice, it did feel less forced than what he'd experienced with Lilith and her group.

It didn't take long before they came to a large door set in the stone wall.

"I want you to be prepared before I open this door," the man said.

"What is in there?" John asked.

"My family," the man said. "The family that my mother is trying to destroy."

With that, the man opened the door and stepped in. John followed, unsure what he would find.

John hadn't expected to see families in the room. He expected to see much the same as he saw when he was in the castle. There were men and women of all ages, along with children from toddlers to teenagers. All of them were huddled in the space, wide eyed and fearful.

"You turn children?"

It was the first thing that came to his mind, and the man answered without hesitation.

"We never turn a child," he said. "These are the children born naturally to my family."

"But aren't you..."

"No," he said. "We are not like my mother. Some things are the same, but not much."

"Then how do you survive?"

"Follow me," he said, making his way through the crowd.

They all watched as John walked past. It was an uneasy feeling, but he didn't feel malice from them, simply curiosity. Reaching the other side of the large room, the man turned down another hall, walking up it to another door. John could feel the eyes of the people even after he turned the corner. The man opened the door and stepped in.

"Grace," he said.

John followed and saw the woman who had warned him about Lilith.

"What are you doing here?" he asked.

"You met my twin, Magda," the woman replied. "She is with Lilith. I am with Gabriel."

John looked at them in clear confusion.

"Sit," Gabriel said. "There is a lot to discuss."

For nearly two hours, John listened to the history of Lilith. The damage she'd caused in the beginning, the way she'd been thrown out of the garden, the threat she'd issued to God Almighty, and the havoc she'd wreaked since. Almost all of what Gabriel told him was not new information. What was new was the manner in which he heard it. First hand knowledge from events that Gabriel had witnessed were astonishing, and the vivid detail that he was able to recall was spectacular.

By the time Gabriel finished with his story and had brought John up to speed on what was currently happening, John knew he needed to take action. What he would do, however, was still unclear.

"She cannot be killed," Gabriel insisted.

"Why not?" John asked. "With as much pain and misery she's caused, I see no reason to let her live."

"Would you condemn the people out there to death?" Gabriel asked.

"Never," John replied. "But what do they have to do with Lilith?"

"If you kill my mother," Gabriel explained, "you kill us all."

"How?"

"We are all linked," Gabriel said. "I am her son, which makes all of my people her grandchildren. When you kill the creator of the family, the subordinate members also die. It's like when you cut the head off the snake."

"And because she's your mother," John said. "Then you would die, which would mean all of your people will die, too."

"My people and hers," he said. "All of this line would cease to exist. Trust me," he continued. "If there were a way for us to live and have her die, I would be a willing accomplice. Unfortunately, the way we are made means that when the top goes, so goes the rest."

"It's like cutting the family tree completely down," John said.

"Exactly," Gabriel confirmed.

"Then what can we do?"

"That's where Grace and Magda come in," he said.

"I don't understand," John admitted.

"Allow me," Grace said.

John had nearly forgotten that she was there, she was so quiet during their discussion.

"My sister and I are not what we appear," she said. "We came after Lilith, even after Gabriel was born. An emergency clause, if you will, created specifically for this purpose. Our only goal is to neutralize a threat of the magnitude like this."

"What are we talking about?" John asked.

"My kind is a much larger portion of society than you could ever imagine," Gabriel said.

"How so?"

"If Lilith dies," Gabriel began.

"Two thirds of the world's population would disappear," Grace finished.

"Two thirds?" John was shocked. Never in his wildest imagination did he think there were that many among them. "How do you hide? How is this not known?"

"Because we continue to change the lore," Gabriel said. "We used to be able to walk among you without you being aware. When the first fictional stories came out, we were pushed to change our way of life. Much of what you know is likely based on misinformation we've been able to put out to keep your kind unaware of our existence."

"But why hide?"

"Because humans are a fragile species," Grace answered.

"And fear runs you much more than you'd like to believe," Gabriel continued. "When we were first 'found,' humans assumed we were just a religious sect. As time passed, your kind saw that we were not growing old like you. They wanted what we had."

"That wasn't possible, though," Grace said. "You are too fragile to take on the attributes that Lilith's children possess."

"What happened?" John asked.

"We were forced to hide," Gabriel said. "Whether it meant moving frequently enough to keep suspicion to a minimum or literally hiding, we weren't able to continue the way we'd lived for centuries."

"Then," Grace intervened. "Someone decided that they would write a book. Tell everyone who we were, what we could do, and why we were a danger."

"Dracula?" John asked.

"That was one of the biggest," Gabriel said. "But it wasn't the first. Well before that we were outed as monsters, dangers to civilized society, and should be destroyed. Mother wanted to remove the human population from the planet."

"Then how would you survive?" John asked.

"Contrary to what you may have heard," Grace said. "They are not required to drink human blood."

"It's better," Gabriel said. "But she's right, not necessary."

"You're saying that we could all die and you'd be fine?"

"He doesn't know," Grace said, looking at Gabriel.

"Know what?"

"You're one of us," Gabriel said.

"I'm... what?" John didn't know what to say. He'd never thought he was one of them, even when he was captive with Lilith.

"Most people don't know they belong to us," Gabriel said. "You walk around without the knowledge that you are greater than the ordinary you think you are."

"But, how?"

"I am only half of what my mother is," Gabriel said. "The other half is my father."

When he didn't elaborate, John asked, "Who is your father?"

"My father was an archangel who fell," he said. "While his fall was his fault in part, my mother's role was much larger. She seduced him, convinced him that she was still in the good graces of God, and that their union was chosen to be a greater part of the world."

"Their children were to rule a portion of the world," Grace continued. "At least that's what Lilith told him."

"By the time I was born," he said. "Mother had killed my father."

"She killed an angel?" John asked.

"They aren't as strong as her," Gabriel said. "It was brutal, and I was nearly lost in her fight. She used me as a weapon, though. Father tried to subdue mother instead of killing her, all to save me."

"If an archangel can't subdue your mother," John began. "What makes you think we can?"

"Because of me," Grace said.

"I still don't know why you are so important," John said.

Grace looked to Gabriel who gave her a subtle nod. When she looked back to John there was something different about her. He couldn't put his finger on it, but he knew there was a difference. Then she shifted. All at once she became pure light, so blinding that John had to close his eyes to her, covering them with his hands to ward off the pain from the light.

As quickly as she erupted, she was back to the small woman she'd been before.

"What are you?" he asked, pure shock in his voice.

"We're angels," she said. "My sister and I were created by God after Lilith killed Gabriel's father. We've all been given free will to choose our path, and most choose to follow."

"My father did not," Gabriel said.

"I thought you said Lilith seduced him," John said. "Doesn't that count for anything?”

“If someone convinces you that driving over the speed limit, even just a little, is no big deal,” Gabriel said. “When you get pulled over, do you use that excuse to get yourself out of a ticket?”

“No,” John said.

“And so it is with this,” Gabriel said. “He knew what was right and he chose to disobey, chose to go against what God had put into place as the rules.”

“By doing so,” Grace said. “He condemned an entire race. All of Lilith’s children, whether they are hers by birth, by conversion, or by chance, are condemned.”

“Then I am condemned, too,” John said.

“In a way, yes,” Gabriel said. “If we kill Lilith, you will die.”

“Then what are we going to do?”

“Grace and Magda will take Lilith to the throne room of God,” Gabriel said.

“What happens then?”

“God will judge her,” Grace said. “And only her, without passing that judgement on to her children.”

“What’s to keep someone else from taking her place?” John asked. “I mean, if she can get to the point of being so corrupt that she is willing to kill her own child, what’s to keep someone else with the same ideals from picking up where she left off?”

“You ask a very good question,” Gabriel said. “The answer is nothing. We cannot assume that there won’t be another to take her place at the head of that faction. What we can do, however, is put that person, and all who follow Lilith, on notice. Once she is gone, their protection is as well. If they choose to follow her path, we can end them, and their line, without any danger to us and ours.”

“So this is a war,” John said. “Supernatural as it may be, it’s still a war. You believe you are right and she believes she is.”

"Except she wants to kill us," Gabriel said. "We don't want her family dead, we simply want her to be judged as we would want ourselves to be judged; on our own merit and not on those of someone we didn't have a choice being connected with."

"If that judgement leads to her death, then so be it," John said.

"It has been her choice," Grace said. "This began long before anyone else was involved. She has her own idea as to what is right."

"So do you," John said. "You are saying that what she wants and needs and does is wrong, but she sees it as right. It's like looking at a cup and one arguing there is a handle and another arguing that there isn't."

"Except the cup either does or does not have a handle," Gabriel said. "One of those people is wrong. Just because they can't see the handle doesn't mean that it doesn't exist."

"And just because you can see the handle doesn't mean the cup would be any less valuable without it."

"If I can see the handle," Gabriel said, "and you can't, I can turn the handle so you can see it. I've done this for my mother. I've shown her that there is a better way to be here, sharing this world with those who are not fully the same as us. She has not only refused to see the truth of it, but she's gone out of her way to destroy any evidence that that truth exists."

"We simply want her to acknowledge that her way is not the only way," Grace said.

"Which we've tried over and over and over," Gabriel said.

"So you're just going to take her to her execution, then," John said. "Without remorse, without thinking of those who may be hurt because of it."

"We're trying to make sure she doesn't hurt anyone else by her actions," Gabriel said. "Once God judges her, it will remove not only the protection her clan has from her, but also remove the lineage issue.”

“I’m not sure what you mean,” John said.

“Lilith is the head of our kind,” Grace said. “If she is removed without causing a catastrophic failure down the line, then that risk is gone. The sins of the father or mother will no longer cause damage to their offspring.”

“Wait,” John said. “If she is taken out without it causing the rest of you to go the same way, then you could die and it would not kill your entire family?”

“Exactly,” Gabriel said. “Once that happens, we can police our own without retribution falling on those who are not even aware of their connection to us.”

“It’s a big if, though,” Grace said.

“How so?”

“God could choose to remove her entire line,” she said. “Take her and all of her offspring from the planet.”

“Then there’s no difference as to whether we kill her or take her to God,” John said.

“But there is,” Gabriel said. “We have a chance to live if we take her to God. If we don’t, we know we’ll die.”

“And God could spare her,” Grace said.

“Spare her?”

“Let her live,” Gabriel said.

“Would he take away her powers?” John asked. “Take away the lineage threat?”

“Maybe,” Gabriel said. “We won’t know until she gets there.”

“Then this could be a fool’s errand,” John said. “It could do nothing but make her angrier than she already is. Give her even more reason to fight and kill you.”

“It’s a chance I’m willing to take,” Gabriel said.

"Even if it means killing your entire family?" John asked. "Even if it means that you lose?"

"I will happily give up my life if it means that my family is safe," Gabriel said. "I'll give it up if it means that the few humans that are left are able to live in peace without the threat of my mother cursing them to a life they never even knew existed."

John looked at the other man. Everything about him said that the man was telling the truth. He just hoped he hadn't hitched his wagon to the wrong horse. "What do I need to do?" he asked.

"They said they'd only talk to Lilith," John said.

"Are you sure they have information?" Decentius asked.

"What they said seems to make sense," John replied. "I have a good feeling about what they are telling me. It hasn't been much, but what they've said seems to be exactly what she said she was looking for."

"I'll let her know and set up a meeting," Decentius said.

"Thank you," John relied, then hung up the phone.

"He bought it?" Gabriel asked.

"I believe so," John replied.

"Then all we have to do is wait," Grace said.

It didn't take long for John to hear back, and the meeting was set for midnight the next night. It barely gave them enough time to get everything into place, but they managed.

"And you're sure I'll be safe?" he asked again.

"Magda and I will protect all who are there," Grace said. "You are included in that group."

"As well as Lilith's people," Gabriel added.

"But…" John began.

"We have everything under control," Gabriel said. "If they

attack, we will subdue them. We will not kill them. I won't be like my mother, killing anyone who opposes me."

"You have your father's soul," Grace said.

"I also have my mother's tenacity," he said. "I won't stop until she is dealt with."

"Even if it means your death?" John asked.

"No matter the outcome," Gabriel said. "I will not subject this world to her reign of terror any longer."

"Why now?" John asked. "I mean, you've been doing this for eons. Why did you decide to make your stand now?"

"You," Gabriel replied.

"I don't understand," John said. "What's so special about me?"

"There was always a chance that you would exist," he began. "Not you, specifically, but your abilities. Grace and Magda were the first to realize. They've been waiting until Lilith made her move. Once she did, they knew that the plan could be put into place."

"I still don't know what abilities I'm supposed to have," John said.

"You're resistant," Grace said.

"To what?"

"Our kind," Gabriel said. "My mother attempted to convert you. That's why you have some memory gaps and why she was feeding you blood. She thought her transformation worked, so she sent you out to find me and mine. If you could be converted, then you would be able to withstand our charms. She didn't count on you not knowing about what you could do."

"She also didn't know that we knew who you were," Grace said.

"Does she know Magda is like you?" John asked.

"My sister is very clever," Grace said. "She and I have the

ability to project exactly what we need the other to see in order to persuade them to our desires.”

“How do I know you haven’t just convinced me to do what you want?”

“Because you can’t be charmed,” Gabriel said.

“I don’t understand,” John said.

“If I wanted to,” Grace said. “I could convince anyone to jump from a cliff, step in front of a bus, or swallow bleach. There is nothing I could do to convince you to do that.”

“Why not?”

“You are the one who can fix this world,” Gabriel said. “My mother is already weaker because she took in some of your blood. She doesn’t realize it, but that has made her vulnerable.”

“And that vulnerability is what we needed in order to stop her,” Grace said.

John thought about what they’d said. He had been weak when he first woke in the castle dungeon alone. The drinking of the blood had strengthened him some, but the regular food that Decentius brought did much more to build him back up. He knew that Lilith needed to be stopped, and what Gabriel and Grace had told him made sense. Still, he couldn’t deny there was an inkling in the back of his brain that said something was amiss. Somehow, something more than what they were telling him was going on.

“I want to go with you,” he said to Grace.

“And you will,” she replied. “I need you to take me to Lilith.”

“No,” he said. “I want to go to the throne room of God. I want to see for myself that what you are saying is true.”

“I’m not sure you’ll survive,” Gabriel said. “Even I am unable to go there.”

“My life isn’t worth anything if I simply take you at your word,” he said. “I want to know that what I am contributing is for a worthy cause. That I'm not simply sending Lilith and her people to their death in a spat between family."

"You know that this will likely kill you," Grace said.

"Yes," he replied.

"As long as you know the chance you are taking," she said, "I am willing to take you along."

"Grace," Gabriel said. "He can't go with you."

"God has a way of surprising even us," she said. "Whether he lives or not is up to Him. All I can do is take him there."

"Thank you," John said.

"Don't thank me yet," she replied. "You know what they say; 'be careful what you wish for.'"

"Is she here?" Decentius asked.

"Is Lilith?"

John wasn't about to let Grace die if he could help it. She'd said that if Lilith didn't bring Magda, then she may not survive the interaction.

"Lilith is here," Decentius said.

"Who else did you bring with you?" John asked.

"Lilith demanded we bring her handmaid," the other man said.

"I suppose that's fine," John said. "Where are they?"

"Just inside," Decentius said.

They'd chosen an abandoned warehouse to do the meeting. Lilith must have arrived early in order to already be inside.

"Where's yours?" Decentius asked.

John turned to the van he'd driven up and opened the door. Grace stepped out and John was worried that Decentius would recognize her.

"Scraggly little thing, ain't she?" Decentius asked.

"But she knows things," John replied, thankful that whatever Grace was using to hide her true nature stood up to the other man.

She stood there, rubbing her fingers together in a rhythmic way, sending an eerie feeling over both men.

"Let's go," Decentius said and turned to enter the building.

John followed behind, with Grace on his heels. She continued the rhythmic rubbing of her fingers as they made their way through the building to a set of stairs. Grace started humming under her breath in time with her hands swishing sound as she rubbed them together.

"What's she doing?" Decentius asked.

"Dunno," John replied. "She's never done it before. Maybe she's nervous."

"Make her stop," Decentius said.

John turned to Grace, but she'd already stopped the noise. She continued to rub her hands together, but no noise came from them now. She also appeared to still be humming, but again it was silent.

As they made it to the top of the stairs, Decentius turned the corner and stepped up to a door.

"Ready?" he asked.

Grace nodded rapidly, still appearing to be a frail woman. Decentius opened the door and stepped inside. John went through next and saw Lilith sitting at a desk, Magda next to her. When Grace stepped into the room, Lilith stood.

"Thank you for helping," she said.

In that moment, Magda stood, sandwiching Lilith between her and her twin. John stepped back and was not surprised when both women burst into light. Covering his eyes, he heard Decentius scream, then heard a sizzling noise. He chanced a peek, keeping the twins light at his back. Where the other man stood, now only a pile of ash remained.

The light faded and John turned to see Lilith slack in the arms of the twins.

"Now we go," one of them said.

He couldn't tell who had spoken, as they now matched in fine white robes that fell to their feet. The one who spoke reached out a hand and he clasped it firmly. The room spun around him and his stomach dropped to his feet. As quickly as it started, John was planted on solid ground again, though he wasn't sure what he was standing on. No walls surrounded him, yet he felt somewhat confined. Before him was a wooden chair behind a battered desk. The chair was empty, but the twins didn't seem surprised.

"We wait," the one who held his hand said.

John barely had time to wonder how long they would wait when a man appeared in the chair.

"Ladies," he said. "What brings you to us?"

"Lilith," the previously silent one said.

The man at the desk stood abruptly, saying, "Why?"

"Gabriel requests a decision."

"Who's he?" the man asked.

"The immune one."

"One moment," the man said, then disappeared. John barely blinked and he was back. "This way," he said, turning to the wall.

Without realizing what was happening, John was suddenly in another room, this one much larger. He hadn't felt like he'd walked, nor had any time passed.

"Here," the man said to John, handing him a set of glasses.

Not knowing anything about where they were or what was going to be happening, he put the glasses on. Blinking in surprise he realized that there were hundreds of people surrounding him. They hadn't been there a moment before. He slid the glasses down his nose, and they disappeared. Pushing them back into place, he marveled at the crowd around him.

"Come," he heard, though he couldn't say whether it was aloud or in his head.

Before him was a large throne, a smaller one set to the right. The man sitting in the larger throne looked at him kindly, but he could feel the power rolling off him. Sitting to his right was a much younger man.

"Speak," the older man said, again inside John's head.

"We bring Lilith," one of the twins said. "Gabriel has asked for a decision."

"And the immune one?"

"Wanted to make sure we weren't simply taking Lilith to slaughter as she did for Gabriel's people," the twin who seemed to be the spokesperson said.

"Then he shall watch," the man said. "Bring her to me."

The twins moved forward, not walking, simply gliding. They approached the throne and set Lilith in front of it, then stepped back.

Looking at the woman he said, "My child."

Lilith jolted, as if shocked where she lay. John saw her eyes widen, fear rippled across her face, followed quickly by rage.

"You," she said glaring at him. "You did this to me. Why would you do this?"

"My child," the man said again.

"I am not yours," Lilith spat.

"I never left you," the man said.

"You threw me out," Lilith screeched. "Turned your back on me when I needed you most."

"You chose to walk away," the man said, now kneeling beside Lilith. "I was right there beside you, waiting for you to come back. All you had to do was ask."

"There were conditions to my coming back," she said.

John watched in amazement as the woman who he'd seen as so strong and confident crumbled to a sobbing child in front of this man, this God.

"I've always loved you," God said.

"But you wouldn't let me back unless I changed," she sobbed. "I couldn't be me if I wanted to come back."

"You could have been so much more," God said.

"It would have made me less," she replied. "I wouldn't be what I am. I wouldn't be me."

"Do you want to come back home?"

"Not if I can't be me," she said.

"Then the answer is no," God said. "If you wanted to come home, you would change. Since you don't want to change, you don't really want to come home."

"Come home," a man said. John wasn't sure where he came from, he was just suddenly next to her. "Please come back to me."

Lilith blinked, then turned her head away from the man. John waited, wondering what would happen next. Nothing moved in the big room, not the people, not Lilith, not even God. Everything was frozen in place. Then the quiet shattered with a thunder so loud John had to cover his ears and a flash so bright he had to close his eyes. In that moment, everything shifted.

"Welcome back," Grace said.

"What happened?" John asked.

"You were there," she replied. "You saw what happened."

"I mean after the thunder and lightning," John said, sitting up.

He was back in the office where he'd met with Gabriel and Grace before they'd gone to capture Lilith.

"You don't want to know," she said.

Gabriel came in just then. "You're awake," he said. "Good. Feeling better?"

"I'm not sure," John replied. "I feel like I've missed something."

"God gave you a choice," Grace said.

"I don't remember that," John said.

"That was part of the choice," she replied. "You saw everything that happened in the throne room. Everything Lilith went through before she was cast out for good."

"Then she's back here?" John asked.

"Never again," Gabriel said. "That was not what she chose."

"Who was the man who asked her to come back?" John asked.

"That was my father," Gabriel replied.

"But I thought he was dead," John said, clearly confused.

"Not exactly," Grace said. "God kept him safe."

"But he disobeyed…" John began.

"And then asked for forgiveness," Gabriel interrupted.

"Just like that," John said. "No harm, no foul?"

"Not quite," Gabriel said.

"God is more than generous with us all," Grace said. "We are given free will, the ability to make decisions for ourselves. Part of that is the ability to turn our backs on Him. He gives us a multitude of chances, but at some point, just like a parent with an errant child, He gives us the final chance. If we choose well, we are given forgiveness."

"And if not," John concluded. "We are thrown away."

"I think that's a bit harsh," Gabriel said.

"How so?" John asked.

"We are lost to God," he said. "We are not gone forever."

"But we're not given another chance," John said.

"That's true," Gabriel conceded. "It isn't easy for God to give us up, though. He mourns deeply, and those of us who have met him know that those wounds run deep."

"Then why does he give us the choice?" John asked.

"So we can live," Grace said.

"And live free," Gabriel continued.

"Until we have to face him," John said.

"That's why we have to tell the stories," Grace said. "We tell everyone we meet what will happen if they choose to disobey. Then it's up to them to decide."

"If God simply wanted obedient servants," Gabriel said, "he would have made us all drones."

"Which he didn't," Grace said. "Now you have to choose."

"Choose what?" John asked.

"Whether you will tell the story of Lilith and what happened to her," Gabriel said.

"Or simply let it fall away and allow another to take her place," Grace said.

"But why me?"

"You cannot be bought," Gabriel said. "You are immune to the call of our kind."

"And you alone are the one who can tell the story the best," Grace concluded.

"How?"

Gabriel handed John his notebook, the one he'd written things down in from his meeting with Lilith. "Share your story," he said simply. "Share it with the world."

SACRAMENT
BY DAVID MECKLENBURG

The way across the desert leads past Clavicula Magna. It is nearly deserted now, and its roster was dwindling even when she was a girl. The track leaves the civilized land and the pavement stones of the Elders disappear into bare rock and sand. Beyond the strong walls of the Clavicula, is the waste-desert, full of acacias, scorpions and witches.

Stella remembered the warnings as the cart full of her and the other girls went up the pass. The Sister pointed out Claviculus Minor and told them of the older monks, who, after achieving a kind of holiness unknowable, were inured in their bottle-like cells for final contemplation. Raw, un-threshed grains, fruit peels, and the resins and gums of various trees were lowered to them along with water. Buckets of fragrant, desiccated shit would be brought up, but the task became less odious the holier the monk became.

The younger monks performed this work. It was a good way to learn the eternity of sanctification: to watch the elder monks deny their bodies and the illusions contained therein. Sometimes an acolyte would be lowered into the bottle to share the cell with the monk and learn his holy words and visions.

"This is how they learn the prayers and devotions."

"How shall we learn?" A girl asked the Sister.

She turned and looked at them. The hood of her habit fell over her face, but Stella could still see her wide leering mouth. "You shall encounter the Eucharist here. Understand the blood and flesh of God. By God you will taste it." A thin band of spit connected her bottom teeth to the soft, purplish upper lip that was split and bruised.

They either huddled against one another in the ass-driven cart or got out and helped by pushing. At last, the cart came to a wide saddle of the mountain—Clavicula because it looked like a collarbone. Built squarely in the middle of the pass, the ancient fortress and college stood a kind of guard over that which could be seen and not be seen. The girls climbed out and went into the enclosure of the thick, high walls topped with shards of glass and iron.

Twenty girls stood facing a line of black hooded robes—The Sisters. Between them on the red sand was a pile of cloth.

"Welcome to the Enclave of Clavicula Major. Here you will be humbled. Before you are your new clothes. Remove the emblems of bitchery you wear now and don the rags that become you."

"*Do it now*" the voice roared. One by one, the girls became naked and moved towards the rags. Stella did not know where the voice came from: it boomed from the walls, the rock, the sky. She, like the other girls had waited all her young life to matter, and now she would. She told herself this as the sun began to cut into her fair skin. But when the first girl touched a rag, the Sisters descended on them with quirts and whips and beat them in expert fashion.

Stella was tall and fair and stuck out like flame in the night. They beat her especially hard and when she pulled on the burlap, her blood oozed into it straight away. Stella looked down and realized it was an old tea sack with the upper corners and a hole for her head cut out of it.

The fastest, strongest girls were covered with few scratches and they stood mocking the rest.

"For those who have dressed first, we have a special prize," The Voice said. It seemed as calming as a mother's, or as seductive as a man trying to sell cheap jewelry at the market.

"Come forward." Stella was not in the vanguard. Five unscathed girls had been chosen and stood before the Sisters. The Sisters bowed slightly and then brought out heavy cudgels from their black and white robes.

"And receive!" And then they beat the five girls mercilessly, hitting them in the stomach first so they doubled over and then they laid in on their backs and heads with the cudgels until all of them were on the ground. "Enough! This is what happens to the haughty. All shall feel the hand of the Lord." Other Sisters came forward and smashed wreaths of brambles down on every girl's head so that no one escaped blood, but Stella was so miserable at this point she hardly noticed.

The Sisters divided the girls up into groups of three and then each was given one of the crippled, unconscious girls to tend to. Stella found herself with Karina, Jennica, and Miriam, who had been a rich man's daughter. Her father had paid the requisite amounts, but he needn't worry. She was well fed and fast and had escaped the first whips but not the cudgels.

Miriam had only one unbroken arm but she also had broken a rib or two and one savage blow had split open her skull. Karina, who had some knowledge of tending beasts, sewed it up as best she could. "But she will never be the same," she whispered to Jennica and Stella.

Three nights after the girls had arrived, Miriam lay in the leather bed retching and screaming in agony. Karina wanted to put her down: "she would have wanted to die, look at her, an idiot now," but the others felt the Love of the Lord was needed. Karina, who had been raised on a farm, agreed, but knew what had to be done.

"We must trepan her. I saw my father do it to a cow. Our prize milker."

"Did she live?"

"Yes, but... that is all Miriam is now anyway. She will be a Motherwife now."

Karina could not perform the necessary task. There were no instruments at hand, and she was afraid. They prayed around Miriam, and it seemed the Lord heard them for Miriam's pain subsided, but she was more an idiot than before. "Why?" Stella asked herself and the Lord but there was no answer.

This is how Stella's life at the Clavicula began. She pretended to be illiterate because no one wanted to be known as a reader, especially a strawhead. The ceremonies of the Shoulder had been learned through whispered paeans of wonder and euphemistic votives of humiliation. Stella had longed to be A Vessel of the Shoulder, to join the Sisters and partake in the Eucharist with them. But when looking at Miriam—whose speech was slurred and could not remember her name—Stella felt a deep and evil seed take rest within her mind.

At night, Stella sensed the seed moving, as though it wriggled into some part of her body where it had not been before. She had restless dreams where ants crawled just under her skin, stretching it, preparing it. The Sisters would come when ready and flay her alive, to make a drum of her. They smeared her with the fragrant resins and gums, the same recipe for the monks and left her eyes and lips whole so that the drum mallet could beat against her cheeks and she would watch the sun set in fire every night. Yet she could not speak since what was left of her meat-body had been thrown down the hill for jackals and ravens.

As this, Stella usually woke. She said her prayers and with each bead of her Rosary, she imagined a chore or some animal that needed milking. But as she went in the circle of prayers, the question kept repeating itself. *Why?*

For a year they would work. They would harvest grain with blunted sickles, threshed it and tended the animals. They prayed through the offices of Matins, Lauds, Prime, Terce, Sext, None, Vespers and Compline. Stella looked forward to their prayers in the Chapel, for it was cool and peaceful there and much time was spent cleaning it. Had she lived there long, she would have seen the decay the other buildings had fallen into.

Unlike the bruised-pink stone of the rest of the Clavicula campus, the Chapel gleamed white for it was pure. Stella understood that as flesh and blood, sinful from filthy conception, she was not pure. While the outside was white, the inside was covered in intricate tiles and murals centering around the elegant vertical scriptures of the Elders, carved into the stone and inlaid with nacre pulled up the mountain from the sea. The writing descended like a rain of salvation, and Stella read the words secretly for they told of the stories and interpretations of the Holy Testaments. Sometimes the Grand Sister's homily matched the inscriptions but sometimes it did not. Stella did not let anyone know. Desiring the distraction of mortification, Stella knelt with her bare, bruised and calloused knees on the hard stone like the other girls.

As their prayers progressed, they could see better in the dark red light of the sanctuary, for a large stained-glass window stood between the girls and the sun. The Lord, the precious vessel of God upon earth, stood before his Rood, holding out his bloody heart with one hand, and pointing to his Spear Wound. The glass gleamed so vibrantly that the Wound and Heart appeared to bleed afresh as the sunlight filtered and rippled through them. Next to him was his

Acolyte, tied to a tree and full of arrows. The Mother of God was on the other side, with her womb still bleeding tears. All wore crowns of brambles, and they were naked to show the bruises, cuts, and other lacerations of Glory.

The Chosen Five, gibbering, drooling, laughing, and now sanctified were allowed a special place at the feet of the Grand Sister. They were destined for Motherwifedom.

The Motherwives of the City married the richest men, but they were all dumber than the bed posts they tied them to. Once a year Priests allowed the Motherwives and their bedposts to march in the parade of the Lord to the Fountain. That is where Stella had seen them, laughing and waving like infants, the most sublime of the City's martyrs. They bore many strong children to rich families and were perfect wives because they couldn't put five words together to talk back. A Motherwife's husband simply mounted her every year and another baby came to be taken away by the midwives.

The days went on.

Jennica was allowed the honor of walking barefoot down to the nearest town. She went with money to buy desired things. She was older than Stella and Karina and wanted to be a Sister someday. But most of all, Jennica was kind and often bought tobacco and peppermints for Karina and Stella to take to the Confessional Box. They knew that girls who went empty handed had to perform milking and ablutions for the Priest who came every week. Stella grew to loathe the smell of peppermint and burnt tobacco in the small, hot box, but she was grateful to not have to milk him. She merely had to tell him her multitude of sins. But one day, Stella discovered that not all Priests were leathery gray old men with half-turgid members and the sins of the world populating their thoughts.

Father Enrico came like a shock to the girls. He was a traveling Priest who went barefoot to the Holy Places. He preached by playing an old beaten guitar and singing about the Love of the Lord—how He reached down and sanctified the most lowly so that the World would know the true path.

The girls were arrayed in a half circle, kneeling as always in the chapel, and Father Enrico stood before them playing. Stella caught the scent of olives that wafted from his curly black hair that fell in ringlets to his spare, brown robe which was open to show his bare, wide chest festooned with more hair. Stella often looked at him and then to the red stained-glass portrait of the Lord and waited, perhaps for Father Enrico to reach into his own chest and pull forth his beating heart.

That night, he even ate with them, chewing on the same bran-filled hard oat-mash they all ate.

"Tell us, Father. What formula of the Lord compels you to wander so? Do you not wish to preside over a proper church?"

"The Lord wandered, and so do I." He looked at Stella and smiled. "The beauty of the Lord's work is not only in chapels, although none are as beautiful as yours. When I had taken Orders," and he paused, "I... was shown a different path than across holy tiles. I wished to feel the hard earth and see the majestic Hand of God at work. And even the Holiest Martyrs need compassion at times, and in my small way, I hope to give it to them. So may some of you find as you leave this sacred place. Let the Lord show you the way." And he looked at Stella again and smiled.

Stella's abdomen had been hurting all day from cramps and she thought that it was the Holy Food they had been eating since it was supposed to scour the insides as the Holy Words scoured the mind. But at that moment, she felt the pain subside and she imagined herself wandering the world as Father Enrico had done, bringing small comfort to martyrs so that they may continue to suffer afresh and with renewed devotion. Whether through the Laying on of Hands, or cooking, or simply singing as Father Enrico had done. Yes. It did not answer the *Why* that goaded her, but it would help her make her way through this terrible, fallen world.

That night, after Compline, she had trouble going to sleep. She knew the *Why* was struggling against the Grace of the Lord. She counted her prayers and imagined the Holy Martyrs and the Lord in the chapel and eventually passed into dream.

Who can say where a dream begins or ends? Only the Lord. Stella found herself naked and running, running through the darkness. The flames of the world and hot sands scorched her. And then she ran through her own miserable hovel in the City, and then through the halls of the Clavicula but she dared not turn to see the *Why* behind her.

She ran all the way to the Holy Hill but the Rood was empty when she reached it. Then she knew. She turned and saw him. His black hair fell around his beautiful face, the blood seeped from his Spear-Wound. She could clearly see the holes in His feet and arms made by the Holy Iron. He reached out to her and she turned to run, but He touched her back and raked it with his long fingernails. Stella felt her own blood flow down her back and her buttocks, and she kept running but He was behind her and called her name.

"Stella, stop, come, and accept my Love."

Her blood had reached her thighs and the back of her knees when she stumbled and fell. When she looked up, He was there and tenderly held her chin. Without effort, He picked her up and she could see how enormous his member had grown. There was a pearl of light glowing at the tip and when He lowered her upon Himself, a splitting rapture overcame her and she wanted to scream, but that was when she felt a great force surge inside of her, the Dove of God opened its wings and burst forth from her mouth.

Stella awoke, sweating and trembling on the rough pallet she slept on. She looked around could only hear the breaths of the girls and the sound of mosquitos searching out for their blood in the darkness. She wanted to be somewhere cool. She wanted to see the blue of the sky and nestle deep within its comfort like the mantle of the Mother of God. But all Stella could feel was the rough scratch of burlap. Her abdomen then cramped and she arose. She did not care. No, no one would hear her and there was only one place she would find comfort and coolness. She moved quickly, silently, like a cat bent on communion with the darkness and went toward the Chapel.

Past columns, past doorways, past the sleeping rooms of the Sisters where she could hear them softly groaning or sighing, Stella crept. She reached the doors of the Chapel and was so thirsty that she begged eternal forgiveness from the Lord as she scooped handfuls of Holy Water to her lips. Yet still she did not make and noise and perhaps that is why the sound of breaking glass was so loud.

One shattering crash. Then laughter. Another crash. Then crying. Although it was not a voice that could command words, Stella knew it as well as her own. She rushed into the depths of the Chapel, and it glittered like gold and rubies in the guttering candles. And there, on the floor, scattered over the tiles was the shattered Heart of the Lord. The glass looked even more sanguine than before and in the middle of a heap of broken crystal, that had once been the images of the Mother, the Acolyte and the Lord, sat Miriam, weeping and laughing and gibbering.

"Miriam!" Stella said, but Miriam merely looked up grinning and rolling her eyes. Then she grew afraid and pointed at Stella. It was then Stella looked down and saw that blood was flowing from her. Miriam screamed again and the sound of the Clavicula rousing in alarm moved past the doors and flowed over Stella like a choking smoke.

Why. The *Why* had won. She was too poor. She was too tall.

Too fair. She would not be merely punished: that would have been a blessing. She would be made into a drum that warned a thousand other phantoms she could see mounting the hill. The Face of the Lord in her dream mocked her. As the cramps crushed her insides, these thoughts crashed through her heart like a herd of wild horses, and so she ran with them.

She ran through the shadows of the Clavicula and she ran through its gates. She ran beneath the stars she was named after as they shone upon the rocks, the dust and the twisted trees. She ran until at last, the sky erupted in scarlet and apricot. She fell and prayed in her passion until the sun blazed behind her closed eyes—then, she turned to lay down to cry and bleed. And there Stella slept through her first day as a woman amongst the acacias and scorpions.

ABOUT THE AUTHORS

JENNIFER DIMARCO

A PNWC and Bumbershoot award-winning poet and Seattle Times bestselling novelist, Jennifer DiMarco first toured nationally as an author when she was nineteen years old. Her resume of publications includes contemporary drama, science fiction, high fantasy, and mystery novels as well as poetry collections and stage plays. For the last ten years, DiMarco has worked as a filmmaker writing and directing more than a dozen feature films, half a dozen mini series, and more than a hundred short films. She lives in the Pacific Northwest with her wife, author and actor Brianne, and their children, author and illustrator Maxwell, and producer and actor Faith. Find out more about DiMarco at www.jenniferdimarco.com.

LAUREN PATZER

Hailing from Tacoma, WA, Lauren has been an information technology guru, actor, writer and film producer among other pursuits. From the earliest days when he could sit up in a chair, he typed happily away at his grandparents IBM Selectric typewriter, writing somewhat less coherent stories than he does now. He feels the best part of writing short stories is the ability to briefly immerse yourself in a brand new world (even if it's modern day America) and tell the reader a complete, entertaining and /or thought-provoking story in just a few short pages. When he's not spending time with his wife, three daughters and grandson, Lauren is pouring over the details of his next pursuit.

HIROMI COTA

Hiromi Cota has been a special operations heavy weapons expert, an adjunct professor, a rave journalist, and the flaming-sword-swinging lead in a heavy metal opera. They (singular) have lived in nations around the world, but have settled down in Seattle with their spouse Randi and their (plural) dog Nasus. Outside of crafting queer science fiction/fantasy, Hiromi writes roleplaying games, produces the inclusive and comedic D&D radio drama podcast "Dear High Elves," programs video games, and gets into sword fights as a member of the Seattle Knights actor-combatant troupe. A reasonably complete list of their work can be found at: HiromiCota.com

AMBER RAINEY

A mom first in all things she does, Amber just happens to also be an author, actor, and award-winning filmmaker. She lives in Texas with her engineer husband, precocious son, and two cats, who vie for her lap while she writes. Amber has yet to find a medium she doesn't enjoy so she writes novels, short stories, and screenplays. Her first novel, *Eternal Willow*, can be found online at Amazon. You can visit www.amberrainey.com and www.tiny.cc/amberrainey for more about Amber and her work.

MARSHALL MILLER

After retiring as a Senior Special Agent/Federal Criminal Investigator, Marshall found a second career in writing and has a published four book series called THE TSCHAAA INFESTATION. These in-depth science fiction/speculative fiction works examine the human condition, and what people would do to survive when threatened with being eaten by an invading intelligent alien species. His thirty years of law enforcement experience and world travel provides him with the basis for the many varied characters which populate his literary works, demonstrating the good, the bad, and the ugly.

ELIZA LOEB

A United States actor, Eliza stepped in to the writing field in 2018, beginning with *Prompt Generation 1*. Originally born on Guam, they had spent their life reading, writing and creating with many artistic influences. Today, Eliza channels their creativity and experiences through their writing and does their best to reach out to their readers with a subtle portrayal of empathy or compassion. Sometimes, by allowing the reader to get close to them through the pages, other times by a means of fiction. Most times with wine that rarely touches the glass. A recently published piece of Eliza Loeb's work can be found on Amazon in the horror anthology *Unnerving*. But for those of you who would like to see the human behind the writer with occasional writing tidbits, feel free to follow Eliza on Tumbler at imelizaloeb.tumblr.com.

SHEILA MENGERT

A transgender novelist, dramatist, and poet, Sheila is also a political commentator. She has a Masters Degree in English Literature from the University of Washington with an emphasis on the works of James Joyce and Virginia Woolf. Her stories in *Prompt Generation 1* are a debut effort for her in a new genre. Her previous books include a non-fiction book on Borderline Personality Disorder and a seven volume epic re-telling of the Sherlock Holmes Saga published under another name. The story of her transition is told in her book *Transsexualism and its Discontents: A Political Profile* available from KitsapPublishing.com under the separate editorial imprint of Trannie-Goddess Press. Sheila is currently at work on an eighth volume sequel to her Sherlock Holmes Saga dealing with The Great European War of 1914-1918 and its critical aftermath in the Peace Conference of 1919 in Paris.

CARRIE AVERY MORIARTY

Born and raised in the Pacific Northwest, Carrie still lives there with the love of her life. She raised two wonderful, if not slightly warped, children who both live close to home. When she's not yelling at her hometown sports teams on the television, she's cheering them on from the stands. She loves nature and spending time enjoying it with her family. And you don't want to attempt to beat her in any board game. They are meant to be played to the death. Find more from Carrie at www.facebook.com/AuthorCarrieAveryMoriarty/ and on Twitter or Instagram @camoriarty13

DAVID MECKLENBURG

Much like his unseen Gemini half/fictional narrator Ada Ludenow, writer & illustrator David Mecklenburg was born in Sacramento, and moved home to Washington to attend the University of Washington. He has worked as a chef, tech support specialist, and capital project manager. You can often find him on the Washington State ferries commuting to and from Bremerton where he now lives. His stories were written "on the water." For more information about David (& Ada) please visit www.hagengard.com.

ABOUT THE EDITOR

BRIANNE DIMARCO

A published short story author, poet, and writer of more than a dozen short films, Brianne has been captivated by the written word from an early age and doesn't even remember when she learned to read. She currently works as a full-time volunteer for Blue Forge Group and is the Senior Editor of their publishing division, Blue Forge Press. Brianne lives with her wife, Jennifer, and their children on the Olympic Peninsula in the Pacific Northwest.